Praise for

The Familiars

'Assured and alluring, this beautiful tale of women and witchcraft and the fight against power was a delight from start to finish'
Jessie Burton, author of *The Miniaturist*

'An intricate and sensitive portrayal of a brave, tenacious young girl carving her place in the world. A must-read'
Heather Morris, bestselling author of *The Tattooist of Auschwitz*

'This is a brilliant debut, pacy and inventive, from a terrifically talented new voice'
Daily Telegraph

'The new Hilary Mantel . . . meticulously researched, beautifully written'
Cosmopolitan

'Historical fiction of the highest order'
Sunday Telegraph Magazine

'An intriguing story about a fascinating period of history and brilliant female characters'
Libby Page, author of *The Lido*

The Familiars

STACEY HALLS

ZAFFRE

First published in Great Britain in 2019
This paperback edition published in 2019
ZAFFRE
80–81 Wimpole St, London W1G 9RE

A CIP catalogue record for this book is
available from the British Library.

ISBN: 978–1–78576–614–5

Also available as an ebook

1 3 5 7 9 10 8 6 4 2

Typeset in Dante by Palimpsest Book Production Ltd, Falkirk, Stirlingshire

Printed and bound in Great Britain by Clays Ltd, Elcograf S.p.A.

FOR MY HUSBAND

PART ONE

THE COUNTY OF LANCASTER (NOW LANCASHIRE), EARLY APRIL, 1612

Be ever well in blood, for otherwise she will not long be at your commandment but make you follow her.

The Book of Falconry or Hawking,
George Turberville, 1543–1597

Prudence and justice

Shuttleworth family motto

CHAPTER 1

I left the house with the letter because I did not know what else to do. The lawn was wet with late morning dew that soaked my favourite rose silk slippers, for in my haste I hadn't thought to put on pattens. But I did not stop until I reached the trees overlooking the lawns in front of the house. The letter I had clutched in my fist, and I opened it once more to check I hadn't imagined it, that I hadn't drifted off in my chair and dreamt it up.

It was a chill morning, misty and cool with the wind racing down from Pendle Hill, and though my mind was in turmoil, I'd remembered to take my cloak from its place at the end of the wardrobe. I'd given Puck a perfunctory stroke and was pleased to see my hands weren't shaking. I did not cry, or faint, or do anything at all except fold what I had read back into its old shape and go quietly down the stairs. Nobody noticed me, and the only servant I saw was a brief glimpse of James sitting at his desk as I passed by his study. The idea that he might have read the letter himself crossed my mind, as a steward often opens his master's private correspondence, but I dismissed the thought quickly and left through the front door.

The clouds were the colour of pewter jugs that threatened to spill over, so I hurried across the grass towards the woods. I knew that in my black cloak I'd be conspicuous among the fields from servants' prying eyes at the windows, and I needed to think. In this part of Lancashire, the land is green and damp, and the sky wide and grey. Occasionally you see the flash of a deer's red coat, or a pheasant's blue neck, and your eye is drawn swifter than they can disappear.

Before I reached the shelter of the trees, I knew the sickness was coming again. I pulled the hem of my skirt away from where it splattered the grass, then used my kerchief to wipe my mouth. Richard had the laundry-women sprinkle them with rose water. I closed my eyes and took several deep breaths, and when I opened them I felt slightly better. The trees shivered and birds sang merrily as I went deeper, and in less than a minute I had lost Gawthorpe altogether. The house was as conspicuous as I was in these parts, made of warm golden stone and set in a clearing. But while the house couldn't keep you from the woods that seemed to draw ever closer and were visible from every window, the woods could keep Gawthorpe from you. Sometimes it felt as though they were playing a game.

I took out the letter and opened it again, smoothing out the creases that had formed in my tight little fist, and found the paragraph that had left me reeling:

You can divine without difficulty the true nature of the danger that your wife has been in, and it is with solemn regret that I impart on you my professional opinion as a physick and expert in matters of childbed: that upon visiting her last Friday sennight, I drew the deeply unfortunate conclusion that she can not and should not bear children. It is with excessive importance that you understand if she finds herself once more in childbed, she will not survive it, and her earthly life will come to an end.

Now I was out of sight of the house I could react with some privacy. My heart was beating furiously and my cheeks were hot. Another surge of sickness overcame me, and I almost choked on it as it burnt against my tongue.

The sickness came morning, noon and night, wringing me inside out. At the most, it was forty times a day; if it was twice I felt lucky. Veins burst in my face, leaving delicate crimson stems around my eyes, the whites of which turned a demonic red. The awful taste in my throat would last for hours, sharp and choking as the blade of a knife. I couldn't keep food down. I had no appetite for it anyway, much to the cook's disappointment. Even my beloved marchpane lay in broad, unsliced tablets in the larder, and my boxes of sugar candy sent from London gathered dust.

The other three times I hadn't been this ill. This time it felt like the child growing inside me was trying to escape through my throat instead of between my legs like the others, who announced their untimely arrivals in red rivers down my thighs. Their limp little forms were grotesque, and I watched them being wrapped like fresh loaves in linen.

'Not long for this world, the poor mite,' the last midwife said, wiping my blood off her butcher's arms.

Four years married, three times in childbed, and still no heir to put in the oak cradle my mother gave me when Richard and I married. I saw the way she looked at me, as though I was letting them all down.

Still, I could not fathom that Richard knew what the doctor had said, and had watched me fatten like a turkey at Christmastide. The letter was bundled in among several papers from my three childbeds, so it was possible he could have missed it. Would he have done right by me in withholding it? Suddenly, the words seemed to fling themselves from the page and wrap around my neck. And written, too, by a man whose name I did not recognise, so wreathed in pain was I when he visited that I could not recall a single detail about him: his touch, his voice, or whether he was kind.

I'd not stopped to catch my breath, and my slippers were truly ruined now, soaked with greenish mud. When one of them got stuck and came off, sending my stockinged foot into the wet ground, that was more than I was prepared to take. With both hands I made the letter into a ball and threw it as hard as I could, taking a brief moment's satisfaction when it bounced off a tree several yards away.

If I had not done that, I might not have seen the rabbit's foot a few inches from where it landed, nor the rabbit it belonged to – or at least what was left of it: a mangled mess of fur and blood, then another, and another. I hunted rabbits; these had not been slain by a hawk or a falcon making a neat little kill before circling back to its master. Then I noticed something else: the hem of a brown skirt brushing the ground, and knees bent, and above them a body, a face, a white cap. A young woman was kneeling a few yards away, staring at me. Every line of her was alert with an animal tension. She was shabbily dressed in a homespun wool smock with no pinafore, which is why I did not see her straight away among all the green and brown. Flax-coloured hair spiralled down from her cap. Her face was long and narrow, her eyes large, their colour unusual even from a distance: a warm gold, like new coins. There was something fiercely intelligent, almost masculine, in her gaze, and though she was crouched down and I standing, for a moment I felt afraid, as though I was the one who had been discovered.

Another rabbit dangled from her hands, one eye resting unblinkingly on me. Its fur was stained with red. On the ground next to the woman's skirts a roughly hewn sack lay open. She got to her feet. A breeze rustled the leaves and grasses around us, but she remained perfectly still, her expression unreadable. Only the dead beast moved, swinging slightly.

'Who are you?' I asked. 'What are you doing here?'

She began bundling the little bodies into her sack. My crumpled letter lay pale and bright among the massacre, and she paused when she saw it, her long fingers hovering, stained red with blood.

'Give it to me,' I snapped.

Picking it up, she held it out from where she stood, and in a few quick strides I'd snatched it from her. Those golden eyes did not leave my face, and I thought a stranger had never looked at me so hard. Briefly I wondered how I must appear, with no outdoor shoes and my slipper lying in the mud. No doubt my face was flushed from vomiting, and the whites of my eyes would be red. The acid in my mouth made my tongue sharp.

'What's your name?'

She did not speak.

'Are you a beggar?'

She shook her head.

'This is my land. You have been poaching rabbits from my land?'

'*Your* land?'

Her voice broke the strangeness of the situation like a pebble tossed in a pool. She was just an ordinary village girl.

'I am Fleetwood Shuttleworth, the mistress at Gawthorpe Hall. This is my husband's land; if you are from Padiham you would know that.'

'I am not,' was all she said.

'You know the penalty for hunting on another man's land?'

She took in my thick black cloak, my gown of copper taffeta peeking through the bottom. I knew my skin was dull; my black hair made it sallow, and I did not wish to be reminded of this by a stranger. I suspected I was younger than her, but I could not guess her age. Her dirty dress appeared not to have been brushed or aired in months, and her cap was the colour of mutton's wool. Then my eyes fell on hers, and her gaze met mine, level and proud. I frowned and raised my chin. At four feet eleven inches, everyone I met was taller than me, though I did not intimidate easily.

'My husband would bind your hands to his horse and drag you to the magistrate,' I said, more boldly than I felt. When she did not speak, the only sound the trees hissing and shuddering, I asked again: 'Are you a beggar?'

'I am no one.' She held out the sack. 'Take them. I did not know I was on your land.'

It was a strange answer, and I wondered what I would tell Richard. Then I remembered the letter in my fist. I squeezed it hard.

'With what did you kill them?'

She sniffed. 'I did not kill them. They were killed.'

'What an odd way of speaking you have. What is your name?'

I had barely finished when, in a flash of gold and brown, she turned and ran away through the trees. Her white cap flitted between the trunks, the sack bouncing against her skirts. Her feet thudded into the earth, quick and deft as an animal, before the woods swallowed her whole.

CHAPTER 2

The sound of Richard's waist belt preceded him everywhere. I think it made him feel powerful – you heard his money before you saw it. Now, as I heard the familiar jangle and the tread of his kid leather boots on the stairs, I took a deep breath and brushed some imagined dust off my jacket. I stood as he entered the room, bright and invigorated from a business trip to Manchester. His gold earring caught the light; his grey eyes gleamed.

'Fleetwood,' he greeted me, putting my head between his hands.

I bit my lip where he kissed it. Could I trust my voice to speak? We were in the wardrobe, where he knew he would find me. Even though nobody had lived at

Gawthorpe before us, it was the only room that truly felt mine. I had thought it very modern that Richard's uncle, who designed the house, had thought to include a room just for dressing when he had no wife. Of course if women designed houses they would be as much a part of the plans as a kitchen. Having come from my own house of coal-coloured stone under grey skies, Gawthorpe, with its rich, warm colour, as though the sun was always rising on it, and three floors of gleaming windows, bright as the crown jewels, and the tower in the middle, had made me feel more like a princess than a mistress. Richard had led me through the maze of rooms, and all the fresh plaster and shining panels and little passageways teeming with decorators and servants and carpenters had made me feel dizzy. I tended to stay at the top of the house, out of the way of everyone. If I had a baby in my arms or a child to take down to breakfast I might feel differently, but while I didn't, I kept to my rooms and my wardrobe, with its pleasant view of the rushing River Calder and Pendle Hill.

'Conversing with your clothes again?' he said.

'They are my constant companions.'

Puck, my great French mastiff, roused himself from the Turkey carpet, stretching and yawning and revealing a jaw so wide it could fit my head inside.

'You fearsome beast,' said Richard, going to kneel by the dog. 'Not for long will you be the singular object of our affections. You will have to share them.' He sighed and got to his knees, weary from a long ride. 'You are well? And rested?'

I nodded, tucking a loose strand of hair under my cap. Lately it had been falling out in great black clumps when I combed it.

'You are troubled. You have not . . . You are not . . .'

'I am fine.'

The letter. Ask him about the letter. The words hung thick in my throat, an arrow poised on a pulled bow, but there was nothing but relief in his lovely face. I held his stare for a moment too long, knowing my opportunity to question him was passing, slipping through my fingers like sand.

'Well, Manchester was a success. James always thinks he should go with me on these trips but I fare just as well alone. Perhaps he is only exasperated because I forget to write down receipts; I've told him I keep them as well in my head as in my jacket.' He paused, ignoring Puck sniffing at him. 'You are in a quiet mood.'

'Richard, I read the midwife's correspondence today. And the doctor's, who delivered the last.'

'That reminds me.'

He reached deep into the emerald velvet of his doublet, his face lit with a childlike excitement. I waited, and when he withdrew his hand he dropped into mine a strange object. It was a small silver sword, long as a letter opener, with a shining gold hilt. But the end was blunt and all over were little spheres dangling from miniature hooks. I turned it over in my palm and it made a pleasant tinkling sound.

'It's a rattle.' He beamed, shaking it so it jangled like horses coming to a halt. 'They are bells, look. It's for our son.'

He did not even try to disguise the longing in his voice. I thought of the drawer that I kept locked in one of the bedrooms. Inside were half a dozen things he'd bought the other times – a silk purse with our initials, an ivory horse that could fit in a palm. In the long gallery was a suit of armour he bought to celebrate the first time my stomach grew. His faith that we would have a child was clear and strong as a stream, even when he was trading wool in Preston and passed a trader selling miniature animals, or when he was with our tailor and saw a bolt of silk the exact colour of an oyster's pearl. With the last one, only he knew if it was a son or daughter, and I did not ask, because I was still not a mother. Every gift he gave me was a token of my failure, and I wished I could burn them all and watch the smoke rise from the chimney and be swallowed by the sky. I thought about where I would be without my husband, and my heart was full of grief, because he had given me happiness, and all I'd given him were three absences, their souls extinguished in the gentlest breeze.

I tried one more time. 'Richard, is there anything you wish to tell me?'

Richard's earring glinted as he considered me. Puck

yawned and settled on the carpet. A deep voice called Richard's name from a distant floor below.

'Roger is downstairs,' he said. 'I should go to him.'

I put the rattle on the chair, eager to be rid of it, leaving Puck to sniff curiously at it.

'Then I will come down.'

'I came upstairs only to dress; we are going to hunt.'

'But you have been riding all morning.'

He smiled. 'Hunting is not *riding*, it is hunting.'

'Then I will go with you.'

'You feel fit for it?'

I smiled and turned back to my clothes.

'Fleetwood Shuttleworth! My eyes, look how pale you are!' Roger's voice boomed across the stable yard. 'You are whiter than a snowdrop but twice as beautiful. Richard, have you not been feeding your wife?'

'Roger Nowell, you do know how to make a woman feel special.' I smiled, drawing up on my horse.

'You are dressed to hunt. Have you accomplished all your ladylike pursuits of a morning?'

His voice carried to every beam and corner of the stable yard as he sat astride his horse, tall and broad, a grey eyebrow raised in question.

'I have come to spend time with my favourite magistrate.'

I pushed my horse between the two men's. Roger Nowell was easy company, and I admit now that I suppose I was a little in awe of him, having no father to compare him to. He had enough years to be mine or Richard's father – grandfather, even – and as ours were both long dead he became a friend to us when Richard inherited Gawthorpe. The day after we arrived he rode over on his horse carrying three pheasants and stayed all afternoon, explaining the lie of the land and everyone in it. We were new to this part of Lancashire, with its rolling hills and shadowy forests and strange people, and he was a wealth of knowledge. An acquaintance of Richard's long-dead uncle, who had been the chief justice of Chester and provided the closest link the family ever had to the Crown, Roger had known the Shuttleworths for years, and settled himself in our household like an inherited piece of furniture. But I liked him from the moment I met him. Like a candle, he burnt brightly, and his mood would flicker easily from one moment to the next, bringing warmth and knowledge wherever he went.

'News from the palace: the king may finally have found a suitor for his daughter,' Roger announced.

The hounds in their kennels were driven wild by the sound of us and were brought out, teeming and panting around the horses' legs.

'Who is it?'

'Friedrich the Fifth, Count Palatine of the Rhine. He

will come to England later in the year and hopefully put an end to the parade of jesters trying for the princess's hand.'

'Will you go to the wedding?' I asked.

'I hope to. It will be the grandest the kingdom has seen in many years.'

'I wonder what sort of gown she will wear,' I thought aloud.

Roger didn't hear me over the barking hounds, and he and Richard moved out of the yard to begin the hunt. With the hounds on leashes I realised the quarry would be hart, and I wished I had asked before. A hart at bay was not a friendly sight, with its antlers slashing and eyes rolling; I would have preferred almost anything else. I thought about turning around, but we were already in the forest so I kicked my horse onwards. Edmund the apprentice acted as whip, riding alongside the dogs. As we went through the trees I heard snatches of their furtive conversation and rode silently behind them, half-listening. An image from the day before came to me: spilt blood, glassy eyes and the strange golden-haired woman.

'Richard,' I interrupted. 'There was a trespasser on our land yesterday.'

'What? Where?'

'Somewhere south of the house, in the woods.'

'Why did James not tell me?'

'Because I did not tell him.'

'*You* saw him? What were you doing?'

'I . . . went out walking.'

'I told you not to go out alone; you might have got lost or tripped and . . . hurt yourself.'

Roger was listening.

'I am *fine*, Richard. And it was not a man but a woman.'

'What was she doing? Was she lost?'

That's when I realised I could not tell him about the rabbits, because I had no words for what I'd seen.

'Yes,' I said eventually.

Roger was amused. 'You do have a wild imagination, Fleetwood. You had us thinking you were attacked by a savage in the woods when really a woman had only got lost?'

'Yes,' I replied faintly.

'Although now even that isn't without harm – you may have heard of what happened to John Law the pedlar at Colne?'

'I have not.'

'Roger, you don't need to frighten her with tales of witchcraft – she already has nightmares.'

My mouth fell open and my face grew scarlet. That was the first time Richard had told anyone about The Nightmare, and I would never have believed it of him. But he continued ahead, the feather in his hat trembling.

'Tell me, Roger.'

'A woman travelling alone is not always as innocent as she seems, as John Law found out and will never forget as long as he lives – and that might not be long, Lord have mercy.' Roger settled back in his saddle. 'Two days ago his son Abraham came to me at Read Hall.'

'Should I know him?'

'No, because he is a cloth dyer from Halifax. The lad has done well for himself, considering his father's trade.'

'And he found a witch?'

'No, *listen.*'

I sighed and wished I hadn't come, wished I was sitting in the parlour with my dog.

'John was travelling on the woolpack trail at Colnefield when he came across a young girl. A beggar, he thought. She asked him to give her some pins, and when he said he would not – he paused for effect – 'she cursed him. He turned his back and next thing, heard her speaking softly behind him, as though she was talking to someone. It sent a shiver up his spine. He thought at first it was the wind, but he looked back, and her dark eyes were fixed on him, and her lips were moving. He hurried away, and not thirty yards on, he heard running feet, and then a great thing like a black dog began attacking him, biting him all over, and he fell to the ground.'

'A thing *like* a black dog?' Richard asked. 'You said earlier it *was* a black dog.'

Roger ignored him. 'He held his hands to his face and begged for mercy, and when he opened his eyes the dog had disappeared. Gone. And the strange girl with it. Someone found him on the path and helped him to a nearby inn, but he could barely move a limb. Nor could he speak. One of his eyes stayed shut to the world, and his face was all fallen down on one side. He stayed at the inn, but the next morning the young girl appeared again, bold as brass, and begged his forgiveness. She claims she wasn't in control of her craft, but that she did curse him.'

'She admitted to it?' I remembered the girl from yesterday. 'What did she look like?'

'Like a witch. Very thin and rough-looking, with black hair and a sullen face. My mother says never trust someone with black hair because they usually have a black soul to match.'

'*I* have black hair.'

'Do you want to hear my story?'

My mother used to threaten to sew my mouth as a child. She and Roger's mother would have plenty to discuss.

'I am sorry,' I said. 'Is the man well now?'

'No, and he may never be again,' Roger said gravely. 'That is worrying in itself, but there is something that troubles me more: the dog. While it is free to roam Pendle, no one is safe.'

Richard flashed me an amused, sceptical look before tearing ahead to keep up with the hunt. The thought of the animal did not frighten me – after all, I had a mastiff the size of a mule. But before I could point that out, Roger began again.

'At the inn, a few nights after it happened, John Law

woke to the sound of something breathing over him. The great beast was stood over his bed, the size of a wolf, with bared teeth and fiery eyes. He knew it to be a spirit; it was not of this earth. You can understand his terror: a man who is unable to move or speak, save for groaning out. Then who should be there by his bed in its place not a moment later, but the witch herself.'

I felt as though my skin had been brushed with a feather.

'So it turned into the woman?'

'No, Fleetwood have you knowledge of familiar spirits?' I shook my head. 'Then I will direct you to the book of Leviticus. In short, it's the Devil in disguise. An instrument, if you will, to enlarge his kingdom. This girl's is a dog, but they can appear as anything: an animal, a child. It appears to her when she needs it to do her bidding, and last week she told it to lame John Law. A familiar is the surest sign of a witch.'

'And you have seen it?'

'Of course not. A creature of the Devil is hardly likely to appear to a God-fearing man. Only those of question-able belief might sense its presence. Low morals are its breeding ground.'

'But John Law saw it; you said he was a good man.'

Roger waved me off, impatient. 'We have lost Richard; he will not be happy with me for tongue-wagging with his wife. This is what happens when women come on hunts.'

I did not point out that it was me indulging him – if Roger had a story, he wanted it heard. We set off at a canter, and slowed down again when the hunt came back into view. We were a long way from Gawthorpe, and now I was here I was not in favour of the thought of a full afternoon's riding.

'Where is the girl now?' I asked as we fell behind again.

Roger adjusted his grip on the reins. 'Her name is Alizon Device. She is in my custody at Read Hall.'

'In your *house*? Why did you not put her in the gaol at Lancaster?'

'She is not dangerous where she is. There is nothing she can do – she would not dare. Besides, she is helping me with some other enquiries.'

'What kind of enquiries?'

'My, my, you are full of questions, Mistress Shuttleworth. Must we *talk* the quarry to death? Alizon Device is from a family of witches; she told me so herself. Her mother, her grandmother, even her brother all practise magic and sorcery, no more than a few miles from here. They are also accusing their neighbours of murder by witchcraft, one of whom lives on Shuttleworth land. Which is why I thought your husband over there ought to know about it.'

He indicated his head at the expanse of greenery before us. Edmund, Richard and the hounds were again nowhere to be seen.

'But how do you know she is telling the truth? Why

would she betray her family? She must know what it means to be a witch – it's certain death.'

'Your guess is as good as mine,' Roger said simply, although I detected something beneath his words. He could be forceful and bullying when he wanted; I had seen it with his wife, Katherine, who was a tolerant sort of woman. 'And the murders she claimed her family are responsible for all happened.'

'They have *murdered*?'

'Several times. You would not want to cross a Device. Do not fear, child. Alizon Device is safe in custody, and I am to question her family tomorrow or the next day. I shall have to notify the king, of course.' He sighed, as though it was an impediment. 'He will be pleased to know it, I'm sure.'

'What if they escape – how will you find them?'

'They'll not escape. I have eyes all over Pendle – you know that. Not much gets past a high sheriff.'

'Former high sheriff,' I teased. 'How many years has she? The girl with the dog?'

'She does not know, but I would say she is seventeen or so.'

'The same as me.' After a moment of thoughtful silence, I spoke again. 'Roger, do you trust Richard?'

He raised a bushy eyebrow. 'With my life. Or what's left of it – I am an old man now, with my family grown and the best days of my work behind me, most regrettably. Why do you ask?'

I'd tucked the doctor's letter into my pocket, deep beneath my riding clothes, and it beat against my ribs like another heart.

'No reason.'

CHAPTER 3

L ent was not yet over and though my appetite was poor, I longed for a cut of stewed beef or a strip of soft, salted chicken. Roger stayed for dinner and rubbed his hands together as the servants brought out silver platters of pike and sturgeon. I knew I wouldn't touch any of it, even though I was hungry after the hunt, from which we had come back empty-handed as a chill mist descended. It pressed in now at the windows, and the dining chamber was cold. I broke my bread into pieces and sipped my wine, wondering when the time would come when I would be able to eat everything on my plate again. I hadn't told any of the servants of my condition, including Sarah, who helped me to dress, but a cook is always the first to know. The other servants would have seen me hold my fingers out to Puck, offering him bits of things on my plate, but I had done that since he was young. My dog was growing fatter as I seemed to shrink. Richard once remarked that he ate better than most of Lancashire.

When I could take the sight of the fish heads no longer, I went to my chamber to lie down. At the top of the house it was quiet, away from the clatter of sauce dishes and knives, and the fire had been lit. Usually I would have drawn the drapes to help my headache but I felt too sick and tired, so I kicked off my slippers and lay down, staring out of the window with my hands on my stomach. There had been too much to think about this morning, but the doctor's letter came back to me, clouding my mind like mist. I suppose in the end it came down to who would survive: would it be me, or the child, or both, or neither? If the doctor was to be believed – and no doubt he was – the baby was fattening like a conker in a spiked green shell, and eventually would split me open. An heir was what Richard wanted more than anything, and where I had failed before perhaps I would not this time . . . but at the cost of my own life? Women carried life and death in their stomachs when they conceived; it was a fact of our existence. To hope and pray I might not join the departed was as useful as wishing the grass blue.

'Will you stay there and kill me?' I asked, looking down at my belly. 'Or will you let me live? Shall we try and live together?'

I must have fallen asleep because when I woke there was a jug of milk next to the bed. I reached over to dip in my littlest finger and lick it. My mother used to say the most beautiful girls had skin like fresh milk, plump and creamy. Next to it, mine looked like old parchment. I thought of the fuss Mother had made when Richard came to Barton for the first time with his uncle Lawrence; she wouldn't settle, fluttering around me like a moth.

'Show him your hands,' she said. 'Keep them folded.'

She didn't need to say my face wasn't my best feature – I knew that already. Still, none of it mattered, because we both knew my best feature was my name and the money it brought. Mother always said Father was tight-fisted, but when I asked why we lived in a draughty house and had to share a bedroom, she drew her lips into a thin line and said an old house was better than a new one.

The night of Richard's coming, as mother and I got into our beds, she asked me if I liked him.

'Does it matter?' was my petulant reply.

'It matters greatly to your happiness. You will spend every day of your life with him.'

He will save me from this miserable life, I thought. *I could not like him more if I tried.*

I thought of his pleasant, unlined face and light grey eyes. The beautiful jewellery he wore in his ears and the rings on his hands, one of which I would take so he could lead me to my new life.

'Do you like the playhouse?' he had asked me in my mother's parlour.

His uncle and my mother stood at the window, talking and glancing over at us. I knew my mother had tilled the ground for this marriage, but if Richard refused, nothing could be done.

'Yes,' I lied, for I had never been.

'Excellent. We shall go every year to London. That's where the best ones are. Twice, if you wish.'

How could I not be charmed and delighted by this young man, who did not treat me like an infant as everybody else did? I thought of his face every waking hour and every dreaming one, too. The wedding date was set in the parish church, and I could not wait for every morning to arrive and the nightfall after it, because each one drew me closer. I thought about what sort of mistress I would be: kind and wise, for I wasn't beautiful. A mother, one day, adored by her children and her husband. Whatever Richard wanted I would give him. His comfort would be my occupation, his happiness my life's work. For he had bestowed the greatest gift on me: accepting me as his wife, and I would live out the rest of my days with gratitude. I heard my mother shifting in her bed.

'Fleetwood,' she said. 'Are you listening? I asked if you liked Richard.'

'I suppose he will do,' I replied, and blew out my candle with a smile.

I rose awkwardly, my limbs stiff, and went into the long gallery at the front of the house to walk back and forth. To my surprise, Roger was there, examining the royal coat of arms above the fireplace, with his hands clasped behind his back.

'*Fear God, honour thy king, eschew evil and do good. Seek peace and ensue it.*' I recited the motif on the mantle from memory.

'Very good, Fleetwood. Consider it a promise from your justice of the peace.'

'Richard's uncle Lawrence had that put in. I think he hoped King James would hear about it and not feel the need to visit.'

'The Shuttleworths are loyal to the Crown, of course.' There was an edge of warning in Roger's tone.

'Faithful as dogs.'

Roger was thoughtful. 'Still, more demonstrations of loyalty need to be made in these parts. But how to make them?'

'I think it is not so much lack of loyalty but confidence. Besides, he would surely avoid these areas, with their old ways of faith.'

'This corner of the kingdom causes His Majesty a great deal of anxiety. A lot more could be done to honour thy king and eschew evil.' He leant forwards and frowned. 'I had not noticed the words around the king's arms. What does it say?'

'*Honi soit qui mal y pense*. "Shame on him who thinks evil of it."'

He made a face, as though he was considering it.

'Indeed. But thinks evil of what, Lawrence will never be able to tell us. Maybe I will ask the king himself.'

'You're at court soon?'

Roger nodded. 'His Majesty requires all of Lancashire's justices of the peace to make a record of every person who does not take communion at church.'

'For what purpose?'

'Oh, Fleetwood, you need not concern yourself with matters of the court, they hardly affect the life of a young gentlewoman. You do your duty and give your husband lots of little Shuttleworths, and I will do my duty in keeping Pendle safe.' I must have looked displeased, because he looked more kindly on me, becoming genial. 'Well, if you must know, His Majesty is still very . . . uneasy after the events at Parliament seven years ago. And you may have heard the whisperings about some of the traitors escaping to Lancashire. Something must be done to demonstrate the county's loyalty to the Crown, because currently the king is very mistrustful of our little part of the north, and the lawless people within it. He thinks us a pack of animals, compared to the genteel lords and ladies of the south. We are very far from society here, and I think he is afraid. But do you know what else he is mistrustful of?'

I shook my head.

'Witches.'

There was a gleam of triumph in his eye, and it took a moment for me to understand.

'You mean Alizon Device?'

Roger nodded. 'If I can convince the king that the people of Lancashire are under threat from the thing he hates most, his sympathies might extend to us, and he might grow less suspicious. If I am seen removing the *bad seeds*, if you will, the county may grow and prosper, and we may rejoin the kingdom with a new reputation.'

'But Catholics and witches are not the same thing. There are plenty of the first here, but not the latter.'

'More than you think,' was Roger's easy answer. 'And the king sees them as the same thing, besides.'

'Well, I doubt very much that the king should worry about us storing gunpowder around here. It's far too wet,' I said, and Roger laughed. I wondered then if I should tell him about my letter, folded deep in my pocket. Might he know already? 'Where is Richard?' I asked instead.

'He has some business with his steward and then he is showing me his new falcon before accompanying me back to Read. Will you join us?'

'He spends more time with that creature than me. No, thank you. But you could tell him to ask the tailor to call. I need some new clothes.'

Roger chuckled as we passed the entrance to my chambers and reached the top of the stairs.

'You and my Katherine are two equal forces. But still,

neither of you are a match for Richard. He has the largest collection outside of the king's wardrobe.' He paused at the top of the staircase. 'You will come and see Katherine soon? She often asks after you and your latest fashions. She is fascinated to see what the young people are wearing.'

I smiled and bowed as he descended the staircase that curled around the tower, but before he disappeared I called his name again, because I felt a sudden ache, and wanted desperately for him to embrace me as a father might. Roger certainly smelt as a father might, or so I imagined – of woodsmoke, and horsehair, and tobacco. He stood waiting below the portrait of my mother and me as a child – the one I would not hang in the long gallery or anywhere else. The reason was that nobody paused for long on the stairs, meaning guests walked past it and often forgot to mention it by the time they reached the next floor. In the picture, which was about the same height as me, my mother dominated in her wide collar and scarletwork gown. I occupied the bottom left corner, my mother's arm bent towards me, as though about to hurry me out of the frame. A little black martlet sat on my hand, the pet I had kept in a cage in my room made immortal. I could still recall the unpleasant silence of sitting for the portrait in the great hall at Barton, and the pointy-faced artist with the coloured oils on his fingers, the blackened tip of his tongue that flicked out of his mouth like a serpent.

'Roger . . .' My voice died in my throat. 'Do you think John Law will live?'

'Do not fret,' Roger said. 'His son is caring for him.'

I went back to my chamber, wondering how Roger Nowell slept with a witch in the house, and decided soundly.

I'd hidden the pan under the bed for when I needed it and covered it with a cloth, but Richard still recoiled when he walked into our chamber. I was lying in my nightdress, weak and empty, what little pike I'd had at dinner clinging to the bottom of the bowl. Richard sighed and came to kneel by me.

'Are you no better? You've barely eaten. I so want you to be well.'

I pulled at my nightdress so the tiny mound of my stomach showed through. Richard gazed at it, resting a gentle hand on the bump. I rolled his gold ring, the one his father gave him that he never took off. I could not decide what was worse: how sick I felt or not knowing if my husband was keeping this great truth from me. At some point that evening it had dawned on me as I sat in my chamber with only the candles' cheerful sputter for company: of course Richard valued his child's life more than mine. Would any man not, who had a great deal to leave behind?

'Richard?' I asked. 'What will happen if I cannot give you an heir?'

I thought of the old kings' wives, their necks on the chopping blocks. What would be better: to go painfully and messily, thrashing about in a blood-soaked bed, or clean and resigned, wearing your best dress? Divorce was decades old, but the word struck as much fear as death.

'Don't speak such things. It will not happen this time – the Lord will be kind to us. We will employ the best midwife.'

'We had a midwife last time; she did not stop it from coming out dead.'

He stood to undress, the candlelight casting off his buttons then settling on his bare skin. I watched him change into his nightshirt, then he came to my side and took my cold hand and held it, pink against grey. Although his voice was calm, his face was worried.

'Until you are well again, I will sleep in the dressing room.'

My stomach lurched. 'No! Richard, please, I won't hear of it. I'll not be sick again. I'll have a maid remove the pan.'

I tried to climb out of bed but Richard stopped me.

'I will only be in the next room until you are better, which will be very soon—'

'Richard, don't. Please. I don't like sleeping alone, you know I don't – The Nightmare.'

When I woke, soaked with sweat and blind with terror,

he would hold me until I stopped trembling. It only happened a few times a year, but he knew I would be terrified if he was not there.

'Please don't sleep in the dressing room. Please stay with me. I'm afraid.'

But he kissed my forehead and, with a pained face, left holding the soiled pan at arm's length. I slid down the headboard, feeling tears press at my eyes. He would never have done this when we were first married. After the wedding, in the house on the Strand, I could not sleep with the chaos outside the window. London was new to me, and everything in it – I'd never seen so many carriages in one place, or heard the cries of boatmen coming ashore, or so many loud bells and crowds of people. Richard would sit up with me at night, reading or drawing or just lying quietly, stroking my hair. When it got colder and we moved further out to the fields and wide skies of Islington, I told him I'd grown used to the sounds of the Strand, and now wouldn't be able to sleep because it was too quiet. He laughed and said I was far too spoilt and the only thing for it was for him to make the noises for me. Night after night, just as I was about to fall asleep, he neighed into the darkness, or gave the cry of a knife sharpener, or juggled like a coal seller pretending to scald his hands. I'd never laughed so much in all my life. Once, when it was snowing outside and the fire was low in the grate, I asked to see what he was drawing in my sketchbook. He told me to wait until he was finished. I watched him work, his face taut with concentration, his hands making quick little movements and soft noises on the page. When he turned the paper around, I saw myself. I was wearing a beautiful trimmed hat, a fine ruff and collar, and elegant Spanish slippers. Around my shoulders was a cloak that flowed off the page, pressed with Paris buttons. I could almost feel its thickness.

'What colour is it?' I whispered, running my fingertips along the lines.

'The cloak is of branched satin and orange wool,' he said proudly. 'I'll have it made tomorrow. This is what you will wear to ride home in. To Gawthorpe.'

Nobody had ever done such a thing for me before. When the winter ended we arrived at the brand-new house that no one had ever lived in, just as he said. The journey took nine days, and all I could think about the whole way was arriving in Lancashire as Mistress Shuttleworth, wearing an outfit the likes of which not a soul in these parts had ever seen. Richard looked equally fine in an outfit he designed himself, a dagger and sword at his hip. Villagers lined the streets as we drew closer to our new home, smiling and waving. But with time the picture had changed in my mind, and all I could see was two children dressed for a play.

I blew out the candle and listened for sounds from the other room. This was the first time in our marriage we were both in the house and I was sleeping alone.

✳

He did not come to me the next morning, going down to break his fast without waking me. He read his correspondence while I sat opposite, trying to force bread and honey into my mouth and keep it down. I watched his face, creasing or brightening as he read; I did not ask who wrote. As the servants passed in and out of the dining chamber, I wondered who knew a truckle bed and fresh linen had been placed in the dressing room next to our bedroom. As though in answer, one of the kitchen girls caught my eye and looked hurriedly away, the tops of her ears turning red. I felt cold, and could not eat or say what I wanted to, so like a coward I went to walk up and down the long gallery and pray, hoping for a sign from God. I watched the trees and the sky, and felt that burning itch to be outside without my thoughts, instead of inside with them.

Much later, I found Richard in the great hall, seated with James the steward, the household ledger open between them. The Gawthorpe ledger was as important in our house as the King's Bible: everything we bought, every bill we paid and everything that came in or out of Gawthorpe, whether on wheels, horseback or rolled in a barrel, was inked on its thick pages in James' immaculate hand. Suits of armour, tapestries and other frivolities that Richard liked to spend his money on were committed in ink, as well as everyday things: stockings for the servants, cork for the wine. But like me, Richard took little interest in it, preferring to leave it to our men, so when I found him I knew he would be impatient; talk of quit-rents and profits bored him. As if reminding him to take the estate's business seriously, the grave portrait of his uncle, the Reverend Lawrence, sat overlooking them, the words *Death is the way unto life* painted at his shoulder.

I swallowed. 'Richard?'

He looked up quickly, welcoming the distraction. Then two things happened at once: James turned a new leaf so the pages were blank, even though they had only been halfway down the last, and I noticed Richard was dressed to travel.

'You are going away?'

'Lancaster. I leave tonight.'

'Oh. Did someone write to you this morning?'

'Only my sisters with news from London. They always write me a letter each but it might as well be one – they only talk of the same people and plays and the latest victim of scandal. At least there is more to entertain them there than at Forcett with my mother; I expect they'll never want to move back to Yorkshire. Did you need me?'

Yes, I need you.

The room rang with silence. James' feather quivered, its inky point eager to scratch.

I wanted to say 'Don't go', but instead replied, 'How are the Mistresses Shuttleworth?'

'Eleanor hints at something that has quite excited her, but Anne refers to it not at all.'

'Perhaps she is engaged.'

'It is not like Eleanor to be subtle.'

'Perhaps she hopes to be engaged, then.'

James cleared his throat pointedly.

'I am going into Padiham this morning for some linen from Mrs Kendall's. Is there anything you need?'

'Why don't you have one of the servants go?'

'They will get the wrong thing.'

'You are well enough?'

Lawrence's grey eyes stared at me from the frame. *Death is the way unto life.*

'Yes.'

I did not want him to go; he was always going, and I was always staying.

'When will you be back?'

'In a few days. Shall I check on Barton on my travels?'

'Why? My mother no longer lives there; there will be nothing but empty rooms and mice.'

'I should look in every now and again to check all is in order.'

James sniffed and shifted in his seat. I was taking up valuable time with his master. Perhaps then Richard looked at me properly, for he came to me, tilting my chin towards him with his finger.

'And how about we fit in a trip to London soon? Eleanor and Anne have made me miss it. We can get you one of the best midwives, and I'll take you to a playhouse, the Lord knows we are starved of entertainment in these parts. This dreary hall could use some joy. James, find out if there are any players travelling in the area that could come and perform. Or send for some.' He wrapped an arm around my waist and held my hand, as though we were about to dance. Puck shuffled up to us, grunting curiously. 'Otherwise I shall have to train Puck to be a dancing bear. Behold!'

He discarded me and pulled the dog up to his height, so Puck's great paws rested on his shoulders and his monstrous head was level with Richard's. I could not help but smile as they sauntered in an awkward dance, Puck's tongue lolling as his feet staggered on the stone flags before he crashed ungracefully to the ground. He came immediately to me for a rewarding pat.

'Useless creature. We will have to work on our performance,' said Richard.

He left me with James, and James with their unfinished business. I knew I was not the only person in the household left disarmed at times by my husband's shifting moods. I watched him go, feeling his kiss feathery light on my cheek, and the weight of everything else heavy as a wet cloak around my shoulders.

CHAPTER 4

I'd heard of wise women, who could give you a cup of something and make you bleed so your stomach went flat again. Just as there were herbs and potions to make the child come out, were there not different ones to make it stay in, make it live? The little I'd heard was in snatches of conversation I was on the edge of, when the servants hadn't realised I was sitting quietly in the next room, or from pursed lips at a dinner table in some hall or other, before the topic swiftly moved on to one more tasteful. If only I had a friend I could ask; I could hardly question the apothecary myself.

The ride from Gawthorpe to Padiham was a pleasant one, through wide-spaced trees until the land opened out on to the road. It was cold and bright, and I was glad my thick wool cloak covered me. I tied the horse outside the clothier's, stroking her coal-black mane before leaving her.

'Good morning, Mistress,' said face after plain face as the villagers passed by.

I returned their greetings, noticing them greedily examining every inch of me, from my hat to my gloves. It was impossible to be inconspicuous.

I paused at the apothecary's door, imagining for a moment entering the dark, narrow little shop with all its scents and the dozens of miniature bottles and tapestries of herbs hanging from the walls. It was very possible that some might stop the sickness coming, stop the child leaving. Stop me from dying, even. But it was a different language, and one I could not speak.

I ordered my linen from Mrs Kendall the clothier and thought I saw her bright little eyes flick down my front. It was hard to tell with village people whether they suspected you were in childbed or were admiring your buttons.

'Mrs Kendall,' I imagined whispering. She would no doubt grow confidential and press her round stomach against the counter, leaning forwards. 'Do you know a wise woman?'

'What for, Mistress?' she'd ask in astonishment.

'To help me grow a baby.'

'All you need is a husband for that!'

And she'd slap her red hands on her apron as tears streamed down her face while she laughed and laughed.

Then the whole town would know, and it might get back to my servants, who would tell in turn how the master had quit my chamber, and us not five years married. No, it would not do.

I rode my horse out of the town and took a shortcut through the woods. It was easier to think there than in the house, which was too quiet when Richard was away. I'd found the scale of Gawthorpe and the silence of it frightening at first. Wherever Richard went I would follow, and he began to call me the little ghost.

I suppose if only I had been more assertive, Miss Fawnbrake would never have arrived. When Richard had called me into the hall that spring morning, I saw her wide back turn from where she was standing at the fireplace so she could regard me with her glassy, vacant eyes that were too far apart, like those of a fish. Ten or more years older than me, she looked all wrong – her ruff was floppy and needed starching, her dress was too tight. Even her name was wrong: 'Miss Fawnbrake' belonged to a coltish, beautiful young woman, and she was none of those. But what unnerved me the most was how she stood at Richard's shoulder as though she had lived at Gawthorpe all her life. Richard was telling me he had found me a lady's-maid, to keep me company in the house. Dread poured into me, filling me from bottom to top as he told me how I'd be like a lady at court, who had women to sit and read with them or play games and music. In my meekness I could only stare at her hands, which were pink and dry like smoked ham, folded patiently with too much wrist showing because her sleeves were short. Richard knew I didn't play music or practise my Latin vocabulary; he knew I liked to hunt and be outside with my dog, did he not?

By this point I'd lost the first baby, but this was worse. I'd gone tearfully into the dining chamber, where Richard came to me, leaving Miss Fawnbrake curling her swollen knuckles.

'I don't want a nursemaid, Richard,' I had told him, my voice cracking.

'You prefer to be alone? Fleetwood, you say the suits of armour frighten you.'

'They do not any more.' Hot, salty tears were falling down my cheeks, and I began to cry like the infant I was. My husband did not see me as mistress of the house. 'I am not a child, Richard,' I'd sobbed.

If only I could go now to that frightened girl, I would kneel on the Turkey carpet and take her cold little hands in mine. If only I could have done it years before that and said things will get worse before they get better, but get better they will. Would I believe myself?

Recalling Miss Fawnbrake's rough pink hands and her bloated, pockmarked face still made me queasy. She was with us for eight months and I lost two babies in that time, one after the other. When I began bleeding and begged her not to tell Richard, she marched from the room to inform her master. Richard raced upstairs to find me hunched over the bed as pain folded me in half again and again. I wish he had not seen how incapable I was, how keenly the child did not want me as its mother. The first time I'd miscarried, before Miss Fawnbrake arrived, we'd been walking in the long gallery, talking about commissioning our portraits, when I felt a strange plucking below, and thought my bowel had opened. I did not know what was happening, did not know there had even been a baby, and Richard had tucked me in bed and washed me with a warm cloth and fed me broth and marchpane. He was sad, but also delighted that we had conceived.

'We will have a baby by Christmastide!' He had smiled, and I had smiled weakly back, believing him.

There had been barely any pain, just sorrow, and love. But then Miss Fawnbrake arrived, and that time there had been a great deal of pain, and even more sorrow, and guilt, and everything else.

The third time was worst of all. Richard was away, and I'd been playing with Puck on the lawn outside the house, tugging him around by a stick he had clamped in his mouth. My stomach was big by that time, as though I'd swallowed a globe. A line had appeared down my front, and in my naivety I thought that's where the skin would come apart and my baby be lifted out when it was ready. That afternoon I'd fallen over more than once, and got muddy and wet, my playful Puck jumping all over me when I was down, licking my face and making me laugh. I remember the laughter dying in my throat when I saw

Miss Fawnbrake watching me from the dining chamber window. Then for a long time the joy didn't come back because that evening, while I dressed for bed, the pains started again and didn't stop for three days. A doctor was called, Richard arrived from Yorkshire, and in a blur of pain and darkness I remember the feeling of something leaving me, and a midwife holding what looked like a white rabbit by its feet. For two weeks I did not leave my bed, and Miss Fawnbrake was a malignant shadow in the corner. One day she disappeared and came back with Richard, who for the first time in our marriage raised his voice at me.

'What is this about you rolling around on the lawn like an animal? Letting the dog trample all over you? Fleetwood, it's like you insist on behaving like a child and have no interest in becoming a mother.'

He may as well have called me a murderer. If there had been a knife with my untouched bread, or a red-hot poker in the fireplace, I would have rammed it into Miss Fawnbrake's pallid chest, and proved him right. Once Richard could see how much passion she inspired in me, and how I ground my teeth when she walked into a room, he finally deigned to make rid of her with the idea that her presence was causing me to miscarry. While I did not think him right, I did not think him entirely wrong either. How I dreaded her face appearing at the door each morning to dress me, and how I hated the low, confidential conversations she conducted with my husband, with the servants. Before I could tell Richard about my day, she had done it; before I could greet him at the door, she'd taken his cloak. If she could have carried his child for him, no doubt she would have done. The night Richard dismissed her, I found one of Puck's turds beneath my pillow, dug from the grounds and carried up four flights of stairs in her chapped, swollen hands. Never again would I have a companion; it was like having a sister who hated me.

Halfway home from Padiham, my horse's steady rhythm jolted to a shuddering halt, and before I realised what was happening it began backing up and rearing, its eyes rolling and nostrils flaring. Surrounded by tree trunks and a chorus of rustling leaves, at first I did not know what had startled it. I knew it disliked harts and even deer, as it was not a hunting horse. Then a movement ahead drew my eyes. A red fox was tensed ten yards away, large as a young doe and just as sleek. I had only a second to take in its pointed face and flattened back, its bristling tail frozen in a perfect line behind it. What I remember thinking before I fell was how unmoved by us it was, as though we had disturbed it in some private reflection.

The last thing I saw before my horse flailed again was the animal's reproachful golden eyes. I hit the ground with a crack, landing on my left wrist and feeling several things at once: the pain in my arm, the wet ground underneath, and the mounting knowledge that the horse was going to crush me underfoot. For it was panicking, rearing and bucking around the clearing I was lying in. I placed my good hand on my stomach and spoke calmly to the horse, but its hooves went on pacing, its flanks sweating. My wrist sang with pain and I thought I might be sick. I tried to push myself up and cried out with the shock of it. There was a tree trunk two or three yards away, so I leant on my elbows and tried to drag myself towards it.

'Damn fox,' I muttered. 'Damn mule.'

'Don't move.'

A woman emerged between two trees. At once I knew her – she was the same strange girl from the woods the other day. Proceeding cautiously towards the beast with her hands outstretched, she did not speak or click her tongue, but the effect of her presence was as though she had, with her clear gaze and steady grip. The mare stopped its twitching and came to a submissive halt, its dark eyes rolling. While the woman held the clammy animal still, I watched her golden hair twisting from beneath her cap, her long face serious. Her hands were slim but too bony to be elegant.

I tried to push myself up again and winced with pain, my wrist burning.

'Don't move.'

She spoke again in that low, musical voice, flickering like a flame in all the green. She was wearing the same old dress as before, the same mutton's wool cap. As she knelt beside me, I smelt lavender, despite her dirty clothes. Carefully she took my wrist in her long, white hands and

I gritted my teeth. Releasing it gently, she looked around, got up and snapped a short stick from the low branch of a tree. The woods whispered and shivered around us, and for a brief moment I thought she might use it as a weapon to strike me with. But she knelt again, ripped a length of fabric from her grubby apron, tied the stick to my wrist and bound it tightly in three places.

'Only a sprain,' she told me. 'Nothing is broken.'

'What are you doing here?' was all I could say. She regarded me with those curious amber eyes. 'Why do you wander about the forest alone?'

'Why do you?' she said.

With my good hand I reached for my stomach, feeling for anything amiss. Her eyes travelled down my front, concealed by folds of velvet and brocade, then flicked over my face: my dry lips, my bloodshot eyes and grey pallor.

As if she could smell the sickness on me, she said, 'You are with child.'

My vision blurred, the forest leapt around me, and as though she had invoked it, I leant over and vomited on the roots of a tree. Sweat drenched my face and I wiped at it with a shaking, muddied hand.

'You live at the big house by the river?' she asked.

'How did you know?'

'You told me last time. I will help you back, Mistress . . .'

'Shuttleworth. There is no need for it.'

'You can't ride, and you are weak. I will take the horse.'

'I'm not getting back on that stupid mule.'

'You must. Here.'

Guiding the horse nearer, she made a cradle for my foot, and with difficulty I hoisted myself up. My skirts were damp and muddy, and made a mess on her hands, but she did not seem to mind, and reluctantly I clicked my tongue and dug my heels in, and we began at a gentle pace.

It was spring, and the trees would soon stand proud and green as a cavalry, though the last of the winter wind bit their trunks and shook their branches. It crossed my mind that when these budding leaves enjoyed their short time on earth before turning orange and falling to coat the floor, I would likely not be here to see it. I closed my eyes and we rode on in silence.

'Thank you for helping me,' I said after a while. 'I may have been trampled to offal by the time my husband found me.'

'Your husband?'

'Richard Shuttleworth. Where do you live?'

After a pause, she named the village a few miles to the north-east.

'Colne is not so close. What brings you to my land again?'

If I sounded peevish, I half-meant it. I had not forgotten the massacred rabbits, the limp form dangling from her bloodied fist.

'This is your land too? I did not know.'

'And if you had not been on it I might not have lived to tell the tale.'

We moved in a more companionable silence, me on horseback, she on foot. I only wondered later how she knew the way, with the trees so thick and the uneven ground showing no clear paths. But I let her lead me, as relieved as the horse was that someone was taking charge. My wrist throbbed and my teeth were thick with sourness.

'Are you ill with the child?' she asked.

'Always.'

'I can give you something to help.'

'You can? You are a wise woman?'

'I am a midwife.'

My heart beat a little faster and I sat up straighter.

'You deliver babies that live? And the women – they live themselves?'

'I do everything I can.'

That was not what I wanted to hear, and I sat back in the saddle, a cloud eclipsing my brief moment of hope. We did not speak for another minute or so, then I asked if she had infants of her own. But her reaction to the simple question surprised me. I saw a twitch of something in her face – was it irritation? – and she kept her eyes on the ground. The knuckles on her hand holding the rein flared bone-white as she gripped it tighter. I had upset her; I always managed to say the wrong thing, and my shame sat heavily on me.

After the longest time, she spoke, so quietly I might have missed it.

'No.'

I sighed inwardly. I knew not how to speak to women my age, having no friends or sisters. Eleanor and Anne Shuttleworth were the closest I had to either, and I could hardly bear to be in their simpering, frothy company for more than a day or so. This stranger was being polite, as a poor village girl might with a gentle-woman. But for once in my life I wished for a normal conversation with a young woman, as equals, sitting across from one another at a card table or side by side in saddles.

'I have just had a thought,' I announced, trying to sound merry. 'I do not know the name of my saviour.'

'Alice Gray,' she answered quietly, before adding, 'The women who do not live . . . It's only when it cannot be helped. I know it to look at them.'

I swallowed. 'How do you know it?'

Alice Gray considered her response.

'It's in their eyes. It's giving over to . . . whatever is beyond. You know the daylight gate?'

I nodded, wondering what dusk had to do with child-birth.

'The light and the darkness are equal forces – partners, if you will – then there is a moment, very quick and quiet, where you can see the day giving in to the night. That's when I know. That's what it's like.'

She sounded like a witch, and I almost told her.

'You think me full of fancy,' she said, mistaking my silence.

'No, I understand. The death is inevitable, like the darkness.'

'That's it.'

Not for the first time, I wondered what the darkness felt like when you were half in the light. I think I may have come close to it before, but the pain anchored me to the earth. I watched Alice Gray's dull cap bob alongside my horse's shoulder, and imagined telling her about the doctor's letter. But as with Richard, the words would not come.

'You are young for a midwife,' I said instead.

'I learnt from my mother. She was a midwife. The best, actually.'

I felt the doctor's words tighten once again around my neck, and with my good hand I adjusted my dirt-spattered collar.

'When you say you know it to look at a woman with child?' I asked. 'Are you ever wrong?'

'Sometimes,' Alice replied, but I sensed she was lying. Where she had been eloquent earlier, now it was as though a curtain had come down over her mood. Without turning, I examined her from the corner of my eye. She was not beautiful but there was some vital quality that made her interesting to look at: the long nose, the intelligent, searching eyes, the hands that brought life into the world. She was quickly becoming one of the most fascinating people I'd met.

I swallowed again, tightening my grip on the rein as though it tethered me to this life.

'Do you know it to look at me?'

Alice Gray glanced up at me, then her amber eyes returned to the floor.

Back at Gawthorpe, the servants made a great fuss getting me off my horse and inside the entrance hall. As they lowered me down, I searched for Richard's face in the four or five gathered on the steps, and more in the windows. But of course, I thought dully as they helped me up the steps like an old duchess, he was away. In all the activity, I remembered Alice, and slapped a maid's hand away as she tried to remove the crude stick-and-rags splint.

'I shall keep it on, Sarah,' I said, as usual managing to sound spiteful rather than gracious.

How queer the servants thought me. For a whole year at first I dared not give them instruction – some of them were forty, fifty years my senior. Once, when I was four-teen or so, and brushing my horse in the stable, I heard one of the yard boys call me the child bride. I had stayed there until dusk, prickling with shame, afraid to come out in case they'd know I'd heard. When Richard asked where on earth I'd been for so long, I told him, tears smarting in my eyes, and the boy had been dismissed within the hour.

Sarah let go obediently, but not before I saw the story

forming in her mind, the one she would save for the buttery. That's when I noticed Alice, almost out of sight, descending the front steps. I called her and she paused, framed in the rectangle of daylight, for the entrance hall with its warren of passages was very dark. The servants came to a collective hush, regarding her with open curiosity.

'Will you come in for something to eat?'

My ears were growing red, and I had to clear my throat, knowing everyone was paying attention.

Alice looked uncertain, as though trying to determine whether I had issued an invitation or a command. But Sarah decided for her, ushering her in with an impatient tut and closing the heavy door behind her to keep out the spring chill. Inside the lanterns flared and settled, and Alice wrung her hands. Burning with self-consciousness, I turned to one of the kitchen girls, who was standing uselessly aside.

'Margery, have bread and cheese and something to drink sent to the parlour, and take Miss Gray there. I will change out of my wet things and see her there.'

Alice was looking with interest at the high ceilings, the dark corners, the sconces. I tried to smile at her before going to the staircase, hoping it was not obvious that this was the first time I'd ever had my own guest.

None of the servants offered to help me get out of my riding clothes, which, given how filthy and trampled they were, was difficult with two hands and almost impossible with one. My wrist ached. Puck sniffed curiously at me, and when I was undressed, out of habit I put a hand between my legs to check I was not bleeding. Almost a full half-hour later I was in a clean skirt and jacket, and went down with Puck padding behind me. Voices were coming from beneath the staircase where the parlour was at the back of the house, and I pushed the door open, to be greeted by two faces.

'Richard!'

He came to me and kissed my cheek distractedly, taking hold of my wrist.

'I was on my way to your chamber – what's this about you falling from your horse, little ghost? And *what* is this invention? A fine improvisation, I must say. Miss Gray, is this your work? Fleetwood, are you hurt? I hope no one else is?'

As always, Richard's bombardment of questions made me feel dizzy, and I knew not which to answer first. Leaving my hands in his, I looked instead at Alice, whose face was expressionless, giving no hint of their conversation. The parlour was not grand, but in it Alice looked twice as drab, her dress dull and dingy against the jewel-like Turkey carpets and honey-coloured panelling. Indoors, she was different – ordinary, almost – and younger, perhaps twenty-two or twenty-three

'You are surprised to see me. Did you forget I was not leaving until tonight?'

Weakly, with Richard's help, I sat down in one of the polished oak chairs by the low fire, which thankfully was crackling cheerfully. Before I could speak, Margery brought a loaf with cheese and fruit and a jug of ale, departing with a swift appraisal of Alice and her muddy fingers.

'Your hands – shall I send for water? I turned to Richard, who had begun pouring ale into two cups. 'Alice helped me back on to my horse.'

'An angel of the forest,' he announced, handing one to her.

She brushed her hands on her apron before accepting the cup and drinking thirstily. I realised Richard was waiting for an answer from me, his grey eyes on mine.

'All is well?'

He was in a good mood, as usual, light of spirit and heart. Sometimes he made me feel as though I wore a cloak of doom and gloom that would never unfasten, yet if the same one was placed around his shoulders he would shake it off as easily as a wet dog.

'All is well,' I replied with a reassuring smile. *For now*, I thought.

He knelt and took my free hand, kissing it, then filling it with the cup of ale.

'I will leave you women to talk of French farthingales while I get out of these clothes. I think I will delay my trip another day. Besides, Easter is almost here so there will not be much business to be done.'

My heart sang at his words, but before I could thank him he was gone, grabbing a fistful of grapes on his way out. I watched Alice, wondering what effect my husband had on her, but she just looked tired, with her hair tumbling out of her cap and her mouth turning down at the corners. The faintest hint of lavender drifted over again. The fire cracked and glowed, filling the little room with its comforting scent of woodsmoke.

Before I could speak, Alice said, 'What is a French farthingale?'

I almost laughed, pleased I could answer her for once.

'It's a wheel you wear under your skirts at the waist, to make them wide. You have never heard of one?'

She shook her head. 'How is your wrist? You will need to bind it tightly with rags.'

I prodded it gingerly. 'Fine. I have come off my horse plenty of times. My friend Roger says you are not a rider unless you come off seven times, and one for luck. I suppose you come off frequently, rushing to women in childbed?'

'I do not have a horse.'

'Do not have a horse?' I was shocked. 'Then how do you get anywhere?'

A trace of a smile lifted her lips at the corners.

'I walk. Or if a yeoman is sending his man for me, sometimes he will bring one.' I must have looked astonished, for she added, 'Babies are often not quick to be born.'

'I would not know.' I felt her eyes watching me from across the room, burning like two rushlights. 'Please, sit down. Eat.'

She obliged. 'I cannot stay long, I have to . . . go soon.' I nodded, watching the delicate way she cut the cheese with long fingers. 'This is your first child?'

'Yes,' I said.

I realised I sounded exactly the same as she did earlier when she said that she did not have any children. As she ate quietly, I twisted my wedding band, considering. What had I brought her to my parlour for, if not just to show her my gratitude? I thought of Richard's concern. *All is well.* For how long would it be well? And there was something about Alice that invited confidence: the way she'd tamed my horse in the clearing without speaking.

'I have lost three children,' I said quickly.

She let go of the knife, sitting back and wiping her hands on her apron, dusting crumbs from her fingers. I could not look her in the face, so I stared at the carpet, noticing Puck's orange hairs scattered here and there, so fine they looked woven in.

'I'm sorry.' Her voice was full of kindness.

I rubbed at one of the wooden lions on the arm of my chair.

'My mother thinks I am not able to have children. She

likes to remind me I am failing to carry out my duty as a wife.'

The silence from the chair opposite was thoughtful and patient.

'How old were they?'

'All of them died before they were born.' I pulled at a loose thread of gold in my skirt, then tried to tuck it back in. 'After the first time, Richard was worried, so he hired a woman to watch over me.'

'Watch over you?'

'To see I was eating right, things like that. He was worried,' I said again.

'About you or the child?'

'About both of us. What did the two of you talk about earlier?'

'This and that. Work.'

A sting of jealousy made me sneer a little.

'He talked to you of his business?'

'No. I work at the sign of the Hand and Shuttle in Padiham. I did not know you and your husband owned it.'

'Do we?' I asked, realising too late how ignorant I sounded. 'I thought you . . . So you have two places of work?'

'Babies are not born every day. Not in Colne.'

'How long have you worked there?'

'Not long.'

'How much do they pay you?'

She took a long drink of beer and wiped her mouth. It made me envious to watch her enjoying her food and drink. My stomach growled.

'Two pounds,' she said.

'A week?'

Alice stared at me. 'A year.'

I knew my face glowed scarlet, but I did not look away. In a whole year she made what I paid for three yards of velvet. I shifted in my seat and adjusted the rags from her apron around my wrist, which was beginning to itch. The smooth oak was cool where it met my skin.

My mouth was dry. I wanted to tell her about Richard moving out of our chamber, about how in February I was sick forty times in one day. 'Can you help me have a baby? A living one?'

'I . . .'

'I will pay you five shillings a week.'

The sum would no doubt send James the steward's eyebrows into his hairline as he entered it into the ledger, but my grasp on money had humiliated me, so I knew any offer had to sit comfortably between generous and fair. Richard had once said that money was impossible to discuss with poor people. Alice was quite clearly poor, and – I looked at her hands for rings – unmarried. I now knew what he meant.

'That's five times what I earn now,' she said softly.

She reached a finger under her cap to scratch at her

hair, and set her beer down gently. My stomach made a noise we both heard; I had not eaten a morsel.

'I will also give you use of a horse, so you can ride here and to the inn at Padiham. Colne is a long way to walk.'

She considered this, licking her lips and staring at the fire, before asking, 'Are you further along now than you have been before? When will it come?'

'Early autumn, I suppose. The last time was . . . somewhere near the end.'

'I would need to examine you,' she said. 'When did you last bleed?'

'Christmastide. There is something else.'

Putting my cup down, I reached into my gown and pulled out the letter from the doctor that I'd shoved into my jacket when I dressed. I'd kept it locked behind a small square panel in my dresser, and the key I hid between the rope and mattress beneath my bed. I unfolded it, smoothing it out and feeling the intimate warmth of my body heat. But Alice did not take it, and a frown had creased between her eyebrows.

'I cannot read,' she said dully.

There was a sudden scratching at the door, and we both sat up straight. I stuffed the paper down the side of the chair but no one entered.

I called, 'Yes?'

When no answer came I got up to open it. Puck stood panting on the other side and, I dropped to my knees.

'It's only you. Good boy.'

He followed me to my chair and I saw Alice's eyes widen at the size of him.

'He is a gentle giant,' I reassured her, letting him settle at my feet. 'I am constantly brushing dog hairs off my skirts, but I don't mind really. Finish your cheese or he will have it.'

'He is very big,' Alice said.

Puck lifted his russet head when she spoke and barked once, loudly.

'That's enough,' I told him.

'What is he?'

'A French mastiff.'

'Was he a gift from your husband?'

Instinctively I reached to scratch his ears.

'No. I rescued him from a bear-baiting pit in London. He was thin and starving, tied up in the street next to a bear warden selling tickets. I went to stroke him and the bear warden kicked him. He said dogs were useless if they were soft and I would ruin him. I asked him how much for the pup and he said he wasn't worth the rope tied around his neck. So I picked him up off the ground and said I would take him. He changed his mind then, said I was denying him a prize fighter. I gave him a shilling, and we left without a backwards glance. I named him Puck, for a character in a play Richard and I saw a few days before – an imp of the forest. Not that there is anything imp-like about him.'

Alice gazed thoughtfully at the spoilt beast on the Turkey carpet. His tongue was the size of a salmon, lolling happily from his jaws.

'How far he has come in life,' she remarked. 'I have heard of bear-baiting but never seen it.'

'I find it dreadful. They are bloodthirsty people in London; perhaps it's because they can't hunt.'

We sat in a silence more comfortable than before, and she nodded at the letter in my hands.

'What does it say?'

'That the next time I am in childbed I will die.' Saying it aloud for the first time, I felt the tendrils loosen around my neck. 'As you can see, I am going to need a miracle. God has blessed me with many things. I am not sure that being a mother is one of them, but today I prayed for a wise woman and there you were. I so want to give my husband a son – he longs for it.'

'And you?'

'I am his wife, and I hope to be a mother. I do not want him to be a widower.'

I tried to swallow the lump in my throat. Alice was openly regarding me with an abject pity, and briefly I wondered how she could: she who was poor, and unmarried, who had two jobs and no horse. Perhaps the fine house and handsome husband and expensive clothes meant nothing to her, and perhaps she could also see that they were of little use to me, who could buy anything I wanted except the thing I wanted most: to succeed as

Richard's wife, and pay him back for what he did for me, for the future he took me away from. For him, I wanted to fill the house with sticky hands and dusty knees. While we had no children, we were not a family; we had a house but not a home. Even spending a lifetime locked up at Barton, with my mother's disapproval the first thing I saw in the morning and the last I saw at night, was preferable to the alternative. Were it not for Richard, I knew where I would be.

'Mistress?'

Alice was looking at me with concern. The fire spat and sputtered, and the knife still stuck out from the cheese like a dagger hurled into a tree.

I leant forwards, urgent for the first time. My desperation had been there since I'd met her, had been building for months, but now it was gushing out of me.

'Please,' I said. 'Say you will help me.' I realised I was gripping the arms of my chair. 'I need you to save my life, and with it another one. Help me live, Alice. Please help me be a mother, and have a child.'

She was looking at me strangely, weighing me up, unsure of the purchase. When she finally nodded, it was like she had taken my hand.

CHAPTER 5

That night, in bed alone, I had The Nightmare. The forest was pitch-black and cold, and my feet crunched on dead leaves when I moved, so I stayed still, unable to see even my hand in front of my face. My heart thudded, and my ears strained for sound. Then the boars came, shuffling and grunting nearby, their greedy breath hot and curious. I closed my eyes to hear better, and felt something brush against my skirts. Everything went still. A bead of sweat trickled down my face, and then the silence broke, and it began. The noises the beasts made were awful – high-pitched, excited screeches and barks. I started running blindly, my hands out in front of me. I was crying, and they were behind me, snarling and gnashing their jaws, their stabbing tusks like knives made of bone. I tripped and stumbled to the ground, covered my head with my hands and whimpered. They found me, circling their fallen prey. They were hungry, they were going to pierce me, gouge me right the way through with their tusks. A ripping, shooting pain cut me in half and made me pull my knees up, but they were bound in my skirts, and I cried out.

I was in my bedroom in bright daylight, soaked with sweat. My heart was loud as a bell, my face wet with tears, but relief drenched me as I realised there were no boars, and I wasn't in the forest. My breathing slowed, and my wrist ached dully. The tight rags Alice had told me to wrap around it had come loose, trailing beneath me in the bedclothes. I yawned, blinking in the sunlight, stretched and turned over.

Sitting next to the bed, watching me like a hawk, was my mother.

She waited as I tried to push myself into a sitting position. I did not look at her, but knew that her mouth would be a thin line as she examined my wild black hair, my skin grey as the ashes that lay in the fireplace. Mary Barton disapproved of illness, weakness or failure of any kind; in fact, she found it offensive. Before either of us spoke, I heard the tread of Richard's boots in the passage, his coin belt jangling.

'Look who is here for a visit,' he announced, coming in and resting a hand on my mother's rigid shoulder.

Mother's black eyes met mine. Her head was bare and

her collar, starched to perfection, fanned out high around her. Her white hands were folded serenely in her lap and her expression was one of great restraint. She was still wearing her outdoor cloak, giving the impression that she had either just alighted her horse or was about to leave. She always felt the cold, which was why she'd moved out of Barton after Richard and I were married, complaining of the size of it, settling at Richard's suggestion into a more modest house further north.

Not north enough.

'Hello, Mother,' I said.

'You missed breakfast,' she said.

I licked my teeth. My breath was rank.

'I will have some food brought up,' Richard said, leaving and closing the door behind him.

I pushed back the thick counterpane, climbed out of bed and went to get a length of cloth to clean my teeth, my mother watching me all the time.

'This chamber is like a pigsty. Your servants should be more attentive – what else could they possibly be occupied with?' she said. When I ignored her, she went on. 'Will you get dressed today?'

'Perhaps.'

Standing sentry above the mantelpiece, either side of the Shuttleworth coat of arms, were two plaster female figurines half my height: Prudence and Justice. Sometimes I imagined them as my friends. My mother's straight back and position in front of the fireplace set her directly in the middle of them, making her look like their third sister, Misery.

'Why do you look amused, Fleetwood? You are mistress of this house – get dressed at once.'

Puck whined to be let in, so I let him. He sauntered towards my mother, sniffing her skirts then dismissing her.

'I cannot understand why you keep that beast in the house,' she said. 'Dogs are for hunting and guarding, not treating like infants. What is that on your wrist?'

I gathered up the ribbon and began to tie it more tightly.

'I fell off my horse yesterday while riding. It's only a sprain.'

'Fleetwood,' she said, lowering her voice and glancing over her shoulder to check the door was closed. I could smell the sickly pomade she dabbed at her wrists. 'Richard tells me you are expecting again. If I am not mistaken, you have lost three children before they came to this earth.'

'I have not *lost* anything.'

'Then I will put it plainly. Three times you have failed to carry a child. Do you in honesty think you should be throwing yourself off horses? You are not being careful enough. You have a midwife?'

'Yes.'

'Where did you find her?'

'She is local. From Colne.'

'Might you have been wiser to employ a woman who came recommended from a family we know? Did you or Richard speak to Jane Towneley? Or Margaret Starkie?'

I stared at Prudence's plaster face. Her stoic gaze avoided mine. I was a wife, the mistress of one of the finest households for miles around, and I was standing in my nightgown being scolded by my mother. Had Richard invited her? He knew how I hated her. I clenched my fists, once, twice, three times.

'Whomever I employ is my decision, *Mother.*'

I coated the last word with honey, and her face, so composed at all times, betrayed a tiny flicker of fury.

'I shall discuss it with Richard,' she said. 'In the meantime, I want you to promise you are doing everything you can to carry this child into life. I am not convinced you are currently. More rest is required, and . . . indoor pursuits. Perhaps take up an instrument instead of galloping around like a squire. You have a fine husband, and if you start behaving like a wife and mother, God's gift will come. I did not unite our families so you could play at being a princess in a tower. Now, I expect you to dine with me. Please get dressed and meet me downstairs.'

I heard her descend the staircase and prayed that her portrait would fall from its hangings and flatten her.

Richard poured a glass of red wine under my nose and passed it to my mother. It was dark as a ruby, the same colour that had leaked from me three times – surprisingly beautiful in its richness, drenching the bed linen and mattress that had to be burnt on a bonfire.

To avoid its heady scent I lifted my face to the ceiling. The plasterwork in the dining room was decorated with dozens of bunches of grapes, their vines climbing out towards the corners, entwining like lovers' hands.

'No wine for you, Fleetwood?'

'No, thank you.'

Richard poured another glass for his friend Thomas Lister, who was passing through on his way to Yorkshire. We were sat around the fire, which was low, and the fug of it was making me drowsy. Not drowsy enough, however, to miss how Thomas' greedy glance slipped to Richard's rings when he handed his friend the glass. His own bare hand flexed in response and he caught my eye, looking immediately away.

In years Thomas was somewhere between Richard's age and mine, and his wealth was somewhere between a plain country gentleman's and ours. He would have admitted to the first but never the latter. He and Richard had other things in common: they had married in the same year; their fathers had died; they had inherited large estates with mothers and sisters to support. Four years ago, Mr Lister Senior had been taken ill at his son's wedding, collapsing during the vows and dying a few days later. Thomas' mother never truly recovered and hadn't left the house in all that time.

I found Thomas Lister a strange and rather interesting

man – he did not easily make conversation, preferring to be somewhere on the edge of it. His wide eyes bulged slightly and he was very small and slim, like a woman. Richard said that his build made him a great rider, that he held himself straight as an arrow.

My mother failed to mix comfortably with young people: she had a way of making them feel like infants, and Thomas stuttered a polite response when she asked after his mother. He was rescued by the entrance of Edmund, the apprentice, who told Richard that a woman had arrived from one of the farms with news of a dog that had withered a ewe. In those days we kept hundreds of sheep in the fields; the soil was too wet for anything else.

There was a pause, in which Richard set his glass down.

'To whom does the dog belong?'

Edmund shook his head. 'She knows not, Master. She found it running around, worrying the flock. She asks you to come quickly.'

Richard hurried out. People were always coming to knock at our door and tell us their tales. Richard was generous, giving them grain when their crops were down and wood to repair their houses. There were two hundred families in Padiham and just as many problems laid at our door since we'd been here.

'What takes you to Yorkshire?' my mother asked Thomas.

She was making the point of being a good hostess,

taking pleasure in illuminating me as being a poor one.

'I am going to a trial at the Lent assizes,' said Thomas.

'A trial?'

The logs in the hearth cracked and burnt. I wondered how long Richard would be gone; it was the daylight gate, and darkness would soon press in at the windows.

Thomas shifted in his chair.

'A murder trial,' he said softly. 'The accused is a woman named Jennet Preston.'

I sat up a little straighter.

'Do you know her?' I asked.

'Unfortunately, very well.' A tendon jumped in his cheek. 'She worked for my family for many years, but since my father died she has not left us alone. We gave her kindness and favours, but she is ungrateful, always asking for more.'

'Who is she accused of murdering?'

'A child.'

Both my mother and I were united briefly in shock. Thomas stared grimly at the fire.

'Are you protesting her innocence?'

Thomas looked sharply at me. 'Her innocence? Her guilt. She murdered another servant's son – an infant, not a year old – brutally and heartlessly.'

Before I could stop it a memory crowded in: a small, cold body, two tiny rows of eyelashes that would never open. I closed my eyes and forced it away.

'Why would she do that?' I asked.

'Because she is a jealous woman,' Thomas said shortly. 'She failed to seduce Edward and so took the thing that was most precious to him and his wife. She is a witch.'

My mother leant forwards. 'Another witch?' Thomas was confused. 'You have not heard about the latest guest at Read Hall?'

'How do *you* know about the guest at Read Hall?' I asked.

She shrugged one shoulder dismissively. 'Richard told me.'

She said it in a way that implied of course he would inform his mother-in-law of every matter of which he knew. But she had a way of drawing things out of people, of picking up on a moment of hesitation or an offhand comment and worrying it like the dog with the ewe. Richard would not have spread his friend's affairs about the county; my mother must already have heard it from someone else and no doubt questioned him while he was occupied and distracted.

'Who is at Read Hall?' Thomas asked, looking from my mother to me.

So she told him about Roger, who Thomas was intimately acquainted with, and the pedlar John Law and the witch Alizon Device. He listened with great interest.

Her version of events was less informed and more speculative than Roger's. Deigning to not correct her gave me great satisfaction, and so that she wouldn't see the smug expression on my face, I turned my attention to the frieze that crowded the top of the dining room walls. Mermaids, dolphins, griffins and all sorts of creatures, half-human and half-animal, fixed their attention on the centre of the room, as though we were at some great mythical court. When I came to Gawthorpe the frieze was my favourite thing about the house, and I would walk around and around, examining each figure, giving them names and little stories. Here were two orphan sisters, who were princesses of the sea and ruled the waves; there was a lion army with their shields, primed to attack. I watched them grow darker and more mysterious as the night arrived, and my mother and Thomas Lister nattered like two washerwomen. My eyelids began to droop; my mouth was dry and my back ached. Until Richard came back I would have to sit here, and there was still no sign of him.

That's when it occurred to me: as long as my mother was here, Richard would sleep in our bed so as not to invite questions, for her beady eyes missed nothing. She had given no sign that she had seen the truckle bed, but perhaps Richard had closed the dressing room door.

I pulled at the rolls in my hair and wondered how long until I could take them out.

'The girl is at Roger Nowell's house,' my mother was saying, her eyes shining. 'He is keeping her there so she can do no harm to others.'

'And she confessed?'

'So they say.'

'And Roger thinks there are others?'

My mother nodded. 'In the same family.'

'Heavens, Mother. Anyone would think you had been walking alongside John Law when he was cursed,' I said.

Thomas was looking thoughtful, clutching his glass against his chest.

'Will you admire our mermaids, Thomas?' I asked. 'Take a closer look. They are quite remarkable, designed by two brothers who carried out all the plasterwork at Gawthorpe.'

Obligingly he stood and approached them, and I turned to my mother and whispered, 'We do not talk of Roger Nowell's business like village wives in this house. He is our friend. Now Thomas is going to take what you told him to Yorkshire, which is further than it needed to go.'

My mother's face grew sour. 'I am merely informing your neighbour of what is happening under his nose. Everyone will know soon enough that there are witches in these parts. And so they should. Do they not say the women are wild here?'

'I know not what *they* say, nor do I care to. And I'm not sure wild is the same as evil.'

'Very skilled work,' Thomas commented politely behind us. 'Extremely intricate. Quite fantastical.' He seemed stirred and didn't come back to his seat. 'I will set out again before it gets dark; I may call at Read Hall before my journey to Yorkshire.'

'Read Hall is five miles in the other direction,' I said.

He reached for his cloak.

'My regards to Richard.'

He left swiftly, his boots echoing in the passage. There was a moment of silence, then I excused myself on the pretence of needing to go to bed.

The candles had been lit in my chamber and I stood in front of the glass to remove the rolls from my hair. It looked weak and thin, and strands fell away to the floor when I combed through it. I went to the window to close the drapes and in the glass I saw Richard's outline in the doorway.

'You'll sleep in here tonight?' I asked.

'I suppose.'

I turned and my heart stopped in my chest.

His hands were scarlet. Blood coated his doublet and there were flecks on his face and up to his elbows.

'What happened?'

'I've sent for a jug.' He wiped his hands along his arms but the blood was dried. The skin around his fingernails was already turning brown. 'It was a mess. If I hadn't seen the dog I would have thought a wolf had done it.'

I walked over to the bed and sat on it to remove my slippers.

'That's impossible. There have been no wolves here for a hundred years.'

I thought about our bodies being close again tonight, his warmth beside me. Maybe I could run my finger down his spine like I used to. Maybe he would turn and put his mouth to mine, his hardness inside me. Even if wc never slept in the same bed again, I would never forget the soft heat of his skin at the tip of my fingers. Then I thought of the secret letter, and the image vanished.

'Was the sheep dead?' I asked, turning to let Richard unlace me.

'No. I had to kill it.'

'And the dog? What was it?'

'A brown mongrel. It ran off before I could catch it. I'll ask around to find out who it belongs to.'

'I have hired the girl who rescued me as a midwife.'

'Oh yes? What was her name? She is a midwife?'

'Alice. She is very experienced.' I did not meet his eye. 'I hope you don't mind – I've lent her a horse from the stables, for as long as she attends me.'

'Not one of mine?'

'No, the grey draught mare. She is quite old now. Richard . . .' I swallowed. 'Will you stay in here from tonight?'

'Many men and their wives sleep in different rooms, it's not unusual,' he replied, not unkindly.

'It should be.'

'Nonsense. Besides, you are already with child. It is not as though we can make another one.'

But I did not hear him, because I'd lifted my smock over my head. A fine thread of scarlet was trailing down my thigh. I halted it on its path with a finger and panic rolled towards me like storm clouds. I closed my eyes and prayed.

CHAPTER 6

I lay awake, stiff as a board next to Richard, who snored softly. I rose finally to walk in the long gallery while the moonlight streamed in. The house was silent, and the polished floorboards gleamed bright as snow. The floor creaked under my silent tread as I went up and down, east to west and back again. I returned to bed before the day arrived. More than once I looked at the dried streak of red that had faded into my skin to prove what had happened, or rather had started to happen, and then stopped. I'd covered it quickly with my nightdress, and Richard had noticed nothing, preoccupied with washing off the sheep's blood. I could smell it from across the room, and my stomach twisted with revulsion and fear, as though smelling blood might bring on my own.

Alice had asked me to give her a few days to collect some herbs that would make me stronger, and it already felt like an eternity, so in the morning while everyone broke their fast, I walked out to give Puck his exercise. I could not eat because my stomach was like a bag of eels again, but with worry this time. We turned right out of the house and went along the edge of the lawn, following the river and passing the great barn and outbuildings. The dogs in their kennels caught Puck's scent and barked themselves senseless. He sniffed around the corners and walls, ignoring them. Sometimes I wondered if he knew he was a dog. I wondered too if he could remember anything from before I rescued him, and hoped he couldn't.

'Good morning, Mistress,' the farming men and apprentices said, laden with tools and ropes and things I had no idea the uses of.

'Good morning,' I said, and walked on.

The house and all its buildings were soon swallowed behind the trees, which closed over it like a green drape. They rustled around me as I followed the narrow road that led away from Gawthorpe, watching Puck as he explored, flitting through trees, his nose fixed to the ground.

A quarter of a mile or so from the house, I could see two figures approaching on horseback. I stepped closer to the trees and waited, recognising the larger shape to be Roger. When they were a short distance away, he spoke briefly to the person on his right – a woman in a plain

wool dress. My eyesight was poor, but I knew it was not
his wife, Katherine. Roger dismounted and approached,
holding the reins of his horse, which I noticed was roped
to its companion. Her spindly white hands were locked
in manacles, which were tied to the reins. A prisoner, then.
As magistrate, Roger was often carting felons around the
county and sometimes took them up to the gaol at
Lancaster. My gaze lingered a moment too long on her
bound wrists, and when I looked up into the shrewd face
of a young woman, with dark eyes and thin lips, she was
regarding me with a hostile sort of pride.

'Mistress, I am pleased to see you out walking on this
fine day. You look to be in invigorated spirits,' said Roger.

'Are you visiting us?' I asked, holding my hand out to
let him kiss it.

'A different kind of visit today – more an invitation for
Richard, in fact. Is he at home?'

'Yes.'

'Does he have free time this morning?'

'He leaves for Manchester in an hour,' I lied. Richard
was not going off with Roger and leaving me alone with
my mother if I had anything to do with it. 'His things are
being prepared. Is everything all right?'

He nodded again. It was strange for him to not introduce his companion.

'That's disappointing. I am going now to Ashlar House.'

'James Walmsley's home?'

'Indeed. I wondered if Richard would be interested in

accompanying me – I have two interviews to conduct and would appreciate his assistance.' He leant closer. 'He is going to do great things one day, your husband. Mark my words, he will be high in government by the time he is as old as I am, and I plan to help him on his way. He has the advantage of birth that I did not, his uncle being well known at court. At some point I will introduce him to the king, and I wish for him to have a hand in these developments at Pendle. They could further him in the eyes of the Crown. I trust his opinion, as does Mr Walmsley, but we shall have to get on without him today.'

He turned to glance back at his companion, whose quiet presence was somehow unnerving.

'I hear you have employed a midwife,' Roger said unexpectedly.

I blinked in surprise. 'I have,' I replied, wondering how he knew. Richard had not seen him since their hunt.

Roger beamed. 'Wonderful. There will be an heir at Gawthorpe before the year is out. Is it the same woman as last time? From Wigan?'

It was hard to concentrate, what with the malicious radiance emitting from the woman behind him.

'No. A local woman.'

'Jennifer Barley? She was Katherine's.'

'No. A girl called Alice, from Colne.'

Then something strange happened. At the mention of Alice's name, Roger's acquaintance made a sudden movement that startled her horse. I glanced up at her, then quickly away when I saw she had not removed her gaze from my face, as though she was reading something quite fascinating.

'We shall have to arrange a gift for your confinement,' Roger was saying. How could he carry on our conversation as though his prisoner was not even here? He looked pleased. 'What to buy for the woman who has everything?'

'Who is your friend, Roger? Will you not introduce me?'

'This,' he said, 'is Alizon Device.'

A chill brushed my skin, and my heart beat a little faster. So Roger was parading the witch around Pendle and had brought her to Gawthorpe. There was something in Alizon's proud stare that led me to believe she knew this, and I felt a twinge of sympathy.

'Don't let the dress fool you – it's Katherine's. Alizon has been staying with me these past few days. We are going to Ashlar House for a meeting with some of her relatives,' he said jovially, turning back to his charge.

The girl did not speak, but shimmered with malice. In the silence that followed, a rook cried out from the trees and a gust of wind moved the forest around us.

'Give Richard my best. And Friday sennight, you'll come to dine at Read? Katherine is so looking forward to seeing you.'

'It would be our honour.'

I curtseyed, and let my eyes flick once more to Alizon Device, who was still as a statue, her gaze resting somewhere in the middle distance. Roger raised his hat and mounted. I watched them go, seeing Roger's many-ringed hand raise up in farewell. Then I called for Puck and started back towards the house.

As it was the last day of Lent and my mother did not care for fish, and the cook always remembered, we sat down to a rich dinner of cheese pies with potatoes, fruit, bread and beer. I nibbled at crusts and crumbs, but was so used to not eating I barely felt hungry any more.

My mother disapproved of all our servants apart from the cook. She had decided that they were surly and ungrateful, and said that it was only a matter of time before the silver and silk began to go missing. Sometimes I wondered if I lived in my own house or hers. I could tell she missed the days of running Barton, which with its large staff was palatial compared to her modest manor. Richard and I used to call her Gloriana of the Manor when she visited us after we were married, trying to direct us as though we were both her children. Until then I'd never had anyone to make fun with. We would stop up our mouths with food when she said things like: 'Really, Richard, I never knew a man to wear as much jewellery as you,' and, 'You should have your crest put on your bottles for serving wine – it's the fashionable thing, you know. They are even doing it in Yorkshire.'

On that afternoon she decided to take issue with the set of panels above the fireplace.

'Richard, I see you have still not had my daughter's name scribed on the overmantel,' she announced, referring to the five solid wood squares engraved with the names of various members of the Shuttleworth family.

Richard's initials were added to the fourth before we married. He meant to have a carpenter put my initials with his but had not found the time, so *R* and *S* floated on their own, waiting for a companion. It was a bruise that my mother could not stop pressing, as though the wooden panel was the only evidence of my existence and not simply decoration.

'There is no great urgency, Mother,' I said.

'Is four years not enough time?'

'I will add it to my ever-growing list,' was Richard's genial reply.

It was decided she would leave the following day, Easter Sunday, and we went all together to church. I might have been imagining it but my waist felt thicker overnight. I sat through the service looking at my hands folded neatly in my lap, wondering where Alice Gray was and what she was doing. All the people from the town were staring at me a beat longer than usual; I knew I looked ill. I stuck to wearing black – colours only highlighted the grey of my face, which was dull as a rain cloud. My mother's presence invited more than a few extra glances too. She kept her face passive with indifference, but I knew inside she was purring like a cat.

During the service as the curate spoke, I moved my eyes over the hats and caps, looking for a twist of golden hair, but saw none. I caught the eye of a young woman sitting a few pews across, dressed in a fine warm cloak, her globe of a stomach pressing through it. She looked at me in the bold, friendly way countrywomen look at one another, as though to say 'we are one and the same'. But we were not, and I looked away.

My hands were like ice, so I sat on them until they were numb. The nausea had crept back that morning, persistent and unwelcome. Colne was a few miles away and had its own parish, so it was unlikely Alice would be a worshipper at St Leonard's. But she worked at the sign of the Hand and Shuttle, less than a mile away; dare I show my impatience and visit her there? I had invited her to come on Good Friday, but she said she could not and would come after Easter.

I saw the apothecary sitting a few pews away with his family, his placid face turned to the pulpit like a flower looks to the light. Would Alice grow the herbs herself, or buy them from him? And if she did, would she be discreet?

John Baxter, the curate, had a high, clear voice that rang up into the eaves of the church, banishing darkness from every corner.

'"And when Herod saw Jesus, he was exceeding glad",' he was saying. '"For he was desirous to see him of a long season, because he had heard many things of him, and he hoped to have seen some miracle done by him."'

Up there with him at the pulpit was the new King's Bible we had bought him in London. It was the first time I'd been in a printer's, a tall building in the city that to me was as narrow as a wardrobe. In the streets outside, children carried baskets of loaves on their heads, as though we were in Galilee. Inside the printer's was a different world entirely, half scholarly with its atmosphere of paper and ink, and half like a torture chamber with huge, groaning wooden contraptions.

"'And the chief priests and scribes stood and vehemently accused him. And Herod with his men of war set him at nought, and mocked him, and arrayed him in a gorgeous robe, and sent him again to Pilate."'

The new Bible had been printed the previous year and we bought three copies: one for the house, one for the church, and one for Richard's mother. All of them were objects of beauty, edged in gold, the paper inside as thin as petals.

"'But they cried, saying, Crucify him, crucify him. And he said unto them the third time, Why, what evil hath he done? I have found no cause of death in him: I will therefore chastise him, and let him go. And they were instant with loud voices, requiring that he might be crucified."'

John Baxter was old, his skin the colour of Bible pages, but his voice carried like a much younger man's over the coughing and shuffling and murmuring of infants. My head felt light, as though I was an hourglass needing to be tipped upside down.

"'For, behold, the days are coming, in the which they shall say, Blessed are the barren, and the wombs that never bare, and the paps which never gave suck. Then shall they begin to say to the mountains, Fall on us; and to the hills, Cover us.'"

I felt my mother move next to me, her dress crushing against mine. My corse was tight and my blood beat in my neck. My head was so empty I thought it might detach from my neck and float like feathers into the rafters.

John Baxter invited us to rise, and the crowd moved upwards, carrying me with it, and the room warped and swam. Then everything went black.

The following morning, instead of waiting for Alice at the windows, I decided to join Richard on the lawn where I saw him training his new falcon. A dark cloud had lifted since my mother had left, but the old one had taken its place once again. Picking my way across the wet grass to where Richard was standing by the steps, I stopped quietly behind him so as not to frighten the bird, which was tied to his wrist by a string. Blinded by its hood, it flapped in confusion above our heads, driven to distraction by the scent of chicken flesh in a pouch at Richard's thigh.

There was an art to the training of birds, and Richard

had mastered of it. He made a clicking noise and pulled the string so the falcon came down with it, scrambling about until it found a perch on his glove. He tossed it a bit of meat.

'I shall never know why you do this yourself and leave the falconer idle,' I said. 'I am surprised you still have eyes in your head.'

'Because it's most satisfying,' he replied easily. 'Besides, she is only ever yours if you do it the long way. Loyalty is earned, not demanded.' The bird took off again, getting a shock when it reached the end of the string and shrieking loudly. 'This one is from Turkey. She will need no bells if she insists on making this noise.'

'She is cursing you,' I teased.

'I did not know you spoke Turkish.'

'You still have much to discover about me.'

We smiled at one another, and my thoughts rushed again to the surface. I pushed them down.

'Something is troubling you?' Richard asked.

It would be so easy to go and fetch the letter from my cupboard.

'Tell me why you have kept this from me,' I would say, handing it to him. 'Tell me it isn't true.'

Instead, I shook my head and fixed my eyes on the bird.

'Roger has invited us to dine on Friday,' I said.

'Yes, he told me he saw you. He had his witch with him?'

'She was a strange creature. I am not sure what chilled

me more – her presence or Roger's indifference. She must be dangerous or she wouldn't be manacled. Why would Roger bring her to our house?'

'He has made her his shadow. As long as she is in his sight, he is in the king's. I'm sure he will dispose of her once she has served her purpose.'

'That's a callous thing to think about your friend.'

Richard looked sideways at me. 'That's an innocent thing to think about yours.' He touched the blooming stain at my temple with a gentle thumb. 'That will be quite a bruise.'

'It already has more colours than my dress. My pride is bruised more than anything – all those people who watched me go down.'

'We shall have to lock you in the house. First falling from your horse, then fainting in church. Whatever will we do with you?'

Barrels of wine were being rolled into the house behind us, tumbling over the stone passage that led into the cellar. Richard's attention moved back to the bird, and I followed his gaze to admire her bright talons, her gentle wings struggling against the string. After a few months of this, a dead hare stuffed with a live chicken would be used as prey, then a hare with a broken leg. I wondered where I might be by the time she went on her first hunt. Buried in the churchyard?

The falcon shrieked and flapped above us, and between her wing beats came the sound of hooves. Richard brought the bird down to his glove, and that's when I felt it for the first time: the quickening. Unmistakable, and yet before I realised it was happening it stopped, so suddenly I wondered if I'd imagined it. But I knew the feeling from once before: like I was a barrel of water and a fish was turning inside me. I gripped Richard's arm, my whole body ringing.

'Fleetwood, are you well?'

'Yes,' I lied. 'The baby . . . I felt it moving.'

'But that's wonderful!' He beamed, and I couldn't help but match his smile.

His bird flapped impatiently, and before it could take hold of my head I backed away.

'Alice should be on her way – I will ride to meet her on the Colne road.'

'Your wrist is well enough to ride?'

I held up my bandaged arm. 'Almost like new.'

In the clean air, with the river on one side and forest on the other, with every jolt of the horse I felt my thoughts slip away from my own life and further towards Alice's. There was so much I didn't know about her. As I accompanied her to the front door, the day she rescued me, I'd enquired after her father, and Alice told me he was ill and unable to work. I wondered if they had a close relationship, or if Alice dreamt of marrying so she could move out.

Poor girls were so unlike rich girls, who only had to wait in their houses for the day a husband arrived, like turkeys fattening for Christmas. Poor girls could choose for themselves, perhaps even as equals: a neighbour might catch their eye, or a shop boy they bought their meat off each week. I tried to imagine Alice with a man – her long, white fingers touching his face, him moving a twist of golden hair from hers – and couldn't.

The trees thinned out and made way for the open sky, and green hills billowed around in the manner of fresh linen being put on a bed. The river rounded in front of me and I had to cut into Hagg Wood, moving out of the open and back into the trees. The horse's hooves were quieter there, and after a minute or so I saw two figures ahead in a clearing – women, wearing dull colours and white caps. They hadn't noticed me. I pulled in the reins to slow down, when I realised one of them was Alice, and her voice was raised and angry, travelling through the trees. I slid down from my horse's back and crossed silently over the mossy ground towards them, stopping behind a tree, where I had a clearer view of the other woman.

She was the ugliest person I'd ever seen in my life – almost frightening to look at. She was poor: that was clear. Her dress was so baggy and shapeless it looked as though she had stitched sacking together, making her appear thin and deformed. But the most alarming thing about her was her eyes: they were set in different parts of her face and not level like other people's. One sat high, gazing up at

the leaves of the trees around her, and the other, lower
in her cheek, examined the roots. Could she see more
that way, or less? She stood with her mouth open, letting
her tongue pass over her lips as Alice spoke, sharp and
low at once.

I could not hear what was being said, and as I strained
forwards, a movement next to me made me jump. A thin
brown dog with ragged fur trotted out from the trees,
skirting past me and going towards the women, who did
not pay it attention. It cut through the small gap between
them and passed on into the trees beyond. The ugly
woman's pet, then. I thought about turning away before I
was seen, but Alice made as though to stalk off towards
me and my horse, and I froze. The other woman spoke in
a raspy, harsh voice, saying some admonishment or other.

The dog barked far off, and its owner looked over her
shoulder briefly, before – chillingly – turning her wayward
eyes in my direction. My skin prickled all over, and I willed
that my dark green dress made me difficult to spy. She
spoke once more to Alice, then lumbered off after the
dog, muttering to herself.

Alice stayed for a moment in the clearing and I saw her
fists clench and unclench. She rubbed the tops of her arms
as though she was cold – a vulnerable gesture that made
me feel guilty for concealing myself. Then she went off
in the opposite direction, making directly for the river.

I could not see her horse anywhere, and did not hear
hooves on the forest floor. Unsure of what to do, for a

minute I watched her go, then climbed astride my horse and cantered the short distance home. Dismounting breathlessly at the bottom of the steps, I turned to look the way I came and after a few minutes saw her bowed form hurrying from the bank of trees east of the park. There was stealth in her stride, and grace, and authority, and she crossed the lawn in front of the house quick as a rabbit, bent into the biting wind. She wore no cloak. Her expression was dark, and she looked troubled.

'Where is your horse?' was the first thing I asked her. Before she could reply there was the sound of a dog barking from the direction we had come. She looked back, distracted. 'Alice?'

The front door opened, and Richard stood at the top of the steps.

'Ah, the two wood sprites are returned from the forest. Good afternoon, Miss Gray.'

Alice nodded, her eyes on the ground.

'You too, sir.'

'You are taking good care of my wife?'

Alice nodded again.

'Fleetwood, is your horse to walk herself to the stable?' Richard asked.

I gathered myself and took the reins, ready to take her the short distance, but Richard stopped me.

'Your midwife can do that.'

I looked anxiously at Alice, who was distracted and paler than usual.

'Unless she objects?' Richard asked her.

With a pained expression, Alice took the reins from me. I watched her go, hunched against the animal, then gathered my skirts and entered the house.

'She does seem young for a midwife,' Richard said as I moved past him into the dark hallway. The wall lamps flared in the draught as the door shut.

'She is about your age.'

'I still think we should go to London. There are hundreds of midwives there, delivering infants every day.'

'Don't make me go to London, Richard. I want our son to be born at home, where he belongs.' That seemed to do it, and he reached for my hand, squeezing it. 'Alice and I will be in my chamber while she examines me.'

Ten minutes later there was still no sign of Alice, and I got up from the floor where I was stroking Puck and went to the top of the stairs. There she was, standing beneath my portrait, staring at it. She did not know I was watching her, and I saw the edges of her lips curve up, as though she was smiling, lost in some fond memory.

'What do you think of my mother?' I asked, startling her.

'She is very . . . pointy,' was her reply, which made me grin. 'That's you?' She nodded at the child in the picture.

'What were you smiling at?'

'Your face is very serious for one so small. You remind me of . . .' She trailed off.

'Who?'

But she did not answer, moving as if disturbed from a daydream, picking up her skirts and joining me at the top of the staircase. We passed the dressing room where Richard had been sleeping, the truckle bed clearly visible, and I noticed that her arms were empty, and she appeared to have nothing with her.

'My husband wondered how many years you have,' I said, closing the door behind us.

Her mouth opened wordlessly, and her shoulders sank a little.

'I do not know.'

I stared at her.

'You do not know how old you are? Well, when is your birthday?'

She shrugged. 'I have slightly more than twenty years, I think.'

'You do not know your birthday?'

She shook her head. 'I am afraid I have to confess something. I lost the horse you gave me.'

'You *lost* it?'

'I tied it outside my house and the next morning, it was gone.'

Every line of her was apologetic, and I cursed silently at my own foolishness. I had not thought to ask if she had a stable, but of course she did not. I should have paid for her to keep it at an inn or nearby farm. She mistook my reaction for intense disappointment, and began again.

'I will pay you back; I will work for free. How much are horses?'

'I don't know . . . A few pounds?' Her face fell. 'Do not worry, it is done now, and I will pay you just the same,' I said without conviction, for Richard's anger would know no bounds.

How would I tell him? Never mind. While Alice was there, we would focus on the here and now.

I asked her what she had brought, and she walked over to the dresser and began lifting up her skirts, taking little linen parcels from her pocket and lining them up on the polished top before opening them to reveal herbs of varying shades of green. With the fire full and friendly, and the dog snoozing nobly on the rug, my chamber had the same atmosphere of purpose as the kitchen, and I went to the edge of the bed and sat on it, not knowing what to do.

'You are like a travelling herb merchant,' I said. 'Richard would be impressed.'

She pointed from left to right. 'Dill, marigold, lavender, camomile.'

She held up the first bunch: soft and feathery with fine waving fronds. 'Have your cook chop this and mix it into butter, which you can put on your meat, fish, anything.'

'What does it do?'

'A lot. These petals,' she held up the delicate golden

flowers, 'can be dried and stirred into hot milk, or used to flavour cheese. Have the kitchen make you a hot cup each morning and night and stir this in, and it will help with the sickness.'

I nodded, remembering: butter, hot milk, cheese.

'Lavender,' she said. 'Infuse it in some rainwater to make a tincture, and sprinkle it over your pillowcase to help you sleep, and keep away bad dreams.'

She looked at me meaningfully, and for a moment I wondered if I had told her about The Nightmare. How could she know? She lifted her apron again and brought out a tiny glass vial between finger and thumb.

'I've made you some already – this is the only bottle I had.'

She went over to the bed and, stopping up half the neck with her finger, shook it lightly over the pillows and eiderdown. Something made her pause, and she leant further over to examine it.

'Your hair is falling out?'

I patted it self-consciously, where it barely covered the rolls beneath.

'Yes.'

I could not see her face, but she appeared to be thinking as she smoothed the lavender water over the bedclothes. A moment later she was back at my side, pushing the vial into my hand, then holding up a fistful of a daisy-like plant.

'"Like a camomile bed, the more it is trodden, the

more it will spread,"' I recited. 'Do you know that rhyme?'

'No,' she said shortly. 'Steep this in hot milk, too, and strain it, then it can be drunk. And the final one.' She held a narrow strip of what looked like tree trunk between her long fingers. 'Willow bark. Chew on this if you have any pain – it will help.'

'Where did you get all these from? The apothecary in Padiham?'

'Women I know,' she said.

'*Wise* women?'

'Most women are wise.'

I could not tell if she was teasing me.

'Are they to be trusted?'

Alice gave me a look.

'According to the king? No. He has driven them into the shadows. But people are still sick, and dying, and having children, and not everyone has a royal physick. The king has muddled wise women with witchcraft.'

'You sound as though you are not a supporter of his.'

She did not reply, and began folding up the little squares of linen. Many people in these parts had their opinions on the king but kept them to themselves for good reason, so I was taken aback by her candour. Perhaps all baseborn people spoke as boldly.

'The king is not a supporter of women trying to make their way in the world any way they can: helping neighbours, and driving off sickness, and trying to keep their children alive. And while he is not, I am not of him.' She brushed her palms together and became more business-like. 'You remember each of the instructions?'

'I think so.'

How glad I was that Richard or the servants had not overheard our words. Alice took out her pocket, folded the linen back into it, then asked to see my wrist.

'I almost forgot . . .' I began as she examined it, pressing here and there and bending my palm backwards and forwards. There was no pain now. 'I bled the other night.'

Alice fixed her large amber eyes on mine and once again I smelt lavender. Where did it come from? She could not have perfume; she must crush it at her wrists and neck. I imagined her pulling on her rough wool dress and tucking her hair beneath her cap before making this small attempt at femininity.

'Was there any pain?' I shook my head. She narrowed her eyes. 'There may be too much blood in your body, which is not good for you or the infant. Next time I come, I will bring something.'

'When will that be?'

'In a few days. Until then, use these as I directed, and you should see an improvement.'

I went to my cupboard, where I kept the doctor's letter, and took out a small cloth bag of coins, handing it to her.

'What's this?'

'The first month in advance. How much do I owe for the herbs?'

'Nothing.'

She held the weight of the bag in her palm, letting the coins slide around. The sound reminded me of Richard, and I glanced towards the door. I had not told him or James how much I was paying Alice – that could wait until later, until I grew bigger and he could see her tinctures were working. Then he could hardly protest.

I saw her out, waving from the top of the stairs, and went back to my chamber to rest. Usually I had to pluck my dark hairs from the pillow and toss them in the fire, met with the anxiety that eventually they would all fall out and I would be bald as an egg. What else would this child take from me? They made fine wigs these days, but a woman's hair was as much an asset as her clothes and jewellery, and one that could not be removed. If Richard did not desire me already, with my growing belly and grey skin, he certainly would not without my thick black hair that used to be shiny as a raven's coat. When I met his sisters I'd envied their soft golden heads. But black was an expensive colour, difficult to dye and maintain. Black meant wealth and power.

I sat on the edge of the bed and ran my hand over the pillow, but no black threads showed on the white. Alice must have removed them. I lay down, closed my eyes and let the lavender carry me to sleep.

CHAPTER 7

From the very start of our marriage, Richard took pride in showing me off. At parties, I would shine under his companions' gazes like a jewel in candlelight, always meeting his eye for approval and finding it, and shining brighter.

I was looking forward to dinner at Roger's, and shining more brightly than ever now Alice's tinctures were working. I was glad, though, that she had not seen me pacing my chamber, building the courage to go down to the kitchen and repeat her instructions to the servants. My mother said I always cared far too much what people thought, but really I cared far too much what people said, especially when my back was turned. Thoughts were private, rumour was not, and as mistress at Gawthorpe

I knew I was the subject of both. The cook listened to me with one eyebrow raised when I showed her the dill for the butter, and scattered the camomile leaves on to the scrubbed wooden table. But listened she had, and a cup of warm milk infused with sweet camomile was delivered to my door at night, and a special butter dish brought for me at dinnertime the next day, and for the first time I felt quite fond of the staff. Richard was still sleeping in the next room, so I hoped to shine so brightly at Roger's that the truckle bed would remain undisturbed.

Friday arrived, and at eleven o'clock we were ready to ride to Read Hall. The days were longer now, and even if we stayed at the Nowells' all afternoon it would still be light by the time we left. I did not much like riding at night, when the edges of the forest couldn't be seen but could be heard shivering and straining from their roots like hounds on leashes. I had been ill for so long I couldn't recall the last time Richard and I went out visiting together, so I put on one of my favourite dresses of dark blue, embroidered with exotic birds and beetles, and a tall silk hat, with my riding things over the top. I decided to save telling him about the missing horse for another day, because it would no doubt spoil the evening. I was determined nothing would.

'Ah, the two turtledoves.'

Roger greeted us in the great hall, handing us each a glass of sack. He was dressed finely but retained an element of the countryman about him in his black velvet suit and soft boots. His wife Katherine made straight for me in her gown of black lace with fine gold embroidery. She was hatless, and her dress was cut very low. I was younger than her daughter, but we had mutual interests in fashions and London, and the best clothiers in Manchester and Halifax and Lancaster.

'What news at Gawthorpe? We have not seen you in such a long time – Richard said you were quite ill. I hope you are recovered?' Katherine said once we had done the necessary complimenting of each other's clothes. Her emerald drop earrings shimmered in the candlelight.

'Oh,' I said. 'Yes, I was confined for some time but now I am better, thank you.'

'Roger said you went hunting with them not long ago? I was surprised – all that mud spoiling your things!'

'Yes, although Richard blamed me for driving the quarry away with my voice – hunting is perhaps not the best opportunity to talk with friends.' I smiled.

'You are always welcome at Read – although we are a chamber short at the moment.'

'Oh?'

'I will leave Roger to tell you at supper.'

At that moment one of the men in the party turned

and I saw it was Thomas Lister. He caught my eye and gave a polite nod.

'Mr Lister was not long at Gawthorpe, on his way to Yorkshire,' I said.

Shrunken old Nick Bannister, the former magistrate of Pendle, also stood with Roger, Thomas and Richard, cradling his cup to his chest.

'And Roger persuaded Nick out of *his* confinement with the promise of a few fat birds and barrels of sack,' Katherine added warmly, before asking us to sit.

Thomas Lister was on my left and Nick Bannister on my right, with Roger, Katherine and Richard opposite.

'We must separate the turtles or they will be crooning at one another all night,' Roger said with a wink.

I smiled, and imagined the effect that announcing these two turtledoves slept in different rooms would have.

The first course was brought out: a spread of mutton pies, fallow deer pasties, and ham and pea pottage. Roger waited for everything to be set down and served before he spoke.

'Now,' he said as we picked up our knives, 'as you will all know, I have been investigating a series of crimes in the Pendle area. What some of you may not know is further arrests have been made after some deeply disturbing interviews.' He moved in his chair and indicated for a servant to top everyone's glasses with wine. 'You may remember I told you of Alizon Device, the girl who performed witchcraft on John Law the pedlar? It satisfies me to report she is now safely in gaol with her family, so the innocent people of Pendle are no longer at the mercy of the Devil's work for the time being.'

'Her family are in gaol too?' I asked.

Roger nodded slowly. 'Her mother, grandmother and brother all confessed to witchcraft and popery. Many lives have been lost to the Device family – they have eluded the eyes of the law for too long.'

On my right Nick Bannister spoke for the first time in his dusty, wheezing voice.

'It is a coincidence, is it not, that Device sounds like Devil?'

Laughter broke out at the table and I waited to speak.

'What did they do?'

'Oh . . .' Roger waved a casual hand. 'A horrible medley of things: dolls made of clay, spells, curses. Each of them has their own familiar spirit, which is proof enough.'

'You saw their familiars?' I asked, recalling that he had never seen Alizon's with his own eyes.

'I did not need to. I know they exist. John Law described Alizon's – the dog. Her mother Elizabeth also has a dog named Ball, and her grandmother has kept one for some twenty years. For two decades she has had a pact with the Devil, carrying out his work across the county.'

'But if you cannot see them, how can you know for certain?' I asked.

There were a few beats of silence as everyone chewed and swallowed around me. Roger regarded me.

'The Devil only appears to those he recognises to be his servants. They let their animals suck blood from their bodies – does that sound like a harmless pet to you? Do you let your dog do that, Fleetwood?'

'Roger,' Richard said coolly, 'I will set my falcon on you and it will suck *your* blood.'

Everyone apart from me laughed.

I took up my knife and moved the food around my plate, but the fatty mutton made my stomach churn.

'What news of the Preston woman?' Katherine asked Thomas Lister, who always needed coaxing into conversation.

He sat up a little straighter at the mention of his servant, clearing his throat.

'It was a blow when she was acquitted.' He spoke quietly, swilling the wine in his cup. 'But I am sure she will be back before she knows it.'

I was not sure I had heard him right.

'Back where?' I asked. 'Surely you would not have her back at Westby if you thought she had killed a child?'

He set down his cup and dabbed his small mouth with a napkin.

'At the next York assizes.'

I looked around at the other guests.

'I'm sorry, I don't understand.'

'Well,' he said softly, 'Jennet Preston murdered my father.'

The table went silent. The only sounds were the wind

at the window and the flames roaring heartily in the great fireplace. The other guests appeared to be as confused as I was. Roger sat back and gave Thomas a paternal nod, as though he had laid bare some deep truth.

Richard spoke. 'Your father died four years past.'

Thomas fixed his eyes on his plate, his small frame rigid.

'I did not tell anyone of the words he spoke at the time he died,' he said softly. 'My mother and I both heard him. He was terrified out of his wits.'

'Of what?'

'Of Preston. My father on his deathbed cried out: "Jennet lies heavy upon me! Preston's wife lies heavy upon me; help me, help me!"' For this part he raised his voice into a high, excited cry. Everyone at the table was silent, and his ringing voice echoed around the high walls. 'He bade us shut the doors, all the doors in the house so she could not escape.'

'She was there?'

'Her *spirit* was there. He could see it, I know. After his death she was brought to my father's corpse and it bled at her touch.'

'The surest sign of a witch,' Roger said with confidence.

'But,' I began, 'if this did happen four years ago, why is she only being brought to the assizes now? And was brought for something else last month?'

Thomas looked to Roger.

'Last week, on Good Friday, when all of us good citizens

were praying, a party was gathering,' Roger said in a slow, revealing way. 'And when all of us were fasting, as is the Lord's wish, this party was feasting on a stolen mutton. It took place at a miserable dwelling called Malkin Tower, the home of Alizon Device's grandmother, Old Demdike. And one of the party was Jennet Preston.'

'Preston is acquainted with the Device family?' Richard asked.

Roger nodded once. 'Because she is a witch. And what did they speak of at this gathering, other than comparing their familiars and blaspheming the Lord Jesus, for whom they should have been fasting? Why, they spoke of young Mr Lister here.'

'Why?'

'Preston was plotting to kill him,' Roger said simply.

Next to me, I could feel Thomas Lister shaking. He began touching all his cutlery and crockery, moving them and lining them up in a meticulous design.

Roger went on. 'That is not the only thing they spoke of. The lot of them were gathered to discuss a plot not dissimilar to the one that almost unseated the king from his throne not so long ago.' He leant in, his teeth shining in the candlelight. 'They planned to blow up Lancaster Castle, where their kin are held. To set them free.'

'How do you know this?'

Roger tapped his nose and, folding his handkerchief neatly in his place, pushed back his chair to rise.

'Allow me to introduce my most valuable witness.'

He left the room, and a little gasp went around the table when he returned with his wide, bear-like grip around the small shoulder of a little girl.

She strode with him into the room and they stopped short of the table. She could not have been older than nine or ten, and had a pale, pointed face with wide, clear eyes. Mousy hair straggled from her cap, which was newly starched, and although her pinafore was tied tightly, her simple wool dress drowned her. She was not afraid to look each of us in the eye, and when her bold gaze came to me I could not look away. What I found disturbing was that she was neither afraid nor impressed, her expression as smooth as a painted portrait.

'This,' Roger announced, 'is Jennet Device.'

'A popular name among their kind,' wheezed Mr Bannister.

'Mr and Mistress Shuttleworth, Mr Lister, allow me to introduce you to my source of all knowledge. Jennet has been helping Mr Bannister and me with our investigations. She is Alizon's sister.'

I saw Katherine glance quickly at the girl with an expression both suspicious and fearful. She looked as though she would put another person between them if she could.

I turned to Mr Bannister and whispered, 'She is staying here at Read Hall?'

'Indeed,' he breathed. 'In one of the children's old chambers.'

I wondered what Roger's grown-up family would think

of that – I barely knew what I thought of it myself. The witch was Alizon's own sister? Nobody was speaking, and the way they were looking the Device girl up and down made my skin crawl, so I spoke.

'Hello, Jennet,' I said. 'How are you finding Read Hall?'

'Right nice,' the child rasped with a strong accent.

'And how long will you stay?'

'She will stay until the trial date is set at the summer assizes.'

Katherine made a small noise. 'August? Roger, she will really stay for that long?'

'Where else would you have her go, Katherine? Her family is at Lancaster gaol and there they will remain until they are called before His Majesty's Justices.'

His words did not seem to disturb Jennet in the slightest; she continued to look around at the guests and the room itself, her wandering gaze absorbed by the portraits, the panelling and family shields on the wall. She had surely never seen such things in her life, nor a fireplace as great as the one that towered above her, nor food so plentiful.

'Will you have some of our second course, Jennet?' asked Roger. 'We have roast chicken and beef, and bread, and some butter that was made this morning.'

Jennet nodded eagerly and was seated at the end of the table next to Katherine, who appeared no less uncomfortable. Though a trace of a hostess's smile played on her lips, it did not reach her eyes. Her earrings glittered.

'Jennet was at Malkin Tower on Good Friday and has told me all that was said – including the plot against Preston's master here,' Roger declared as he returned to his seat. 'There were quite a number of people present that her brother James told me of, and Jennet has confirmed all the names on the list. We work well together, do we not, Jennet?'

The child was eyeing the half-finished food at the table, and I could not help but glance at her every few seconds. Her head was so small I imagined Roger could crush it with one hand. She did not appear at all affected by the incarceration of her entire family, and I could not decide if that chilled me or made me pitiful.

The second course was brought and Roger and Richard talked of other things that interested them: the price of salt; what their cattle fetched at market. Jennet ate like a wild animal, with grease smeared all up her face and hands. I was still watching her when I heard Richard tell Roger he had ordered a gun, which made me look around sharply.

'A gun? Richard, you did not tell me that.'

Richard glanced at Roger.

'Fleetwood, I hardly think I need consult you,' he said. 'Unless you have an expertise in flintlocks I know nothing of?'

The table tittered, and I flushed.

'Won't it go off in the house?'

'Not if it is handled correctly, which it will be,' Richard said in an insolent way.

He turned more directly to Roger, indicating the subject was closed.

I tried to speak to Thomas on my left but he was acting very strangely and would not make eye contact: I think the presence of the child frightened him. Katherine squirmed next to Jennet and did not speak to her once.

Before long the topic came back to Roger's witch hunt.

'Let us speak of it away from the child in case it should give her nightmares,' Roger said. 'Jennet, go up to your chamber and I shall send for you in the morning.'

The little girl slid sideways from the table without even removing her chair, she was so thin. She made no noise as she left and the moment she had gone, it was easy to believe she had never been there at all.

Roger turned back to us and grew confidential.

'Her mother was beside herself when she found out the child had handed them over. I thought she would go mad before my eyes.'

Mr Bannister burped beside me and pardoned himself, covering his mouth with a brown-spotted hand.

'She is a sight for sore eyes, Elizabeth Device,' he said. 'She'd give you a fright if you saw her: one eye set up in her head and the other looking right down at the floor.'

I felt as though a bucket of icy water had been thrown over me. I stared dumbly at Mr Bannister, and he mistook my disbelief for fascination.

'She does sound like something from a comedy play,

but I'm not being fanciful. How she has three children by two men I'll never know.'

My mouth was dry as sand.

'Where do they live, the Devices?'

'Just outside Colne. A horrible, damp hovel is Malkin Tower. How folk live like that I don't know.'

CHAPTER 8

'This will not be pleasant. You will need a strong stomach.'

Alice took up one of the items she had set on the dresser in my chamber: a knife that folded in on itself, encased in a horn shell. For a terrible moment I thought she meant to perform surgery on my stomach, but she saw my expression and her scowl softened.

'I will breathe your veins,' she explained. 'It is the only thing for too much blood.'

She drew the dull-looking blade from the horn handle and showed me how the point of the knife was flat, not sharp, and how a small triangle shape jutted down from it at a right angle. It was a curious-looking thing. She told me it was called a feam. I had seen enough of my own blood and felt enough pain not to fear it.

Alice had appeared as mysteriously as ever, crossing the lawn in front of the house with round-shouldered purpose. She offered no chit-chat, but nor did I. We'd grown easier in each other's company, however – as easy as two women can be who could not be more different. I liked her soft voice, and wondered if she read to her father by the fire. Then I remembered she couldn't read. Her voice was the only soft thing about her, though, I thought idly as she moved about the room with a brisk directness, her back straight, her neck long and equine. She'd have made a fine mistress of a house like this in another life. Probably better than I. Working in an alehouse might harden a person. Being poor almost certainly did. Still, she would leave here wealthier than she'd arrived.

She told me to take off my jacket and layers so that my arms were bare, then pulled a chair over to the window and nodded for me to sit in it. She tied a length of ribbon tightly around the top of my arm and prodded the white skin at my elbow.

'Alice,' I said, 'do you think that it will have eyelashes by now?'

'Eyelashes?'

'Do you think the baby will have eyelashes?'

'What a strange question. It's hard to say.'

I nodded and eyed the things she had asked me to have

ready for her: a large bowl, fresh linen, water, a needle and some pale thread. I'd acted on instinct and turned the key in the chamber door, what with Richard downstairs with James and the ledger. When I turned to Alice, she was standing at the fireplace, looking at the plaster figures on either side.

'Are they your family?' she asked.

'No. *Prudentia.*' I pointed. '*Justitia.*'

'What does that mean?'

'*Prudence and justice* is the Shuttleworth family motto.' I nodded at the feam. 'Where did you get that?'

She wiped the blade on her apron for a few moments, then said, not unkindly, 'You take such an interest in where my things come from.'

'Well, I am glad you did not ask me to find one. Firstly, I would not know where to look. Secondly, I can imagine James' face if I told him I'd ordered one.'

'Who is James?'

'Our steward.'

'Why would you have to tell him?' she asked.

'Everything we buy goes in the household ledger he keeps, and everything that leaves Gawthorpe, whether it's beer from the brewery or chickens from the farm or midwives for the mistress.'

'Even me?'

'Yes, even you.'

My hand throbbed as the blood collected in it. Alice asked me to pass the bowl – a pretty brass one decorated with flowers, given to us by Richard's mother – and set it on the dresser, placing my arm above it.

'Are you ready?'

Before I could say yes she had driven the feam into the crook of my arm with the wooden stick, and I yelped like a puppy as she drew it out. Warm, red blood began gushing immediately from the hole she had made. I clapped my other hand over my mouth but could not take my eyes from the grotesqueness of it.

'What does prudence mean?' asked Alice, adjusting her grip on my arm.

Clear, light pain was flooding through my whole body.

'Ah . . . Prudence. Prudence means . . . How long does this go on?'

'Until the bowl is half full.'

'Half full?' It was coming out so fast.

'What does prudence mean?' Alice said again.

'It means cautiousness. Proceeding with care.'

'And justice means freedom?'

'No,' I said, trying to look at anything but the bowl filling as easily with my own blood as if it was wine pouring from a bottle. My head felt as light as it did in the church when I fainted. 'Justice means fairness. Lack of prejudice.'

Working as quickly as she had before, Alice pinched the skin either side of the piercing and drove a needle through it. I looked away as she stitched it with thread, wincing every time it made a puncture.

'I will look like a cushion,' I said, feeling her breath on my arm. 'This will work, do you think?'

'Breathing the veins is the best way to bleed while you're not having monthlies. Bleeding can be healthy from the right place.'

She washed the blood from my arm and pressed a ball of linen to it, instructing me to hold it. Puck lumbered over, curiously. I pulled the pad of linen away from my arm and saw fresh blood leaking through the slapdash thread. Puck sniffed and licked at the wound a few times before deciding it was not as tasteful as he imagined.

Immediately I recalled Roger's words: 'Do you let your pet suck blood from you, Fleetwood?'

I almost laughed at the absurdity of it. Alice wrapped my arm in a strip of linen and tied it, before leading me to the bed and instructing me to lie down while she tidied up. The wound was on the same arm as my sprain – I had quite the inventory of injuries since meeting her, and I told her so. She smiled and closed the drapes.

'I do not feel any different,' I said after a while.

'Give it a day or two,' came her voice. I heard the tinkle of glass. 'If you feel no better we can try the other arm, with more blood. You still have the willow bark I gave you?'

'Yes.'

She appeared in the curtain fold with a piece of cloth no bigger than my hand, and took from its folds a single green leaf. She ripped a tiny edge off it and handed it to me.

'Suck this,' she said. 'It will stop the blood coming so quickly. But don't have any more than that, and spit it out – don't swallow it.'

I lay with my hands on my stomach, sucking the bit of leaf like a farm apprentice on a summer afternoon. It seemed to dissolve on my tongue, and a sense of peace washed over me. Though I'd only known Alice a fortnight, with her here my worries seemed to fade to dying embers, only to flare up again at night. She could not promise that she would save my life. She had not promised anything, in fact. But knowing she was trying to help me, I felt safer than I had perhaps since I married Richard.

'Alice, am I safe to keep riding in childbed?'

There was a pause while she considered.

'I have not known many women who have horses, but my mother knew plenty, and she always said they could. Do you ride regular?'

'Every day,' I replied.

'Then you've no reason to stop if you've always done it, as long as you don't come off again. I expect for a skilled horsewoman it's as safe as walking.'

'Richard seemed to think the last time that . . . it was my fault for being rough, riding around and playing with Puck. He thinks it's not good for a woman. The truth is I'd die if I had to stay indoors all the time, sitting in hard chairs embroidering cushions, though he thinks that is the safest place to be.'

'Perhaps he wants to keep you where he can see you, like all husbands. Until they want you out of their sight, that is.'

Her bitter tone made me raise my head. 'I thought you said you weren't married?'

'I'm not,' she said quickly, and then as though she'd said too much, added, 'Oh, I found your horse that ran away. It's back in your stable.'

I was too surprised to reply, and stared at the closed drapes.

'Did you hear me?' she called from behind the drapes.

'Yes. Where was it?'

'A neighbour found it grazing in a field and brought it back.'

'You're sure it's the same one?'

'With the triangle of white on its nose? And a black tip on its ear? I'm sorry but the tack was gone; it probably threw it off.'

Or more likely someone stole it, I thought, seeing as I'd never known a horse to rid itself of a saddle, bridle, halter and reins. Before I could reply, a noise at the door startled me, followed by Richard's voice.

'Fleetwood? Why is the door locked?'

I pulled open the curtains and Alice was already halfway towards me with my jacket, which I pulled on to cover the wound.

'Fleetwood?'

Richard was rapping impatiently, and stepped immediately into the room when I finally unlocked the door.

'Why was the door locked?' he asked again, directing the question at Alice.

She looked helplessly at me, and, panicking, I swiftly glanced over at the dresser where her things had been moments before, but it was empty and gleaming as usual.

'Richard, you must understand we do not want to be disturbed when Alice is doing her work.'

I tried to sound soothing, but he was still glaring at Alice.

'And what work is that?'

I grasped wildly for an answer. 'Feminine exercises.'

There was an awful period of silence that lasted perhaps five seconds, and Alice cast her eyes down to the floor. Where had she put her things so quickly? I eyed the corner of the room and the fireplace, but there was no sign of the bowl of blood.

'Very well,' Richard said finally. 'Roger is downstairs and wishes to see you. He has . . . someone with him.'

'Who is it?'

There had been a coolness between us since Roger's dinner, though I could not say why. I wondered if I had irritated him by asking too many questions.

'You will soon find out.' He turned on his heel, but not before his eyes searched the room. 'There is a strange smell in here, is there not?'

His eyes lingered on Alice, then he left, closing the door firmly behind him.

'He meant the blood. I can smell it, too,' I told Alice, but her expression was smooth. How changeable her mood could be, like clouds scudding across the sun. She and Richard were alike in that way. 'Will you wait here while I see which guest has arrived?' I asked her.

As I descended to the bottom of the house, I thought of the curious exchange I'd just witnessed. Richard had acted as though he found Alice's presence offensive, revolting even. I remembered their first meeting, when he was laughing and joking with her. But Richard was a man who liked to be flirted with and deferred to, and Alice's silent reproachfulness when he asked her to stable my horse no doubt stung. Our female servants grew shy and pink-cheeked when he spoke to them, whereas Alice was indifferent. Well, he had chosen a woman as my companion once, and now it was my turn. But all thoughts of my husband and midwife evaporated when I turned the final corner of the staircase, for standing in the entrance hall were two figures: the expansive Roger Nowell and the parchment-thin Device child.

'Roger. Jennet.' I tried not to look so startled. 'What a pleasant surprise.'

Jennet was not looking at me, but appraising everything in her sight with her wide eyes – the oak banister, the portraits hanging in the gloom of the stairwell. She was still wearing the same old dress and starched white cap, which made her face look all the paler. Without saying a word, she walked to the picture window at the back of the house. I blinked at Roger.

'Do you have business with Richard?'

'Yes, he is waiting for me in the hall. I came to ask if it would not be an inconvenience to show Jennet around Gawthorpe while Richard and I discuss matters? She has never seen such a palace and would greatly enjoy a tour.'

I touched my arm where the feam had punctured it; the linen was making it itch. I thought of Alice upstairs in my chamber, and looked over at Jennet's small silhouette at the window. Without waiting for an answer, Roger gave me a fatherly wink and departed, his polished boots echoing across the stone floor. I swallowed and went over to where the child was standing.

'That's Pendle Hill.' I pointed at the looming mass in the distance. 'And this is the River Calder. Sometimes you can see salmon jumping upstream.'

Her face was quite delicate, and not ugly. Her small upturned nose was spattered with freckles, and her eyelashes were long and grey.

'Which rooms would you like to see?'

She shrugged, and in her broad accent said, 'How many are there?'

'Do you know, I've never thought about it. I don't know. Perhaps we could count? Though there are many more for the servants, and I don't think we should disturb them. How many rooms are in your house?'

She stared at me. 'One.'

'Oh. Well, then. Let's see.'

I showed her around the ground floor – the dining room, the buttery and servants' working rooms, where the study was. In the great hall, I pointed up to the gallery and told her how minstrels and players sometimes came to perform, and we would watch from below. She paced around mostly in silence, occasionally asking who was in a portrait. The mermaids and mystical figures in the dining room appeared to fascinate her, as did the polished swords and suits of armour, and she examined each one with her hands behind her back, like a miniature Roger. Then we went to the outbuildings: the great barn, which I told her was one of the largest in the country, and the stables and farm offices. Sure enough, as we walked through the yard, and the stable boys and apprentices nodded and wished us good day, I saw the grey mare with the white triangle on her nose chewing hay languidly in her stall.

'Are you enjoying staying at Read Hall?' I asked as we returned to the house.

Jennet wanted to see upstairs, and after a moment's hesitation I agreed.

She shrugged again. 'It is not as big as this house.'

'But Roger and Katherine keep a lovely home. I'm sure they are looking after you well.'

I wondered how Roger could keep her one way and her family another, taking responsibility for one and disposing of the rest.

Jennet had turned on the stair to face me.

'Can I live here instead?' she asked.

She left one hand on the banister, like a little lady of the court. I opened and closed my mouth, disarmed by her forthrightness.

'I'm afraid that's not possible. You are a guest of Roger's.'

There was nothing childlike about the intensity of her stare, and it gave me the oddest feeling that I had said the wrong thing, and would regret it later. Then she turned on her heel and continued her climb up to the top of the house. After her request, I was embarrassed to show her all the empty bedrooms, made for guests that never stayed.

'My mother often comes to visit,' I lied. 'And Richard's family, who live in Yorkshire. He has lots of brothers and sisters, and I have none.' We were back at the staircase now.

'Who is that?' She was pointing at the Barton family portrait.

'That's my mother and me.'

'Why do you have a bird on your hand?'

'That was my pet, Samuel. He didn't live for very long. I kept him in a cage in my room.'

'Why does your mother have no bird?'

'She did not have a pet.'

'My mother has a dog.'

I thought of the ugly woman Elizabeth Device, who I'd seen in Hagg Wood with Alice, and the brown mongrel that had slipped past me, and what Roger had said about Elizabeth's familiar spirit. Surely it was nonsense – I'd seen the creature with my own eyes and there'd been nothing devilish about it. But the woman had turned to me when it passed her . . . My skin prickled at the memory of her eyes.

'What is its name?' I asked.

'Ball.'

'That's a strange name for a dog. Do you have a dog?'

'No, mine hasn't shown itself yet.'

What an odd child she was.

'I have a large dog named Puck. He is somewhere in the house,' I said.

'Does he talk to you?'

'No, but we understand each other.'

Jennet nodded. 'My sister has one too. And my grandma has a boy.'

'A boy? You mean a son?'

'No, a boy. His name is Fancie. He wears a coat that is brown and black, and sometimes he comes to our house and they go for a walk.'

'Oh, you mean a dog.'

'No. He is a boy. She's known him twenty years and he's never grown up.'

I couldn't help but stare at her.

'Have you told Roger all this?'

'Oh, yes. He is very interested in my family.'

We stood in an awkward silence, looking at my portrait,

then Jennet mounted the last of the stairs and I showed her the long gallery. It was a bright day, and the floor had just been polished, so the windows reflected on to the wood like the sky in a lake. I felt that Jennet was growing bored with her tour, though her gaze continued to rove over every cupboard, every chair, as though she was a merchant assessing it for sale. Once we were back in the tower staircase, she pointed.

'What's that room?'

'That's my bedroom.'

'Can we go in?'

I laughed nervously. 'Not today.'

'Is someone in there?'

'No.'

After a pause, she nodded and began her ladylike descent. My palms were slick with sweat, and my heart had begun beating a pattern in my chest. If Alice knew her mother, would Jennet know Alice? I realised I did not want to find out, because I had a peculiar feeling that Jennet Device was dangerous, and I could not say why. How ridiculous that sounded, though – she was a child.

I took her into the hall and she scampered over to Roger like a granddaughter. He and Richard were sitting either side of the table with papers spread between them, and Roger was pouring the dregs of a jug of wine into his cup.

'Did you enjoy your tour, little one?' he asked. Jennet nodded. 'Fleetwood, you are looking better every day.' I smiled and nodded. 'Richard,' he went on, 'might I trouble you for a mouthful of something before I begin the journey to Lancaster? Is there any of that chicken pie your cook makes going spare? We wouldn't turn down a crust of that, would we, now?'

He winked at Jennet, who was standing behind his chair like an attentive servant.

'Fleetwood, would you mind asking the kitchen?' Richard asked.

'Of course.'

I curtseyed and went back through the house, feeling cold even though almost all the fires were lit. The kitchen was a part of the house I rarely visited. Along the length of it was a long, low table covered at intervals with flour and pots. Baskets of vegetables stood on the floor and the open range glowed and threw warmth around the room. Above it, 'Waste Not Want Not' was spelt in stone letters each the size of a forearm, a reminder left by Uncle Lawrence. A rabbit hung framed in the window, swinging gently. The kitchen staff regarded me in the way I'd grown used to: a quick glance, then away.

'Barbara?' I called to the large-framed cook at the table, brushing pies with egg yolk.

She had not noticed me enter, and my voice was so small in the clangs and clatters of the room, one of the younger servants had to fetch her. I passed on Roger's request, and she went off to the larder to fetch some things to wrap in a parcel. As usual, the kitchen was busy with purpose, and I watched various servants roll and chop and brew. As she handed me a warm folded cloth stacked with cold pies and meats, I lingered for a moment.

Then I said, 'Thank you for carrying out my instructions with the herbs so well. The butter is delicious and the camomile milk sends me straight to sleep.'

A smile swept her red face.

'You are most welcome, Mistress. I am glad to see your cheeks fattening. We are almost finished with the herbs you gave me, so I can ask James to order more?'

'No,' I said quickly. 'I will have my midwife bring more.'

I thanked her and turned to go, but she said, 'Mistress, is it true the witch child is at Gawthorpe today?'

'If you mean Jennet Device, she is a guest of Roger Nowell's.'

A few of the servants nearby had their ears pricked.

'I have no mind to look at her,' Barbara went on. 'They say she is the Devil's daughter.'

'I am sure there is no truth in that.'

'I'm sure Mistress knows what she is doing opening the door to such folk, but I hope she doesn't bring a curse to this house. Just this morning the milk began to turn. Fresh from the farm, it was.'

Wishing to end the conversation, I nodded again and made to leave, but Barbara called me back at the door, her voice raised.

'That midwife of yours,' she said. 'Where's she from?'

Impatient now, I replied, 'Colne.'

Barbara's mouth turned down at the corners.

'I ain't never seen her before, and my sister's a midwife. You might have asked down here if any of us had someone to recommend.'

'Yes, well, it was Alice's idea to introduce the herbs to my diet, and they are working very well.'

The tips of my ears were hot, and I felt a blush creeping up my neck. Did servants usually question their mistress's hiring decisions? Did they advise on whom to invite into the house? I held up the parcel.

'Thank you for this.'

I tripped on the way out, causing stifled laughter to ripple through the kitchen. By the time I reached the hall, I was flustered and irritated, my goodwill towards the household soured once again. The two men were standing now, clearing the papers between them. Jennet was crouched at the fireplace, looking up into its corners – she could have stood inside comfortably, like I could in the fireplace at Barton when I was her age.

'This is the list for Nick Bannister,' Roger said, separating a sealed document from the sheaf in front of him. He tossed it on to the table. 'I have a copy at Read, but as I'm away he will call here to collect it.'

Richard nodded, sliding it towards himself and tucking it into his waistcoat.

'I shall leave it with James.'

'Don't get too close to that fire, Jennet,' Roger warned. 'Fire is for stew pots and heretics, not children.'

'And witches?' the child asked.

'In His Majesty's homeland they are thrown on the fire. I am of the opinion that England should follow in Scotland's lead, but unfortunately the penalty here is the rope. Perhaps His Majesty can still be persuaded to change his mind. Now, we must be on our way to Lancaster.'

She shot up. 'To see Ma?'

Roger glanced at me, indicating I hand him his parcel of food, and I crossed the room.

'Your mother is still at the inn, where they don't allow children. Thank you, Fleetwood.'

'What about Alizon? And Grandma?'

'They are there, too. You will see them before long, in a grand room in a castle with lots of important people who will ask you questions about them. And you remember what to say, don't you? Everything we talked about?' She nodded, taking the cloth parcel from him and unfolding it to stuff a fistful of pie into her mouth. 'This one has a belly bigger than her eyes. Well, we'll be on our way.'

Richard saw them out, and I watched Jennet follow them into the passage, quick and soundless as a shadow.

Alice was sitting quietly by the window in my chamber when I returned, looking out at the hills.

'Sorry I kept you in here so long,' I said, closing the door behind me. 'I hope I've not held you from your work at the alehouse?'

She shook her head. 'I start later on. Did I hear a child's voice?'

I licked my lips, deciding.

'My friend Roger Nowell brought a child named Jennet Device. Her family is awaiting the assizes at Lancaster, accused of witchcraft.'

I watched her face for a flicker of recognition, but none came – her face was blank and smooth.

I waited a beat, then said, 'Do you know them?'

She stood, brushing down her skirts and tucking the chair back against the wall.

'No,' she said. 'I don't.'

I'd lost count of the nights Richard had slept in the room beside mine, so much that waking up alone was beginning to feel normal. Thanks to the lavender tincture on my pillow, I hadn't had The Nightmare, and my hair had stopped falling out at such an alarming rate. I found Richard eating breakfast in the dining room, and took my seat opposite him, accepting a roll and some honey and breaking it into pieces.

'Richard,' I said once the servants had left the room. 'I have been feeling much better lately. Might you consider moving back to our chamber?'

He read his correspondence for a moment or two longer, then looked up.

'What was that?'

'I said I am feeling much better, and I wish you would

join me in our chamber. I haven't been ill in almost a fortnight.'

'That's wonderful news.'

When he continued reading and chewing, and it became clear he would not respond, I remembered something that had bothered me that morning.

'I can't find my ruby necklace, the one you gave me when we had been married a year.'

Now I had his attention, and he folded the letter he was reading and tucked it beneath his plate.

'Oh? Where do you keep it?'

'In the cupboard in the wardrobe. I looked for it last night and again this morning, and seem to have misplaced it. I can't remember when I last wore it.'

His grey eyes were thoughtful.

'Your midwife spends a lot of time up there, does she not?'

'She does, but she would not have taken it.'

'Would she not?' he asked lightly. 'Does she have plenty of her own?'

I put a tiny piece of bread into my mouth and swallowed.

'I know she would not. I trust her.'

'You seem to trust her much more easily than Miss Fawnbrake.'

'I will go and look again.'

I pushed my plate away and left before he could protest, trying to ignore the creeping feeling of doubt that plucked at my thoughts like a needle. I turned my rooms upside down that morning, and looked in all the guest chambers and cupboards that I had keys to. Although my most precious jewellery was locked away, I kept the keys in a vase on the mantelpiece in the wardrobe – not the most discreet of hiding places. The rest of my jewellery was as it should be – my favourite opal rings, the velvet and pearl choker, the emerald drop earrings given to me by my mother on my thirteenth birthday.

Hot and bothered, I went downstairs to ask the chambermaids if they had seen the necklace recently, when I heard a commotion. At the last turn of the staircase, I almost bumped into Richard flying towards me, looking thunderous.

'Have you found it?' he demanded.

'No, I—'

'That necklace was my father's sister's,' he fumed. 'He gave it to me when she died. It's an insult to his memory; it belongs in the family.'

'I'm sorry,' I faltered, but he shook his head. That's when I noticed the servants flocking out of doorways and passages towards the hall, throwing us nervous glances.

'Come with me; we will put an end to this.'

He took my hand and pulled me in the same direction, and I was alarmed to find the entire household gathering beneath the high ceiling: fifteen or twenty people, plus one I was not expecting.

'Alice!'

She glanced over at me, and her face was anxious. In her hands she had a parcel tied with string: more herbs, as she had promised to bring when I told her the kitchen was low. There were high spots of colour on her cheeks, and her golden hair fell more untidily than usual around her face, as though she had hurried here.

Richard had left my side and was climbing the narrow stairs up to the minstrels' gallery. Clearly he was about to make an announcement.

'My wife has informed me a precious ruby necklace has gone missing,' he declared. 'This is the first time anything like this has happened at Gawthorpe, and I am loath to suggest one – or some – of you might know its whereabouts, because you are a loyal staff.' As I watched him speak, sweat pricking at my armpits, I felt several pairs of eyes on me. 'There is every possibility it has been mislaid, but Mistress Shuttleworth has assured me she has checked every usual place. Now, that necklace was given to my father,' he went on, his tone melting from stern to appealing, which always made the servants melt in turn. 'It is very important to me that we find it. I will ask the chambermaids to carry out a thorough sweep of the rooms, and everyone else their usual habitats. This time tomorrow I would like it placed in my hands. I will ask no questions when it is.'

A few of the servants straightened in response – he'd even called the stable boys and carter in, I realised. Why not the farm apprentices, too? I thought in exasperation.

Then I noticed someone had raised a hand: Sarah, one of the bolder chambermaids, who liked to bask in Richard's approval. And who, I'm sure, took delight in the fact he was sleeping alone, and possibly even imagined going to him in her stockinged feet at night.

'Sarah?' Richard nodded, indicating she speak.

'I'm sure you know those of us who've worked here such a long time would bring anything we found to you or the mistress straight away,' she said. 'So maybe you should look at those who haven't worked here so long.'

A ripple of interest broke across the room – half surprise, half amusement at her brevity.

'What makes you say that, Sarah? Might you know something you wish to share?'

Richard's tone was inviting. I imagined them alone together, then pushed the thought away. He was a good businessman, skilled at getting the deal he wanted. Nothing more.

I glanced at Alice, who was shifting her weight on her feet. She was not looking at Richard, but directly at Sarah. Her eyes were hard, and there was a flush of colour in her cheeks.

'All I'm saying is,' Sarah chattered on in her girlish, broad accent, 'it might not be a coincidence that someone new starts working here and two minutes later the mistress's jewellery goes missing.'

The two or three young girls standing next to her shone with barely concealed glee.

'The saucy baggage!' muttered an older voice from over my shoulder.

'Thank you, Sarah, that's enough. While there's no need to throw accusations around, I trust my household's loyalty in the main. Some, however, could be more demonstrative with their allegiance.' Did Richard look pointedly at Alice? He began to move towards the staircase. 'I will leave it with you. Remember, noon tomorrow, that necklace will be back in Fleetwood's possession. That is not a request.'

As the hall filled with chatter and the servants filed out, I went to Alice and took her arm.

'Will you come upstairs?'

She shook me off.

'I don't think I will.'

She shoved the package into my arms. The scent of herbs and lavender drifted up, but now the strength of the mingling scents made me feel sick.

'Why not?'

'I have brought the things as you asked. I can't see what else I am needed for.'

'The parlour, then. I will have the kitchen send up some—'

'No, thank you. I need to go to the Hand.' Her voice had lost all its softness.

The hall was quiet now, with the last footsteps squeaking in the passages. Richard's ancestors watched keenly from their portraits on the walls.

'I hope you don't think I was accusing you of theft.' I tried to coat my words with ridicule, but it came out as pleading.

'You have nice jewellery, but I'm not sure any of it would suit me. I trust you aren't in need of my service any longer?'

'Pardon? Alice, no, you can't leave. I know you didn't steal it.'

Do I?

I remembered her closing the drapes around me after she drew my blood. How, an hour after I left her, she sat thoughtfully at the window in my chamber with her straight back and fine angular features, as though she was posing for a portrait. And buried beneath was another thought: what did she do with my blood? There was a whole bowlful of it, and when Richard demanded to be let in, it was gone. Had she thrown it on the fire? I'd heard no sizzle of burning liquid, no stench of scorched blood. Now was not the time to wonder; Alice was watching me, and I knew my face betrayed my doubt.

'I must go,' she said coolly. 'I cannot work where I am not trusted.'

And before I could move, she had slipped into the passage. By the time I reached it she was at the front door, hauling it open and flying down the steps, barely avoiding a collision with the figure dismounting his horse at the bottom.

'Mistress Shuttleworth!' said Nick Bannister, turning to watch Alice's narrow form grow smaller.

'Mr Bannister,' I managed to say, catching my breath.

I felt as though I was coming apart; something terrible had happened, and I had no idea what to do about it. Over a stupid necklace that meant nothing to me!

'You look as though you've had a fright – who was that woman?'

The magistrate approached hesitantly, placing a wrinkled hand on my arm where the feam had been driven in. The wound smarted at his touch, and I pulled away, stammering my apologies. In just a few days the injury had almost sealed itself into a neat scar the shape of a crescent moon.

All I could see of Alice now was her white cap bobbing towards the edge of the forest. As usual she had not gone to the road via the outbuildings, but straight into the trees.

'Mistress, are you quite well?'

I sighed, and felt the chill wind creep its fingers down my gown. My stomach pushed at my corse; it would not be long before I could no longer wear them.

'Yes, quite well, thank you, Mr Bannister. Have you come to see Richard?'

'Only if he is available. I am here to collect a message Roger left when he was here last.'

'Yes, I know it. I will find it for you.'

I'd heard Richard say he'd leave it with James, but I would not fetch him; I did not even want to look at him.

Nick followed me into the house and I instructed a passing servant to see to his horse. James' study was only a few steps from the front door, and he was out for the day with the bailiff. As though sensing I was upset, Puck came to me, pushing his wet nose into my hand.

'Forgive me, Mr Bannister, what is it I am looking for?'

'Perhaps Mr Shuttleworth knows its whereabouts—'

'No. I can help you,' I said, more sharply than I could help. 'Richard has done enough for today.'

I pushed open the door and went to the large desk in the centre of the room. James kept a neat office, with only a jar of quills, a single bottle of ink and a neat stack of parchment on its surface. Behind the leather chair was a shelf containing several bound household ledgers, dating back twenty years to when Richard's father first began to keep the Shuttleworth family records. I searched the stacks of letters organised and filed in some unknown method, remembering how James had brought me the neat parcel of correspondence about my failed pregnancies. Another rage was burning inside me: Richard did not think it prudent to inform me of my impending death, and now he had removed from the house the only person I could trust to save me. I realised I was shaking, and hot tears were blurring my sight. I sniffed, and Nick Bannister cleared his throat.

'Fine beast you have, Mistress,' he said.

I wiped my eyes and scanned the shelves once more, finding what I needed: the letter sealed in wax with the

Nowell crest. I turned it over to find Nick Bannister's name written in Roger's cursive script, and handed it to the shabby old man stroking my dog.

'Thank you.' He nodded. I know I had made him uncomfortable, and he was looking for something to say. 'Nasty business, this.'

'What is?'

'These Pendle witches. Trust Roger to root them out, though. I doubt he shall ever retire from the king's service. I said to him: "Roger, have this last hurrah and then live comfortably. Let some young blood take over, like your Richard." He trusts your man, you know. Hopes he'll carry on his work one day, as Justice of the Peace.'

'Yes,' I said dully.

'Roger doesn't do things by halves – he's not content with sending a whole family to trial, oh no. He wants the glory days back; he wants his name in the London pamphlets. I swear he's after a knighthood. He is already known at court, but he won't stop there. You know him as well as I.'

I wondered how far Alice had got – whether she had reached the alehouse yet. Should I have gone after her?

'"Best get them all", I said,' Nick continued. 'There can't be harm in questioning them.'

'Questioning who?'

I was being awfully rude, but wanted Nick to finish his monologue and go, so I could think about what to do. Perhaps in the months it took for me to grow,

Alice's temper might cool, and she could be persuaded back?

'The gathering of witches at Malkin Tower. He found quite the rats' nest there. Not just the Devices but friends of theirs, the ones talking about killing Thomas Lister, and blowing up the gaol. There are a few local names on this list; no doubt it will cause a scandal in the community. Who would have thought, so much Devil's work in this wet little corner of the land? And on Good Friday – ha! It won't be a good one for them, not now.'

'You have the list there?' I nodded at the paper in his hand, something in his words making me curious. 'What does it say?'

Relieved by my interest, he asked for a knife, and I found one in the top drawer of James' desk. He sliced open Roger's scroll, letting it fall and holding it at arm's length to read the words aloud.

'"Jennet and James Device said they rode off on white foals after the meeting, and Jennet Preston bade them come to her house in Gisburn for their next meeting in a year's time. Preston brought her familiar to the meeting: a white foal with a brown spot on its face."'

I felt my heart pumping in my chest.

'The other people at the gathering on Good Friday: who were they?'

It took an age for the elderly magistrate to find the names with his cloudy squint.

'Let me see . . . ah, yes, here we are: "the wife of Hugh

Hargreaves of Barley; the wife of Christopher Bulcock of the Moss End, and John her son; the mother of Myles Nutter; one Mould-heels, of Colne; and one Alice Gray, of the same."'

CHAPTER 9

The sign of the Hand and Shuttle was a short distance from the river, before the road split to go north or west. I had passed it many times before but barely given it a glance. As I tied my horse in the yard, I realised that its name, of course, came from the Shuttleworth coat of arms: a shield of three shuttles, with a hand rising from it grasping a fourth. The same symbol was carved on a wooden sign on the side of the low building.

The place went silent as I stepped through the door, and what felt like a hundred pairs of eyes came to rest on me, even though I wore one of my most modest outfits with a black wool cloak, and a simple black hat with a gold band. The place was small and low-ceilinged. A few groups of men sat around what looked like creepie stools laden with jugs, their faces hard and blank. A man behind a partition like a stable door waited to see what I would do, perhaps thinking I had walked into the inn by mistake. I moved towards him.

'I must speak with Alice,' I said.

He had a ruddy face, and his mouth hung open, displaying unpleasant teeth. 'Alice . . .'

'Alice Gray,' I whispered. 'Is she here?'

He nodded dumbly. 'I'll fetch her, Mistress. Might you want to go somewhere more private?'

'Thank you.'

I followed him through a curtain of cloth and he led me into a narrow, dimly lit passage to the dining chamber, which was empty. The whole place was cold, with no fires lit, and stank like the brewery at Gawthorpe. I pulled my cloak around me and went to the window that overlooked the yard, where barrels were being rolled into the store-house. I recognised them to be the ones from the house, stamped with the Shuttleworth crest. A door banging and footsteps in the passage made me jump.

'Stop coming here.'

It took a moment for me to recognise the raised voice as Alice's. I placed a protective hand on my stomach and stepped into the doorway to look out. At the end of the passage was a dark-haired young man, whose grubby shirt and threadbare trousers did not detract from how hand-some he was. He looked almost foreign, like a pirate or a prince, with black hair and tanned skin and fine, dark eyes. Alice was standing with her back to me, her hands on her hips.

'You think you can just leave me?' he demanded.

'Leave a horrid drunk like you? Why on earth would I do that? Go home.'

'There is nothing for me there. Not now.'

His face crumpled, and he looked as though he might cry.

At that, her shoulders sank, and she held the tops of her arms like I'd seen her do in the woods. I drew back in the doorway in fear they should see me. When Alice spoke next, her voice was thick.

'We have to put it behind us.'

'Easy for you to say, with your work and your new . . . *position.*'

'Get out, will you.'

He pushed his face into hers, and his dark eyes shone.

'I can ruin that for you, if I like. I could tell them things . . . People have been asking.'

'Leave me alone!' she shrieked, and the hairs on my neck stood up. 'Don't you dare come back.'

With a final withering look, he stumbled down the passage, past me and out into the yard. The unmistakable smell of ale clung to him. I took a few hesitant steps to where Alice was standing, facing away from me, still hugging herself.

'Alice?'

She spun around, her face a paler shade than usual. Her

eyes were large and fearful – more fearful than I'd seen
her earlier in the hall full of servants.

'Fleetwood. What are you doing here?'

I took her hand and led her into the room.

'Will we be heard in here?'

'Who by?'

'Anyone.'

She shook her head, and I closed the door.

'Who was that?' I whispered, my voice trembling.

She shook her head. 'No one. If you've come about the
necklace—'

'No, I haven't, forget all that. Alice, I read a letter just
after you left, from Roger Nowell to Nick Bannister. Do
you know either of them?' She shook her head again, and
her face was so open and confused I did not doubt for a
moment she was telling the truth. 'Well, Roger knows
you, or he will. Alice, how do you know the Devices?'

Alice swayed like a felled tree and had to grip the back
of a chair.

'How do you know them, Alice? How?'

'I do not know them.'

'What were you doing at their house on Good Friday?
They are accused of witchcraft, Alice. The grandmother,
the mother, Alizon . . . The youngest daughter, Jennet,
she is staying with Roger, telling him everything.'

Her eyes darted around the room. 'I . . .'

'Alice, you have to understand: your name is on a list
– a list that is in the hands of a very powerful man who

makes the law around here. You will be arrested, and almost certainly arraigned for witchcraft.'

All the colour drained from her face. I thought she might fall, so I ran to her, holding her by the arms and sitting her carefully in a chair.

'I am . . . I will be arrested? And arraigned . . . But what does that mean?'

I swallowed. 'It means you will face trial at the assizes. Lent has happened, so summer, perhaps.'

'Trial,' she whispered. 'But witches are hanged.'

'*Most* of them are.' I knelt before her, and took her hands in mine. 'But you have not yet been arrested, and there is time to change Roger's mind. Alice, you *must* tell me what you were doing with the Devices at Malkin Tower. I can help you; Richard can help you.'

Still frozen in shock, she ever so slightly shook her head in disbelief. Then she balled her hands into fists, shoving them under her armpits, making herself smaller.

'Who gave him my name? Elizabeth Device?'

'Her daughter, Jennet, I think. What took you there, Alice? You have to tell me so I can tell Roger he has it wrong.'

There were footsteps in the passage. My heart pounded with them until they went away, and Alice looked up briefly, distracted with fear.

'*Was* he wrong?' I asked.

After what felt like an age, she sat up straight and tucked her hair beneath her cap. Her wide mouth was solemn.

'I do not know those people,' she said.

'Alice you have to understand they will think you *do* if you were there. They will see you as a witch.'

She bit her lip and blood bloomed under her tooth. The pink tip of her tongue came out, serpent-like, to lick it.

'Tell me. I will tell Richard, and together we will go to Roger and tell him he has made a mistake.'

But she was not looking at me, her gaze somewhere beyond.

Then she said: 'No. I do not trust him. And neither should you.'

'Trust who? Roger?'

She closed her eyes and rubbed at them, as though she was suddenly very tired.

'Richard?' I said. Her mouth remained closed. 'I can't trust Richard? My husband?' I rose to stand, but my meagre height meant I was only a head or two above her. 'Is this because of what he said about the necklace? He knows you didn't steal it – I'm certain he does. He was just angry.'

Something was starting to make me tremble and I realised it was fear. I wanted to prise Alice's hands away from her face and make her look at me.

'I do not think you comprehend how much danger you are in.' My voice shook with emotion. 'Roger is on a witch hunt. He is collecting women like cards at a table. I have come to warn you, and offer my help. That's if you want it, which I think you do. And I would advise you stay away from Colne for now.'

'But that is where I live.'

'And that is where they will look for you. You should stay with a friend, or family. Roger and Richard know your first name, at least. It won't take them long to realise you're the same Alice on Roger's list.'

'Then why have they not burst through the door to arrest me?'

'Because they do not know yet, and I will not lead them to you.'

With that she made a noise that sounded like a scoff. I reached for the door handle.

'I will go home and explain everything to Richard, and he will go to Roger.'

'You adore your husband.' Her voice rung out clear in the cold, empty room.

'Of course I do. What do you mean by that?'

'Do not go to him.'

'Why?' Hot fury bubbled up again. 'Do you not comprehend how much influence my husband has? Are you saying you do not *need* our help? That you will somehow get through this on your own? Alice, your *life* is at stake. Roger will not be made a fool of in front of the London justices if I know him at all. He made a list of people to arrest, and *your name is on it*. What of this do you not understand?'

Again she put her head in her hands. She had aged ten years in one afternoon.

'Alice, are you listening to me? Do you not trust me?'

'Yes, I trust you,' she said.

It was a small triumph, and despite my anger, her words glowed in my chest. They'd never been said to me before, or needed to be.

'But you don't trust Richard? Why?'

Very slowly, she turned her face to look at me.

'The ledger,' she said.

'What?'

'The ledger your steward keeps. Everything you buy and everything that leaves Gawthorpe goes in there, you said. Is that right?'

I nodded, bewildered.

'Look at the ledger.'

'But . . . How do you know what's in there? You can't read.'

In her wide amber eyes there was an inexplicable sympathy.

'I don't need to read things to see them.'

I went straight to James' study. Even though the fire was lit, I was cold as stone and my teeth chattered as I drew out the thick book bound in calfskin. In James' neat hand-writing was a list of everything bought and paid:

March: two loads malt; roundlett of sack; three great salt lings delivered to Thomas Yate in London . . .

What was I supposed to be looking for?

April: Michael Thorpe to Colne with bacon; half a year's rent for Ightenhill Park; the carriage of a gun down from London.

Could it be the gun? I knew about the gun.

Mr William Anderton to bring marriage licence from York.

I paused on this, my finger holding the place. Why would anyone at Gawthorpe need a marriage licence? No one was betrothed, as far as I knew.

That's when I noticed a word so familiar to me I had overlooked it altogether:

Sweet soap to Barton.

Coals from Padiham pit to Barton.

Chickens bought at Clitheroe to Barton.

Barton.

Barton.

It had been my name and also my home. But nobody lived there; it had been empty since my mother and I moved out four years before.

'Mistress, here you are.' James stood in the doorway, his usually composed face a mask of concern. I closed the book. 'Was there something you needed?'

'No, James, thank you.'

I slammed it shut and moved around the desk, embarrassed. But when I brushed past him into the passage, suddenly the rage returned: how was *I* doing something wrong by looking at my own household ledger? Why *shouldn't* I care how the property I'd brought to this family was being kept? Something told me I had to be careful.

When I'd left Alice in that dank little room at the alehouse, these were my parting words to her, too.

'Where will you go?' I'd asked.

She had only shrugged, and stared at the empty hearth. I'd been too consumed to offer my help, and galloped the short ride home in a fog of my own turmoil.

'The master has been searching for you,' said James.

I noticed with alarm that he was not just concerned, but very pale and grave.

'Is something wrong?'

'One of the servants has been taken ill: Sarah, the chambermaid. Richard has asked me to send for the doctor.'

'Very well. What is the matter?'

'She complained of a headache, and now is in a fever. She is delirious and asking for her mother.'

'Then send for her mother. Or can she be sent home?'

'I think it might be best, once the doctor has seen her. In case it's catching.'

I frowned. There was far too much in my head at once, with supplies being sent to Barton and servants being struck down with illness, and Alice's association with the Devices, and the ruby necklace. More had happened today than in a year.

'She seemed fine earlier,' I thought out loud, remembering how she spoke up in Richard's household meeting.

Then I remembered Alice's pink cheeks and hard gaze, and my stomach sank. I prayed silently that the sweating sickness or some other deadly disease had not come to this house.

The passage outside was dark, and James' study friendly and warm. I had no wish to make a twenty-mile ride, but it had to be now.

'James, I need you to do two things for me: have my horse saddled, and pass Richard a message.'

'The master is due to return any moment—'

'The message is this: I am going to Colne, where I will take a room at an inn for a night or two and try to persuade Alice to return as my midwife.'

He looked at me in astonishment. 'But, Mistress—'

'I feel Richard handled the necklace business quite poorly. He humiliated our loyal staff. You saw it. But of course you won't tell him I said that. I am afraid he has cost me a skilled midwife, who I trusted and liked very much, and I will have no one else deliver my child. Tell him what you will. The real reason, James, is that I cannot stand to look at my husband for the way he treated the servants. You are all loyal and precious to me, and I hope you won't think badly of him for it. That is why I am staying away from Gawthorpe, because I am upset. Please tell him not to follow me, and I will be back in the morning.'

After a moment's hesitation, he nodded smartly.

'Yes, Mistress.'

I turned, and then, as though I'd just remembered, half-turned back, hoping my face was hidden in the darkness and did not give me away.

'Oh, and James? How are things at Barton? All in order?'

His face fell at once, and he went quite grey. It was all I needed. He opened and closed his mouth a few times like a dying fish while I waited calmly.

'Might you need something fetching from there, Mistress? It has been shut up for—'

'Four years, has it not?'

His Adam's apple quivered as he swallowed his words. 'Yes, that's right.'

'Very well. I will get my cloak.'

I arrived shortly after nightfall. There was no moon, only cloud, so everything was black, but I saw the vast shape of the house lurking ahead, and warm light burning merrily in a room on the ground floor. I had not wanted to come back here ever. I did not want to see the chamber my mother and I shared. I did not want to see the parlour where my childhood ended in the time it took my mother to fetch something. I did not want to see the creaking staircase, the high, cold ceilings or the empty cage where I had found Samuel dead one winter morning after he'd been left too close to the fire.

I had dismounted outside the house when a noise – or rather a presence – made me turn my head, and something very low and slim crossed the grass to my right. It was no more than a silky shadow, but it paused, its brush-like tail straight out behind it: a fox. It froze, still as a statue, and we stared at one another, and my skin tingled. But then it bolted and disappeared in the blackness, and I carried on alone, stumbling on the front steps and cursing the clumsy pattens protecting my slippers. I flung them off and they clattered to the ground.

The door opened with no resistance, and the entrance hall was very dim, with no torches lit and that familiar old chill caressing me on the threshold.

'Hello?' I called.

I could not – dared not – think of what, or who, was in the room I knew to be the great hall. At worst it might be a vagrant – or would that be best?

My feet were almost silent. The only sounds I could hear were my breath ragged in my chest and my blood pounding in my ears. I walked blindly in the dark, my hands out in front of my face, to where the door for the great hall was, feeling my way along the walls. I tried to ignore the creeping thought that I might touch the face of a person waiting for me noiselessly. After combing the walls from top to bottom, I found the handle I'd been searching for and pulled it.

A warmly lit scene met my eyes. The sconces were glowing around the walls, and the glass above the fireplace cast light back into the room, which reflected again off the chandelier. At the great fireplace that measured ten feet across – the one I used to walk inside and be scolded for, ruining my slippers on the ash – a woman was seated.

I felt as though I was dreaming, floating, as I approached her, for she did not seem to get any closer. She noticed me, and stood. She was older than me by a few years, and her dark head was uncovered. She looked afraid, and I did not understand, and then I did, and my heart fluttered and stopped.

A noise in the passage behind should have startled me, but did not, so when James appeared there, breathless and steaming from the galloping journey from Gawthorpe, I barely reacted. My eyes were fixed on the woman before me, because her cloak had fallen open when she stood. Her stomach was round like mine.

The floor tilted. The stone flags rushed to welcome me as their old mistress, and I was grateful for their embrace as my world came crashing down, and my body with it.

PART TWO

WESTMORELAND (NOW CUMBRIA),
MAY, 1612

Laws [are] like cobwebs, where the small flies
are caught but the great break through.

Sir Francis Bacon

CHAPTER 10

J ames had escorted me back to Gawthorpe, through the wind and rain, and as soon as I reached my chamber I locked the door. It stayed locked for a full day and night, and I grew used to the sound of Richard pounding at it because it was difficult to mind anything with my stomach so empty. Prudence, Justice and I waited, for what, we didn't know, but then late on the second day, when I began to think seriously about having my fire lit and some food sent, one of the chambermaids came to the door and said there was a messenger arrived from my mother.

Through the keyhole I bade her tell him that I wished to be left alone, and her voice became more anguished as she returned and introduced a male voice I did not know.

'Mistress Barton wishes me to inform you that a carriage is waiting outside Gawthorpe,' the voice said. I waited. 'She insists that it will not leave until you are in it.'

'Then it will be there until it rots,' I said.

The man cleared his throat. I wondered who else might be standing with him in silence.

'Mistress Barton is inviting you to stay with her at Kirkby Lonsdale. She thought you might wish for a change of scenery.' There was a deferential pause. 'I am to wait here until you are ready.'

I returned to the bed for quite some time, sprawled in and out of the bedclothes.

Eventually, my voice choking, I said, 'Are you there, Richard?'

After a pause the messenger said, 'I am quite alone, Mistress.'

With an almighty effort I dragged myself back to the keyhole. All I could see was a clothed thigh and sword sheath. Even after a day and night, I still had not been able to comprehend the scale of betrayal. It began in my bed and spread down to the brewery that was sending her beer, the study, where our loyal servant James committed each individual blow to ink. It had travelled to the Hand and Shuttle, where I assumed Alice had heard of it. And it even seeped into my past, spreading its stain on my already unsentimental childhood. That was almost worst of all: that Richard was keeping his woman in the house I grew up in, that was handed over to him like a parcel the day we married because he knew I would never go there again.

That was when the thought occurred to me: did my mother know about the dark-haired woman with her full belly? As the afternoon wore on the question hummed in my ear like a fly, and then I heard Puck barking on the other side of the door. He scratched and whined outside it, and I realised I had not given him a thought, concerned with only myself. I knelt closer to the door.

'Puck,' I said in a small voice. 'Puck, stop. I am here. I am here.'

Tears streamed down my face as he howled, a sound that felt as though it was ripping me in two, and no matter what I said he would not be quiet. The need to hold him overwhelmed me, so I turned the key in the lock and he fell inside, knocking me to the floor. His huge tongue wiped my face and I could not help but laugh as he climbed all over me, whining and panting and making noises of pure pleasure. When he had quite finished I pulled myself up to sit. The messenger stood away from the door, waiting diffidently.

'I will come but only on my terms.' I said. He bowed graciously then stood up straight, expectant. 'I will bring my dog. And there is somewhere we must stop on the way.'

'Should I send for a servant to pack your things?' he asked.

'I will pack them myself.'

*

During the journey north, Alice and I came up with a plan. So Roger could not find her, she had left her position at the Hand and Shuttle, telling the landlord her father was ill, and needed caring for. I waited a few streets away in the carriage, so as not to be seen. There was a nervous urgency about us both, because she was running away in all but name – I'd asked if there was anything she needed from home and she just shook her head. As the road fell away behind us, we decided she would come to my mother's as my companion Jill, which she told me was her mother's name.

'Would you like something to eat?' I asked.

We were waiting in another inn yard while the carter changed horses, the smell of supper cooking and roasting meat wafting over. It was a pleasant May evening – warm and still – and we listened to the sounds of the yard, of horses' hooves and people chatting and going about their normal lives, with the curtain drawn across the carriage door so nobody could see in.

Alice shook her head.

'You said your mother was a midwife,' I said. 'Is she . . .'

'She died.'

'I'm sorry.'

'It was years ago.'

Alice sat very straight; she had good posture even without a corse.

'How did she die?'

After a moment, she replied.

'She had a fever. She was ill for a long time, then that carried her into the next life. There was nothing I could do.'

'Did you learn about herbs from her?'

She nodded. 'She had a garden . . . her kitchen, she called it, because we did not have one. She grew things to eat, herbs . . . I try to keep it going because I know how she loved it. She told me the names of everything. We would go out walking and she would show me things and tell me what they could do. She said it was useful for a woman to know, for a wife and mother to keep her family together in this world. She loved to think of me with a family,' she finished softly.

'Where did she learn her trade?' I asked.

'Where does any woman learn it? By doing it, I suppose. She and her friend Katherine did it together, they would go where they were needed. Mould-heels, they called Katherine, because she took so long over everything, making sure it was all right. She always got her things out carefully, even if the mother was screaming to high Heaven.' She smiled at some private memory. 'She would build a fire as if she had all the time in the world.'

'And you would go with them?'

Alice nodded.

'How many babies have you birthed?'

'I don't know . . . Twenty? Maybe more?'

Her answer surprised me – I had thought her more experienced, but then I hadn't asked. After a while I asked if her father would miss her while she was away. She thought about it, then shook her head.

'No. What I do, perhaps, but not me.'

'What do you mean?'

'Cooking. Feeding the chickens. Keeping the house. Earning money.' Her voice was flat.

'You never thought of marrying and having a house of your own?'

Her face darkened so briefly I wondered if I'd imagined it. She appeared to consider her answer, then said, 'There is no difference in it, really. It's the same life for a daughter as it is for a wife – just a different man telling you what to do.'

'I suppose you are right. But you would have infants of your own. Every woman wants that; it's our purpose in life.'

She lowered her eyes. 'Children are more trouble than they are worth.'

It was a strange answer, especially for a midwife. Then the carter climbed up on to the roof, jolting us in our seats, and we set off again.

When Alice did not speak again, I thought I may have offended her, until a few miles later, when I'd begun to doze, and I heard her say in a quiet voice, as though to herself, 'I have never been in a carriage before.'

Darkness had fallen when we arrived. The manor itself

sat high on the side of a hill in the midst of a copse of thick woodland, and the ride up was steep, so I had to press my feet against the seat opposite to prevent sliding down. The park stretched to the top of the valley, where scree and heather met the sky. Puck was asleep, as was Alice. She was an odd sleeper and still somehow looked alert, her neck long, her face impassive, as though she had just closed her eyes.

The carriage drew up and I climbed exhausted from it, dog-tired after my second long journey in as many days. Puck dropped to the ground behind me, yawned and stretched, and Alice after him. Henry unloaded my trunk, and at the top of the steps the wide front door opened, spilling light on to our strange party and framing the unmistakable silhouette of my mother.

'Fleetwood,' she said, her thin voice carrying into the night. 'I thought you would never come.'

I glanced at Alice and together we ascended the steps.

The house my mother lived in was owned by the Shuttleworths, bought by Richard's uncle some two decades before as a place to rest or hunt on the road to Scotland. I had been only once before, when my mother was ill with a bad chest and Richard persuaded me to visit.

I decided I would get straight to business. Before my trunk had even been set down on the stone flags of the entrance hall, I turned to face my mother.

'Did you know of Richard's woman?'

'Of course I knew, Fleetwood. Now get inside before you are dead on your feet.'

Though she'd only confirmed what I suspected, still I felt as though she had driven a sword through me then pulled it straight back out again.

Alice took my arm and almost carried me through the stone-flagged corridors to a snug room that was sparsely furnished. There were no books, vases or jugs, just bare surfaces, as though they were waiting to have their things replaced after dusting. Mary Barton had always taken a Calvinist approach to furnishing, but here the carpet needed replacing, the fire sweeping, the windows washing. She took her seat by the fire and indicated I take the one opposite – even these were old and tired. I wondered if the furniture had been updated since Richard's uncle bought the place twenty years ago. But the room was warm, and a low coal fire burnt in the grate. There was a mildly unpleasant smell, cloying and meaty, and it took me a moment to realise the candles here were tallow, not wax.

'My midwife will need a chair,' I said.

My mother stared at me, then looked Alice swiftly up and down, before rising and striding from the room. Alice was taking no interest in her surroundings, staring absently at the threadbare carpet at her feet. My mother returned with a servant behind her, carrying a sturdy chair, which he set against the wall before bowing and quietly closing the door on his way out.

There was complete silence as we both waited for the other to speak. It did not take long for me to lose my temper.

'You invited me to travel fifty miles but have nothing to say?' I snapped.

No matter how rude I was, my mother's face remained inscrutable. She was white as chalk and I noticed she had more lines at her eyes and lips than the last time I saw her.

She sighed deeply, closing her eyes.

'I hoped this day would not come,' she said.

'Did you think I would not find out?'

'Yes,' she said simply.

'Why? Why would you not tell me if you knew? Richard has betrayed me, he has *broken* me and our marriage, and you knew. My own mother!'

'I was trying to protect you,' she said slowly. Her eyes were dark.

'How can I trust you? I cannot trust anyone. Not one person,' I said.

Apart from Alice, added a voice in my head.

I started to cry, and my mother watched, her expression awful, as I held my face in my hands.

'I hate you!' I screamed at her. The sound ripped through the small room, bouncing from the wooden walls. 'I hate both of you. You have both betrayed me.'

She allowed me to gather myself and I slumped back

into my chair, a sullen child again. My breathing slowed and I wiped my face dry.

'You will stay here,' my mother said eventually.

'Until when? Until *she* has the child?' I asked.

'What child?'

Understanding dawned on my mother's face. She reached for the arm of her chair with one white hand and her face turned paler.

'She . . .'

'She will have his child,' I said.

She closed her eyes. 'The stupid fool,' she whispered.

I did not know which of us she was referring to.

'And you know she is at Barton?'

My mother nodded. Absently she flexed the finger that held her plain gold wedding band. I saw her mind working. From the corner of my eye I was aware of Alice, silent and perfectly still. My mother had not asked her name or even acknowledged her presence.

'Do you know the woman's name?' I asked finally.

'Judith Thorpe.'

'How did you learn of her?'

'It is not important.'

'It is to me.'

'What *is* important is that you succeed in carrying this child, as you have not done before.'

My stomach dropped. 'Why?'

She licked her teeth. 'Fleetwood, listen to me. If you do not produce an heir, she will.'

Her voice rang clear in the room, and we stared at one another, reaching an understanding for possibly the first time in our lives. I felt suddenly cold all over.

'But she is not his wife.' Alice spoke, surprising us both.

'An illegitimate child is as good as an heir,' my mother said darkly. 'They may not be able to inherit directly, but a man can bequeath all kinds of things to his bastard: estates, land, property. Especially if there are no others. The only other way a bastard can be legitimised is if his father and mother marry,' she added dismissively.

James' writing swam before my eyes: *William Anderton to bring marriage licence from York*.

I covered my mouth with my hand.

'He means to marry her. He knows I am to die.'

'*Die?*'

I told my mother about Dr Jensen's letter, about the order of a marriage licence I found in the ledger. I was shaking violently now.

'Fleetwood!'

My mother was shocked and appalled as I twitched and shivered.

Alice was suddenly at my side.

'Have you *rosa solis*?' she asked my mother.

'What is that?'

'Brandy and cinnamon. Have it made for her, it will help.'

My mother fled from the room and Alice took my hand in hers: pink flesh against grey. Presently my mother returned with a servant bearing a tray on which sat a pewter cup. Alice took it and handed it to me, and I choked back the drink, the pewter clattering against my teeth. The concoction fired my throat and warmed my insides, and gradually the jittering slowed to a gentle twitch. My mother replaced the cup on the tray and asked for bread and wine to be brought.

'Mistress,' the servant said softly, 'there is no more manchet, just cheat.'

'Bring it whatever,' my mother snapped. Then she turned to Alice, and her dark eyes were interested. 'What is your name?'

'Jill, Mistress.'

My mother nodded once, to indicate both approval and dismissal, and returned to her seat before me.

My head was thick with thoughts. I felt the child in my stomach move, as though reminding me it was still there. It felt like when a carriage runs over a dip, not entirely unpleasant, and I cupped my stomach with my hands and rubbed as though to warm it, remembering the spidery words of the doctor's letter that were now as familiar to me as my own name: *Her earthly life will end.*

CHAPTER 11

Alice and I shared a room at the top of the house because it was warm – the start of summer had not yet reached this far north. She was on a truckle bed brought in and set next to mine, and she slept in a peculiar way, curled around on the mattress, without using the pillow. I knew because I barely slept. Not wanting to wake her with my rolling and creaking, I eventually got up and sat at the window.

All I could think of was Richard's woman. The more I tried to picture her, the less clear her face became, but I was sure I had never seen her before that moment, that she was not someone I had met. I wondered if she slept in my old bed at Barton, and if Richard did too when he was there. All the times he had kissed my forehead before going away, and I had watched from a window as he departed on his horse to Halifax, Manchester, Lancaster, and further: Coventry, London, Edinburgh. But really: Barton, Barton, Barton.

Tears came easily now, and I tried not to sniff too hard or make much noise. I could not imagine going back to Gawthorpe but I could not stay here either, forever a guest in my mother's house. I was stuck in the mud, and sinking. But for now, sat at the window looking out while it was still dark outside, I would not think of the next day, or the day after that. And I was still alive, and my child too, for it was squirming like a newborn kitten now, and I felt it all the time – I was never truly alone. Then I realised that if it was born, and if I lived and became a mother, I would never be alone. The thought came like a ray of warm sunshine on my face. I may have lost Richard – or a part of him – and my marriage was no longer what I thought it was, but I would have a lifelong friend.

I turned to look at the sleeping form of the woman who was my only means of achieving this. Her golden hair fell over the pillow and down her back, and her chest rose and sank peacefully. I thought of the man who'd upset her in the Hand and Shuttle, how she'd said children were more trouble than they were worth. I felt as though she was the first person I could call a friend, but how much did I really know about her?

As though aware in some part of herself that she was being watched, Alice shifted in her narrow bed and

whimpered. I watched her settle again, then she stiff-
ened, her hands scrabbling at her covers.

'Leave her,' she whimpered quietly. 'Leave her.'

But before I could decide whether or not to wake her,
as suddenly as she'd began, she melted into peace, her
body relaxing and her face smoothing back into sleep.

I sat with my hands on my stomach and watched the
inky blue sky grow darker before it got lighter, and it was
only when the birds began to pierce the silence that my
eyes grew heavy and I climbed back into the bed sheets,
which were cold.

Breaking our fasts that morning, we made a sombre group.
Alice went as though to eat with the servants but I asked
that she sat with my mother and me, and when she refused
I insisted. Neither she nor my mother were happy about
it, and sat with their faces pinched as their eggs were set
down in front of them. The bread was brought, but it
was different from what I was used to. I remembered what
my mother's servant had said the night before, that they
only had cheat flour, made of bran not wheat.

I scratched at my clothes and cap where they felt tight
and yawned. Alice was nibbling at a boiled egg, and I took
one from the bowl and held its warm weight in the palm
of my hand. Against the thick white of it, my skin looked
almost yellow.

'Fleetwood, is there something wrong with your egg?' my mother asked.

I bit into it and found it surprisingly delicious: salty and solid, not like the trembling, watery things my kitchen served in their shells. I had to put it down though to scratch my arm, rubbing the material of my dress hard where I could not reach the skin.

'Fleetwood,' my mother said, 'do you have lice?'

I thought I might, although I hadn't seen any. It felt as though I was being tickled very softly and finely all over, from my ankles to my ears. I scratched at my neck, my face, my wrists and my stockings: anywhere I could reach.

'Perhaps I do,' I said.

Poor people got lice, unclean people, not me, who rubbed myself with linen every day and dabbed rose oil at my wrists and throat.

'Eat your breakfast,' my mother said. 'If only you had the appetite of your midwife.'

Alice coloured and paused buttering her bread, setting the knife down slowly.

'I prefer manchet to this cheap stuff,' I said, hoping to make her colour in turn, which she did.

But I was lying: the seed loaf was warm and nourishing, and delicious with the home-made butter. The itching started up again and my knife clattered to the table as I sprang up to relieve the backs of my legs.

'Fleetwood!'

'I don't know what's the matter with me.'

I stuck my fingers down the back of my dress, but while that brought relief, my arm tingled again where I'd rubbed it a moment before.

'Control yourself. You are causing a display.'

'This has not happened before, and the moment I come to stay with you I itch from head to toe. Do you wash the bed linen, mother?'

'Of course it is washed, don't be absurd!'

'I need to get out of this dress.' I stalked away from the table, then stopped in the doorway. 'Jill, will you help me?'

Alice looked relieved to abandon breakfast and followed me out of the dining chamber and upstairs. I was impatient as she unlaced every ribbon and lace that she had tied not half an hour before.

'Hurry, please!'

Finally the gown fell down around me and I stepped out of it; then my corset had to come off and the French farthingale be pulled from my hips. By the time I could sit down to untie my stockings, I was shoving up the sleeves of my underclothes to tear at my skin with my nails. I reached under my nightgown to get to the flesh at my stomach, which felt hard and smooth where before it was doughy. I pulled a pin from my hair and used it to scratch down the back of my neck.

Alice watched, rubbing her neck thoughtfully as I contorted myself in front of her.

'Perhaps a bath would help?' she suggested.

A tub was brought and jugs of water from the kitchen. Then a chambermaid knocked on the door with a slice of soap, which was soft and black and home-made, not like the solid white cakes we bought. I did not know how to ask Alice to turn away as I undressed, but she did anyway. As my underclothes fell to the floor, I half-expected to see tiny black things crawling up and down my flesh and in and out of my clothes, but there was nothing. My skin was white all over, not flaming red as it felt. I started to laugh. Alice half-turned from her truckle bed.

'What is it?'

'There's nothing there. No lice. No rash. I must be addled.'

I lowered myself into the water and splashed it all over, extinguishing the itching like so many little flames licking my skin.

'Would you like me to leave?' Alice asked, still facing the wall.

'No, stay,' I said.

She kept her back to me, folding her legs beneath her to become more comfortable. The water settled and I stared down at my stomach, which was much bigger than the last time I'd bathed. I couldn't see the coarse black hairs below it. I moved the soap all over my skin, making it slick as an eel, and the itching dulled. I filled the jug and tipped it over my head, lathering my hair so it tangled into a knotted mess. The water lapped gently around me and I sighed, letting my mind wander back to something that I'd been thinking about ever since I rode out with Richard and Roger on that misty hunt in April.

'Alice, have you heard of familiar spirits?'

I heard her weight shift on the bed.

'Yes,' she said.

'Jennet Device told me her mother had a dog, and I saw a dog with her when you were . . .'

Alice went still. 'When I was what?'

I swallowed. She turned and looked straight at me over her shoulder, her eyes bright and clear.

'When I was what?'

'Alice, do not look.'

I attempted to cover myself in the tub, but her gaze did not stray from my face.

'Were you spying on me?'

'No.'

'When?'

'I . . . I went out riding to meet you. I saw you with her in the forest.'

She turned again to the fire and reached for the poker, pushing it into the splintered coals.

'What did you hear?'

'Nothing.'

'Why did you not make yourself known?'

'I . . . I was afraid. Of her. Of the woman. Elizabeth Device.'

'Why?'

'Her eyes. They frightened me.'

How awful she had looked when she turned towards me, staring wildly in different directions.

'Her daughter, Jennet,' I went on. 'I cannot fathom why Roger believes everything she tells him. How can he? She is just a child.'

As I said it, I thought of myself at that age, and how I'd told no one about what happened to me, knowing no one would believe it. But that was different – Jennet's stories were full of magick and spirits, like a tale told to a child to get them to sleep.

'Maybe he wants to believe it. Maybe he is telling her what to say.'

'Roger would not do that.'

'How do you know?'

'He is a good man. He has been good to us.'

As my words rang out into the room they sounded hollow. Did Roger know of Richard's woman too? That would be a betrayal twice over, and worse even than my own mother's. He called Richard and me the turtledoves. Either he was ignorant or cruel.

'Alice, I am sorry for spying, I did not mean it,' I said after a long silence.

My thoughts were becoming too tangled for me; I needed to separate them and follow each of them in turn. I watched Alice pick at something on her skirt. Her old dress badly needed mending and washing, and her cap starching. I decided I would have it done here. I wondered when the last time she bathed was – if she too longed to scrub herself clean.

'Alice, would you like to bathe?'

'No, thank you.'

'I can have more water sent up.'

She bristled. 'Do I smell badly? Do you think *I* have given you lice?'

'No, of course not. There are no lice. I imagined it . . .' I looked at the white pile of my underthings on the floor and watched them again to see if they crawled. 'Alice, do you think my skin looks yellow?'

She glanced dismissively at me.

'I couldn't say – it does not look healthy, but then it never does.'

She was full of resentment, and for the first time I wondered if I'd been right to bring her here with me. Something had shifted in her the day Richard implied she had stolen my necklace. Still, I was used only to being deferred to, and she treated me almost like an equal. Yet I realised I did not mind.

I scooped water over myself once more then stood up, meeting myself in the mirror at the dresser. My hair was wild, bunched up around my ears like a bird's nest. My paps were full with dark rings around the nipples, the buds of which were also dark, and shadows hung beneath my eyes. I pressed myself with clean linen towels and wrapped a bath sheet around me to sit on the bed. Alice had not moved from where she was. I thought about where she might want to be. It was not here, but instinct told me she did not pine for the place she had left either – impossible anyway, now it was unsafe. Perhaps the place she felt most comfortable was somewhere I had not pictured her: in a lover's arms beneath old sheets, or sitting comfortably with her father outside on a warm spring evening.

'Alice, tell me,' I said as I pulled a clean smock over my head. 'Am I keeping you from your father?'

'No.'

'Or anyone else?' She shook her head. 'The man in the alehouse . . .' I hesitated.

She looked sharply at me. 'You saw him?'

For the second time I'd admitted to spying. I coloured slightly, and nodded.

'Just in the passage as he was leaving. Did he upset you?'

'I don't want to talk about it.'

She turned so I could not see her face.

I combed my hair and picked up my corse wrapped in pearl-coloured silk, rapping it lightly with my knuckles. I decided I would wear my gown without it today; I could not bear to bind my stomach again. Alice saw me playing with it.

'Do you ever tire of wearing clothes you cannot put on yourself?' she said.

'No,' I said truthfully. 'I only dress once a day. Apart from today.'

We smiled at one another, and I felt I was forgiven. A knock came at the door and someone collected the bath-water, while another servant brought sugar biscuits and hot milk, which I shared with Alice. She said that she had eaten better in twenty-four hours than she had all year. We sat eating the biscuits and feeding crumbs to Puck, and with sugar crystals on my lips, my hair clean and soft, and my gown fresh, it would have been easy to forget why I was here, but I couldn't quite manage it. The reason Alice was with me was because I was growing heavy with child, and the reason *I* was here in this bright, airy chamber fifty miles away from my own was because my husband had another woman. It was all such a mess, but somehow it didn't feel completely hopeless. Not yet, anyway.

Before long my mother came in, and made no attempt to hide her displeasure at the sight of Alice sitting on her bed, her legs tucked to the side, a cup of milk resting on her skirts that were dusted with sugar. Alice coloured slightly and sat properly.

'Will you dress again today, Fleetwood?' my mother asked.

'Perhaps.' I saw her eyes flick momentarily to my stomach, which was more pronounced in my shift with no layers of silk or velvet or wool piled over it. 'Have you no wood for the fires? We are like two servants hunched over these dying coal embers.'

Her eyes shone very black.

'We keep a good economy in this house. If you prefer a wood fire I can fetch you an axe.'

We glowered at one another, then she left, closing the door firmly behind her.

'No wood, no wheat and no wax candles,' I thought out loud. 'I am beginning to think my mother is growing cheap in her old age.'

Alice prodded the ashes in the hearth.

'How does she get her money?' she asked.

'I have never thought about it, but I suppose . . . from us.'

A bird sung in the canopy of trees beneath the window, sweet and clear. Us. I had always known that word to mean my husband and me, but all along he had been living two lives. Which of his women did he think of first? I slid my wedding band off my finger and slipped it on again. Off, on, off, on.

'You grew up here?'

'Here? No. I grew up at Barton. My mother has only lived here a few years.'

'Barton? But isn't that . . .'

'Yes.'

Her eyes were wide. 'Your husband keeps his mistress at your house?'

'I don't see it as mine, but yes.'

'Why not?' I felt her golden eyes on me.

'It was not a happy place.'

She let out a laugh, curling her feet beside her once again.

'How can a manor house not be a happy place? Did you not have fancy gowns, and fine food, and servants?'

I did not smile. Earlier she had allowed me a glimpse into her life – a keyhole's worth, but still a glimpse. Now she waited for me to decide how much to tell her, her clever eyes never leaving my face. I sighed, and crossed my legs to mirror hers.

'My father died a few years after I was born. I don't remember him. Then it was just my mother and me. I had no friends or cousins or anyone to play with, apart from my bird, Samuel. One day I left Samuel's cage too close to the fire and he died. He was the only friend I had. I was a miserable child. Whenever I misbehaved my mother threatened to send me to my husband. I should have got another pet, something to keep me company, but I didn't.'

'Your husband?' she asked suddenly. 'You mean Richard?'

'I was married before Richard.'

Before I could stop it, the memory that I had fought so hard to forget leapt into focus: the parlour, my mother's skirts disappearing around the corner, my husband's deep, cracked voice: 'Come to me, Fleetwood.' His large hand reaching to sit me on his lap.

'You were married *before*? So you were . . . You are divorced?'

'Heavens, no. The marriage was annulled so that I could marry Richard. My mother decided the Bartons and the Shuttleworths made a more advantageous match. If

Richard had not agreed I would still be wed to Mr
Molyneux.' I had not spoken his name aloud in such a
long time. 'And I do not think he was a good man.'

Alice was quiet and thoughtful.

'How old were you when you married the first time?'
she asked.

'Four.'

Alice was shocked into silence. Then she said, 'How
old was he?'

'About thirty.'

'How awful,' she whispered.

'I only met him twice: once at Barton, and the second
time at our wedding. After that, my mother took me home
to live until I was ready to be his wife. Thankfully that
day never came.'

There was pity in every line of Alice's face, and something else: a grave kind of understanding, as though she,
too, knew what went on in the world, and had seen some
of it.

'Why do you look like that?' I almost laughed. 'Did you
think I could choose a husband? Catch someone's eye in
the alehouse?'

'I suppose so.'

'The thing is, if I could, I would still have chosen
Richard.'

'You must love him a great deal.'

'I do,' I said simply. 'He rescued me from a different
future, and gave me a new one. I had no say in the matter.

But you – you are lucky. *You* can choose whomever you like.'

She gave a small smile. 'I have never been called lucky before.'

'Do you meet lots of men at the inn?'

'Drunks, plenty.'

'A world of choice, then.'

We both laughed, and there was a comfortable pause. I wondered if this was what friendship felt like.

'I can't imagine going home,' I said after a while, growing serious again.

'What will you do?' Alice asked.

'I have no idea.' I twirled my wedding band around and around. 'Do you want to hear a story?'

'Yes.'

'I do not know where it came from but people in the village at Barton, where my house was, say that a wild boar was running around causing havoc in the forest. My father offered up my hand in marriage to the person who could slay the boar. A hunt followed, and on St Lawrence's Day, the eldest Shuttleworth son slew it. There is an inn on the site called the Boar's Head, though I'm not sure which came first, that or the story.'

Alice was confused. 'But your father died before you were . . .'

'It's just a story. And do you know the best part? I am terrified of boars.'

'Why?'

I shrugged. 'I have nightmares about them chasing me. I must have heard that story when I was a child because I've been afraid of them for as long as I can remember. The Barton family crest is three boars.'

I had never told anyone but Richard so much about myself, and felt slightly exposed. Alice was quiet.

'I bet you are not afraid of anything,' I said.

'Of course I am,' she said, and she pulled at a loose thread in her apron. 'I am afraid of lies.'

That night, in the early hours, I woke suddenly. The room was black, with the faintest smell of burnt candle wick. Something had woken me – a noise or a movement. It might have been Puck – he had taken to sometimes sleeping in the room with us. I closed my eyes again and tried to get comfortable beneath the counterpane, but could not dismiss the feeling I was being watched. I pushed off the covers and crawled to the edge of the bed to look over at Alice's truckle bed, letting my eyes adjust to the darkness. There the white linen glowed faintly in the moonlight. The narrow bed was empty.

A breath of noise stirred behind me, and I knew immediately that there was someone else in the room. I turned slowly, searching here and there in the dark, and almost jumped from my skin to see a tall figure in a white nightdress standing directly beside my bed, where my head had been. A scream died in my throat.

'Alice?' I whispered, barely able to hear myself over the rushing in my ears.

She did not move, apart from swaying slightly. I could not see her face.

'Alice,' I said, louder. 'You are frightening me.'

Silently, she walked back to her bed and climbed into it. It took so long for my heart to stop racing, the edges of the window were light by the time I went to sleep.

'Do you remember what happened last night?' I asked her in the morning as she scrubbed herself with linen. She stared at me. 'You were standing over my bed.'

'Was I?'

'Yes. You frightened me. I thought my heart would stop.' She appeared surprised, and told me she did not remember. 'You sleepwalk?'

'Yes, but only . . .'

She fell quiet, and began scrubbing again.

'Only what?'

'Nothing.'

A few nights later, I woke with that same feeling again, and there she was, ghostly and moonlit, and then again a few nights after that. It was always unsettling, because it felt almost as though she was guarding me from something, and I could not say if even she knew what it was.

The cook at my mother's house was a woman named Mrs Knave, and it was thanks to her that after a long winter of hibernation, my appetite returned. She fed me apple pie, bread and butter, biscuits, gingerbread and marchpane. At mealtimes we had flaky salmon with creamy parsley sauce, oyster pies, and beef that was soft and pink in the middle. There were fluffy potatoes and buttery carrots and cheese pasties that burnt my tongue. Each night I had *rosa solis* – brandy with cinnamon – and slowly the colour began to return to my hollow cheeks. I hadn't been sick once. After my conversation with Alice about my mother's housekeeping, I had the coal in the fireplaces replaced with wood and the tallow candles with wax, instructing the suppliers to bill Richard directly.

One morning the movement in my stomach woke me before it was fully light. I lay with my hands on my rounded stomach, taut as a drum skin, thinking how strange the sensation was and listening to Alice's steady breathing. Dr Jensen's words came back to me as they often did in the early, lonely hours, so I slipped out of bed and went to the window. The sky was a beautiful deep blue but the forest of trees that surrounded the house was still in shadow. Beyond them was the village.

The chamber was warm and the air stale, so I found my cloak and put it on over my nightdress. The passage outside was silent, my mother's chamber door closed at the far end. I went quietly down to the kitchen, my mouth parched for a ripe pear or juicy apricot. I found a pear in a basket on the floor and went to the back door, turning the key to step outside and eat while dawn broke and birds sang above me. The juice coated my hands and chin as I stood beneath the wide sky, thinking about everything but wishing my mind was still. My stomach rolled and tiny fists and feet pummelled and kicked.

'Good morning,' I whispered. 'Shall we watch the sun rise?'

My skin itched again and I scratched absent-mindedly, my attention caught by something at the edge of the bank of trees. It was an animal, weaving in and out of the trunks. In the morning light it looked the same colour as Puck, but he was fast asleep on the Turkey carpet. I stood still against the wall and watched it come all the way around, looping through the trees as though making for the house without wanting to be seen. It was a fox. It held my gaze as we each waited for the other to move first, then a large bird, a rook or raven, burst out of the treetops and flapped, cawing into the morning. By the time I looked back the fox had gone, but something about it pulled a thread in my head somewhere. It wasn't until I went back upstairs and

found Alice in our chamber making her bed that I realised what it was. She looked up when I came in, and I
saw it: her eyes were the same colour as a fox's, like
coins in the sun.

CHAPTER 12

Two letters arrived at once: one for me, one for my mother, both from Richard. Even though they were only slips of paper, I felt that somehow he had arrived at the house, barging in where he was not welcome. His slanted handwriting always looked rushed no matter if a letter took him all afternoon, and there it was, spelling out my name. While my mother pulled hers open straight away, I put mine in my pocket.

Alice was outside. She had been spending time in the woods, searching for plants she could grow in the kitchen garden, and I'd often look out of the window to see her kneeling on the soil, her skirts bunched underneath her, her white cap bobbing among the green. A few days after the itching started, I watched her go from the garden to the kitchen door with a fistful of flat green leaves, then bring them to me in my chamber. She told me to rub them on my skin where it itched, and soon after it stopped altogether and my skin grew milky again.

'When we travelled here, you said children are more trouble than they are worth.'

I was standing outside, watching her at work in the soil. Dirt streaked her face. She sat back on her heels and wiped her cheek with the back of her hand, warm from her industry despite the chill spring day.

'And here you are planting a bed to help grow one that is not yet born,' I considered. 'I wonder if you are afraid of having them, knowing what you do about the delivery of them. Usually midwives are old and past their child-bearing years, or those I have seen are.'

'Perhaps.'

She seemed thoughtful and distracted at the same time. I watched her pull up a weed and toss it in her basket, and decided to go inside, because the fresh breeze was no longer pleasant, but then she spoke.

'How many children do you want to have?'

I wrapped my arms around myself.

'Two,' I replied. 'So that they will never be on their own like I was.'

'A boy and a girl?' she asked.

'Two boys. I wouldn't wish a girl's life on anyone.'

198

Richard's letter stayed where it was in the pocket of my gown, and though I forgot about it, two days later my mother decided that it two days after his word came was the appropriate time to discuss him. I knew what was coming from the way she set her spoon down; I could see her tasting his name in her mouth.

'Fleetwood,' she said. 'Have you thought about when you will go back to Gawthorpe?'

'No.'

'You have not thought about it?'

I glanced at Alice, sitting directly across from me, stirring distractedly at her meal and honey.

'I have not.'

'Tell me then.' My mother took up her spoon again. 'What have you been thinking of?'

Until that moment I had not noticed a copy of the King's Bible lying next to her hand. She saw me looking and lifted it, opening it at the ribbon marker.

'While we eat, let us consider the gospel according to Luke. "Judge not, and ye shall not be judged. Condemn not, and ye shall not be condemned. Forgive, and ye shall be forgiven."' She placed the book next to her bowl and took up her spoon again. 'What do you think to that passage, Fleetwood?'

I pretended to consider and licked my teeth.

'I think that it is remarkable how with his Bible, the king has a presence in every household, and on every bookshelf. He encourages us to not condemn others, yet seems to do little else. Papists, witches . . .'

'The king has not *written* the Bible, Fleetwood. This is the word of God. The king writes about witches in his own publication.'

'He does?'

She got up and left the room, coming back a few moments later with a slim volume bound in black calfskin, which she handed to me. I pushed my bowl away and lifted the soft cover. The word *Daemonologie* was printed below an ink depiction of the Devil. Flames licked his body and great wings expanded behind him. I looked up at my mother, who indicated for me to read on.

'"Written by the high and mighty Prince James,"' I said.

Alice was looking at the book in my hands and I remembered she could not read. I turned the page and followed the king's words.

'What does it say?' Alice asked.

'"The fearful abounding at this time in this country of these detestable slaves of the Devil, the witches or enchanters, has moved me, beloved reader, to dispatch in post this following Treatise of mine . . ." He has written a book about witchcraft?' I asked my mother, leafing through what appeared to be a very thorough treatise.

'Twenty or more years ago, a ship he was travelling in to Scotland was cursed by witchcraft. He put around a hundred witches on trial for treason. There are witch trials held there twenty times a year. One of the stable boy's distant relatives was executed not long ago; here in Westmoreland we are not far from the border. Your friend Roger Nowell is only keeping abreast of the times, Fleetwood. The execution of heretics is nothing new.'

Nick Bannister's spidery handwriting came into my mind: *Alice Gray, of the same.*

It had been easy not to think of it since we had arrived here, or at least it had been for me. I wondered if the child Jennet was still at Read Hall.

'But the definition of witch is new.' Alice directed this at my mother. 'These are peaceful people, carrying on as they have for centuries. It's only since the king came to the throne that people became fearful. Have *you* never needed the help of a wise woman?'

Mother shimmered with hostility.

'How dare you address me in so insolent a manner in my own house? Are you a midwife or an authority on politics?'

I gave Alice a warning glance. A flush was creeping up her throat.

'Jill merely means that perhaps not all those accused of witchcraft are guilty,' I said quickly.

My mother's neck was mottled a furious scarlet.

'You defend these Devil worshippers who use blood and bones and hair to carry out their sorcery? What is peaceful about that? They are godless people.'

Alice's eyes were on the table now – she knew she had spoken out of turn.

'Enough,' my mother went on, straightening her napkin on her lap and addressing me. 'Let us return to the matter in hand: when you will return to Lancashire, and to your husband. You have had time apart, and now it is only right that you go back. You are a wife, and wives live at home, not with their mothers.'

'What if Richard has moved that woman in?'

'He would do nothing of the sort.'

'So I suppose she will go on living at our house?'

'Where else would you have her? She is not in your parish, not in your way. She is out of sight and out of mind.'

I threw the king's book on to the table.

'She is not out of *my* mind. She might be out of yours but it is not *your* husband who has a woman. How can you defend her? And him? If he is such an angel, why does he have you furnishing your house like a yeoman's wife?'

'I am content with my lot, as you should be yours,' was her cold reply. 'That nasty temper of yours is no doubt what drove him away.'

'What drove him away is his need for an heir, and his wife not being able to give him one.'

My eyes stung and my throat was tight.

'Fleetwood, do you think Richard is the first man to have a mistress and a bastard?'

The ghost of an itch sent my fingers to my scalp, my neck.

'Next you will tell me that Father had twenty.'

'Of course he didn't. My father did, though.'

I stared at her.

'My father had three wives, and all of them had his children by the time they were married. When his first two wives died the next set was ready to move in. Not me,' she said quickly. 'But I had many brothers and sisters. Father's will was ten pages long – he left something to all of us.'

'So you are telling me,' I said slowly, 'that if I die, this woman will easily take my place and move her children in, and nobody will remember me at all?'

'The things that come out of your mouth!' my mother cried. 'That is not what I am saying. While you can have children, your place in the family is safe. Deliver your husband's heir and nobody will give a thought to this other woman, just as nobody gives a thought to the hundreds of other women and their bastard children in homes all over the country.'

Her chair screeched against the floorboards as she forced it backwards and strode from the room. I waited until her feet were on the stone flags outside, then I took the king's book and threw it at the wall.

But *Daemonologie* turned up again later that day on Alice's bed. I asked her about it when she came in from the garden, her palms dirty.

'I thought you could not read.'

'I can't,' she said, pouring water from the jug into the bowl on the dresser. 'I wanted to look at it. Would you read it to me? I want to know what he says. The king.'

'Why do you?'

Brown water lapped the sides of the bowl as she rubbed her hands and wrists.

'Please,' she said, and then, 'I spoke out of turn with your mother. I should not have been so bold.'

'Think not on it. I don't.' I sat on the end of Alice's truckle bed, reaching for *Daemonologie* and leafing through it. 'I have no idea why it is written in dialogue.' Alice looked blankly at me. 'Dialogue, like what is spoken in plays.'

'I have never seen one.'

I opened it at chapter three. '"Epistemon says: I pray you likewise forget not to tell what are the Devil's rudiments."'

'Rudiments?'

'"I mean either by such kind of Charms as commonly daft wives use, for healing of forspoken goods, for preserving them from evil . . . by curing the worm, by healing of horse-crooks, by turning of the riddle, or doing of such like innumerable things by words, without applying anything, meet to the part offended, as mediciners do."'

'What does it mean?'

'Doing things by words without applying anything. Curses,' I said. 'Healing things or maiming them from afar. I find it hard to believe the king found time to write this when he was ruling Scotland.'

'I don't understand why he would write a book about it. But then, if I could write a book, maybe I would,' Alice said.

I laughed. 'You? Write a book? Women do not write books. Besides, you have to learn to read first.'

'If you can write a letter why not a book?'

'Alice,' I said gently, 'it's not what is done.' I had a thought. 'Have you seen your own name?' She shook her head. 'Would you like to?'

She nodded, so I took out Richard's letter, still wrapped in ribbon, and brought a feather and ink from the desk in the corner of my mother's room. I sat down beside her on the truckle bed. In one quarter of the paper, bordered by ribbon, I wrote Alice's name and blew on the ink before handing it to her. She smiled and took it from me, holding it up as though it shone in the light.

'What does that say?' she asked, pointing to the letters curling up around the red ribbon.

'That's my name.'

'Why is it longer than mine when they take the same time to say? Fleet-wood. A-lice.'

'That isn't how it works. Each of those things is a letter. A-L-I-C-E. They each make a different sound, but when you say them all together they sound different again.' In the top right-hand square I wrote her name in widely spaced letters, then handed her the pen. 'You try.'

She gripped the feather in a way that made me smile. 'No, like this.'

I showed her. In a shaky hand, she copied the *A* in a new square followed by the other letters. I burst out laughing when she showed me.

'What?' she demanded.

'The way you've written it with the *A* so far away, it looks like a lice.'

'A *lice*?'

'If you separate the *A* from the rest of the letters, your name becomes "a lice".'

'What?'

She screwed her face up in such a way that I could not help but laugh. Then she began smiling, and before long we were rolling about like two daft milkmaids, clutching ourselves as tears ran down our faces.

'Get the *A* right first,' I told her. 'Then the other letters after.'

That night as I undressed for bed, I saw the paper on the desk with the quill lying next to it. Richard's words remained unwrapped and unread, and in the one remaining corner a little army of *A*s travelled across the page, like an infestation of lice. An infestation of Alices. It made me smile.

CHAPTER 13

The window of the chamber Alice and I were staying in overlooked the front of the house, as well as the approach uphill and the woodland either side that was thick with partridges and pheasants. One morning I heard hooves outside, and thought Richard had finally come. But standing at the casement, peering through the glass, I saw a young woman wearing a beautiful pea-green gown, with a waist I could only dream of, dismounting her horse while another, plainer woman in scarlet waited beside hers. I gasped as I recognised them.

'Richard's sisters are here,' I told Alice, choked with panic.

I'd got up late that morning, feeling hot and lazy, and had only just finished breakfast in my nightgown. I jumped back from the window and began putting my hair in rolls. My mother had gone to the village, but I did not know when she would return, so I would have to be the hostess.

Mrs Anbrick, the housekeeper, came to the chamber door and rapped smartly.

'Mistress, your sisters-in-law have come to pay you a visit.'

The housekeeper was a warm, pleasant woman with soft skin and twinkling eyes – how she and my mother rubbed along together I had no idea. Now her tone was excited, impressed, even; visitors were rare at this house. I thanked her and when her footsteps had died away, I turned to Alice, keeping my voice low.

'Do not show yourself to them. You would be wise to stay in here.'

'They don't know who I am, do they?'

'No, but they are dreadful chatterboxes and have noses for rumour like hounds, so keep out of their way.'

I closed the door behind me.

Eleanor and Anne were seated in my mother's parlour, which was always chilly. There was a pleasant view of the old-fashioned knot garden at the back of the house though, the purpose of which was more functional than stylish because only the hardiest flowers survived on these high, windy fells.

Both Richard's sisters shared his fair hair and clear grey eyes, but Eleanor was pretty and Anne plain.

'Fleetwood!' they cooed as I entered.

Both immediately noticed my stomach, where my sleeveless gown parted around the cloth of silver stretching in a sphere. We kissed and I sat at the window with the weak sun on my face.

'We heard a rumour you were here, and it was true!' Anne said saucily. 'And without Richard?'

'Yes, without Richard.' I tried to force a smile. 'From whom did you hear?'

'We were staying with friends at Kendal – do you know the Bellinghams of Levens Hall?' I shook my head. 'One of their servants is cousin to one of yours here in the kitchen. We did not dare believe it when she told us you were staying here for the summer, but how many women are called Fleetwood Shuttleworth? And here you are! All alone?'

'All alone.'

Relief allowed me to sit back more comfortably. I had not yet rubbed my teeth and there was still the sour taste of morning in my mouth.

'Not for long.' Eleanor indicated my stomach. 'You are a funny little thing, staying away from your husband when you are about to have a baby. I suppose wives of the gentry can do what they like around here.'

She gave a little tinkling laugh. To listen to her, you would think she'd lived all her life in one of the London mansions.

Before I could ask what else the servant had said, she went on.

'How very exciting: a new Shuttleworth heir. Are you prepared? Do you have a midwife?' I nodded. 'Well, you shall have to pass her on to me when you are finished. I did make a hint to Richard in my last letter, but nothing was confirmed then. I am to marry before the year is out!'

I made a delighted face.

'That's wonderful news – who is your husband?'

'Sir Ralph Ashton.'

Both Anne and Eleanor were older than me. When Richard and I married I had been thrilled to spend six months with them in London, but after thirteen years on my own I was not used to being spoken to, petted and teased at all hours of the day. All my life I had wanted sisters, and as soon as I got them I could not wait to be rid of them and their chatter, and their darting little hands and boundless inquisitiveness.

'Fleetwood?' Eleanor chided. 'I said the wedding will most likely be at Michaelmas. Will the baby be born by the end of September?'

'Perhaps.'

I wondered what they knew – if anything – of Richard's other woman, Judith but before I decided whether to ask, Mrs Anbrick brought a jug of sack and three Venice glasses. She looked approvingly at our little feminine party, pleased that the house had opened its doors to society. I poured a generous amount into each of the glasses and toasted Eleanor's forthcoming marriage. Anne was smiling but I could see that really she was downcast, with no husband arranged. Like Alice, I could not help but think her lucky. I drank deeply; the sack was sweet and burning at the same time.

'Fleetwood, why *are* you here without Richard?' Anne asked, wearing a thin smile and shifting in her dress.

With their pale faces turned to mine, and their white ruffs gleaming in the sun, they looked like two daisies.

I reached down the back of my own ruff to scratch.

'I . . .'

Suddenly the baby kicked, and my hands flew to my stomach in response.

'Is it the quickening?'

'Yes.'

'Can we feel?'

I was too surprised to say no, and within a moment four small, white hands were pressed to my gown. I moved uncomfortably, wanting to pick their palms away.

'How wonderfully strange,' they said, their eyes wide and staring.

I willed the child to be still, and it was.

'How is your mother? She will miss you, Eleanor, when you leave Forcett.'

'Yes, she is quite well but visits less often now,' said Eleanor. 'I expect she will pine for me. Anne will still be there, of course,' she added smugly.

'What news from Yorkshire?' I asked.

'Nothing much of interest. Not like in Lancaster.'

'What do you mean?'

'You will know all about them, of course – the Pendle witches? They say there will be a trial and upwards of a dozen hangings. The servants at Levens say it will be the most England has ever seen. You must have heard something of it.'

I swallowed. 'Something, yes.'

I thought of Alice upstairs, bent over the cupboard with her quill. We had no parchment so she had been practising inside my mother's copy of *Daemonologie* and, having mastered her first name, was now inking her surname.

'Well, what do you make of it?'

'I would not know because I have been here,' I said coolly. 'And I pay no mind to servants' chatter.'

That made Eleanor flush, and Anne gave a shudder.

'I wonder what they look like. I am glad we do not have witches in Yorkshire, I would not sleep in my bed.'

Eleanor gave a high, tinkling laugh.

'I do not think *you* are in danger, Anne. They only seem to curse each other and their strange little neighbours. Apparently they bury cats in their walls and prick babes to drink their blood. And Lancashire is positively full of them, by the sound of it. Are you sure you wish to return, Fleetwood, and raise your son there?' Eleanor teased.

'They murder *children*,' Anne said gleefully. 'And they're said to have animals that are the Devil in disguise.'

'Like toads and rats and cats!' Eleanor shrieked, and the two of them writhed with giggling.

'Do you know a woman named Judith?' I interrupted them.

'Judith? No, is she a witch?'

I did not answer and filled our glasses again. The sack was going down easily and making me feel loose-tongued.

'Shall we walk around the garden? It's quite warm out.'

The truth was I could not bear another moment sat in that poky room with them. The three of us stood, and I realised that I was giddy. I led them outside, where the sky was pale and the air warm and windy. We walked around the side of the house, and Eleanor picked a fistful of flowers and held them at her breast.

'Do I look like a bride?' she asked.

'The most beautiful bride I ever did see!' said Anne.

They flounced in their skirts, twirling around and around, but Anne stopped when she saw me, for I was not laughing or playing along.

'Fleetwood, you are different, you know,' Anne said. 'I cannot think exactly why; something about you is more . . . *something*.'

'Eloquent as ever, Anne.' Eleanor snorted like a pig.

'In what way?' I asked.

'You have always been quite melancholy, really. But now you seem to . . . carry it better.'

'Melancholy?'

'Yes, a little mournful and sad. But now you seem different, older somehow . . . More *knowing*.'

'I wish I was not *knowing*,' I muttered. 'I would rather not know.'

Eleanor looked blankly at me.

'Know what?'

There was stillness around us; the wind had died for a moment. I felt quite light-headed from the sack and the bright sunlight and the green hills leaning all around.

'About your brother,' I said, my face innocent. Anne had stopped too and they were both looking at me dumbly. 'And his other woman. About the infant she is expecting. You did not know?'

The pretty bouquet fell from Eleanor's hands, splaying on to the path. Their faces were identical masks of shock.

'You aren't serious.'

'I saw her with my own eyes. She is at Barton, at my father's house. That is where he keeps her.'

A flock of birds flung themselves from a group of trees nearby, their wings cracking above us. I had sown the seeds, and now they would grow whether I liked it or not.

'You are sure about this?' Anne asked, her voice quivering slightly.

'Quite sure.' I swallowed.

'But you have only been married . . .'

'Four years.'

I was seventeen now, but for all I'd been through I might have been twice or three times that. My husband already had a lover, but I was no old matron, with greying hair and wrinkles at my eyes. I suspected I was younger even than her, but every time I thought about her she only grew more beautiful. The baby I'd wanted to give as a gift to Richard was now a much more precious commodity: it secured my place in the home, and in the family. Without it, I would be an ornament, a wife in name only. I knew this now. If this baby died inside me like the others, I may as well move permanently into my mother's house, for I would be less than useless. The thought of that made a hard kernel of dread in my stomach. I had to have Richard's child to secure my future, for if it died, I may as well die with it.

We walked twice more around the garden in gloomy silence, with Anne and Eleanor making occasional uncomfortable little comments about the inclement weather, and how Westmoreland was so far behind Yorkshire with its fashions, and had any of the Bellinghams had a new frock made in the past five years?

They did not stay much longer, and said they would not wait for my mother to return, but would go and collect their steward from the inn in the village and start on the journey back to Yorkshire. But as we were walking to the stables, we passed the kitchen door at the back of the house, and it opened, and suddenly there stood Alice.

Her mouth was a little 'O' of surprise, and she had a basket on her arm, and an old apron over her clothes. We stared at one another for a long moment, and Anne and Eleanor noticed something was odd between us, for usually servants went unnoticed.

'Who is this?' Anne asked.

I licked my lips.

'No one. Alice, go inside.'

I gave her a tight smile, and went to continue on our path. Only when she did not move did I realise what I had said. I felt as though I'd missed a step, and the ground beneath me tilted, then righted itself. After a moment, Alice retreated, and the kitchen door closed.

Dread grew in my stomach, twisting and sliding like an eel, and I dared not look at Anne or Eleanor, for I did not know how much or how little they knew. What I did know was that I had to act as though nothing had happened, and Alice was no one.

'Do you know, I am suddenly very tired,' I said weakly. 'Shall we get your horses? I think I need to lie down.'

Once they'd said their hurried goodbyes and gone back down the windy slope, I returned to the parlour, where I finished the jug of sack. Something had gone badly wrong, and I could not tell how badly. I had been foolish to tell them about Richard; it would do nothing for my position, and everything for his temper. And saying Alice's name like that . . . Surely they could not know she was the same Alice Gray, whose name was on a list in the next county, who may or may not be wanted for inquisition. Could they?

By the time I went upstairs to my chamber, I was drunk and it wasn't even noon. Alice was nowhere to be seen, so I sat on the edge of the bed and kicked off my slippers.

Richard's sisters and mother – if she didn't already know – would no doubt have something to say to him about Judith, and he might now be even more furious with me. Probably I would be the talk of Yorkshire as well as Lancashire, my name mentioned in great halls and dining chambers. Well, I was more furious with him than myself. All this was his fault, and my mother's too, knowing what she did about Judith and keeping it from me, always pressuring me to produce a child, as if I did not want to, as if I did not know how important it was. I used to think I was letting everyone down with my failure, but as I lay on the bed with the warm light pouring in, I realised they had let me down too.

Not quite everyone.

I must have fallen asleep because I felt something damp being pressed against my face. When I opened my eyes Alice was standing over me with a bowl and cloth.

'I thought you had a fever,' she said.

My tongue was dry and I still had the woozy feeling from earlier. Sweat gathered at my armpits.

'I drank too much sack,' I said.

The child inside me was still, too, lulled by the sweet wine. Richard's sisters' words echoed in my ears: *in Lancaster plenty is happening.*

'I am worried,' I said, sitting up.

A small frown threaded between her eyebrows, and her eyes grew troubled.

'About earlier, in the garden?'

'Yes. I said your name. I'm sorry. I don't know if they know . . . I don't know *what* they know. Or, more worryingly, who they will tell.'

'But there is nothing to tell. They would think nothing of you talking to a servant.'

'Only if they did not know who you are. Oh, why could I not remember Jill? I wish I could sew my mouth shut.'

She swirled the cloth in the bowl. Her expression was uneasy.

'Alice,' I said. 'My mother will be back any time, so I must ask you this now. I want you to tell me what you were doing with Elizabeth Device that day in the woods.'

Her hand stopped on the water, her fingers balancing lightly on its surface. As well as her usual scent of lavender, there was an earthy scent too, of soil and things nourished and growing.

'I would not ask if I did not think it important.'

After a pause, she went to the court cupboard and set the bowl down on it. With her back to me, she sighed.

'Do you remember when we sat in your parlour and you asked me where I worked, and I told you the Hand and Shuttle? And you asked me how long I had worked there and I said not long?'

'Yes.'

'I'd been there about a week.'

I waited, hardly breathing.

'And do you remember when you caught me with the rabbits the first time we met?'

'Yes.'

'I really was lost. I had just started work at the Hand and Shuttle and was finding my way.'

She did not look at me, and I watched her long neck, her narrow back, as she spoke, still facing the wall.

'Before that I used to work at an alehouse in Colne. One morning I was walking to work and I came across a man lying on the ground. It was a quiet road and there was no one else around. He was a pedlar. All his things were cast in a trail behind him, pins and needles and scraps of cloth, as though he'd staggered about dropping them. I thought he was dead, but he was alive, muttering and mumbling. One side of his face was collapsed, and his eye wouldn't open. I'd seen it before with my mother.'

I could not breathe; the air in the room was thick and I tried to swallow but there was a lump in my throat.

'I took him to the inn and the landlord helped me put him upstairs in a chamber and called a physick. The man kept muttering on about a black dog and a girl he'd met on the road, but his speech was slurred and we didn't know what he meant. Then later that night a girl arrived.'

Alice had both hands on the court cupboard, as though steadying herself.

'She was in such a state, sobbing and begging for forgiveness. I did not know what she meant until she spoke of cursing a pedlar that same day. She was filthy, like she'd spent all day tramping about in the rain. I asked her to come in and get dry, but the landlord would hear none of it, telling me she was a beggar and he didn't let her sort in. He told her to make herself scarce. Before she went, she told me her name was Alizon and she would come back tomorrow to check on the man.'

'Alizon Device,' I whispered. 'And did she?'

Alice nodded, her back to me still.

'And the next day, and the day after that. But Peter the landlord wouldn't let her in; said she was trouble. By that time the man had woken up, and I could make out that his name was John. I sat with him, giving him beer and food and wiping his mouth when it fell out. His face was still all melted, like only one side of it worked. I don't know if it will be right again. He got some of his speech back and told us his son's name and to write to him, so Peter sent a man.

'One day I was sitting with him on my own and the girl had been again that morning as usual, standing in the yard, wringing her hands and crying, asking to see him. She was distraught, kept saying that it was all her fault. I decided to tell him that she was there to beg for his forgiveness, and asked did he want me to let her in, and he nodded.

'Peter was out so I had to look after the customers. So I went down and told her to be quick. I stayed downstairs. Not long after she'd gone up she came running through again, so I went back upstairs to see John. He was in such a state, sobbing and shaking and pointing at the door. "She's a witch," he was saying over and over.'

At this point Alice walked to the window and looked out. The sound of the moor drifted in through the glass: a lonely wind whining at the casement.

'Then what happened?' I asked.

'He told me she had a black dog with her, the same one she'd had on the road. But I hadn't seen one; I didn't know what he was talking about or if he was dreaming. Then someone else turned up: the girl's grandmother. She made the whole place go cold, she did. Everyone felt her coming in. Everybody knew who she was.'

'Who was she?'

'They call her Demdike. She keeps to herself most of the time but local folk know her. I'd seen her around, heard what people said.'

'What did they say?'

'That she's an oddball, a witch, she's this, she's that. Stay away from her, they said. But she wasn't there to see John Law. She was there to see me.'

'But why?'

'Alizon must have told her that I'd found John and was looking after him. That's when she started threatening me. She told me she'd put a curse on me if I didn't lie for Alizon. She wanted me to say I'd never seen her, that the old man was making it all up, that his mind was weak and he couldn't tell up from down.

'But Peter had already written to John's son and he arrived not long after, from Halifax or somewhere. John told him he'd forgiven Alizon, that he was a God-fearing man who believed in mercy and that's what God wanted him to do. He's a good man, John Law. But his son Abraham wouldn't hear of it. He sent for Alizon and questioned her. Demdike came with her and they put the shivers in him, I think. Demdike was denying everything, screaming and cursing all over the place, and Alizon was crying. I was just stood there, not knowing what to do. And the son turned to me and said, "Have you seen these here women before? Did this girl curse my father?"

'I couldn't speak, and John was squealing like a pig in the corner. His son, Abraham was red in the face and looked like he was about to kill someone, and I was frightened. So I said yes, I'd seen them.

'He tried to make them break the curse but Alizon couldn't, and Demdike said only the person who'd put it on could take it off. So that was that. Abraham sent for the magistrate, and Peter asked me to leave because of all the trouble I'd caused.' Her voice was thick. 'I worked there for nearly ten years. He knew I was a good worker so he found me a job at the Hand and Shuttle. His brother-in-law is the landlord.'

My mind was empty. My thoughts were still. I stared at my stockinged feet, small and dainty in white silk. Alice did not speak, and we were silent for a long time, until a thought came to me.

'But how does that involve Elizabeth Device? What were you doing with her that day?'

'She came to the Hand and Shuttle one night.

Somehow she found out I was there, I don't know how. Alizon and Demdike had been arrested, so she'd already lost her daughter and mother. People were giving her funny looks when she came to see me. Well, you can see why. I was afraid I'd lose my job there as well, so I said she had to leave. She asked me to go to her house that Friday, said she was having some neighbours around to talk about what they could do to help those that'd been arrested. She said I had to help, that I was . . .' Her voice shook. 'She said I was the reason her daughter and mother were in gaol.'

I shook my head. 'But you were only trying to help.'

'She was desperate . . . angry. I could tell she just wanted to do something. And I wanted to help. Like a fool I went. I had to do something to stop them turning up at work and getting me in trouble. And even after that, after I went to Malkin Tower, she was waiting for me near your house in the forest. I cannot escape them.'

There was real fear in her voice now. I remembered her whimpering in her sleep.

'But what happened at Malkin Tower? What did they speak of?'

Alice shrugged. 'We ate a meal and they talked about how they could help Alizon and Demdike. It was just a meeting of people who knew the family, neighbours and the like. Apart from me and one other person.'

'Who was that?'

At this, Alice bowed her head.

'My mother's friend Katherine. Mould-heels.'

'Why did she go?'

'She was with me when—'

We both jumped out of our skins when the door was flung open and my mother swept in, her face hard with displeasure.

'You did not think to send someone to the village to fetch me?' she demanded.

I sat up straighter and glowered at her, resenting the interruption.

'Richard's sisters did not stay long. They were travelling from Kendal back to Forcett.'

'How did they know you were here?'

'A servant here is a cousin of someone at the house where they were staying.'

Her black eyes were penetrating.

'What did you tell them?'

'Nothing,' I lied.

The silence that followed indicated her deep disbelief.

'Supper is almost ready,' was all she said, and she left the door open behind her.

I went to close it quietly, and crept back towards Alice. All the questions I could have asked were ripe, hanging in the room. I could have reached anywhere and plucked one easily, but I chose the first one that came into my head, from the last thing she had said.

'Alice, you said Mould-heels was with you when . . . what?'

Alice was silent now, and outside the window the wind

rushed down from the moor, sounding almost like a child crying. She covered her face with her hands.

'Alice! What's the matter?'

'I cannot speak of it,' she whispered. 'I cannot bear it.'

'Whatever it is, it cannot be so bad.'

But she would not tell me, and I could feel the waves of my mother's irritation lapping at the door. The last thing I needed was another afternoon of combat. I felt troubled as I went downstairs to dinner, as though something apart from the wind was pressing in at the windows, wanting to be let in.

CHAPTER 14

That night I had The Nightmare. I woke, paralysed with fright, to a candle at my side, a familiar but frightened face behind it. My legs were twisted in the sheets and I was soaked with sweat. I was so scared I thought my heart would leap right out of my chest, and Alice sat with me until my breathing calmed and the shadows at the corner of the room grew less frightening. I hoped I had not been screaming, but the alarm in Alice's eyes and a tightness in her jaw made me think I had.

'It's all right now,' Alice whispered. 'Was it the boars?'

I nodded and gasped, and that feeling of dread arrived again, so I checked between my legs for a trickle of blood, but they were dry. Eventually Alice went back to bed, and her breathing began to slow too. We had been at my mother's for a month, and in all that time I'd been free of The Nightmare.

Since that breakfast, my mother had not mentioned my going back to Gawthorpe, and neither had I, but I should have known her better than that. Perhaps if I'd had the plaster figure of Prudence with me in my chamber, I might have remembered to exercise it once in a while, but my old friend remained miles away in my room at Gawthorpe.

I was sitting in the kitchen with Mrs Knave, eating biscuits hot from the oven, when Mrs Anbrick arrived to tell me someone was here for me. I'd known it from the moment I woke up: a change in the atmosphere, a shifting sense of unease in my stomach. My time was running out.

'Who is it?'

I did not need ask. The black skirts of my mother entered the kitchen before she did, smooth as a fish gliding across a pond. Her face was set for battle.

'Fleetwood, come out of the kitchen now,' she said.

The dread stirred in my stomach, pinning me to the chair.

Mrs Knave bowed her head, her chubby hands brushing awkwardly at her apron. I fixed my mother with the most hateful look I could summon and rose, stepping past her, remembering how she had untied Richard's letter then kept the contents to herself. I had not thought to ask her what he had said, and his letter to me remained unopened on the desk in my chamber.

'You cannot avoid him forever, Fleetwood.'

Her voice rang behind me in the hall as I went to wait in the parlour. I had decided I would not speak to her again.

I sat shivering, even though the room, with its high, narrow window, was close and stuffy. Dust danced around in the watery beams of light, and a chessboard lay on a stool by my chair. My mother sometimes played chess with the housekeeper and sometimes with herself. It was something she had always done, but for the first time I realised how pitiful that was, with her alone in this room and me upstairs. Well, she could have asked me if she wanted to play; I would not feel sorry for a woman who chose so often to be alone. I drew my sleeveless robe around my stomach, put my hands in my lap and waited.

Puck came in first, greeting me with his tongue when he saw me and coming to sit beside me. My mother came in next, her pattens clacking on the stone flags, with a deeper, heavier tread of soft calfskin boots and that familiar jangle of coins behind her.

'Fleetwood.'

I heard and saw him at the same time. His earring caught the light and his clear grey eyes shone. He looked first at my face, then my stomach.

You are still with child, I heard him think.

I had forgotten how conversations could be held in silence when you are married, when you know the flesh and bones of someone and could know them in a dark room. Why not their mind too? My mother looked unblinkingly from one of us to the other.

'You look well,' Richard said.

I said nothing.

'Fleetwood?' my mother spoke.

'You may go,' I said coldly.

She looked appealingly at Richard, but his grey eyes were fixed on my black ones as intensely as if I might disappear at any moment.

She closed the door. I did not hear her pattens in the hall, so after a few moments I said 'Mother' and she went clacking off.

Richard took the seat opposite mine and, to both our surprise, Puck gave a low growl and then barked.

'You have turned the dog against me too?' Richard said in a light way, but his eyes were sorrowful.

'He has a mind of his own.'

Richard swallowed and removed his black velvet hat, offering it to Puck to sniff as a sign of peace.

'Remember me, boy?' I felt doubly betrayed when Puck went to him, nuzzling into his hand and grinning broadly. 'There we go,' Richard said softly, rubbing him all over and patting him in the hard way he did.

'I forget how long a journey it is up to these parts,' he said eventually, resting his hat on his lap.

'You do not mind when you have a hunting trip.'

'I did not say I minded.'

'Your journey did not take a month, though.'

My boldness surprised us both. Richard opened his mouth then closed it again, changing position in his chair.

'No. I had some business to attend.'

'That came before your wife? How could you do it, Richard?'

'I'm sorry. Come home, please.'

I pressed at my eyes and remembered the last four years: us riding together, shopping together, lying together, laughing together. It felt like a lifetime of happiness.

'Gawthorpe is not the same place without you. It's our home; we should be there together.'

'You are never there!'

'I am. I want to be there, with you.'

'All these secrets, Richard. And lies.'

I remembered Alice's words: *I am afraid of lies.* Now I knew what she meant: lies had the power to destroy lives but also create them, as Judith's belly was round with the ones Richard had spun.

'I am happy here.'

'Happy? With your mother? You cannot stand your mother.' He did not lower his voice. 'What is there for you here apart from idle servants and dusty rooms?'

'If they are dusty it's because you do not give my mother enough money,' I whispered. 'Something I would never,

ever have suspected seeing as I brought an awful lot of it to this family.'

He reached into his pocket for his purse.

'How much more does she need?'

'How much do you pay for your mistress?'

He pulled the bag open and set some coins on the mantel, as though he was paying my lodgings at an inn.

'That is four women to pay for now, is it not?' I went on. 'Two mothers and two wives? I suppose it's no coincidence that standards slipped here when you added another household to your stable. Did you know the poverty you were keeping her in?'

'Of course not. If she needs anything, she need only ask. I will make it right. Perhaps James made some adjustments to balance the books that I was not aware of.'

'Then I will ask James why he has been sending sweet soap to Barton while my mother's staff make hers.'

A smile played at the corners of Richard's lips, and I knew he was amused that I was defending her. My chest churned with rage and I waited with my hands clasping the arms of my chair. He could not tease me into forgetting he had taken a month to come to me.

Dressed in his fine black velvet robe and doublet, he must have been warm, and I noticed the colour in his cheeks, from heat or shame or frustration.

'I have come to bring you home,' he said finally.

'How long have you kept her?'

He exhaled, as though I was testing him.

He was not used to me disobeying him. I was not used to disobeying him.

'Not long.'

'How long?'

'A few months?'

'So she is fertile, then. Success at last: a prize breeder. And you the sire of a fine calf, which is more than your wife can give you.'

'Don't make yourself ridiculous. People are not cattle.'

'Women and cattle are very similar, actually.'

'You are being absurd.'

The chessboard caught my eye and I lifted an ivory pawn, holding it up to catch the light. I recognised it immediately as being my father's set from Barton. I set it back in its place and saw it was before the queen. Using the pawn I bumped her off, sending the piece crashing to the floor, where she rolled on the threadbare carpet underneath the table. I imagined my mother on her hands and knees searching for it later.

'Will you have me executed, like the king?' I said.

'Fleetwood, I *care* about you. Do you think I wished to see you so ill? Every time you have carried a child you have almost died, and it is my fault for making you that way. I did not mean for this to happen – I turned to Judith as a way to stop it from happening, to protect you.'

'To protect me? Keeping your mistress in my house was to protect me?'

'You hate that house; I knew you would never go there.'

'And you were right. You know me better than anyone, Richard. Except you forgot one thing: that I could read. You thought I would never go in James' study and find out all the betrayals committed in ink. They were there for me to see all along.'

'How did you know to look in the ledger?'

My heart began to beat faster.

'I needed to check something.'

'What?'

'An order of linen. It is not important.'

I tried to act dismissively but he was a hunter, and he had caught the scent. His eyes narrowed.

'Who did you come here with?'

'No one.'

I stared him down, and he did not like what he saw, for he said, 'You have changed, Fleetwood.' I waited, but he said no more, only impatiently, 'Are we not to be given refreshments?'

I did not speak, and turned my face to the grey window. Richard shifted uncomfortably in his seat.

'Roger came not long ago with a parcel for you.' I watched him from the corner of my eye. 'The ruby necklace.'

'The one that went missing?'

'His maid found it at the bottom of Jennet Device's bed. She is an opportunist, clearly.'

'She is a thief. But she had no opportunity – I did not leave her for a moment.' Then I remembered my journey down to the kitchen for Roger's cold pie, and my heart sank. 'Did she leave the hall at any point?'

'I suppose she must have.'

'And you apologised to the servants?'

A flicker of shame crossed his face, and as we sat in furious silence, the other events of that day flooded back to me – how so much had happened.

'And the chambermaid, Sarah – how is she?'

'Not recovered, but better. The doctor arrived in time. She is still being cared for by her mother.'

'Are you sleeping in our chamber?'

He shifted again. 'Yes. I have brought our carriage here, for you to take back to Gawthorpe. I have some business with my agent on the border, so I will go on to Carlisle before coming home. You can leave tomorrow.'

I thought of Alice, resting upstairs on her truckle bed. I thought of what might be waiting for her if we returned.

'I cannot come back.'

Something seemed to stir in Richard, and he spread his fingers wide, his rings glittering, then clenched his fists.

'As sorry as I am for the way you discovered what you did, my patience is wearing thin. No man wants an unruly wife. There is a fine line between being tolerant and being made a fool of.'

Tears sprung in my eyes, hot and angry.

'And I suppose you have not made a fool of me? I am no different from one of your precious falcons. You have me on a leash, then with a flick of your wrist I am back at your arm.'

At last he had the modesty to look aggrieved. Even as I spoke, I knew I was acting outside the boundaries of womanliness, of wifeliness. I did not have a beautiful face nor the manners to go with it. It was hardly a surprise he left our bed and with it our union, I thought miserably.

'It is time for you to settle into your new role,' was all he said.

'As a neglected wife?'

'As a mother.'

'I wish to stay here a little longer.'

At that moment, as though she had been waiting, there was a sharp knock on the door and my mother came in.

'You have readied her things?' Richard asked.

She nodded, and glanced at me.

'I will not go,' I said.

Light and thin as a knife through butter, my mother's words sliced through me.

'You will not stay here while your husband needs you. It's time for you to leave.'

I stood up from my chair, drawing myself up to my full, unimpressive height, and said coldly, 'If that is your wish, so be it.'

✳

Richard left to go further north on his horse, and I went to my chamber. By the time I had reached the top of the staircase a plan had formed in my mind, and immediately I relayed it to Alice.

'You can return to Gawthorpe with me, as my midwife and companion, and those are the terms on which I'll forgive Richard.'

But Alice looked unsure, and twisted her cap in her hands. Her hair was a mass of sprung gold, coiled and twisted like a lion's mane.

'Does he ask for forgiveness?' was all she said.

'He betrayed me, Alice, come back with me and I will see to it. I'll see that your name is cleared – that will be my price. Richard will meet it. We will go back to Gawthorpe and have you a bed made, and in a day or two Richard will arrive home and I will lay out my terms: that for me to stay, you must stay too. I cannot deliver this child without you.'

Doubt was written all over her face, but, despite everything, I knew my husband.

We packed our things – or I packed mine, because all Alice had was what she stood up in. She had no trunk, no wedding ring, no husband calling her home and no sisters-in-law who paid visits. No child in her stomach, no heir to produce. She could go anywhere, any time, and if she had wanted to I would have let her, even when

I knew I needed her. But she climbed in the carriage beside me, just as she had on the way here. I decided I would give her a horse again when we got home – never mind the business with the other one, for I knew now that I trusted her – and she could ride to visit her father when Richard agreed my terms, and tell him she'd found a permanent position. But what would we find at home? For the first time since Alice told me her story, I thought of the Pendle witches and what would become of them. Perhaps Roger had not been able to build a case against all the people at Malkin Tower; perhaps he was satisfied with the Devices and their neighbours, and tossed Nick Bannister's list in the fire.

I held my stomach, and as the wheels rocked on the uneven road and my child bucked and rolled with them, I wondered how anyone could consider coaches safer than riding. Puck whimpered at my feet, tired of the constant motion. I told him we would be home soon, and I would have milk and bread brought for him, and he licked my hand with a comforting tongue.

I lost interest in my surroundings after a few hours; the sky grew more grey, and the rain fell very lightly, making everything dull again. Alice's eyes were closed, her head tipped back against the seat. I wondered if she was really asleep, or worrying like I was about what would happen when we were back. Even my child, who often made sleeping uncomfortable, was still.

The last part of the journey became a race against the

creeping dark, and it was after nightfall when I felt the carriage slow and turn into the approach to Gawthorpe. The darkness had a blacker quality here, with the woods dense on both sides. The horses' hooves clattered on cobbles; we had reached the barn and outbuildings. We slowed to a stop and I heard the carter tell someone in the yard he was instructed to take me directly to the door. By that point, thick with sleep, I'd forgotten Alice was there. We'd spent so much time together I no longer knew what it was to be on my own. The carriage was so dark I could not tell if she was awake, and I longed for my bed. I would put Alice in the next-door room where Richard had slept, so that she was close by. Perhaps he and Alice might even become friends, with the necklace mystery resolved.

We came to a halt. The horses exhaled and shook themselves. The coachman moved around above us, then I heard his feet hit the ground. I moved first, but the carriage door sprung open before me and I almost tumbled out.

Richard was standing there. His face was hidden in shadow, and before I could speak or even exclaim in surprise, he took my wrist and guided me down. My feet hit solid ground, and I heard Puck jump out behind me, and then two things happened at once: Alice stepped out of the carriage behind me, and I saw Roger Nowell standing at the top of the steps.

Neither he nor Richard had spoken, and I could not

see their faces properly in the darkness. The torches flamed either side of the doorway, twisting this way and that. I felt as though someone had poured cold water down my back.

'Richard, what are you doing here?' I said.

He still had hold of my arm.

Roger's voice came from the steps.

'Alice Gray, you are under arrest for the murder by witchcraft of Ann Foulds, daughter of John Foulds of Colne, and will be a prisoner of His Majesty until your time of reckoning.'

In a moment he was upon her, moving quick as a shadow.

'Roger!' I cried. 'What are you doing?'

But Richard began to pull me up the steps into the house. I twisted wildly, trying to shake him off.

'Alice! What is this? Roger, Richard, tell me at once. Get off me!'

I pushed him with all my strength and managed to loosen his grip, but before I could run down the steps he took hold of me once again, locking my arms behind me.

'Fleetwood!' Alice cried, her cap and face the only visible things in the glow from the torches.

Roger's dark bulk was forcing her back into the carriage. She was sobbing and frightened, and disappearing before my eyes, but I could still hear her, muttering, 'no, no, no'.

One of the horses whinnied in fright, straining against its harness. Then I was in the house, and Richard was closing the door, and I was within, and she was without.

PART THREE

A man also or woman that hath a familiar spirit,
or that is a wizard, shall surely be put to death:
they shall stone them with stones: their blood
shall be upon them.

Leviticus 20:27

CHAPTER 15

Richard dropped me like a hot coal and disappeared down the passage into the great hall. I threw myself at the door and felt for the handle, wrenching it open to see the dark bulk of the carriage moving away, out of the pool of torchlight. I ran down the steps, almost falling over my trunk that was lying at the bottom, and raced to catch up with it, shouting her name at the window, but the drape remained closed.

'Stop!' I called. 'Stop!'

The carter remained facing forwards, hunched over the reins. I fell back as it picked up speed and watched as the night swallowed it whole, the sound of the wheels and horses' hooves growing fainter, the trees shivering around the clearing.

I stood for a long time in the blackness until the chill soaked right through to the deepest parts of me. My body felt as though it was submerged in water, anchored to the ground, my gown impossibly heavy. I heard two boys come from the house to lift my trunk and carry it inside.

I had led her right to the centre of the web, to where the spider was waiting.

I found Richard in the great hall, waiting for me at the empty fireplace. All I could do was stare at him, and he returned my gaze with the same expression.

'You tricked me. You lied to me!'

'And you tricked and lied to me.'

'How so?'

'You told me the girl was not with you.'

'You laid a trap – you had us ride into it. How *could* you . . . ?'

'Alice Gray is wanted for a crime. Whether she was arrested here or at your mother's, it matters not.'

'It does matter. Who told you she was there – your sisters?'

'No, your mother. Inadvertently, of course; I'm not sure even she would betray her own daughter. She wrote to me and spoke of a lively young midwife named Jill, who you had brought with you. She wanted to know if Mistress Starkie had recommended her. You might do better to cover your scent next time; I thought you were a skilled huntress.'

I breathed in deeply, and out, trying to control my anger.

'Why has Alice been arrested?'

'I do not know all the details.'

'Roger said she murdered a child? What nonsense.'

'You know that, do you?'

'Of course I do. She would not harm a fly.'

'Then she will have nothing to fear.'

'Roger is on a quest for power,' I said. 'He is only doing this to appease the king and display himself at court like some painted peacock. He does not care about the consequences, that people's lives are at stake. How many more *witches* has he found since I've been away?'

'I don't know.'

'How many?'

'About ten. It has not been difficult for him: they are giving him the names, thinking it will buy them their freedom. They are doing the accusing, not him.'

'We must do something.'

'We must do *nothing!*' Richard bellowed. 'You have done enough!'

His temper had boiled over. He had been pacing in front of the fireplace, and now he fixed me with the full force of his wrath. I thought back to that rainy day in April when Roger and I stood in the long gallery. *Shame on him who thinks evil of it.*

I reached for a chair and held the back of it, reluctant to do something so domestic as sit down.

'You have left me without a midwife,' I said eventually.

'There are plenty of others, Fleetwood. I do not know why you insisted on using some local slattern, who may or may not have killed a child. Is that who you want delivering our heir?'

'Yes.'

'We will send for another midwife.'

'I will not have another.'

'Then you may die. Is that what you want?'

'Perhaps. It's what you want.'

'Don't be so ridiculous.'

I gripped the chair harder.

'Alice is irreplaceable. Tell me, Richard: why are you allowed to keep a woman and I am not?'

Blood pounded in my ears, and I squeezed, willing the oak to splinter under my fingers. When he didn't say anything, his face tight and furious, I went on.

'Alice Gray saved my life, not just once but many times. When I itched, she brought me plants to rub on my skin. When I was sick, she made me tinctures. She kept me company when I was at my lowest. She planted a garden for my health.'

'Sounds like a witch to me,' Richard said bitterly. 'How else would she know those things?'

'She is a midwife, like her mother before her. Are you like the king now, thinking all wise women and poor women and midwives are carrying out the Devil's work? Why, he must be the largest employer in Lancashire.'

I suddenly felt very tired, and was forced to sit. My

gown was dusty from travelling, and part of my mind was still in the carriage with Alice and Roger, journeying into the darkness. My head ached with it all.

'Where will he take her?'

'Perhaps Read Hall. Perhaps straight to Lancaster.'

'But the assizes aren't until August.'

I heard his boots on the flags and the next thing, he was kneeling beside me, his gold earring glinting in the candlelight.

'Forget Alice,' he said. 'You have done enough for her.'

'Forget her? I have done nothing for her! What can you mean? The only thing I *have* done is lead her directly to the rope!'

'My only concern was your safety. Once I heard who Alice was, I acted straight away, of course I did. What has *happened* to you, Fleetwood? You are a different person since she came along.'

He sounded so hateful. I wiped my nose with my sleeve. I wanted desperately to lie down.

'I want to go to Read Hall,' I said.

'You will do no such thing. It's late.'

Again, I was thwarted, bound by my invisible leash. It was strange: I was sitting in my house with my husband and dog, but had never felt more wretched. For a long time they had been enough, but now I felt like a visitor in my own life. I looked around at the dark windows, the shiny panels and the gallery where players and minstrels had performed in happier times. There were the coats of arms above the fireplace – mine included; there were the pair of doors, so two people of the same rank could enter at the same time. Was this really my house?

Richard helped me to my feet and I kept one hand on Puck's head to go upstairs. The staircase was dark, and I was already half asleep.

So much had happened since the last time I was in my chamber that it felt like a new room. I stared at the bed I'd designed as a fanciful young bride, with its headboard decorated with knights' helmets, crowns and serpents. In the centre, two crests were carved in one: the three shuttles and the mullet for Shuttleworth, six martlets for Fleetwood. I had refused to use the Barton crest here.

Richard slept next to me that night, whether in solidarity or guilt, it did not matter to me. Puck slept on the floor at the foot of the bed, snoring loudly, and for once Richard did not complain. I stared for a long time at the canopy, and my thoughts raced from one side of my head to the other.

Alice was accused of killing the daughter of a man named John. Had the child died in birth while she was delivering it? Or could it be a tale, born of revenge from the tongue of Elizabeth Device? Perhaps John Foulds was a friend of Roger's, with a long dead daughter in the churchyard, made richer for agreeing to peddle his lies.

I waited for sleep, and knowing there was no figure curled at the foot of my bed, it did not come easily.

✳

The next morning I took my time getting ready, washing properly after so long on the road. I soaped my hair and combed it, letting it dry down my back before I dressed. Prudence and Justice watched vacantly as I got into my things; I had little need for a maid now I did not wear a corse. I took a clean collar from my wardrobe and a pearl headdress and fixed them in place. I tied my silk stockings above and below my knees, even though my swollen legs kept them up easily, and put on my slippers. A dab of rose oil went behind my ears and at my wrists, and I rubbed my teeth with linen and spat into the used bathwater that was scudded with sweat and grease and dust. Then I opened the door for Puck to go with me to breakfast. I was still tired and sick from the jolting journey from my mother's and all that had happened last night, and all I could think of was Alice.

As usual, Barbara's food was bland and I picked at it, thinking of the cherries and gingerbread and butter pies we'd eaten at my mother's. Everything was duller here. On the other side of the table, Richard ate with his Turkish falcon sat on his shoulder, like some mythical knight of the realm. If he was trying to provoke me after I'd compared myself to his bird, it had the desired effect. I watched him, not touching my plate. He seemed cheerful and occupied, oblivious to my presence. Perhaps he had grown used to my absence, like I'd had to with his.

I swirled my spoon around in my oats and pretended to sip my beer.

'I wish you would not bring that creature in the house,' I said eventually.

Though I'd attempted to sound concerned, it came out spiteful. The bird regarded me with one serpent-like eye.

'I am getting her used to me. She likes to see where her master lives, don't you?'

'What if it breaks free of its leash and flies up into the rafters?'

'"Be ever well in blood, for otherwise she will not long be at your commandment but make you follow her."' I stared at him, and he grinned. 'The first rule of falconry and hawking. All it takes is a bit of meat to coax her down.'

'What if that bit of meat is a servant's finger?'

Richard winked; he was in a careless mood. The fact that he was capable of that, with everything that had happened, made me loathe him. Never would he brush up against the law; never would he be bundled into a carriage by a magistrate drunk on power. I watched him with a clear, steady hatred.

'I will go to Read Hall this morning,' I announced a few minutes later.

'To see Katherine?'

I licked my dry lips.

'Yes.'

'I won't join you. I have leases to draw with James.'

'What for?'

'I am buying up some land left by a farmer. Do you know, his son said he buried a cat in the wall of his house when he built it?'

'Why would he do that?'

He shrugged. 'To ward off evil? These local folk can be very queer. Glass windows would do it just as well.'

I realised he'd made a joke and forced my face into a smile. He had given me an idea.

I rode slowly on horseback to Read, glad of the fresh air that gave me space to think and plan. Passing the same old dwellings and farmhouses on the same old roads, I saw face after face, all of them wearing their hard lives in every crease and wrinkle. People trudged along, their heads wrapped, their shoulders hunched against pain and illness and grief. Their houses were made of mud; their backs stooped from hard work. I hoped they had moments of brightness in their lives; I hoped they bit into cherries and felt the surprise of the stone. If they would only build a playhouse here, there would be no need for witch hunts. Perhaps I would build one.

The sky was cloudy and the land green, and once you grew tired of looking at one or the other, there was not much else to see on the road to Read. I drew up to the house, and apart from a boy carrying hay to the stable, there was no one about. I gave him my horse and went to the door, knocking and waiting for what felt like a long time before knocking again. When the door opened, I expected to see Katherine, but no one was there – then I realised the person who opened it reached only to my chest, and I looked down into wide, watery eyes.

'Jennet,' I said, trying to hide my surprise. 'I am here for the master.'

The little girl stared.

'E i'nt home. E's gone,' she whispered.

Her skin was so pale it was almost silver.

My stomach twisted.

'Gone where?'

'Jennet?' came a voice within the house.

Katherine appeared behind her. Her face was tighter and thinner than when I'd last seen her.

I swallowed. 'Hello, Katherine.'

'Fleetwood.' She wrung her hands together and stopped a few feet short of the door. 'Jennet, get away from there. I told you not to answer the door. Get upstairs now.'

Although her words were scolding, her voice sounded anxious. The child leapt away and disappeared into the house.

'Katherine, is Roger home?'

'No, he's gone to Lancaster.'

'With Alice?'

'Alice?'

'Alice, my midwife. Alice.'

Katherine blinked, her white hands clutching at each other.

'I don't understand. Would you come in? I'll fetch some wine . . .'

'No, thank you. I need to know if Roger has taken Alice to the gaol at Lancaster.'

'He went out last night and hasn't returned – he told me that's where he was going.'

So he didn't put all his charges up in his house like an innkeeper. Just the ones he wanted something from. I took a step back and sighed, thinking of what to do.

'Do you know a man named John Foulds?'

Her face crumpled in confusion.

'I'm afraid not. Should I?' I shook my head. 'Roger said you were with your mother in Kirkby Lonsdale for a spell,' Katherine went on pleasantly. 'Was it . . . enjoyable?'

'Very. I have to go. I'm sorry, Katherine.'

She wavered on her doorstep like a woman on the edge of a drop, as though she might jump and come with me.

'Fleetwood,' she called, and I turned. She appeared anguished, as though what she was about to say was causing her great torment. 'He said he was taking a prisoner to the castle. I did not know it was a woman until I saw her in the carriage. She was your midwife?'

'Alice *is* my midwife. Thank you, Katherine. You have been helpful.'

'You won't stay for dinner? Have some wine, at least.'

I shook my head and said goodbye, going straight to

the stable, where my horse was still drinking from the trough. I waited for it to finish before going back the way I had come. My head was thick with trying to understand all the implications of this dreadful situation, and the ride back to Gawthorpe was a slower one.

When I arrived I dismounted and stood in the yard with a frown on my face, my hands still holding the reins. There was something I needed from the house before I went on the road again.

Richard was in the great hall with James, surrounded by papers.

'You are back early,' he said. 'Was Katherine well?'

'Fine,' I said absently. 'Have you seen the dog?'

Richard told me he'd last seen Puck in the parlour.

'I am going riding,' I announced.

'Is that wise?'

'Alice said so, and she has not steered me wrong thus far.' I held his stare. 'I'll be back in a few hours.'

Richard's face was half amused, half annoyed.

'Do you know, James,' he said to the steward, 'I wonder if the king has some sense in wanting to tighten the reins on Lancashire's women. They are lawless, are they not?'

There was a hint of malice about my husband as he looked closely at me. I'd seen the same glint of it at my mother's house in the moment he decided he would tell me what to do, for the first time in our marriage. Now he was exercising his authority like a muscle, testing my limit and his.

'I know not, Master,' James replied soberly.

'They are wild, are they not?' he asked me.

'They are also harmless,' I replied carefully.

'And who will be the judge of that?'

Richard did not look away, so I smiled clumsily and left the room, but before I disappeared he called me back.

'I am on business in Ripon today and will be away for the night.'

I paused with my hand on the door.

'When will you be back?'

'Late tomorrow, or the morning after. But worry not – James will be here to keep an eye on you.'

I went to find the dog. Walking across the bottom of the staircase, I felt the presence of my mother's portrait at the top of the tower, as though she was standing on the gallery looking down at me. I shuddered and stepped back out into the chill morning.

CHAPTER 16

I t was market day in Padiham, and the village was lively with people and animals and thick with the cries of traders and groans of cattle. I rode into the stable yard at the Hand and Shuttle, barely registering the curious glances that fell on Puck and me. I took him inside and asked a young boy with a rag in his hand for the landlord. He went off into the corridor I'd walked down not so long ago, before Alice told me to open my eyes. Now I wished I could close them.

The same man as before, with a ruddy, inquisitive face and rotten teeth, appeared.

'I did not introduce myself last time I was here,' I said quietly. 'My name is Fleetwood Shuttleworth. I live at Gawthorpe Hall.'

'I know who you are,' he replied, not unpleasantly. 'I'm William Tufnell, the landlord.'

That was when he noticed Puck at my side and almost jumped out of his skin.

'No dogs allowed in here, Mistress. I'm sorry. Even yours.'

I nodded, glancing around and noticing the fireplace Alice would have swept and the tables she'd wiped.

'I won't take a minute of your time, I only have one thing to ask,' I said. 'Have you ever heard of John Foulds or his daughter Ann?'

He looked blankly back at me.

'No one of that name in Padiham. And if he's got a hand to lift a tankard, he'll have been in here.'

'There is an inn at Colne. The Queen's Arms?'

'Aye,' he said warily.

'I believe your employee Alice Gray came from there to here, looking for work.'

'My brother-in-law passed her on, aye. She's not here any more, though.'

'What is your brother-in-law's name? Is he the landlord there?'

'Peter Ward, Mistress. And yes. You'll find him there if you seek him.'

The Queen's Arms was on the edge of the village a few miles upriver, and I imagined Alice helping a feeble and petrified John Law along the pack road here. It was a small inn, no bigger than an alehouse, with the same smell of damp beer once I crossed the threshold. The place was empty, the benches and tables old but well scrubbed, and there was fresh sawdust on the floor.

I left Puck outside, tying his leash to a post. A woman with a broom stood in a doorway behind the bar, telling a loud story. I waited for her to finish, my hands clasped in front of me. The woman realised she was being watched and as she turned to see me, her mouth fell open in a rude way.

'Can I help you?'

She looked me up and down, clasping the broomstick in her red hands.

'My name is Fleetwood Shuttleworth. I am looking for Mr Ward, the landlord.'

She could easily have called, but the woman went through the doorway and I heard her whispering. A moment later, a great barrel of a man with a shock of white hair stepped through. He was so large I felt his boots hit the packed earth floor.

'Can I help?'

'Are you Mr Ward, who employed Alice Gray?'

'If I had a feather in my hat for every person who came in here asking for Alice Gray, I'd look like a chicken. What's she done now?'

His choice of words surprised me.

'She has done nothing. I wondered where I might find her father.'

'Joe Gray? What do you want with him?'

'I wish to speak with him.'

'He don't say much worth listening to.' I waited. 'He lives about half a mile that way along the woolpack trail, then right, a little way up where the trees stop. What'll you want with him?'

'That is my business. Who else has been asking for Alice?'

'Oh . . .' He waved a large hand. 'Some magistrate, t'other week. I said, "Are you sure you've got t'right person?" Before that, you don't even want to know – a beast of a slattern with one eye on Heaven and the other on Hell. And her mother, screeching like a pig in a slaughterhouse. God knew what they wanted with her.'

'You mean Demdike? And Elizabeth Device?'

'Demdike, aye. It means demon woman, did you know that? Two families around here have been locked away for witchcraft now, would you believe – the Devices and old Chattox and her daughter. Some folk were telling me they're neighbours at war with each other, both of them in with the Devil. And that little 'un who was here a few month ago, asking after that poor sod she'd cursed. Good riddance, the lot of them. I'm not having their sort in here – folk won't come if they know witches have been in. That's why I had to let Alice go: they were always asking for her. Years, she worked for me. But she were scaring the customers, the ugly wench.'

'So you let her go,' I said coldly.

'She were caught up in it, rightly or wrongly.'

'All she did was bring that poor man back here.'

'I wish she hadn't bothered. Brought me nothing but grief, he did. Wailing and weeping about dogs in his room and needles and curses. He's the one needed locking up but she begged me to let him stay.'

I looked around at the empty tables and chairs, the full barrels waiting to be drained into men's bellies. He had a business to run, and there might have been some truth in what he was saying, but he was wrong to get rid of Alice, because in doing so he'd implicated her of wrong-doing.

'Do you know John Foulds?' I asked eventually.

'You want him as well then, do you? She has bad luck with men, does Alice, what with her old dad and John Foulds.'

The hairs on the back of my neck stood up.

'I beg your pardon?'

'He comes in here, now and again. Well, he used to, until . . . He's not been in for a while. I don't know where he is.'

'Until what?'

Peter reached around to scratch the side of his large belly.

'His daughter died not long ago. How long would it be now, Maggie? Six months or so, I reckon.'

'And he and Alice . . .'

'Well, they were courting. He'd been married before – his wife died. She kept her cards close to her chest, did Alice, never did let on much. But they never did marry. You'll not find Alice around here anyway, sorry to disappoint. If you're asking her dad, he might not have much idea either. You could try at the Hand and Shuttle – that's where she works now, in Padiham.'

'What does he look like?' My mouth was dry.

'John? Dark hair, tall. Handsome chap, until the drink takes hold of him, eh, Margaret? I've seen you having a look.'

Margaret rolled her eyes and slapped his arm.

So the man who'd upset her in the passage at the Hand and Shuttle was John Foulds. The idea that Alice had murdered his daughter was impossible. And she his lover? He'd had a fine face, but idleness and wastefulness radiated from him like light from the sun.

I thanked Peter and his wife flatly, and before I went to get my horse, I looked up at the little windows on the second floor of the inn. I wondered which one John Law the pedlar had looked out of from his sick bed.

The road at the side wound down to Colne one way and ran out into open fields and copses of trees on the other. Birds sang around me, and the joyful chorus they made rang empty in my ears as I rode slowly away from the village. The road was muddy underfoot, and my horse's feet were unsteady. Puck padded heavily beside me, and in the quiet and clear air I imagined Alice on this same path, as familiar to her as the woods at Gawthorpe were to me.

I knew so little about Alice, yet she knew so much about me. She told me once that she came close to marrying, and that must have been John. She missed her mother dearly, and had found a kindred spirit in her old friend Mould-heels. She did not speak often of her father, and when she did it was not with warmth. All these little things I knew, but they were like brushstrokes at the corners of a picture: I could not see the full thing.

The road cut through a wooded area, with trees that would dwarf Gawthorpe. I shivered as I thought of John Law meeting Alizon under their whispering leaves. I kept my eyes straight ahead until the trunks and boughs opened into wide fields again, trying to shake off the feeling that I was being watched. Just as Peter had said, the land began to rise up on the right, and a low, dark house squatted on the hillside. A mud track led to it, and I turned my horse uphill, guiding it around the worst of the bog. A thin thread of smoke drifted briefly out of a chimney into the air, only to be carried in all directions by the wind. The house was not much taller than I was, smaller even than the buttery at home, made of wattle and daub with a thatched roof. The windows were not glazed but had shutters that were open to let the light in. A low wall surrounded the cottage, and flowers lay dying or dead in their beds. A few colourful heads peered from beneath the weeds like lanterns. I remembered Alice talking of her mother's herb garden and thought it must be around the back. The house was exposed on the hillside; it would have been difficult to protect growing things from the wind and driving rain here.

I rapped smartly on the door and a few moments later it opened. Joseph Gray was older than I expected: older even than Roger. Or it might have been that he looked that way because he was poor. Hunched over, he gave the impression of constant movement even when he was still; his body trembled and his mouth worked around his teeth. Like Alice's, his cream-coloured hair spiralled down to his shoulders. His eyes were a clear blue, and he was thin: his clothes hung off him and looked as though they needed leaving in lye for a week.

'Mr Gray?' I said. 'I am Fleet—'

'I know who you are,' he muttered. 'She worked for you, didn't she? Come in. I suppose you've got summat to tell me.'

It was very warm in the house: the fire in the middle of the room burnt as merrily as if it was December, not July. The rising smoke escaped from a hole in the centre of the roof of the cottage, and I thought how cold and draughty it must be with an opening to the weather. Two low beds stood either side of the fire – one unmade – and lengths of cloth hung over the earth walls that would no doubt be damp and cold to touch. A table, two stools and a cupboard were the only furniture. By the fire on the rush-covered floor lay some pewter pots and pans that looked used but not washed. So Alice and her father cooked, slept and lived in this house full of holes that the wind whistled through all hours.

Joseph spoke. 'I suppose you're here about the nag?'

'The nag?' I asked.

'The nag you give our Alice. You've got it back though now, so I don't want no trouble.'

I stared blankly at him.

'The horse that went missing?'

'Aye.' His mouth kept moving even when he was not speaking and I wondered if he was chewing tobacco. 'I give the money back to the fella. And was she grateful? Was she fuck.'

He ambled over to his bed and sat on it. I remained where I was, struggling to breathe in the fire's oppressive heat. Joseph licked his lips and picked a tankard off the floor, examining its contents and throwing them into his mouth.

So that's what had happened to the grey draught horse: Alice's father had sold it. And she, somehow, had got it back. My chest felt heavy suddenly, and for a brief moment I felt overcome with emotion. But I straightened my skirts and stood straighter.

'Mr Gray, I am not here about the horse. I have it back

now, so no matter. I am here because Alice has been arrested by the magistrate Roger Nowell, who seems to be under the impression she has murdered a child.'

His eyes remained glazed and vacant, resting on the fire, and after a few seconds he pulled them towards me.

'Eh?' he said.

'Mr Gray, your daughter is in a great deal of trouble. I will do everything I can to help her but I thought you must know about these fatal claims. She has been taken to Lancaster gaol to await the assizes next month, but it can't get that far. I won't let it. Mr Gray, are you listening to me?'

'Bet you don't even need that horse, do you? What's one more nag to you? Bet you have a whole stable of 'em lined up like soldiers, waiting to be called to attention.'

He gave a half-hearted salute and again tipped his grubby tankard into his mouth, though it appeared to be empty.

'Mr Gray! Are you listening to me? Your daughter is accused of being a witch and is in gaol. Do you know anything about this?'

He burped. 'Guess she'll be going same way as her mother then.'

With one finger he drew a line across his neck.

My mouth fell open.

'She could be hanged, and you don't care? You have no interest in helping her?'

'What I have an interest in . . . is . . .' He lost his words and grew vacant again. 'Where is my ale coming from?

Cos it i'nt from her! Or that tight-fisted bugger Peter Ward. He is only down the road, but now I have to go further 'cause he won't serve me. I'm an old man, Mistress What's-Yer-Name.'

The heat was so intense, the fire blinding, and Joseph Gray so infuriating and strange, I felt I couldn't stay for a single second longer in his hovel. But I had come for a reason, and I owed Alice everything. I rose slowly to go to the unmade bed in the dampest corner of the room. Even the great barn at Gawthorpe was warmer and drier – no wonder she had taken so easily to the idea of going with me to my mother's.

There was something lying on her bed – a bundle of rags, though it might have been something a cat dragged in. I lifted its damp, lifeless form – not a creature, but old wool, crudely sewn. Made as though from a handkerchief, it appeared to be a human form, stuffed with hair, with a head, and two arms and legs. There was a curious mass attached to it, and though the smoke and the heat were overwhelming, my skin went cold when I realised it was the figure of a child bound with hair to a woman. Black hair. I remembered the strands covering my pillow, and how they had disappeared. There was the faintest scent of lavender, then it disappeared. Inexplicably, my eyes filled with tears, and I set the poppet back on the bed.

'Mr Gray,' I said, going back to where he sat, jerking and muttering. 'Alice told me about her mother, Jill.' I waited for a response, and something stirred in his blank blue eyes. 'She misses her very much, as I'm sure you do. You have already had one member of your family taken away. Would you not do everything in your power to stop it happening to Alice? She is the only family you have.'

His head snapped as though he was dreaming. He was staring wildly at something I could not see. With difficulty, I crouched down, my skirts bunching around me.

'Your daughter has been very loyal to me, and helped me greatly over the past months. I am sorry that I took her away from you,' I lied. 'I will help her; she has helped me and now I must return her kindness.'

The smoke was badly stinging my eyes now; perhaps Joseph thought I was moved to tears.

'Mr Gray,' I said again.

His gaze cleared and he focused. His lips parted and I thought he would speak, but instead he showed all his brown teeth, and it was a moment before I realised he was laughing.

'They burn witches, don't they?' he wheezed, pointing at the fire.

'What?'

I stood, even more alarmed.

He pointed at my skirts.

'They burn witches!'

Flames were licking the bottom of my gown. Puck began barking, and horror hit me with such force I was almost blind with it. I ran to the door and flapped my skirts desperately in the open air. The fire seemed to falter but did not go out. I looked around in desperation for a trough, anything, and found an old pail against the wall filled with rainwater. With Puck barking and tearing around me, I tipped the whole thing over the side of my gown, and as the brown water puddled around my feet I saw the bright flames were gone.

Inside, Joseph Gray was still laughing. I stood there panting, Puck circling with his back to me, as though fending off an invisible army. The wind pulled at me from every angle and drew fine, dark threads of smoke away from my ruined gown. The ruby red of my skirts had gone black and gaped in a horrible wound. I don't know how long I stayed like that, but Joseph Gray did not come out, and it took me a long time to stop shaking enough to climb on to my horse. I broke into a canter, with Puck streaking behind me. I could not have gone faster if I was running from the Devil himself.

That night, something visited me in my chamber where I slept alone. I woke up because I felt warm fur brush against my hand. It was pitch-black, and all I could hear was my own breathing. I felt a weight shift on the bed somewhere near my feet. My breath died in my throat as it moved again, as though getting comfortable. I imagined Joseph Gray standing in my dark chamber with a dead rabbit hanging from his dirty fist.

I closed my eyes and willed my heart to stop hammering. *It's only a dream.* Yet I knew it was not.

Through the spaces between my heartbeats I felt the weight disappear from near my legs, then there was the softest, slightest sound of something landing on the floor. It was too light to be Puck, too silent. My hands stayed where they were on top of the bedclothes; I was too afraid to move them. My child kicked, as if to say, *I can feel it too*.

I waited: either nothing would happen or I would die of fright. Though everything was black, I saw something move towards the door, and then it was gone.

Earlier, I'd crept into the house and hurried upstairs, wrapped in my cloak like a smuggler. After shoving it into the wardrobe, I'd gone to my chamber and noisily pretended a candle had fallen, burning my dress.

'Oh!' I shouted, hearing myself and almost believing it. 'Oh, oh!'

I blew it out so it would still feel hot and placed it on the floor by my feet.

'My gown!' I cried when one of the chambermaids came in.

She was frightened; she probably thought I was losing the child. She guided me to sit down, and I puffed and panted and pretended I was scared, which wasn't difficult: all I had to do was think of Joseph Gray's wide, glassy eyes and the flames clawing at my hem.

I lay awake as my face dried and my heart slowed and

the child inside went back to sleep. I thought of Alice. My nightmare only happened when my eyes were closed, but Alice was living hers. Her father's words came to me in the darkness: *They burn witches, don't they?*

I tried to picture Alice as a child, growing up in that draughty house with her strange father and kind mother. Though I'd now met two people from her life, I had no better understanding of her, the girl who did not know her own birthday and could not spell her name, but who had a masculine intelligence, and knew the properties of everything in the earth, and could still a bucking horse with the palm of her hand.

I closed my eyes and prayed she was safe.

CHAPTER 17

The next morning I rose in the moments before sunrise and dressed quickly in the near dark, hoping I wouldn't meet any servants on the way out. I unlocked the front door and slipped outside, closing it gently behind me and pocketing the key. The summer morning was before me, and I would have thought it glorious in another year, another lifetime. I yawned and watched the trees rustling awake, then I went to the stables. The cattle were lowing in the great barn, eager for their feed, and the river sighed behind the house. I had to walk much more slowly now, so I noticed these things. One of the stable boys was dressed, a pail in each hand, and I sent him to saddle my horse. When he came back, I told him I had a message for him to pass on.

'Please go and find James later, and tell him I will be out all day, and he is not to tell the master about it when he returns. Tell him if the master finds out, I will throw his precious ledgers on a fire and he will have to rewrite them from memory. Can you remember that?'

The boy, whose name was Simon, and who was probably only three or four years younger than me, nodded gleefully, thrilled at the prospect of delivering a threat to his superior.

I strapped on a pack of food I'd taken from the kitchen and wrapped in a napkin – bread smeared with honey, cheese and grapes, with biscuits for later – and before the light had come up fully I was on the road north. If Richard was back tonight, I would need to be back, too.

Several hours later, I welcomed the sights and sounds of a busy town. It was a bright summer's day, and warm, and the journey uphill to the castle was slow, for the streets were crammed with carts and horses. Before I reached the gatehouse I looked back behind me, where Lancaster was spread far below, down a steep, winding street. Buildings were crammed in everywhere, with the hills rising up in the distance hemming them in. From the castle, you could see everything. On my horse I approached two helmeted guards standing with swords at their thighs like suits of armour.

'I am here to visit a prisoner,' I said.

They regarded me lazily.

'Name?' one said.

'Mine, or the name of the prisoner?'

'Your name,' he said impatiently.

'Fleetwood Shuttleworth, of Gawthorpe Hall near Padiham.'

He looked me up and down, taking in my swollen stomach. Then he turned and disappeared under the great yawning gate. My back ached and my legs burnt from the long ride, but if I dismounted I thought I might never get back on the horse again.

Just as I began to wonder if the guard would return, he came striding out with a plump, slightly younger man with black hair. He was dressed finely in soft black boots, breeches and a black doublet with silver buttons fastened over his well-fed belly. Wide sleeves billowed at his wrists.

'Mistress Shuttleworth?' he asked politely. 'Should I be expecting you? My name is Thomas Covell. I am the coroner and keeper of this castle.'

I decided to stay on my horse to keep the advantage of height.

'I am here to visit Alice Gray, Mr Covell, if such a thing is possible?' When he looked no more enlightened, I said, 'She was recently arrested by Roger Nowell, who is a dear friend of mine. I was in the area and wanted to . . . enquire after her welfare.'

Clearly prisoners' visitors were not a daily occurrence

at the castle gatehouse, for Mr Covell was intrigued and suspicious. He placed his fingertips together.

'Ah . . . We do not permit callers at the castle, I am afraid to say.' His eyes slipped to my stomach. 'Especially under certain circumstances – the prisoners can get quite excited by it, and it does no good for their dispositions.'

'Mr Covell,' I said, 'I have travelled a long way – over forty miles.' His face was impassive, as were the two guards' either side, gazing into the distance. 'My husband, Richard Shuttleworth, would be very disappointed to hear I had been turned away, especially considering his late uncle Sir Richard's generous contribution to the Crown not fifteen years ago – that and the fact he was chief justice at Chester, and knighted at court. So I am not sure that my late relative would look with agreement at his nephew's wife being refused entry. I would hate to have to take the matter further.'

Mr Covell opened his mouth and then closed it again.

'What is the name of the prisoner you seek to visit?' he asked.

'Alice Gray. She was brought here not two days ago.'

Thomas Covell regarded me again coolly, taking all of me in from my hat to my rings. His fat chin wobbled and he sighed.

'You have two minutes. I will have one of the gaolers escort you.'

And so I passed under the gatehouse, just as Alice had two days before me, and thousands more would after.

There was only one way into the castle, and one way out.

I left my horse tied behind the gatekeepers. A thin, wheezing man with a pointed face like a rat took me across the castle yard – but not the way I was expecting, towards the main part of the castle. We followed the interior wall around to the right, towards a cluster of huts and stone outhouses. His gait was very wide, his legs sprouting from his hips, so he walked with difficulty, but also like a man determined not to show it.

'What'n' ya want wi' these wenches 'en, eh?' he said conversationally.

I ignored him and stared up at the height of the stone, feeling the chill of the place even though it was a warm summer's day. I was not expecting us to stop so suddenly, and not outside: we were next to a low arch at the foot of one of the towers, covered by an iron gate. But the door did not lead out to the other side of the castle walls – the blackness inside meant it only led one way: down.

I frowned. 'Why are we stopping?' I asked.

'This is the Well Tower,' said my companion through a gummy smile.

'I don't understand. Alice Gray will be in a cell awaiting trial. Can you take me to her, please?'

'She's in 'ere.'

He pointed at the arch. It was so dark I could see why it was called the Well Tower – it was like looking into one. I could not see beyond one or two steps; it was as though a black curtain covered the rest. The gaoler extracted a large bunch of keys from his hip and spent a long time considering each one as, slowly, the absolute horror of what I was seeing dawned on me. Behind this gate, in this hole, was my friend. I had never been to a gaol and did not know what a cell might look like, but this was not a cell. It was a dungeon. It was as though the sun had gone out; all the heat and light left me, and I stood shivering, staring at the entrance to Hell itself.

A curious sound came from somewhere behind the gate, and I realised it was a bird chirruping. Hopping from one spot to another on the top step was a robin, trapped behind the gate. It might have been small enough to get through the bars, but it was asking for us to set it free.

'Bloody stupid vermin,' the gaoler muttered, unlocking and pulling open the gate. 'Get out of it.'

He moved towards the bird and finally it took flight, flitting past us to freedom. I reached for the cool stone wall to steady myself.

'In't nowt to be scared of. You wanted to come, din't yer?'

No. I did not want to go down there for anything, not even Alice. But I had to, because unlike her, I could come out again.

The gaoler closed the gate at the top of the stairs, and when I heard it clang and the key turn in the lock, every nerve in my body was set jangling, my head light with terror. It was like going down steps into black water, so dense was the darkness. They went down and down into the earth, and at the bottom was another door of solid wood, or iron – it was too dark to tell.

'Stand back,' he wheezed, using another key in the door at the bottom. 'Or the smell'll knock you out.'

I went back up a few steps, my pattens echoing on the stone. I heard the gaoler's barking on the other side of the door, and waited, and then a pale face appeared in the dim light at the bottom of the steps, and a slim body slipped through the narrow gap.

'Alice.'

I am ashamed to say I started crying: me, in my fine clothes, with my stomach full of cheese and bread, and my horse waiting for me outside the walls. She did not cry. I had not seen her in two days but it could have been years: she looked so different. Her long face was whiter than the moon, and there were shadows under her eyes that had not been there before. She blinked furiously, as though the gloom of the staircase was blinding. Her dress was filthy and looked damp, and her cap was streaked with dirt. Dark blood spotted the front of her dress, and no doubt the back too where she'd sat.

She said nothing, only held herself weakly against the wall, as though she had no strength. The gaoler appeared at her side, closing the door, and I heard shrieks and cries of protests from behind him as what must have been the only light was shut out. He was right: the smell was incredible. Alice had used to smell of lavender, and clean her hands in a porcelain bowl, and now she lived in a cesspit beneath the earth.

'Who else is in there?' I breathed.

'All of 'em,' the gaoler wheezed. 'All the witches awaiting trial.'

'How many people?' I asked Alice.

'I do not know,' she whispered. 'It's too dark to see anything.'

Her mouth was dry, her tongue peeling from the roof of her mouth as she spoke. Her pupils were large as marbles.

I had travelled for hours and now I could not think of a single thing to say. In that moment, I think I might have given the child in my stomach for her freedom.

The gaoler looked from one of us to the other, disappointed.

'Well, this is quite the reunion, is it not? Do you have nowt to say?'

'Do you have food?' I asked.

'A little,' she said.

When the gaoler looked away to sort his keys, she shook her head.

'I will help you.'

My voice echoed on the walls. My words sounded as pathetic as a child's.

'They got Katherine as well,' she said, her voice thick.

'Who?'

'Katherine Hewitt. My mother's friend.'

That's when she started crying.

Mould-heels: her mother's partner in midwifery. I remembered her telling me about her in that warm, lofty chamber in my mother's house, long ago in a different life.

'It's my fault,' she said.

'What do you mean? What's your fault?'

'Now, now,' said our acquaintance, uncomfortable.

I turned to him.

'Will you leave us for a moment?' I demanded.

'*Leave* you? I shan't be doing that.'

I fumbled at my skirts and took out my purse.

'Here.' I held out a penny and he fell on it like a starving dog. 'You can leave us locked in, just come back when I call. Don't go far.'

He staggered up the steps, breathing raggedly, shutting the gate behind him and locking it again. His figure blocked the light momentarily, and only when he moved away could I see Alice again.

'Come up,' I said, retreating up the staircase. 'You need air and light.'

She followed me and we sat on the top step with our backs against the gate. I tried not to breathe in the stench coming off her: stale sweat, vomit and dried blood, plus something else that I knew at once to be fear. I'd never smelt it before on a human, but somehow I knew it right away. She had stopped crying now but the tears had carved clean paths down her mucky face.

'Tell me about Katherine,' I said gently, taking her hand.

'She is accused too, of the same thing. It's my fault – she's done nothing.'

'Alice, you have to tell me everything. Why are you accused of murdering John Foulds' daughter? He was the man I saw you with at the Hand and Shuttle, wasn't he?'

She nodded and licked her lips, though her tongue was dry.

'I loved him,' she said in a very faint voice. 'And I loved Ann. I loved them both. Me and John were . . . together. He used to come to the Queen's Arms, that's how I met him, a couple of years ago. He had a daughter; his wife had died. He was funny, and kind. At first I thought we would get married. Ann wasn't two years old when we met. I used to look after her when he went to work. She was like a little angel, with fat cheeks and yellow hair that wouldn't lie flat no matter how much you combed it.'

She was almost smiling now, her face lost in memories. Then it clouded over and she sniffed.

'John said he wouldn't get married again, not after losing his wife. It was too painful, he said. So I stayed, and it was like we were married. I lived with him, and my dad as good as disowned me. He called me a whore. He said I'd never be a wife, that I was good for nothing but lying down for John after he'd been drinking. But I was happy, with John and with Ann. We were a little family.' She swallowed. 'Then he started staying out longer, and later. Me and Ann were on our own a lot of the time. Most of the time. John was either at work or at the alehouse, while I was pretending to be his little wife at home. I was lying to myself.'

She shifted her feet and wrapped her arms around her knees. I looked again at the blood on the front of her dress, at her unwashed hair trailing from under her cap. I wished I could wash her and put her in a clean nightdress, tuck her in bed like a child.

'Even when folk started telling me he had other women, I didn't want to believe them. And life went on, and he got meaner, and cheaper, and me and Ann were living off my wage because he spent all his. And she started having these . . . I don't know what you call them. She would go stiff and her eyes would roll in her head, and her tongue was too big for her mouth. I thought she was doing it because her dad wasn't around. He didn't believe me when I told him. He thought I was making it up to get him to come home. I tried all the plants I could think of, all the herbs. I went to Katherine for help, but even she couldn't do anything. She was fine most of the time, it was just when this happened she was . . . It was like an evil spirit was choking her.

'One day I had to go to work and leave Ann at home on her own. John was nowhere to be found. He was supposed to come back. I was close to losing my job.'

Tears began leaking again from her eyes. Her face was carved with sorrow.

'I still loved him. I always loved him, even when he

wouldn't come home. If we hadn't had Ann, though, things might have been different. I might have left. Anyway, I went to work and asked Katherine to keep an eye on her. The next thing, she came running in saying, "Alice, Alice, come quick, you have to come now." And we ran to John's and she . . .' Alice buried her face in her knees. 'I shouldn't have left her.'

I put my arm around her, feeling her thin shoulders. As I grew, she shrunk. My heart felt like it was breaking. It was a different pain from when I had discovered Judith. That time there was anger; this time there was only sorrow.

'There was nothing you could have done,' I whispered, pressing my cheek to hers.

Our tears mixed together and ran down to our lips. I tasted salt: mine and hers. We stayed like that as she shuddered beneath my arm, then after a while she grew still.

'I think that's why I wanted to help you so much,' she said softly. 'I thought maybe if I could keep your child alive, it would go some way to . . .' She stopped, struggling to explain. 'I'd failed to save one child, so I thought if I could give life to another . . .'

'If the child is a girl, I will call her Alice Ann.'

She did not smile, but there was a shadow of comfort in her eyes.

'I thought you wanted two boys.'

'I do.' I looked down at our skirts – shiny maize taffeta

against filthy brown wool, and I held her hand again. 'That has not changed.'

'It's awful in there,' she whispered. 'It's like Hell. You can't see a thing, and it makes you feel like the room's turning. There's a woman dying. Demdike. She'll be dead before the trial. There's no food.'

I closed my eyes and thought of the food I'd had that morning all to myself. I hadn't even thought . . .

'I'll get you out of here,' I said. 'I promise. I will get you out.'

More tears slid down her cheeks.

'I can see what all this has cost you,' she whispered. 'I can't have you sacrifice any more.'

'To Hell with what it costs me.'

As I said it, I felt the baby move, and was aware at once that while all three of us were here and alive now – Alice, the baby and I – one day very soon we might not be, and there was no way of telling which of us would make it. We were bound together in some dreadful destiny, and it was clearer now than ever that to survive, we needed one another just as equally, and just as desperately.

'I will save you,' I said again, gripping her fingers in mine.

She squeezed them once, and let go, then she looked sadly at me, and her lively golden eyes were empty.

'I am not a dog you can save from a bear pit.'

'I *will* save you from death, like you promised to save me. You will live.'

'And Katherine,' she whispered.

'And Katherine.'

At that moment a great wail came from behind the locked door at the bottom of the steps, making us both jump. Then fists began banging and the wails turned to screams. Alice and I leapt to our feet as the gaoler hurried over and fumbled with the lock.

'You've set 'em off, have you?' he demanded.

'What's all this?' another voice echoed down the staircase.

More men were approaching now. The gate clanged open and an iron grip held my arm. Alice and I were wrenched apart and suddenly I was outside the gate and she was being marched back down into the darkness.

'Alice!' I cried. 'I'll come back! I'll come back!'

While a fierce bulk of a man escorted me back to the gatehouse, the door to the dungeon clanged open and the shrieking grew louder.

'She's dead! She's dead! She's dead!'

The words flew out like crows from a forest, echoing around the walls with nowhere to land.

Before beginning the long journey home, I stopped at an inn in the town, where I ordered three roast chickens, twenty meat pies and two gallons each of ale and milk to send to the dungeon. I had four boys carry the food and roll the barrels up the hill to the castle, and made sure that the same wheezing gaoler carried them down those steep stairs and came back with empty arms. I left him with another penny to shine his palm and gave one to each of the miserable guards too. I told them I would be back, and they smiled at me as though they knew better.

CHAPTER 18

The next morning there was a crowd of servants at the front steps when I came down to breakfast. Richard's bare head was at the front of the crowd, so I pushed my way through. Then I realised everyone was looking down at the ground. I stepped back in horror.

Richard's falcon had been slashed to pieces. Lying in a pool of her own blood, she had been left as an offering on the top step, her wings folded, her eyes glassy and unseeing. The servants were hovering like a pack of flies on rotten meat, so I sent them away. Richard's face was a mask of grief and anger, and I knew that one would soon surrender to the other, so I urged them back inside and closed the door.

'Do you know who did this?' I asked.

'No, but when I find out I will kill them,' he said quietly.

I allowed him to collect himself, thinking suddenly of the slash of fur, the glistening red of those butchered rabbits I'd seen in the woods all those weeks ago.

'One of our tenants? Have you rowed with anyone of late?'

He shook his head and gazed on the pitiful creature. As he knelt, I watched his narrow shoulders slope in sadness, his hair stir in the damp wind, and felt a powerful surge of love. But also something else: a despondency – a shame, previously unknown to me – that he could feel something so strongly for a creature, and not for me, or for Alice. I felt like leaving him on the doorstep and going to where my breakfast was waiting in the dining room, but then an idea arrived. I asked a servant to bring a bathing sheet, then knelt to wrap the carcass up. The sight of it did not stir me – I had seen plenty of death. But something did cause me to hesitate: a few very fine orange hairs were caught in its wounds. I folded the sheet and bound it carefully around the bird.

We crossed the lawn as the skies opened. I stood with my husband in the downpour as he buried the bird behind the great barn in a sheltered spot by the river. I felt the rain run down my neck, soaking my jacket, and my child kicked inside me. When we got back into the house, and Richard pulled off his drenched jacket, I took his face in my hands. His hair was plastered to his head, and his eyelashes were wet. His grey eyes burnt.

'Richard,' I said. 'I need your help.'

I spent a long time getting dressed, and for the finishing touch added my black velvet choker with the plump pearl hanging ripe as a peach that Roger had bought for me one Christmas. My cheeks were fatter than the last time I saw him. I pinched them and dabbed rose oil behind my ears, at my wrists and at the dip in my throat. When I heard him arrive downstairs, I stared into the looking glass for another minute or two, tweaking my collar, patting my hair and trying to breathe normally. I was pleased to see my hands weren't shaking, and said a silent prayer.

I heard Roger's voice before I saw him, telling Richard some tale or other. They were in the dining room, and I paused in the doorway to take a deep breath before gliding in. He looked the same as ever – shiny boots, wide sleeves, glittering rings. It might have been any day in our friendship, but the memory of the last time I saw him returned. Something told me to be very careful.

'Mistress Shuttleworth,' he said genially, with a graceful bow of his head.

I went to him and kissed him, trying very hard to act as I might have done months ago. So much had happened since that supper at Read Hall, but you would never know it from his easy grin, his beaming cheeks.

'You are looking very well,' he said evenly.

'Thank you. Will you have some wine?'

'I will always have some wine, if there is wine to be had.'

I went to the draw-leaf table to pour it and found myself glancing at the panels above the fireplace. Empty, gleaming wood filled the space around Richard's initials.

'The tower lies empty,' Roger was saying. 'I told him I imagine it will be difficult to find a tenant afterwards.'

'I could ask the bailiff,' Richard suggested.

'Tower?' I asked, going back to serve the wine.

'Malkin Tower,' was Roger's reply.

I tried to appear lightly curious.

'What is that?'

'The home of the Devices, near Colne. It's a very strange place to look at. You hear tower and think it to be grand but it's like a spike coming out of the earth. It's tall and round and made of stone, with one room at the bottom, and they climb rotten ladders to sleep around the walls. But they won't have use of it for much longer – it's been empty a month or more. Since Constable Hargrieves found the teeth and clay dolls under the ground there, I shall be surprised if anyone wants to go in there again.'

Silence fell as the food was brought in: a joint of roast beef, with fallow pasties and cheese. Roger eyed it hungrily.

'Fleetwood,' he said, helping himself to sauce, 'a friend of mine saw you in Lancaster the other day. What were you doing there?'

I kept my eyes on the food, cutting the beef into strips.

'I was visiting a clothier,' I said.

'All the way in Lancaster? Must be some fine material.'

I smiled and licked my thumb. Roger was always two steps ahead of everyone else: no doubt he had already asked the guards or Thomas Covell, who had confirmed I'd been there.

'I stopped by the castle, too,' I said thickly. 'I thought I might visit my midwife.'

I glanced at Richard. I'd told him of my whereabouts in case Roger did first, and was glad of it now, though he was not at all happy I'd ridden some eighty miles in a single day. I'd reminded him of Alice's advice: that if I had always ridden, then riding was as dangerous as walking, so that was balm at least.

Roger speared his meat with his knife and did not look up. He knew, then.

'And why ever did you do that?' His voice low and dangerous.

I pushed my plate away and reached into my pocket for my handkerchief to dab my eyes.

'I have been feeling very unwell,' I said in a small voice. 'I am worried for my health and the health of my child – I wanted to ask her advice.'

'And there is not one other midwife within forty miles that could assist you?'

'Alice has been a very good midwife – the best I've had.' I stopped dabbing and looked meekly at him. 'I have never reached this far in childbed before, and I believe that is down to Alice. My lying in will begin soon, Roger,' I went on. 'If you could just consider allowing Alice to live in custody here at Gawthorpe, for my own sake and for that of my child's. Without her, I am afraid. Richard?'

I glanced at my husband, praying he would play his part.

There was a pause, in which Richard licked his lips.

'Fleetwood was very ill,' he said quietly. 'You saw her. She could barely eat a morsel. Her hair fell out in clumps. Somehow she is better than ever now. Alice would of course still face the assizes next month but we would keep her here under lock and key. She would not escape.'

'And you could guarantee that how?'

'The same way you could guarantee it with Jennet Device, who I believe is still at Read,' I said.

'Jennet Device is not on trial for murder,' Roger said calmly. He picked up his knife again. 'You would invite a child murderer and a witch under your roof?'

'She is not . . .' I whispered, but Richard gave me a look, and I went silent.

'It is impossible,' Roger announced, returning to his food.

I hated him more than ever in that moment. He was

like a cat placing a powerful paw on a mouse's tail before letting go and catching it again. Roger enjoyed letting people wheedle, and persuade, and beg, letting them think they were in with a chance, when his decision was already made.

'I think the pair of you fail to grasp the seriousness of the allegations against the Pendle witches,' he went on. 'Witchcraft is punishable by death, but their crimes are altogether more serious. They have not only practised witchcraft, but their actions have caused the deaths and madness of many people. They are a danger to society. How would it look to the king, to ask for their pardon until the trial? No, it will not do.'

He dabbed at his beard, where beads of sauce clung to the silver hairs.

'Which brings me to my next point,' he said, this time speaking directly to me. 'There is no use visiting the castle again, because you will not be let in. Visitors excite the prisoners, and what with your . . . condition . . .' He gestured vaguely at me. 'It whips them into a frenzy. Shortly after you barged your way into the Well Tower and had that door opened, a woman died.'

'You are not suggesting—'

'I am not suggesting anything; I am telling you,' Roger interrupted. His eyes were fierce now, every line of his body taut with malice. 'Do not go to the castle again. If you do, you will not be let out.'

My knife clattered against the table. I turned to Richard,

who was pushing strips of fat miserably around his plate. He would not challenge Roger; I knew it. And I needed him on my side. Trying to disguise the fact that I was shaking, I sat back in my chair and let my hands fall to my lap.

'Do you mean to say I would be a prisoner?'

'That is exactly what I mean. Be under no pretence: your advantage of birth is the only thing that stands in your favour. Had you not this house and husband, do you think you would be permitted to tear around the county unchecked, making your enquiries? You are no threat to the course of justice, as much as you design to be. But if you think you are free from the grip of the manacles, you are quite mistaken.'

At this, Richard interrupted. 'Roger, be reasonable.'

My blood had turned cold, but Roger was not yet finished.

'One of the accused is Myles Nutter's mother. She, too, is a rich woman, a fine lady of standing. Land-owning, with educated sons. The problem is she curses her neighbours and they fall down dead.'

If only it was that easy to kill you, I would do it, I thought, but my mouth remained shut.

Roger leant in slightly to deliver his fatal blow.

'In fact, Jennet told me you reminded her of Mistress Nutter. She can always be persuaded to think a little harder about who was there at Malkin Tower on Good Friday.'

His pale gaze rested unblinkingly on me, and I think

that was the first time I realised who I was pitting myself against. This was not Roger, my father figure, who dined and hunted and played cards with us; this was the former sheriff, the magistrate, the Justice of the Peace.

'That's enough,' Richard cried, stabbing his knife into the table, with a sickening crack.

We all jumped, and Roger sat back. I had not seen Richard this angry before.

'I'll hear no more of it.'

He pulled the knife from the wood and began eating again.

'I am leaving this afternoon for Jennet Preston's trial at York,' Roger spoke quietly now. 'The same judges who are hearing the case will be at Lancaster in August: Sir James Altham, who is very experienced and discreet, and Sir Edward Bromley. Do you know Bromley, Richard?' Richard ignored him, his jaw still set with fury. Roger did not seem to notice. 'He is the nephew of the former Lord Chancellor, who oversaw the execution of the Scottish queen. He is also the man who acquitted Jennet Preston at the Lent assizes.'

He took a noisy sip from his glass.

I remembered how Thomas Lister had seethed and shaken next to me at dinner at the mention of Jennet Preston; how he had succeeded in committing her to trial twice in the space of a few months. One of the judges had found her not guilty a few months before; he could do it again.

'How many weeks until the trial at Lancaster?' I asked Roger.

'Three or four. I expect both of you will want seats in the gallery? I am expecting it to be busier than the Rose on play night.'

Later, when the two men went out to look at Richard's new gun, I stood for a long time at the window, thinking. Demdike was dead. Jennet Preston would be tried for murder by witchcraft tomorrow. While Alice was alive, and there was time before the trial, I could still save her.

The next morning I set out to find Malkin Tower. I rode in my travelling cloak, my skin slick with sweat, even though it was cool for July, and my mother's voice ringing in my ears:

Fleetwood, you are making yourself ridiculous. Fleetwood, you are making a mockery of your family.

I thought back to those gentle, light-filled days at her house – a place I would never have imagined myself comfortable. The reason I found it comfortable was Alice. If I had sat night after night embroidering or reading Bible passages with only my mother's sour face for company, I might have been driven mad. No, how could I think that? What would drive someone mad was night after night in a dank, pitch-black cell, surrounded by other sweating, weeping, vomiting bodies, with no water or food or place to relieve yourself.

The reason Alice was in prison was Elizabeth Device, who had wanted to save her child so desperately she had shackled herself to everyone around her. Perhaps she thought there was safety in numbers. She might never have expected her other daughter would bring about their downfall. I wanted to see where she came from, this astonishingly ugly woman with her spirit dog and bastard child. She had already lost her mother, and now the rest of her family were at stake – apart from the child Jennet. What life had this child experienced, which made her deliver her kin to Roger Nowell? Roger had said Malkin Tower was a miserable place, but it was the only home she had known, with the only people. The lure of a feather bed and meat pies at Read Hall would surely not be enough to make her betray her family.

But you *hated your home*, a voice persisted. *And your mother.*

As much as that was true, I told myself I would never have betrayed my mother. But then, I was not sure what it would take for a child to do so. Neglect? Cruelty?

I did not know where to find the tower, nor whom to ask, so I set out on horseback towards Colne. I left Puck at home, knowing I might regret it later when the wind whistled on the moors and Joseph Gray's wind-battered hovel came back to haunt me.

They burn witches, don't they?

With my cloak covering my head and stomach I might have been anyone, or no one, so nobody paid me much attention on the quiet road. Three or four carts passed me, piled with vegetables and bolts of cloth, but I kept my eyes down, remembering how I'd been seen in Lancaster.

I have eyes in the forest, you know, Roger had said.

I knew that if I stayed on that road, eventually it would lead to Halifax, and to John Law and his son Abraham. To think a simple pedlar who was asked for some pins started all this. To think what might have happened if he had given them. But even if he had handed them over to Alizon Device, Alice would still have lived with her grief, would have gone on working at the Queen's Arms, cooking what little they could buy for her miserable father under the hole in the roof. And where would I be? I may have been dead; I may not. I may have never found out about Judith. But wherever I was, I would not be on the road searching for a stone tower sticking like a spike out of the will.

Grey and green, grey and green, as far as the eye could see, now and again passing the odd home made of crumbling stone or crudely slapped together from mud. Long, low farmhouses stretched along the hills like cats, but there was no tower. I decided to ask the next person I saw: a man travelling in the opposite direction on an exhausted-looking mule.

'Excuse me, do you know where I can find Malkin Tower?' I asked.

He shrunk back in alarm like I had told him I was a witch, and without saying a word shuffled away on his dusty beast, glancing back over his shoulder.

I sighed and came to a stop. Just when I was deciding what to do, two more figures appeared on the road: a woman, dressed plainly, tugging her daughter along.

'Excuse me,' I tried again. 'I am looking for Malkin Tower.'

The woman stopped, and her daughter, dozy with the heavy summer air, almost walked into her.

'What do you want with Malkin Tower?' she asked.

Her dark eyes glittered suspiciously.

'I've heard of the Devices and have a bet with my sister – she doesn't think they are real, or their house. I have a penny on finding it.'

'It is real all right, and so are they. Tell your sister she should believe what she hears, folk aren't likely to repeat falsehoods around here. They've been an odd family for years, and now we know why. My mother used to buy remedies from Demdike but I was having none of it. I leave the Lord to do his good work, I don't dice with the Devil.'

She licked her lips. Her daughter stared silently at my cloak, my face.

'Where are you from?'

'Burnley.'

'You've come a way to settle a bet.' She nodded in the direction behind her. 'Leave the road half a mile up and join the path up to the top of the moor. You'll find it up there. I don't like it myself; there's something not right about it. Like I say, my mother used to go up there when we were ailing; she took me a few times. I wouldn't take my own there if the Lord told me to himself.'

I thanked her and went the way she said, leaving the road for a narrow path between two dry-stone walls. A dog barked in the distance, and I thought of the one I'd seen in the forest with Elizabeth and Alice, and how Jennet had said hers had not yet appeared to her. Could there be truth in familiar spirits, and did Roger really believe in them? I leant backwards on my horse as the land rose up slightly with wide fields on either side. The brow of the hill came closer but there was no sign of the tower, and then I was at the top and looking down the other side, and there it was: a dull, grey, tall-ish building, like a short table leg. It was in the old style of towers, like the one built at Gawthorpe hundreds of years before. But the Devices were not a noble family or even yeomen – they were poor as church mice, so how they came to live in this place was a mystery.

As I came closer I saw great chunks of the building had fallen off and were scattered around the ground. I went to what seemed to be the entrance: a large, thick door at the bottom. Arrow slits in the walls would be the only source of light, and probably a hole in the roof for the smoke to get out.

I climbed off the horse and walked once around the base of the tower. An odd little garden had been attempted doubt Roger would pawn her off to a farm in need of labour, or a house not unlike ours for a brewing or laundry maid. And how would she live the rest of her life? Would she believe herself elevated by fortunate circumstance, or be racked with guilt until the end of her days?

By the time I reached where the path met the road, it was only mid-morning, and the sun was high but dim in the watery sky. I looked left towards Colne, and right to Gawthorpe. A moment later my mind was made up, and I clicked my mouth and squeezed with my heels to walk on.

CHAPTER 19

'You!' said Peter.

I stood once again before the counter on the straw-covered floor of the Queen's Arms.

'We never have ladies in here at all, now it's twice in one week.'

A few drinkers were straggled around the tables, porters finished their shifts or deliverymen breaking for the day, but they didn't take much notice and went back to their solitary tankards.

'I am looking for an address,' I said. 'You wrote a letter in March or April this year to a man named Abraham Law, a cloth dyer from Halifax.'

Peter eyed me warily, his rotund middle denting a little where it butted against the counter.

'I might have. What's it to you?'

I drew myself up to my full, insubstantial height.

'I need to speak with him.'

'What for?'

'I have a large quantity of cloth on order from Manchester and I would like a quote to have it dyed. Alice mentioned Mr Law, so I thought I might try him.'

Peter exhaled. 'Well, the Lord knows you gentry folk have needs the likes of us mere mortals can't fathom,' he said. 'I'll go and find it, give me a minute.'

I clasped my hands together and waited. Presently he was back with a single sheet of correspondence, which I all but snatched from his hand to read the address.

'Many thanks, Mr Ward,' I said. 'I shall write to him at some point.'

Five minutes later, with the sign of the raven, Haley Hill repeating in my mind, I was on my way to Halifax, having left Peter Ward with a palm of silver. I thought about all the coins I had pressed into hands recently and wondered how I would explain all my travelling to James. Then I remembered he would probably never question me on anything again – even looking at me sent the tips of his ears red. But I would take a much closer interest in the household management once all this was over – if I was here to. Soon there would be extra linen, towels, milk, caps and miniature gowns – not one set but two. It interested me to realise that thinking this didn't send me into a blind rage; it was a fact, and not even an important one at this moment in time.

I had to go fast, and by the time I reached the next county I felt as though I had been put in a pillowslip and shaken within an inch of my life, as the baby inside me squirmed and kicked. Briefly I wondered if this constant journeying was doing it harm. But while it was moving, it was living, so I pushed the thought from my mind, dismounted and paid the nearest boy to mind my horse and fetch it something to drink.

The timber house at the sign of the raven was crammed in by others on both sides and hung over the street on its highest floors, so you had to lean back to see it. Here, children ran barefoot up and down in the mud, and people walked with purpose in and out of the shops and houses.

I knocked on the door, my knuckles making a rhythm that sounded more confident than I felt. It opened into a dark hallway and a young girl appeared. She looked at me in surprise: I was wearing my travelling cloak and everything was covered, from my hat to my hem.

'I am looking for Abraham Law,' I said. 'Is he at home?'

'He is at work, Miss,' she said. 'I'm his daughter. Me mum's home if you want to see her?'

'Oh. I . . . Yes, I better had, then.'

She stepped back so I could enter, and I followed her into a warren-like low corridor with rooms leading off the left-hand side.

'Wait here, I'll fetch me mum,' she told me.

I stood, listening to the sounds of a busy household as well as the households on either side. To my great surprise, I heard someone cough on the other side of the wall. After a minute, a slender woman approached from the end of the corridor, wearing a corn-coloured gown and an apron that needed darning. She had a kind face and several strands of fair hair straggled out from beneath her cap. She was wiping her hands on a rag.

'Can I help?' she asked.

In that moment, seeing her distracted politeness, I was suddenly startled by the sheer weight of my own task, but also the indulgence of it. This woman would have no idea who I was, or why I was here, and the effort of explaining myself suddenly seemed exhausting. But she must have seen this, for she asked me to come in and have some beer, so wordlessly I followed her into a wide room that was dim despite the bright day. Heaps of things were piled on every available space, and several children and a dog occupied the floor space, moving constantly, so I had to step cautiously. There was a man in a chair looking out of the window: I could see the top of his balding head.

I unfastened my cloak and held it, unsure of where to set it down. The air in the little room was stifling. The woman returned with a cup of beer for me, and I drank it gratefully.

'I am Liz,' she said. 'You were looking for my husband?'

'Yes,' I managed. The beer was light and good. 'My name is Fleetwood Shuttleworth. Forgive me for trespassing like this . . . I hardly know where to start.'

'Please, sit down.'

She indicated a chair on one side of the empty hearth and I waded through the children to sit down. She took the other seat.

'I wanted to speak to Abraham about something that happened a few months ago in Colne.'

Liz Law's face instantly took on a different expression, one of tiredness and even pain.

'A matter involving your father-in-law? What happened to him set off a series of events that . . . I'm not sure if in Yorkshire you're aware of what is happening in Lancashire?'

She shook her head, and one of the children wailed for her attention. She spoke to him kindly but firmly and turned back to me. Of course she knew nothing: she was up to her eyes in running her household.

'What's happened is . . . My midwife is a woman called Alice Gray.' I swallowed and saw her eyes flick almost imperceptibly to my stomach, then back again. 'She has been caught up in accusations of witchcraft, as have many others. About twelve, at the last count.'

A small child was using Liz's skirt to pull itself up, and

began banging on her knee with a chubby fist. Was there no nurse or maid to take them off her hands for a single moment?

'Alice Gray worked at the Queen's Arms, which is where your father-in-law was taken after he was . . . After he met Alizon Device. She found him on the woolpack road and cared for him there, but the Device family began threatening her to change her story. Now they have dragged her into these horrid accusations, and there will be a trial in a few weeks at Lancaster.'

Liz was still listening but I could sense she was distracted. She removed the child from her skirts and tried to put its hands by its sides. The child began to cry.

'Sorry, I know you are very busy. I wondered first of all how your father-in-law is, and secondly if I could ask him some questions about what happened that day in Colne?'

She sat up straight and picked the child up on to her lap.

'You can ask him yourself, but you won't get much sense from him. Dad?'

She went over to the man I'd noticed before, positioned in the weak light from the window. I followed her, and my mouth fell open.

John Law was shrunken like an old apple, crumpled into his chair. One side of his face looked as though it had melted, with the eye closed, and the other roved wildly over me and Liz, as though he was frightened. I had the impression of a much larger, stronger man, who had lost a lot of weight quickly; his skin sagged, and I could have grabbed fistfuls of fabric from his clothes.

'Hello, Mr Law,' I said, failing to hide my shock.

He moved about, but the side closest to me remained limp and heavy.

'Whaaant,' he said loudly.

I looked at Liz.

'We understand him but no other folk do,' she said. 'Dad, this lady is here to see you. Do you know her?'

'Nnnnnnn,' he cried.

'No, he doesn't.' My voice faltered and I cleared my throat. 'Mr Law, my name is Fleetwood Shuttleworth. I am a friend of Miss Gray's, the woman who took you to the Queen's Arms after you were . . . After you were attacked.'

He gave some lamentable cry, and I had no idea if he understood.

'Alice Gray?' I tried, but he squirmed and his eye moved away to look out the window again.

'He's been like this ever since,' said Liz.

The infant in her arms was tugging bits of her hair from under her cap.

'I thought . . .' I swallowed. 'I thought he could speak.'

Liz shook her head. 'He could at first, but he's got worse as time's gone on. Some days he makes more sense than others but . . . Today isn't a good day. I can leave you with him, so you can try and talk to him – he might say something. I have things to get on with. Could you just hold this one for a moment while I clear this cloth?'

She handed me the small boy, smocked and sticky, and began lifting piles of cloth from every surface and taking them from the room. It was the first time I had ever held a child. He dangled like a sack of flour from my rigid arms, staring at me with astonishment, and I at him. In no time at all Liz Law was taking him back, before leaving the room yet again. I looked around. With most of the cloth moved, the surfaces were clean – the table was polished and free of crumbs, and I realised too that the children's faces weren't dirty like the others I'd seen in the street. The Law household was one of modest respect-ability, and the addition of Abraham's father was stretching them beyond their means. They might have left him in a bed all day, but he had been placed before a sunny window overlooking a yard, where women did laundry and more children and dogs ran about. I pulled my chair up to the old man and sat beside him.

'Plenty to see, isn't there?' I said. He made a noise of agreement. 'Mr Law, I do not mean to upset you or cause you further grief, so please forgive me for troubling you. But I was trying to find out what happened that day on the woolpack road in Colne, when you met Alizon Device.'

'Hmmmza-tch. Seeurst me nnnnn kamme.'

I watched him speak from one side of his mouth, trying to understand, but it was hopeless. His blue eye was fixed on me, willing me to comprehend. When I didn't, he dropped his gaze sadly and seemed to hunch even further. I covered his nerveless hand with mine. He looked at my rings, the gold and rubies and emeralds fastened around my fingers.

'Mr Law, do you know Alice Gray? Nod if you do.'

His chin went down into his neck, then up again.

'Do you think she is a witch?'

His face went off in the opposite direction, then back towards me, and again.

'Would you be prepared to say that at the assizes? Are you going to the trial?'

His head did not move; his eye roved wildly.

'Have you been invited to speak at the trial?'

He nodded, or what I understood to be a nod. If only he'd regained his speech, he could speak freely for the others' innocence.

'Do you think Alizon Device is a witch?'

He nodded, then shook his head. He looked greatly pained, and his searching blue eye filled with tears that spilt on to his face. His right hand moved as though to wipe them, but only got so far as his chest. I took a handkerchief from my pocket and did it for him. Poor John Law was a living puppet; he would be carried in as proof of what had happened, then carried out again, unable to use his own voice. Alizon Device could have walked away and none of this might have happened, had she not turned up day after day at the Queen's Arms and admitted her own guilt. No wonder her family wanted to change the story: it was *her* story. This man had none.

I sat a while longer with John and we watched the women outside, bending over tubs and brushing sweat from their foreheads. The sun was high, and their work was hot. They were not afraid of their skin browning; they had no choice. On a day like today I would be riding by the river under the cover of trees or even sitting by the window like an ornament, no more useful than John Law. An almighty crash sounded from another room, and Liz began scolding someone.

'Jennie!' I heard her shout.

One of the women in the yard looked towards the house, holding her hand over her eyes. It was the young girl who had answered the door, but really she was not much younger than me. I watched her walk back into the house, the smell of lye coming with her. I thought of her life here, with infants to play with and a mother whose lap she could rest her head on at night while her father read them a passage from the Bible.

There was banging at the door to the street, and shortly afterwards Jennie came through to tell me the boy I'd paid to mind my horse had to be getting home. I rose stiffly and thanked John Law, and went to thank Liz too, who was feeding a child with a spoon in the hallway, crouched on the floor.

'I'm sorry to have troubled you,' I said, having to step around her.

'Not at all. I hope you aren't too disappointed. John wishes he could talk, I know he does. We all do.'

'Will he or your husband be at the trial in a few weeks' time?'

She looked up distractedly.

'What trial?'

'The assizes at Lancaster, where the witches are on trial.'

'Oh, yes, Abraham did mention something about that. I will speak to him.'

'Good day to you, Mrs Law.'

I stepped out of the dark and dingy house into the bright street, where at least there was a breeze. Sweat ringed my armpits and sat above my lip. I was no closer to anything; I felt as though I was walking around the centre of it all in ever-widening circles, gaining nothing. And with little Jennet sitting high in her tower at Read Hall spinning stories, she was tying the family's nooses one by one. But she was a *child*.

I could not see a way out of it for Alice. John Law did not think she was a witch but could not clearly say it; her own father was indifferent to her fate; and her landlord cared only about his business. Who else was to speak for her, then? I thought hard all the way home, but I felt like I was staring at a wall.

By the time I arrived back in the stable yard at Gawthorpe, I was as exhausted as if I'd been carrying a sack of bricks. But there was an idea burning in my mind like a tiny ember. I just needed to give it enough space to catch alight.

CHAPTER 20

Richard was away again when I got home, gone to Preston, which I assumed meant Barton as it was the nearest town. He left no note, and I wondered if he was angry with me; then I remembered that I had every right to still be angry with him, but somehow anger was difficult to summon. At least while he was away I did not have to be discreet about my 'wild ways', as he called them. Before all this, he had indulged and even admired my lone wanderings, my propensity to leave the house tidy and arrive back muddy and wet. Could he not see that those pursuits were girlish, and now they had purpose? I went to the study and took ink, a quill and paper to my chamber.

The next morning, the sky was a bright blue and there

were no clouds. I collected the two letters from my desk and tucked them into my jacket. Overnight my fingers had swollen, and there was a funny feeling in my chest, as though inside it was being pulled taut like a sheet. I ignored the persistent thought that these could be the symptoms of the sun setting on my earthly life: that the next one was drawing ever closer. Perhaps death was right behind me, stepping with me, moving in my shadow, and at any moment it would gather me in its cloak. I summoned my nerve, glanced at Prudence and Justice, and went downstairs.

Katherine Nowell answered the door, her eyes wide with concern.

'Fleetwood? Back so soon? Do come in.'

I leant on the door frame with one hand; with the other I cradled my stomach.

'Katherine, please . . . I need help. My child . . . I am in pain. I need my midwife.'

'You are alone? Where is Richard? Fleetwood, you are full-bellied, you should not be riding now, surely.'

There was fear in her voice, and she helped me into the house. I gave another groan.

'Where is the pain?'

'It started yesterday. I tried to ignore it but . . . It's not time yet, Katherine, it's too early.'

'How badly does it hurt? Does it come in shocks?'

'No, it's constant.'

I let her guide me to the great hall, where she had been embroidering a cushion. There were pins and thimbles and lengths of thread strewn over the draw-leaf table, and I thought of Malkin Tower, and how all Alizon Device wanted was some pins. Katherine helped me into a chair.

'Should I call the physick? A doctor?'

'No. I need my midwife, Katherine. Ever since Alice was put in gaol I have got worse. I felt fine until she was arrested. Roger said he would try and get her out, but I need her now with me at Gawthorpe. I asked him if she could stay with us until the trial – I will not let her go anywhere, you have my word and Richard's. Please, ask Roger.'

This I said through laboured breaths, and Katherine handed me a cup of ale brought by a discreet servant. Compared to the life and chaos of the Law house, here it was as quiet and restrained as Gawthorpe. Roger's father frowned sternly down at me from his portrait.

'Roger is away – I forget where. Oh, Fleetwood, I am so worried. Tell me, what can I do?'

'I need Alice,' I said weakly. 'I need to get her out of gaol. Only she can cure me; she knows the herbs, and the right tinctures.'

'Perhaps the apothecary could help in the meantime? I will have our man ride out for him.'

'No. I need Alice. Only she can help me. Only Alice.

There is no time to write to Roger, or to the castle – I must go myself so she can help me.'

'No, you should go home – but not until you have rested here. I will make up a room for you and I will tell Roger when he gets home that Alice should be released for your health.'

I thought of being shut up in one of Roger's chambers. It would be little better than the gaol at Lancaster: he might lock me in and throw away the key.

'Katherine, do you think you can persuade him to let her out?' I asked feebly.

Her eyes were wide with compassion, her lined face grave. She cast around helplessly for some words of comfort.

'I had an excellent midwife from Liverpool, but this was many years ago, I would not know how to reach her . . .'

'No, it has to be Alice.'

She wrung her hands together.

'Fleetwood, I . . . She is a prisoner of His Majesty, I don't see how . . .'

'Just until the trial,' I said hurriedly. 'I am worried my life is in danger.'

For the first time there was fear in my voice, because for once I was telling the truth.

'But the woman is on trial for witchcraft. The penalty for that is death; she will not be allowed to roam free before the trial. She will disappear!'

I knew suddenly that we were being watched, and not by one of the painted faces around the hall. I looked towards the doorway and saw a pair of wide pale eyes staring back. Jennet Device did not look away, and her gaze was full of judgement beyond her years. I knew it was ridiculous to be frightened by a child, but there was something very strange about her. After all, she had stolen my necklace, and how without being noticed? I would not have wanted her staying in my house, gliding soundlessly over the floorboards, appearing in doorways like a ghost.

'Katherine, might you have your man check on my horse? I quite abandoned him on the doorstep in my haste to reach you; I hope he has not wandered off.'

Katherine leapt up, hurrying from the room in her effort to help. With her gone, Jennet slipped inside and went over to the fireplace, kneeling in front of one of the stiff-backed oak chairs. She appeared to be carrying some scraps of cloth, and began arranging them on the seat. Unable to disguise my curiosity, I stood and went towards her.

'What are those, Jennet?'

I noticed they were knotted in such a way they resembled human bodies – a large knot at the top for a head, with more knots and lengths between to represent arms and legs. I had seen these poppets before in church, stuffed into the fists of infants to hush their crying. Having seen her house, I felt certain Jennet was not a child who had grown up with toys.

'Who gave you those?' I asked. 'Was it Roger?'

'I made 'em,' she rasped in her scratchy little voice.

'And you've stuffed them too, how clever. What with?'

'Mutton's wool.'

I felt certain she had only brought them in here to show them to me, like a cat bringing a mouse to its master. I looked at her thin, shapeless dress; unhappiness and neglect in every line of her. Because of this child, my friend was rotting in a place that light never reached, and was facing her death at the rope. Because of this child, so many others were in there with her. I wanted to grab her bony shoulders and shake her so hard her teeth rattled and her eyes rolled. I wanted to scream at her to take back every word, every lie she had told with her sharp little tongue. I could barely look at her. I went back to the chair.

Jennet was whispering something, and the sound of it made the hairs on the back of my neck bristle.

'What are you saying?' I demanded, so sharply she turned in surprise and regarded me with those wide, contemptuous eyes.

'A prayer to get drink,' she replied, the picture of innocence.

'What do you mean by that?'

'*Crucifixus hoc signum vitam Eternam. Amen.*'

I stared at her, piecing the vocabulary together. My Latin was poor because I had no attention for reading. Something about a cross, and eternal life? I wondered where she had learnt it, because the words were pure popery. Had she said them in front of Roger? And if so, were the Devices in gaol only because they were Catholic? But it made no sense – half the families in Pendle were. Roger knew that, and as long as they presented themselves at church each week and kept their eyes to the ground, he gave them no trouble.

Jennet came towards me and took the empty pewter cup at my elbow. She held it to the imagined lips of her poppets so they could drink.

'Where did you learn that, Jennet?'

'My grandmother,' she lisped.

'You say that and she brings you a drink?'

'No,' she said flatly. 'Drink is brought.'

'In what sense?'

'In a very strange manner.'

Everything she said was so peculiar. Had I been this precocious as a child? Almost certainly not. But something about the way she had corrected me made a distant memory stir, and then it came to me. Dead rabbits; Alice crouching over them.

I did not kill them. They were killed.

What was the reason for their careful distinction? Perhaps a different approach was needed with Jennet. As Richard had said about his birds, loyalty was earned, not demanded. I remembered too Roger's threat: that Jennet might be encouraged to 'remember' others present at her home. The idea was too grave to consider.

'Jennet?' I glanced at the doorway. 'I think you may know my friend. Alice Gray?'

She stayed hunched over her poppets. Her lank, colourless hair spilt down her back from beneath her cap. She did not reply, and neatened her cloth figures, brushing imaginary dust off them.

'Do you know her, Jennet?'

She lifted her shoulders: an acquiesce.

'You do know her?' I leant forwards. 'Do you think you might have got it wrong about her being at your house that day, at Malkin Tower?'

'James stole a sheep for us to eat,' she said, pointing at one of her toys. They leant drunkenly on one another. She pointed at another. 'Mother told him to.'

I licked my lips.

'Do you remember Alice being at your house? Is she a friend of your mother's, or had you not seen her before?'

At that moment I heard feet on the flags, and Katherine appeared bearing a tray.

'More ale. Are you recovered, Fleetwood?'

I sat back, disappointed, and eyed the child in front of me. Jennet was smiling, and when I realised what about, a chill saturated me, creeping over my flesh.

'Drink is brought,' she said happily, and turned back to her toys.

'Jennet, will you leave us?' Katherine asked in a strained voice.

The child gave her a look, and swept up her toys in an

armful, sending the pewter cup clattering to the floor. She did not pick it up, and glided silently from the room. Katherine sighed deeply, and I noticed properly the lines around her mouth, the dull exhaustion in her eyes.

'How much longer will she stay with you?' I asked gently.

Katherine shook her head.

'Roger cannot tell.'

'Surely it is his decision?'

'While she is here she is . . . useful to him. So I suppose when she stops being useful.'

Her bluntness took me aback. Katherine sat back and sighed, reaching for her cup and drinking thirstily.

When she had finished she wiped her mouth and said, 'I cannot tell you how glad I will be when the assizes leave and all this will be over.'

'But how can you wish haste on the sacrifice of innocent lives?'

'Innocent?' Katherine was bewildered. 'Fleetwood, neither you nor I can make judgement on that.'

'Do we not have eyes and ears like our husbands, and the men who will condemn them?'

'You speak as though you know the outcome already.'

'But I do, everyone does! In history when have witches ever been treated with leniency? Katherine, we *must* do something.'

Katherine gave a pleasant little chuckle that made me want to slap her.

'Fleetwood, your head is full of fancies. You speak as if we are in a play, all with a part to act. You and I have no role in the king's justice; we support our husbands.'

'We cannot stand by and let this happen!' I cried. 'We must do something!'

'Fleetwood, please,' Katherine coaxed. 'You will exert yourself and cause harm to yourself and your child. May I speak frankly with you?' It was unexpected, and all I could do was nod. 'Richard loves you very much. He is very fond of you. The pair of you are lucky to be companions in marriage, not like most of our kind.'

Briefly I wondered if she knew about Judith, or if Roger would have kept that from her, too.

'You must concentrate on raising a family, and being a wife. People talk, you see, Fleetwood. And I know we are out of the way here as gentry folk. We are far from large cities, we have a certain privacy in this corner of the land, but that does not mean we can behave without propriety.'

I shifted in my seat, the silence of the hall ringing in my ears. I waited for Katherine to wet her lips before going on.

'You are very young, and very earnest, and endearing. You are mistress of the finest house around. This child will make your life so full, and rich, and happy. You must take care to involve yourself in the right things, like the family and the home, and not be so upset by things that you have no agency over.'

I felt as though she had crushed me like a carriage

wheel. My words died in my throat, were lost in my sinking heart.

'I want to help my friend,' was all I could say without choking. 'Or she will die. And I will die with her.'

The realisation was lapping at my edges again – the knowledge that without Alice, I may as well have a rope tied too. She had promised to save me, and I had promised to save her, and the chances of those things happening were now so small they had almost vanished from significance. I realised I was thinking in days now. When I tried to picture what my child might look like, and me holding it in my arms, I could not. Neither could I picture my life in five, ten, twenty years' time. The date of the summer assizes loomed, and my life as I knew it was contained in these short weeks.

'There is nothing I can do, Fleetwood.' Katherine's voice was gentle. 'Roger will not release her. She is on trial for murder by witchcraft – a crime punishable by death.'

'Roger has it wrong. She has been cheated, by almost everyone in her life. I cannot let her down like the others. You must come with me to the castle, and plead for her release. You are Roger's wife – you must have some authority.'

I heard myself, and knew it was hopeless, and my shoulders sank in abject misery.

'You are distressed. You need to rest. Let me take you to one of our chambers.'

'No, thank you. I must go.'

'You cannot ride home, you are unwell.'

'I will go slowly.'

Katherine smiled. 'You are more like a man than a woman. I insist on having someone ride alongside you.'

I reached into my skirts for the letters I'd written by the light of my candle.

'I have a favour to ask of you, Katherine.'

'Oh, Fleetwood . . . What have I just said?'

'Please. I ask nothing of you but this.'

I pressed the papers into her hands. The sealing wax was like bloodstains.

'When is Roger next going to Lancaster?'

'In a day or two, perhaps. Are these for him?'

'No, and he cannot see them. I want you to go with him, the next time he goes. Say you wish for a change of scenery and want to visit the shops – I don't know. But go, and when you are there, you must find a way to visit the castle, alone. They know who I am; Roger will have warned them, which is why I can't do it. You must give these to the coroner Thomas Covell's clerk at the castle. Don't give them to anyone else – put them into his hands, and tell him to send them *with urgency* to their intended. If the clerk asks questions, use Richard's name, and say they are from him.'

Katherine's eyebrows were knitted with anxiety.

'I don't understand.'

'Please, Katherine. I would not ask if it was not a matter of life or death.'

'And there is nothing deceitful in this? Nothing that

slanders my husband's name? Why can he not know about it?'

'He just can't. If you do not wish to have my blood on your hands when I die in childbed, then you will do this for me.'

We stared at one another, and there was a flicker of something like defiance in Katherine, but not towards me – I could see her tasting it, examining how it sat on her.

'I will do it,' she said, nodding.

I could have kissed her, and almost did, but settled for taking her hands in mine and squeezing them. She tucked the letters into her skirts.

'A thousand times thank you,' I said.

'Roger will be back from Yorkshire tomorrow, I think, unless the execution is delayed.'

'Execution?'

'You have not heard? They found the woman Jennet Preston guilty of the murder of Thomas Lister's father. She hangs today.'

Over the next days, I occupied my old role as the ghost of Gawthorpe, waiting at various windows for Richard. When I saw him approaching from the stables, I watched for a moment his easy swagger, the lightness of him after his trip to Preston. How untouchable he was, how easily he glided through life. I went to let him in. He seemed surprised to see me opening the door, then read something in my face, because he stopped.

'What is it?'

'Come inside.'

His face turned ashen.

'You are not . . . You have not . . .'

'No, nothing like that, the baby is safe.'

Relief swept through him and he mounted the steps, removing his gloves while I helped with his cloak. I led him through the house to the parlour and closed the door. Puck was dozing lazily beneath the window, and forced himself up to greet Richard, licking his hands with his large tongue.

'Do you remember the other day when Roger came to dinner and told us about His Majesty's justices at the assizes – Altham and Bromley?'

'Yes,' was his weary reply.

'I have invited them to dine at Gawthorpe.'

There was a pause, in which Puck wandered back to his warm spot. The baby adjusted its position in my belly, and I rested a hand on it.

'You invited them to dine here. At this house.' I nodded. Richard stared. 'For what purpose?'

'For the purpose of illuminating the plight of the Pendle witches.'

Richard did not blink. His voice was calm.

'You are making things very difficult for yourself, Fleetwood. For both of us.'

'This is not about me, or us. This is about Alice and how she did *not* murder a child.'

'That is for the jury to decide, not you, or Roger.'

'Roger has already decided for everyone!' I cried. 'He has already decided!'

'Lower your voice!'

Richard began pacing, his fury a clear, high note in the room. Pockets of red bloomed on my cheeks and I felt hot rage fizz in my head. I felt for my chair, sitting back down slowly. Puck whined and whimpered next to me, trying to reach my hands. I rested a trembling palm on his head and covered my face with the other.

'When are they coming?'

'When they pass through Lancaster next week.'

'And Roger knows about this?'

'No.'

He gripped the back of the chair and shook his head.

'You are making a mockery of the Shuttleworth name. For far too long I have let you run around like an infant, and now this.'

'*I* make a mockery of our family? *You* are the one with two families!'

'Damn you to Hell, Fleetwood, I thought we were finished with that. Plenty of men have mistresses; it is not uncommon.'

'We are common, then, are we? And it is not the sort of thing that can be finished. I am trying to help an innocent woman – what is so wrong with that?'

Richard began pacing through the dust motes illuminated in a shaft of daylight, stepping into the beam then out again; lightness then darkness.

'Why must you constantly undermine your own husband? Do you know how you make me look? And over a low-born local girl you barely know. Is she worthy of your attention? You have known her mere months. Why must you make such a spectacle of yourself, of us, for a woman who gave you some herbs?'

'If you do not understand this now then you never will: *Alice is innocent*. And nobody believes it but me! Nobody wants to help! I *need* you, Richard. Who will you choose – your wife or your friend?'

'Roger was your friend too!'

'I cannot be friends with that man after what he has done, and you shouldn't either.'

'How can you say that? Roger is the closest thing to a father I have. He has looked out for us; he has helped us through so much. He thinks I have what it takes to be sheriff; he sees me in Parliament one day. He *believes* in me, Fleetwood, like no one else ever has.'

'You should see the gaol he has them in, then you would not think so highly of him. It is a corner from Hell – dark and damp, and they are locked in there with no light, sleeping in vomit and waste, and there are rats and Lord only knows what else. One of them died in there! Where is your heart? Do you have a hole in your chest where it was? Where is the man I married?'

What Richard said next made my blood run cold.

'Your lying-in starts now. You will not be seen out of your chamber. You will stay there until our son arrives. It is mindless and foolish of you to go galloping around, making a nuisance of yourself and putting yourself in harm's way. You are not thinking of our child, you are thinking only of yourself.'

'So you will punish me for trying to save my friend's life? You were more grieved for your bird than the fate of an innocent woman. And you would prefer me dead anyway, would you not? Your life would be easier without me here, your friendship with Roger intact. You could marry Judith and forget I ever existed.'

Puck whimpered and I stroked him absently. Richard's face was filled with a private sort of agony. Before he could reply, I left the room, shutting the door behind me so he would not hear me cry.

CHAPTER 21

The day of the dinner arrived, and the house hummed with purpose, but I did not. I'd followed Richard's wishes and stayed in bed, though my heart raced even when I was lying down. The thin sheet of pain was still wrapped around my chest, fine but tight, and my neck pulsed.

I had a new nightmare. In it, I was in the witches' dungeon. Even when I opened my eyes it was blacker than black, darker even than when they were shut. There was the sound of dripping water, and someone was sobbing quietly in the corner. I did not move, because the floor was wet, covered with what felt like straw, crunching gently. Just as I thought I would die from fright, close to me, very nearby, there was the sound of something eating. Not a person – something bigger, like a dog or some other creature. I listened as teeth ripped easily through flesh, the beast savouring every mouthful. That sound sent my stomach churning, my skin crawling, and I woke up drenched with sweat and fear, my heart battering my ribcage.

I had no reply from the Lords Bromley and Altham, though I was not expecting one. In my confinement I had not been able to ask Katherine whether or not she had carried out my request. By the time the morning arrived, my nerves were jangling like a bunch of keys. I sat in my chamber and imagined what was happening two and three floors below: the kitchen servants would be plucking, chopping, peeling and braising; James would be selecting wines from the cellar; glasses and cutlery would be polished, knives sharpened. If they didn't come, it would be a splendid feast for two.

There was no sign of Richard: he was not speaking to me. I climbed out of bed and went to the looking glass, deciding to tackle my hair that hadn't been combed in a week. My arms ached, and I felt as though I hadn't slept in days, when really it was all I'd done. I cleaned my teeth and went to my dressing room, where I no longer took enjoyment. My sketchbook gathered dust in the corner.

Once I'd dressed in pale gold taffeta, the idea of going downstairs after so many days in my chamber felt strange – I had grown used to the size of it. Just before midday, there was a knock at my door. Richard put his head in, his face tight.

'Are you coming?' he said.

I stood up. 'Are they downstairs?'

'No, but the mistress who invited them should be.'

The great hall was laid out for a feast, glinting with silver and glass and fresh linen napkins. Bowls of fruit brimmed with strawberries, plums, apples, pears and peaches. A very low fire crackled to take the slight chill out of the large room, and the sky blazed blue at every window. Richard and I stood in unhappy silence looking at it all, and then James appeared in the far right doorway.

'Master, your first guest has arrived.'

Roger stepped into the great hall.

Richard moved forwards to greet him.

'Hello, Fleetwood,' he said after shaking Richard's hand. His expression was mild. 'Are you much recovered?'

I glanced at my husband, who had betrayed me yet again, choosing his friend over me, but he kept his eyes on Roger.

'A great deal improved, thank you,' I eventually managed to say.

'You have Katherine to thank for that.'

He smiled placidly. Richard went to fetch him a glass of wine.

'His Majesty's justices are not arrived?' Roger asked.

'Not yet. What time did you tell them dinner would be served, Fleetwood?'

'Noon, I think.'

'It is unfortunate today is a fish day,' Roger said to Richard. 'That was a fine fellow you killed on Thursday.'

'That was thirsty work. I think I shall wait for the weather to break before going out for that long again. The heat makes the horses grow stupid.'

'Your skill surpasses stupid horses. You would hunt well on a mule.'

Richard laughed and clinked his glass with Roger's. He had not handed me one, so I moved towards Jacob, our red-cheeked, bright-eyed young server, who had noticed Richard's slight and was flushed with embarrassment. I took a glass.

We made an odd triangle as the two men stood close to one another and I away from them, breathing deeply to calm myself. James appeared again through the low doorway.

'Sir Edward Bromley and Sir James Altham.'

He gave a little bow and retreated, and as though appearing on either side of a stage, both doorways into the great hall were filled.

On the left, Edward Bromley stood poised, a thumb hooked behind the velvet sash that cut through his middle. His doublet was very finely embroidered, with slashes through his sleeves, and his fan collar was tied beneath his chin with a green ribbon. A wide black hat completed the ensemble, and beneath it his eyes twinkled merrily. He was past middle age – at least forty – but handsome with it.

Standing ten feet from him in the other doorway was James Altham. Perhaps ten years older than Bromley, he was taller and slimmer, enhanced by a voluminous sleeveless gown thrown over one shoulder. His jacket was a pretty cream silk, cut close to his body with wide cuffs. His breeches were black velvet with gold stitching to match his jacket, and rosettes were tied around each of his slender knees. He was hatless, and had grey hair and serious dark eyes in a lined face.

As though hearing some silent cue, they both stepped forwards. Richard went to Sir Edward first, so I hurried to the older Sir James at the same time, as was proper with guests of equal rank.

'My Lord, thank you for coming to Gawthorpe,' I said. 'I trust you had a pleasant journey?'

'Mistress Shuttleworth, thank you for inviting us. It was very generous of you to entertain us while we are in the north.'

His dark eyes fixed on mine as he kissed my hand.

The steward's voice interrupted, surprising me.

'Mr Thomas Potts,' he announced.

I looked towards the door, my hand still caught in Sir James', and saw a tall, slim young man standing in the entrance.

'Mistress Shuttleworth, I hope you do not mind my taking the liberty of inviting our constant companion during our tour? Mr Potts is the clerk of the assizes.'

The young man directed an elegant bow in my direction.

'Of course, welcome, Mr Potts,' I said.

The clerk moved inside and looked around the room, appraising the coats of arms on the wall and the minstrels' gallery at the ceiling. He might have been younger than Richard, perhaps twenty-one or twenty-two.

'Gentlemen.' It was Roger's turn to greet our acquaint-ances, and he slid smoothly over to shake their hands. 'It has been an age since we were last in each other's company. When was it . . . Tuesday?'

They all laughed heartily and the three arrivals were handed wine.

'Mr Potts, you are travelling with the assizes?' I asked the youth.

'Yes,' he replied in a gentle voice. Was there a hint of Scot about him? 'We have just left York, and begin the Westmoreland assizes the day after tomorrow.'

'Ah, my mother lives in Westmoreland, outside Kirkby Lonsdale,' I said.

He nodded politely.

'Tell me.' I lowered my voice, but the other men had moved towards the table and were talking loudly. 'If you were at York, then you must have been present at the trial of Jennet Preston.'

'Indeed,' he said pleasantly, as if we were talking about a shipping merchant we had in common. 'Are you an acquaintance of Thomas Lister of Westby?'

'Yes.'

I trailed off, expecting something else would come to me, but it did not.

His dark eyes darted around the hall.

'This is a very modern house.'

'Thank you,' I replied, knowing it was not a compliment.

'How do you like living in the north?'

'I have never really lived anywhere else.' We walked towards the table, where a sixth setting had been discreetly made. 'Is this your first tour?'

'Yes, and very interesting it has been, too. I must say I find the people in the north very . . . *different*. Everything is different: the food, the humour, the towns. I am craving London already.'

He smiled with sharp teeth like little pins. I smiled and took my seat, further back than everyone else because of the size of my stomach. Roger was introduced to the young clerk.

'Pleasure to make your acquaintance,' said Mr Potts, dropping the handshake to reposition his glass of wine.

Roger's eyes flicked towards mine then away.

The first course was brought: salmon poached in beer, with pickled herrings. My own glass of wine had helped me overcome the shock of Roger's arrival, and I turned to the two justices.

'How does your tour fare so far?'

'Very well, Mistress,' said the genial Sir Edward. His

moustache framed his rosy cheeks, plump as apples. 'We are over halfway through, with Kendal next and Lancaster after that, as you know.' I coloured slightly, hoping desperately that he would not mention in front of Roger the request I'd made in my letter, but he stopped there. 'So far we have completed Durham, Newcastle and York, and Carlisle is after Lancaster. And then we are on the long road home to the south.'

'Tell me,' I said. 'You must have seen all sorts of fascinating arraignments in your work. For how long have you been justices on the northern circuit?'

'Two years,' replied Sir Edward.

'And I just under ten,' said Sir James.

'And this is my first time on the circuit,' announced their clerk importantly.

The men's eyes fell to their food and we began to eat. I could feel Roger's intense presence from across the table.

'I recently heard the news . . .' I tried to keep my voice steady, 'that you found a woman guilty of witchcraft at York?'

'Indeed,' said the older justice. 'That was an interesting one, because the woman was also at the Lent assizes accused of the same thing, not four months before.'

'Again by Thomas Lister,' I said.

The table fell silent. A piece of herring trembled before Sir James' lips, having failed to reach its destination.

'Quite right,' he said. 'You must take an interest in the laws of the realm.'

'But this time she was found guilty.'

'The woman was found to be guilty of the felony of murder by witchcraft of Thomas Lister Senior, yes.'

James Altham's voice was quiet, almost soft. No doubt he saved its full impact for the courts.

I nodded and dislodged a salmon bone from the back of my mouth, trying not to gag.

'Sir Edward, however, did obviously pardon her at Lent, so her life was graciously extended by some months.' He spoke to his colleague. 'I wonder if you had an idea then of how very *disparaging* her supporters were, and that was how you reached your verdict.'

Sir Edward's eyes twinkled.

'I knew nothing of the sort. They're a loud bunch, the Prestons,' he explained to the rest of the table. 'Poor Altham here has been vilified at every town from York to Gisburn. And that's quite a few.'

I tried to imagine people crowding the streets in Padiham and Colne to protest against the arrest of the Pendle witches, and could not imagine so much as a single raised fist.

'And have you tried a person for witchcraft before this year?' I asked.

The pair looked at one another, considering for a moment.

'Never,' said Sir Edward in a tone of surprise. 'In fact, this is the largest group of people to be tried for witchcraft in this country.'

'Ever?'

He nodded. I could not help but glance at Roger, who had been waiting for his turn to speak.

'They have successfully hidden themselves all over the country, until now,' he announced. 'It's like catching mice: when you find one, you know there's a nest. The king has long suspected Lancashire to be the hiding place of delinquents and sorcerers, so I am only happy to help root out the evil before it spreads and infects the rest of his kingdom, delivering it into your capable hands.'

'Would that imply you think evil is like a plague?' asked Sir Edward.

'In certain neighbourhoods. Look at the Devices and Redfernes: they live not a hundred yards away from each other. Whether one household began with witchcraft and the other took it up to protect themselves, or something else, it's no coincidence. But old Demdike has been practising for, oh, decades.'

I realised I was glaring at him and lowered my eyes. Thomas Potts spoke.

'Why do you think the old woman has avoided detection until now, if that is the case? Has no one accused her before this?'

'Not to my knowledge.'

Our plates were removed and the second course of oyster pies was brought. I had three more courses to persuade the justices to . . . What, exactly?

'Where are you staying tonight?' asked Richard.

'A modest inn not far from here.'

'Oh, but I insist you stay here.'

'We will not intrude. We leave very early in the morning.'

'Although a feather mattress would be quite welcome after so much straw,' said Thomas, leaning in conspiratorially. The men laughed. I cleared my throat.

'I suppose you were relieved to cross the border and escape Jennet Preston's supporters,' I said.

I could feel Richard's eyes on me, but did not look.

'Quite, yes.'

'And you have met no such protest on behalf of the so-called Pendle witches?'

'We have only just crossed into Lancashire,' said Sir Edward, spilling open his pie with his fork. 'We are not so familiar with those cases yet, with Westmoreland to come first. How many women are accused?'

'A dozen or so. But unfortunately one passed away,' said Roger, without a hint of regret. 'However, I am investigating another case of a woman at Padiham.'

'*Another* one?' I failed to control my voice.

'A woman named Margaret Pearson. My colleague Mr Bannister is taking evidence tomorrow from her servant, who swears that she has seen Mrs Pearson's familiar spirit.'

'What is it?'

'A toad.'

There was a pause, in which I'm sure a sound like suppressed laughter escaped from Thomas Potts. Roger ignored it.

'Mrs Booth, the servant, says she was carding wool at her employer Pearson's house and asked her for some milk. They added wood to the fire to warm the milk pan, and when Mrs Booth removed it, a toad – or a spirit disguised as a toad – came out of the fire. Margaret Pearson removed the creature with a pair of tongs and carried it outside.'

'I am curious to know,' I began mildly, 'if you have yet seen any of these familiar spirits yourself, Roger?'

There was an awkward silence, in which Roger chewed thoughtfully.

'The Devil appears only to those who crave his company,' he said eventually.

'Did you not say,' I went on before I could stop myself, 'that a familiar spirit is the surest sign of a witch? Does this mean if a witch does *not* have a familiar spirit, they are likely to be innocent?'

Roger regarded me through heavy-lidded eyes. He took a sip of his wine.

'Or they keep it well hidden.'

'Gentlemen,' I addressed the table, '*I* have a very large dog, who accompanies me everywhere. Should *I* not be accused of witchcraft?'

The table went silent, and my gaze landed on Roger, who watched me coolly.

'It sounds almost as though you are inviting accusation, Mistress. I would be very cautious, if I were you. You have your husband's reputation to consider. His name, Sir

Edward and Sir James have told me, has already been heard of at Whitehall for the right reasons, so let there not be a wrong one.'

The two men exchanged an uncomfortable glance.

'Is Padiham in the forest of Pendle too?' Sir Edward asked politely.

'The boundary is that river there.' Richard indicated with his knife. His tone was generous, but his mood unreadable. 'So you are safe in this house.'

'You cannot swear to that,' Roger said. He was looking directly at me. 'Seeing as one of them has been a guest here.'

Several powerful, intelligent gazes turned on me at once, and my voice died in my throat. Roger's presence commanded the table, and the men peeled their eyes from me to look at him in disbelief.

'One of the accused is a woman called Alice Gray, and she was Fleetwood's *midwife*.'

He said the word with the same incredulity as if she'd claimed she was a mermaid.

Sir James pulled a puzzled face.

'How very unusual.'

'Quite.'

Roger did not move his eyes from my face. In that moment, I despised not only him but Richard for inviting him, when he knew my mission. Things would have been entirely different with them both out of the way. I could have pleaded Alice's case and perhaps made some difference. But here we were, all together like one unhappy family. At that moment, the main course was brought out: a huge pike curled gracefully on a platter the size of a carriage wheel. Richard's eyes met mine, and there was danger in his look, but also something that looked like guilt. Perhaps he realised now the consequences of what he had done.

'Gentlemen, before we enjoy our next course, may I speak with my husband's permission?'

I glanced again at Richard, who gave a quick, solemn nod. Roger cleared his throat, but I went on.

'The woman who has been a guest here was my midwife, and friend, and her name is Alice Gray. She is arraigned at the Lancaster assizes, accused of murder by witchcraft.'

An attempt at a protest came from Roger, but I continued. My voice was high, and nervous, and I prayed it wouldn't falter.

'Alice was working for me for some months, and she is an exceptional midwife. She is highly skilled, and learnt her skill from her late mother.'

I swallowed and looked at each of them directly. They were all staring back at me, rapt. I knew I was standing on the edge of a cliff with one foot dangling over.

'Alice is very generous, and obedient, and kind. A long time ago she was . . . She . . .'

I faltered, then I felt the most curious thing: waves of encouragement radiating from somewhere close by, like heat from a fire. I breathed in and carried on.

'A long time ago she found herself in a terrible situation no woman should be unlucky enough to experience. She has few family and friends; her only friend is sitting with her in the dungeon at Lancaster. I hope that . . .' I blinked as tears came to my eyes. My throat was thick with emotion. 'I hope that you will not punish her for the tragedy she endured, because she has already suffered immeasurably.'

Roger cut me off, shooting up in his chair.

'I think we have heard quite enough. This is not a courtroom and the woman's own statement will be heard where and when it is appropriate.'

His face was puce, his eyes little beads of malevolence.

I nodded and turned again to the others.

'I invited these men to my home, and I hope they do not consider it impertinent of me to talk fondly of my midwife, who they will soon meet in different circumstances. Are you offended, gentlemen?'

They shook their heads, bewildered but polite. Silence covered the table like a dust sheet.

'Gentlemen, when we are finished eating I will show you around the house, if you would like to see it,' Richard said.

Everyone was glad of the change in atmosphere, and the mood lifted as Richard served the fish and told a brief history of his uncles. Only Roger and I sat like dark clouds, wondering which of us would burst first.

CHAPTER 22

One dreary, rainy afternoon a few days later, I was lying in my silent confinement when Richard knocked on the chamber door. He told me Lord Montague's players were in the area and would perform at the house that evening. Usually this would thrill both of us, but things were different now.

'Why in heavens would James agree for them to come at a time like this?' I asked, moving to sit upright.

Richard sighed. 'I asked him to invite them months ago. They only announced their arrival this morning.'

He left, and wearily I forced myself out of bed to get dressed.

I should have been surprised to see Roger sitting in the great hall a few hours later, his hands knitted together, resting on his large belly. But when I walked in, with Puck at my hand, my eyes were drawn not to Katherine, pale and drawn-looking on his left, but instead to the dark-haired woman sitting on his right. Her eyes were cast down into her lap, but her white collar lifted her features and pulled them from some distant corner of my mind. Behind the table, she had attempted to conceal her huge stomach beneath folds of brocade and taffeta. My head swam.

'Mistress,' Roger said pleasantly. 'May I introduce Judith, the daughter of my great friend Jeremiah Thorpe of Bradford; not to be confused with the Thorpes of Skipton, but perhaps a distant relative?'

There was a stunned silence, broken moments later by footsteps in the passage. Richard appeared in the other doorway. It took less than a second for him to take in the scene before him, and the colour drained from his face.

What little courage I had – the kernel of hope that had embedded inside me and had got me this far – vanished, like some minuscule object being pulled into a great, powerful river. I knew it the moment it went, and I knew too that it was gone for good.

'Roger,' Richard managed to say.

But he was not angry; he was as breathless and surprised as if his friend had stabbed him.

Then several things happened at once: Puck began barking, unsettled by the awful feeling in the room; James arrived in the doorway to announce the Lord's

Players, who could be heard assembling in the hall; Richard regained his colour and turned an unsightly beetroot purple; and Judith looked up. As I watched her, all the noise in the room and in my head quietened. Her heart-shaped face was the colour of cream, and her plump cheeks the delicate, warm orange of roses. Her liquid dark eyes gazed fearfully at Richard, but there was also guilt there, and respect, and I could not deny it: love.

The chaos of the room returned and I put my hand to Puck's head, which silenced him instantly. He whimpered once and stood still. James teetered in the doorway, his mouth a perfect hole of surprise.

Richard strode over to where Roger was sitting at the table, a thorn between two trembling roses.

'Roger, what do you mean by this?' he roared. 'What on *earth* possessed you to do this?'

Katherine looked tearful. She had lost more weight since the last time I saw her. With a distant pang of guilt, briefly I wondered what it had cost her to defy Roger for me. Judith looked terrified, her lovely features arranged in an expression of anguish.

'Answer me now before I get that sword down and run it right through you. Damn you, Roger, answer me!'

Roger's eyes travelled uneasily to the monstrous weapon that glittered above the fireplace.

'As you know, Richard, Judith is a friend of the family, and I invited her to stay at Read Hall for a spell. So when

Lord Montague's men announced their arrival in Pendle and enquired as to whether I would enjoy a private performance at Read, I found out they were also performing at Gawthorpe, so naturally I saw the opportunity to bring our families together for the . . . occasion.'

He spread his hands wide to encompass everyone in the room.

'Master?'

James tried timidly to thaw the frozen scene before him. The only person at ease was Roger, drumming his ringed fingers. Behind him, where the low voices of the players had buzzed a minute before, there was a hush as they awaited instruction.

Very slowly and stiffly, Richard turned to look at me. His face was a mask of grief. It probably mirrored mine.

'Fleetwood, will you join us?' he asked, his voice thick with emotion.

I blinked through tears at Judith, the woman with whom I shared a husband and now a home. She had returned her gaze to her hands, which were folded in her lap. I sniffed and nodded, taking a seat next to Richard.

While wine and sack were brought, six or seven men trooped into the gallery and took a bow.

'Good evening, ladies and gentlemen.' A young, handsome one in the middle spoke. He had a wide mouth and a clear, gentle voice. 'Mr and Mistress Shuttleworth: thank you for inviting us into your splendid home. Tonight's play is a national favourite from one of the greatest living playwrights, and it is certainly one of *our* favourites to perform. A tragedy of ambition, a maze of morals and with a touch of magick, cast your imaginations to deepest, darkest Scotland – which should be relatively easy in these climes.' He paused in anticipation of a titter of appreciation, which did not come. 'Ladies and gentlemen: William Shakespeare's *Macbeth*!'

With a flounce of his cloak, the assembled men left the gallery, save for three, who had pulled their cloaks up over their heads and sat hunched in a tight circle. I was vaguely aware of all this, but my mind was occupied by a dull kind of numbness. I had seen the play before.

> '*When shall we three meet again*
>   *in thunder, lightning or in rain?*
> *When the hurlyburly's done,*
>   *when the battle's lost and won.*
> *That will be ere the set of sun.*'

While the players chanted, from the corner of my eye I was aware of Judith, sitting still and upright, her face turned towards the players but perhaps looking about at the room too: at the china vases in the cabinets, the polished sconces on the walls, the portraits – all ordinary things, but no doubt of great interest to her eyes. She would be drinking in every detail of Richard's house to savour and think of later. Unless, of course, she had been here before.

Rain lashed at the windows; the players could barely be heard and were raising their voices, sounding slightly hysterical.

'I come, graymalkin! Anon! Fair is foul, and foul is fair: hover through the fog and filthy air.'

The rain kept coming, and Judith's presence too was loud as a bell. I could feel her casting glances at me, but I kept my eyes on the gallery. How lifeless we must all look, how dull and bored. The clock ticked loudly. I thought of the stairs down to the dungeon, and the door closed on the darkness. Tick, tick, tick.

When the battle's lost and won.

A servant taken ill. A rag poppet on a bed, tied with black hair to a child. A bowl of blood, vanished. A falcon ripped to death. A nightdress in the dark, floating palely, coming ever closer.

'Stop!' I shouted. 'Please, stop.'

Richard leapt up in alarm and clapped his hands.

'Gentlemen, my apologies, but my wife has been taken ill.'

I was vaguely aware of confusion, and the gathering up of things. I sat staring at my hands that were ice-cold and dead-looking. Soon I might actually be dead, and Alice too, but this room and these people would remain, and the year 1612 would become a distant memory. Wine would be poured for Richard and his new wife, and Roger and Katherine would play with their pink-cheeked child. I could feel the other child's presence in the room too, feet away from me, waiting to be born, waiting to claim its place, and Judith mine.

Even in life I had been the little ghost, and now I was consigned to death. I held my stomach, and imagined disappearing. It would come soon, no doubt, but it would not be gentle, like the light leaving the sky. It would be painful, and terrifying, and lonely, with no cool hand on my head, no amber eyes willing me calm. There would be a trial, and Alice would die, then I would die, both of us killed in an outbreak of misfortune. I closed my eyes, and thought of my child, of how much I wanted us both to live. My earthly life was coming to an end, and the end was nigh.

CHAPTER 23

It was the day before the assizes opened, and almost every man and woman in the county and those surrounding it had come to see the fates of the Pendle witches unfold. The streets of Lancaster were thronged with horses and carts and people and dogs and cows and chickens and children and all kinds of obstacles that led our carter to curse audibly and repeatedly behind Richard and me as he navigated the trap carrying our luggage and a travel-weary Puck. I kept my eyes down as we crossed the cobbles on our horses to join the throng moving up the hill, feeling my skin prickle with stares. I wanted to disappear, but with the size of my stomach I was as conspicuous as if I'd grown a beard. The narrow streets were a mass of brown clothes, white caps, black hats and unwashed skin. I watched a little boy of one or two stumble into the road in front of me and be wrenched back by his mother before my horse's plate-sized hooves claimed him. She caught my eye, and I think she was surprised at how indifferent I seemed, how un-motherly.

Richard and I had travelled all the way in a numb sort of silence, with Puck padding at our sides or trundling behind us on the cart, whining occasionally. It was a welcome relief when the noise and distraction of Lancaster arrived.

By mid-afternoon we were pulling into the yard of the Red Lion, a modest inn shielded by trees, tucked away down a narrow road leading to the river. I barely noticed the room we were shown to on the third floor, but it was clean and well furnished, with carpets on the cupboards and a handsome four-poster bed. When my trunk was set down with a thud, I jumped, and the porter looked at me with curiosity. The baby bucked and rolled inside me, invigorated by the long and bumpy journey. I was so big now my skirts hung inches away from my legs.

Bread and milk was brought for the dog, which he ate gratefully before settling on the Turkey carpet in front of the fireplace. I could not rest so easily: I was cold and shivering, and lay on the bed on my side, drawing my knees up to meet my stomach.

Richard stood at the window, his hands clasped behind his back. Since the dreadful dinner a week before, I had barely spoken. I had barely eaten or slept either. I drifted up and down the long gallery, my legs planted wide on the polished wood to balance my massive stomach. Or I sat at various windows, facing out, and the baby moved for both of us. I could tell Richard was still anxious I would lose it, and I felt like telling him there was no need to be so worried about things that were out of our control, when there was so much that we could have done, and had not. The appeals we should have made; the help we should have offered. I dared not think it was too late, but part of me knew it was: for me, for her, for everything.

'How do you think it will go?' Richard spoke.

I stared at the wall.

'They cannot be found guilty,' I replied. 'Their only witnesses are each other. They are like children telling tales.'

'People are hanged for a lot less. Do you really think they know the Devil?'

I thought of Malkin Tower poking up from the moor-side like a finger from a grave. How the wind had howled there; how it would drive you mad. I thought of Alice's home, open to the sky; the damp streaming down the walls; the child she knew as a daughter buried in the thick, wet soil. What was there for them in this life? In the shadows cast by their fire at night, perhaps they did see things they wanted to.

'If the Devil is poverty, and hunger, and grief, then yes, I think they know the Devil.'

Richard went to the castle to find out when the witches'

trial would start. For the rest of the day I lay fully dressed on the bed, staring out of the window at the trees, with Puck lying next to me, thumping his tail happily at being allowed on the counterpane. Even with the glass separating me from the street, I was aware of a strange quality to the air outside. I realised it was excitement. The trees shivered with it, and it bounced off the walls and flags of the yard like rain. More carriages were arriving at the inn now, and the yard was full of people with brightly expectant faces talking to one another. Women carrying babes jiggled them patiently; men stood astride the cobbles with a sense of purpose. I knew that if I could listen I would hear a hundred different opinions, all of them certain. Neighbours denouncing neighbours – it was the most reliable trait of humanity, and was how the dungeon was filled in the first place. Rumour spread faster than disease, and could be just as destructive.

A maid brought a tray of food and set it on the cupboard, bowing clumsily, flinching when she saw the dog. I didn't look at the tray, let alone touch it. I felt for the paper in my pocket I had put there the night before – my statement defending Alice's innocence that I hoped to read aloud before the judges. A more eloquent version of my speech at the dining table, I had written it at least five times, the paper blotting with ink and tears. If they would not let me speak, I would try to have Richard stand for me. He did not know this yet, because I could not face him refusing me this one kindness, though I would never ask anything of him again. I did not know if they would let me read it at the assizes, did not know of any time when a woman had been allowed to stand up and speak when she was not in the dock. The idea of doing it sent my legs to melting, but then I thought of Alice's face, blinking in the light after being kept in the dark. She had to be at the trial, yet I had a choice. Roger had said no witnesses would be brought, but Bromley and Altham could surely not ignore the polite request of a member of the gentry, when they had dined at his house? I would leave it until the last moment to ask Richard's permission to speak, because I was not convinced myself that my words would be enough, and until I was, I could not persuade him with conviction.

As more people arrived at the inn, the passages filled up with voices and the sound of boots on stone. I listened vacantly over Puck's snores as women chatted and scolded their children, men bellowed, trunks scraped and dogs barked.

I was clutching the paper so tightly I thought it might tear, thinking of how, not so long ago, I'd held a different letter – one that gave death, while this one could give life. A noise in the passage: much closer. A man's voice drawing near; a door opening and closing.

Suddenly I was wide awake. I pushed myself up on my elbows, bringing my head in line with the top of my stomach. The child must have been sleeping, for once. I went to the window and looked at the sky; I did not have a watch. Where was Richard? It would soon be dark, and from below came the sound of the kitchen getting the supper things ready. Barrels rolled in the yard and the traffic in the streets had eased. I had what felt like a hair's breadth of time to make a decision: it had to be now. I did not need more than that.

I woke Puck from where he lay next to me and beckoned him to the floor, before going to one of the trunks. Thanking Prudence for blessing me with her gift earlier, I pulled out the long, wrapped package I had buried among several nightdresses. Then I went to the cupboard and scrawled a note for Richard, finally casting a swift look around the room, making sure I had got what I needed. With my dog at my heel, I left for the stables, the package slim and inconspicuous at my side.

CHAPTER 24

J ohn Foulds' house was down a dank little alley in
Colne. By the time I arrived it was almost midnight,
and I was breathless from navigating the horse along the
black paths. But the moon was on my side: full and bright,
it had shone all the way from Lancaster, lighting the way
for our ghostly procession. And I had Puck with me, so I
felt safe, and I held his head with one hand and knocked
on John Foulds' front door with the other.

The street was silent and there were no lights in the
windows. I'd knocked on four doors where I saw the
yellow glow of rushlight, and the last occupant – a woman,
her face creased with tiredness – told me in surprise that
John Foulds lived one row behind the market street, three
doors from the right.

Here, I knocked again, and Puck gave a low growl from deep inside his throat. I looked around, and could see no figure at either end of the passage, but did have the sense of being watched. It was too dark to see into the shadows pushing up against the houses. I shivered and set my eyes on the wooden door in front of me, knocking more impatiently this time. Then, suddenly, all the hairs on my neck stood up, and I knew there was someone in the alley. Puck immediately began barking, straining from my grip and directing his aggression to our right, and in the gloom I saw something low and rangy slink around the last house. I banged furiously on the door, and a man's voice shouted from behind it, and then I was looking into the face of John Foulds.

Tousled dark brown hair hung down either side of his face, and he was dressed for bed, wearing a loose cotton smock, untied at the neck. He was as handsome as I'd remembered, but there was something in his eyes that was not – a coldness, perhaps, that impacted on his features, like an imperfection in a portrait. Whatever arrogance he had, though, died when he saw what I held to his stomach: Richard's musket, which I'd carried with one aching arm beneath my cloak. And then he saw the dog, and there was fright there, and even resignation.

He angled himself so that he was standing between the door and the wall, and I could not see into the small house. I pushed the barrel of the musket into his chest, and was thankful for how heavy it was, because I was shaking so badly.

'Will you let me in?' I said.

'Are we to fight a duel?' he said drily, his lip curled.

Puck growled, and he eyed the massive dog anxiously, then gave me a look and opened the door wider. I went in, Puck padding behind me.

The tiny house had one room downstairs and one up, accessed by a steep set of narrow stairs against the back wall. John Foulds held the only rushlight in the room, and from its glow I could see a few shapeless objects: a couple of chairs by the fireplace; a low cupboard covered with a cloth and pots and pans. John went to light another rush and set it in a holder on the cupboard, and the fatty fumes were choking. But I watched his every move, because I had no idea how to use Richard's gun.

'Who are you?' he asked, holding his torch up to my face.

'You don't know me,' I said. 'But we have a mutual friend.'

He made a noise like forced laughter.

'I wouldn't call him a friend.'

'Who?'

'Roger Nowell. Is that not who you are here for?'

'No.'

I stared at John Foulds' flickering face, half-hidden in shadow. He scratched his neck and glanced about fretfully. If he moved suddenly, could I move quicker?

'Did he give you money?' I asked.

'What if he did?'

I let the musket fall, heard the mechanisms clink inside. The weight of it was exhausting. Just as I'd reached Colne, it had started to rain very lightly, and now I could hear it coming down harder, thudding into the dirt in the street. John Foulds' eyes glittered in the candlelight.

'Why is Alice Gray on trial for murdering your daughter?'

'She's a witch,' he said simply.

His neck was warm and brown in the rushlight, the top of his chest smooth.

'She loved you,' I said, trying to stop my voice from shaking. 'And she loved Ann.'

'Who are you?'

'It matters not.'

'Who is your husband?'

'It matters not. But you will give me something tonight. I will not leave here without a written testimony from you that says Alice Gray did not murder your daughter.'

He looked at me as if I was crazed. Then he started to laugh. I smelt something else then, masked under the dripping grease of the rushlights. Ale. Fermentation. Decay. John Foulds was still a drunk.

'If Alice is hanged, it will not bring your daughter back. Why would you see an innocent woman killed?'

'Innocent? She's a bitch,' he spat. 'Anyway, I can't write.'

My heart sank. A signed testimony had been my only

hope – I'd brought paper and ink and a quill, and tucked it in the pack of the horse. How naïve I had been to assume he could read, or write, or even sign his name, when Alice could not. The musket was so heavy, it was making my arms hurt. But I could not turn my back on him.

John Foulds had checkmated me.

The stairs creaked, making me jump, and someone began walking down them. A long white smock descended from the ceiling, then the rest of a plump body, and a plain-faced woman in a cap appeared, her mouth a little round 'O' as she took in the scene before her. Her eyes widened when she saw Puck; he might have been a wolf in the dim light, and certainly looked monstrous in the little room.

'John?' she said.

'Go back to bed.'

'Who is this?'

'Now,' he barked.

The woman turned with difficulty on the dark, narrow staircase, holding the wall with one hand.

Before her head disappeared, I said, 'Wait.' She stopped. 'What kind of knife does John use to sharpen his quill?'

She gaped at me.

'An ordinary one, Miss.'

'Just as I thought. There is a horse tied outside. In its pack you will find a quill and paper and ink. Will you bring them to me?'

She looked quickly at John, and nodded, but did not move.

'Now,' I said, and she disappeared through the front door into the rain. 'You are literate, then,' I said to John. 'Your wife?'

He regarded me with vicious hatred.

'No.'

'How much money did Roger give you?'

'None of your business.'

'It is the business of the king's peace. How much?'

He moved his jaw; his eyelids lowered.

'What is of more use to you: money or ale? I have a brewery. If you do what I want, you will have a hogshead sent every month.' His eyes widened. He was listening now. 'I presume that's what you spend your money on. Unless you prefer brandy? Wine? What will it be?'

'How do I know you will keep your word?'

I loosened my grip on Puck's collar and he lurched forwards, snapping his mighty jaws. John Foulds leapt back and gave a cowardly whimper. What had Alice seen in this weak, selfish man?

The woman padded back inside and handed me the things I'd asked for, never moving her eyes from the dog. As soon as I took them she ran back upstairs.

'They say dogs can smell fear,' I told him. 'I would try to mask it, if I were you. But I know how hard it is when you're terrified. I am scared, John. I am scared that my friend will be hanged for a crime she did not commit. And not only her: *her* friend might be hanged, too, for trying to save your daughter's life.'

I looked around at the unhappy room, with its stench of fat and ale, and the chill that came from the bare walls, and shivered. It was no place for a child. Maybe it was cheerful once, when John's wife was alive and they had their new baby wrapped in fresh linen, with the front door open to the street so the neighbours could come in and tell them how blessed they were.

'And what if I don't?' He sniffed. 'You'll shoot me?'

'Yes. Unless you would prefer to be worried by the dog?'

His dark eyes went from one to the other. I handed him the paper and quill, and nodded. He sighed and carried it to the low cupboard, bending over to flatten it out in the pool of light.

'What do I write?'

'The truth.'

I stood shivering and waited as he scratched down his words in an untidy, barely legible scrawl. I listened to the horse exhaling outside and the rain on the street. My chest was tight with fear, and relief, and I thought of the long way I had to travel in the morning. I would ride back to Gawthorpe tonight and sleep for a few hours, then leave for Lancaster before dawn.

John Foulds handed me his testimony, and I read it through quickly.

'Add a line about Katherine Hewitt,' I said. 'She is arraigned for the same thing.'

He rolled his eyes. 'I am not writing a whole book.'

'You will do what it takes. Add a line.'

'There,' he said. 'Good enough?'

'I don't know,' I said, taking it from him and folding it into my pocket. 'You had better hope so.'

'Meaning?'

'If it isn't, I may pay you another visit, and don't expect me to be in a bargaining mood. The assizes start in the morning, should you wish to face what you have done like a man. Goodnight.'

I turned to leave. The rain teemed down outside.

'If that bitch hangs, I'll still get my ale, won't I?'

I stopped in the doorway and, without turning around, released my hand from Puck's collar. All John Foulds would have seen was a streak of copper and a flash of teeth as the dog threw himself at him and sunk his mouth into his arm. He cried out in high-pitched terror, then cursed, rolling about and gripping his elbow. Blood bloomed dark on the dirty white linen. I called Puck softly, and he came back to me. I turned to face the weak, trembling, cowardly man whom Alice once loved.

'Yes, you will still get the ale,' I said. 'Because if my dog doesn't kill you, that will. And the slower the better.'

An hour later, I realised I was lost. I meant to head west along the river to Gawthorpe, but the rain was coming down so hard and was so loud I couldn't hear the water, let alone see in the darkness. There were only trees, and mud, and clouds flitting across the moon, making it impossible.

I was soaked. The horse was soaked too and plodding ahead miserably, stopping now and again in protest. Puck trudged on next to us, exhausted as I was, his drenched coat a dark brown. My stomach felt heavier than ever, and my heart was racing despite the slow pace. I turned left and right and left again, hoping to find the wide roads that ran between villages. All I could think of was the two pages in my skirts: my testimony and John Foulds'. If they were wet, they were ruined. Something was lodged in my stomach, and I thought it might be despair, but I would not submit to it. I would not cry; I would find my way home, even if it took all night. I would go to Lancaster tomorrow and stand up in court and hear my own voice ring through the hall, pronouncing Alice's innocence, and everyone would listen, and her chains would clatter to the floor, and she would be free.

I was slumped forwards over my stomach, riding at a snail's pace through the woods, with tall black tree trunks surrounding me on all sides, and the rain seeping down my neck, and then The Nightmare began.

The horse stopped suddenly, as though startled, and that's when I heard the grunting. It was low, but distinguishable even over the rain. Cold fear drenched me from the head down, and I felt dizzy with it. I closed my eyes and opened them again in case I was dreaming, but that sound: I knew it, had heard it many times throughout my life, but always in my sleep. Now I was awake, and alone in the woods. Puck barked, and there was a low squeal, and another chomping, grunting noise, and I knew the beasts had come closer, but I could see nothing on the ground. I kicked the horse and shouted for it to go, but it staggered about in terror, and then I felt it land against something, and it neighed, and reared – and I began to slip down.

I screamed and the horse bucked again, and I jerked sideways. The soaked musket that had been in my lap clattered to the ground, and I gave a cry, searching desperately for the reins but finding only the damp mane and neck. It reared once more, and I kicked my feet out of the stirrups lest I get dragged for miles, but then I was falling backwards into the darkness. The world tipped upside down and there was a moment, a clear, pure moment of free fall, where my mind was empty, and I was flying – no, falling – and then I hit the ground, landing on my side, my stomach smashing into the mud.

I lay with one cheek to the ground, and somewhere close by Puck was barking furiously, and the sound of hooves grew quieter as the horse galloped further away, and the rain continued to fall. I could not move, but I could hear, still listening for the grunts I knew would come. And then I heard them. There was more than one – a boar coming from somewhere behind me, and one in front, and Puck was nearby, thrashing and barking and growling and snapping, and there was an explosion of squeals, and I had no idea how many of them there were, or if Puck would survive their ivory tusks.

I closed my eyes because I knew they would reach me – they always did. It was what happened after that I did not know. And while Puck wrestled with one or two or three, I felt a curious nudge on my leg, then heard the sound of grunting, greedy with hot breath and blood-soaked teeth. I was wet, with rain or blood or my own piss, and my legs were damp under my skirts, and that's when the pain started.

Perhaps a tusk pierced my stomach, because it was instant and explosive, a great crashing blow, and my heart pounded in my chest, and I could not move. But then, just as quickly, I was empty, my body ringing with the shock of its sudden absence. And then it came again, and something was nuzzling my neck, my face, some-thing hairy and then soft – was it Puck? Something else? And I closed my eyes, and the pain came again, harder, driving right into my body, into my spine, and I could not move, with agony or terror I did not know, but I was blind with it.

I was dreaming, I had to be – I had been knocked out, or I was sleeping. I was at home, at Gawthorpe, in my bed, and the window was full of stars. No, I was lying on the forest floor, in the rain, miles from home, miles from anywhere, and I was alone, and about to die.

Her earthly life will end.

I was too frightened to cry, but this was a different kind of fright from how I felt in my nightmare. There was knowledge now, and understanding, but still terrible fear, and I could not decide what was worse: the fear or the understanding that this was it.

My dog. Where was he? I had once saved him from a life of violence and misery, and I loved him. I opened my eyes to look for him, and there was a streak of copper, bright as a flame before my eyes. I closed them again. I knew Puck was near, fighting for me, that great beast I had carried around and petted and kissed and told secrets to, who could kill a bull but wouldn't hurt a fly.

My baby, who I would never meet, and who would never meet me, but we knew each other, and that was enough. Agony seared me again like a branding iron, creasing me in half, and I hoped my child did not feel it, and was not afraid.

Her earthly life will end.

The sounds seemed to fade away, but I was pinned to the ground, still pinned to this life under great rolling waves of agony. I might have been under a carriage wheel going back and forth, back and forth.

The rain was soft now, like Richard kissing my shoulder.

The papers in my pocket would be soaked.

Alice. I had to save Alice.

I opened my eyes, but it was as black as if they were shut. I closed them against the pain, and waited for the real darkness to come.

'Mistress?'

Birds were singing. The sound of them was so cheerful. Arms lifted me as another stab of pain coursed through me.

'My God, look at her.'

'Is she dead?'

They sounded afraid, and I had no wish to open my eyes and look at whom they were talking about.

'Is she bleeding?'

I was being lifted up, but I was heavy, my dress soaked with rain. More pain, too much to make a sound, and cold – so cold.

'She's shivering.'

'Quick, be quick, man!'

Then I was moving, with a steady rhythm like a baby being rocked in a cradle, and I could see green leaves and dark branches waving above me, and hear the wind sliding through the woods. I liked the woods, and felt safe there, and I must have fallen asleep because suddenly I was being carried upstairs, laid across a powerful chest like an offering. Strong arms held me, and we moved upwards, and I wondered if this was God taking me to Heaven.

Then I was in my chamber, being lowered into bed, and the counterpane was pulled back, and all the drapes opened, and people were standing around the bed, but I did not have time to see who they were because another crease of pain was starting, and it brought me back to life, because although I was awake, I felt as though I was dreaming. And that's when I realised where I was, and what was happening to me.

The baby was being born.

I screamed and tried to sit up, and saw that at some point my gown and jacket and farthingale had been removed and I was lying in my smock, which was stained red from my waist to my ankles.

'No,' I murmured. 'No, no, no. Richard! Alice! Where is Richard?'

'We are fetching the master,' said a timid voice beside me.

I saw one of the boy apprentices from the farm standing inexplicably by my bed.

'The boars,' I told him. 'I need Alice. Send for Alice.'

The boy wrung his cap in his hands, frightened out of his wits.

'George, go back outside and wait for the midwife,' said another voice.

It was James, the steward, who was standing at the foot of my bed. His face was grey.

'Midwife?' I asked, aware that another roll of pain would soon knock me sideways. 'Is Alice not coming? Only she can help me. Where is she?'

And then I remembered. I had left Lancaster to visit John Foulds and get his statement, because the trial was today, and Alice was there, and I was here, bleeding, and that only meant one thing. My earthly life was ending, and so was hers. A great roaring wail came from somewhere in my stomach and escaped from my mouth.

'Alice! I must get to Lancaster to the assizes. Am I too late?'

'The master is on his way, Mistress, he is almost here, and a doctor, too, and a midwife.'

James' dark eyes were shining with terror.

'Where is my gown? Fetch my gown.'

Someone – not James – brought it to me from where it must have lain crumpled on the floor, wet with soil and blood and rain.

'The pocket, open the pocket.'

I could not do it myself; I was braced against the pain, propped on my elbows, trying not to look at the blood coating my smock and the sheets, trying not to cry. But I was so terrified, and no one knew what to do, least of all me, and if I was going to die on this bed I at least wanted to hold my husband's hand while doing it, because I loved him, and I forgave him everything, and hoped he did me. Bits of paper were being drawn out of the ruined gown, and I snatched them from the woman's hand – a kitchen servant – and cried out with relief, for they were dry, protected by the lining.

And then I was being trampled, again and again, by

this great wheel of agony, and then it went away, and someone came and told me to sleep, and bathed my head with a cloth, but it was not Alice, and it was not the same.

'Alice is innocent. I saw John Foulds,' I muttered, and the voice said, 'Shh, I know, I know.'

Then perhaps I did sleep, because the next thing I was awake, filled again with panic. Then Richard was in the room, filling it with his dynamic power and authority, as if the king himself had walked into my chamber.

He fell on me, taking my hands. His face was wet.

'My little ghost, what have you done?'

I was vaguely aware that there was another woman with him, a stout, wide sort of presence, with pink skin, and I thought in horror that it was Miss Fawnbrake. But Richard told me it was a midwife from Clitheroe, and she would—

But I was not listening, because now he was here, something strange was happening, as though I was sinking into sleep. But I had something to give him – I felt around on the bed for the papers and thrust them into his hands.

'Richard, you have to go now, you have to read these at the assizes.'

My mouth was very dry, and my voice faint.

'What is this?'

'Richard, *please*, listen to me. These statements could set Alice free.' Another bolt of pain seared me like an iron white from the furnace. 'You have to go and insist they be read, or read them yourself. It's my statement, and John Foulds'.'

My head was spinning, my vision blurring.

Her earthly life will come to an end.

'Of course not, Fleetwood, I am staying here, with you.'

'*You have to do this!*' I all but screamed. 'Get her out, Richard. Get her out! Only *she* can save me, and only I her!'

'Enough!'

His voice was like the voice of God now, swimming around in some great cavernous darkness, because I was drifting away from him, from my chamber, from everything. I thought I knew the pain, but it turned out I'd only had the best of it, and the worst was to come.

I was being stabbed with knives. I was being washed with flames. Chains covered me, and kept me down, though I tried to lift myself, and couldn't. My limbs: full of water. My body: cut in half, sliced from the scalp. Every inch of me screamed, except for my mouth, because when I opened it nothing came out. Water, I needed water. Water to extinguish the flames that licked along my spine. I was on fire. I was dying, I was dead, and must be in Hell. I could feel liquid streaming out between my legs, then darkness came again, mercifully wrapping me in its thick, black cloak.

'Fleetwood.'

'Fleetwood.'

'Fleetwood.'

There was love in the voice, and grief, and it was shaking with both of those things. A woman's voice, or was it a man's? The pain – I *was* pain, it was not separate from me, was not something happening to me. Darkness came again, and I was grateful.

A streak of fur against my arm. I knew it was a fox before I opened my eyes. It was standing on the floor by my bed, staring at me with wide amber eyes. It looked as though it was desperate to tell me something.

I laughed, and said, 'What is it?'

And then the strangest thing happened: the fox opened its mouth and spoke, and it was female, and what it said was: '*Honi soit qui mal y pense.*'

Shame on him who thinks evil of it.

The darkness went on for so long, I could not remember what light looked like. But then there was candlelight, dotting my vision like pearls on a black velvet dress. A cool hand on my head brought me out of the darkness. It was the hand of light, but darkness tugged at my feet too, at my arms.

No, I want to stay in the light.

I tried to brush it away, concentrating on the small, cool hand – or was it a cloth? – on my head that was anchoring me to the room as the wild, dark sea raged on inside me.

'Push,' a voice said. 'You have to push.'

A white cap. A twist of golden hair tumbling from it. It was the girl from the forest with the bag of rabbits. What was her name?

A wave of pain crashed into me, and to end it I had to strain against it, to push it away and out of my body.

'Push!'

Something spilt, and there was a gush like a barrel of fish knocked over. The wave was coming again, building slowly, then crashing, and I strained harder, harder, harder, until I thought I might burst.

'When it comes again, push!'

Oh, did it have to come again? Yes, it was coming now, and I was ready for it this time, braced against it like I was about to do battle with some ancient deity. There was a horrible cry, an agonised groan, and I wished whoever it was would stop, but then I realised *my* mouth was open and *my* lungs were emptying, and it felt good, like I was wringing myself out, because it was louder than the pain.

And as my cry died, another one started up. But this one was much softer, and came in short little bursts rather than one great long note. The crashing waves had stopped, and were coming now in little lapping motions. That strange noise again, almost like a lamb, or a kitten. Suddenly I felt more tired than I'd ever been in my life. I wanted to sleep, and although my limbs were heavy as lead, my heart drummed on furiously, going *bang bang bang*.

But there were people in the room, and they were being loud, even though I wanted to sleep. I heard the word 'blood' over and over, and they sounded panicked. Had they never seen blood before?

Sleep – I needed sleep.

'Fleetwood, stay with me. Fleetwood, stay here.'

Where else was I going? I was too tired to move. The darkness that had been tugging me earlier had now wrapped my hand in his, ready to take me with him. Ah, that's where they meant. Don't go with him.

I can't go, I said. *I have to stay*.

Another tug, more insistent this time, and with it I knew it would be quiet there, and peaceful, and safe. I was already lying down – it would be so easy to surrender to warm, thick darkness.

'Fleetwood, drink this.'

Just wait a moment, I need to have a drink.

A drink would be good. With difficulty, for he was strong, I removed myself from his silky grip, and felt a cup at my lips, and something warm and sweet in my mouth. Then the liquid was replaced with something hard and earthy, and I was told to chew.

As I came to my senses, the room was mercifully quiet and bright with daylight. A single bird sang outside the window and the fire burnt merrily, filling the room with the scent of woodsmoke. A woman was bent over the fire with her back to me, stirring a pot, and the sharp tang of herbs fragranced my chamber. Pain echoed around my body still, and every part of me wanted to sleep. I watched her, and saw the creamy curve of her neck, and the mischievous way her hair refused to go neatly in her cap. She stood and went to look at something at the foot of the bed, and made a gentle noise.

'Alice,' I whispered, and I don't know if she heard me, but she looked up, and I saw she was crying.

She moved towards me, and knelt beside my bed. I went to sit up, but she put a firm hand on my arm We looked at one another for a long time, and I wanted to ask her things, but the effort of speaking would not be worth the answers, because for now they did not matter.

'Willow bark,' she said.

I realised the bitter wood was still in my mouth, and it was perhaps helping, for my mind felt clearer and my heart no longer galloped. I wanted to wipe her cheeks, because tears were falling down them freely now.

'You should sleep.'

She moved to stand up, her skirts rustling.

Obeying like a child, I closed my eyes. There was another rustle, and the comforting scent of lavender, and I felt her lips on my forehead, very softly, and her breath on my cheek.

When I reached again for the darkness, it was not there.

PART FOUR

Kind friends know and keep

Shuttleworth family motto

CHAPTER 25

Richard Lawrence Shuttleworth was born just before dawn on the twentieth day of August, 1612, the same day that ten witches were hanged on the hill overlooking Lancaster.

Alice Gray was not one of them.

It was only because Puck had run from that deep pocket of forest to Gawthorpe, that was actually only a mile away, that all three of us – Alice, my son and I – survived. His barks at the cellar door roused the servants, who woke James, who woke some of the apprentices, and my dog led a torchlit procession through the trees back to where I lay in the mud, arriving as daylight broke on the first day of the witch trials. One of the men – the best rider on the fastest horse – raced forty miles to the Red Lion at Lancaster to fetch Richard, who was worked into a frenzy not knowing where I was, having asked at every door in the town if anyone had seen a small woman with a large stomach and a huge dog. All I'd left was a note saying I'd be back before the trial started. He had even gone to the home of Thomas Covell, the castle keeper, but the words had died in his mouth as he realised Roger might be sitting in the parlour with an ear to the door, so he stammered an apology and left.

When his man from Gawthorpe arrived before breakfast, he said he'd heard the hooves on the cobbled yard beneath the window and knew it to be a message about me. He wasted no time, and rode home without stopping, sailing like an arrow in the wind. He told me how the skies were peach and blue, and how he made a deal with himself that if I lived, he would have me a gown made in each of the beautiful colours he saw that morning. He said he made all sorts of bargains with himself – if I lived, he would refurbish my mother's house from cellar to gables, with fresh plaster and paint and rugs and more books than she could read in a lifetime. If I lived, I would never sleep alone in our bed again, if that's what I wanted.

The servants had also fetched the cook's midwife sister from her bed in Clitheroe. When Richard arrived, breathless and shining with perspiration, she'd told him in plain terms that she did not hold out much hope, and that the Lord seemed ready to take my child and me into the next life. And Richard was white with rage, and dismissed her, and bid the servants find someone else. As she left with her nose in the air, she passed him the papers from my skirts that lay discarded on the floor, trampled by so many feet going in and out.

And that was when Richard decided the only person who could save me was sitting in chains in the castle. So without changing riding habits or even stopping to eat, he rode all the way back to Lancaster, knowing he might never see me alive again. He left his horse at the gate, both of them almost expired, and burst into the castle, and demanded that His Majesty's justices allow him to read two testimonies relating to the trial of Alice Gray, which had already begun.

He was barely aware of the ripple of astonishment from the gallery, or Roger's thunderous expression from his seat by the judges, or the grand, high ceiling and rows of gleaming benches, or the jury. All he knew was the papers in his hand, and his heart hammering in his chest, and Alice's wretched face where she stood with the other prisoners, with chains around her wrists and ankles.

Lord Bromley granted his request, and Roger almost exploded with anger, rising up to protest, but the law prevailed, and Richard faced Alice at the bar and read my words, though his hand was shaking and his voice trembled. And after that he read the words of John Foulds, though he struggled even more with them, because the man's writing was so poor.

When the jury went out, Richard had to wait in the

gallery, soaking wet and exhausted from riding almost eighty miles in less than a day. On their return he searched their faces, every last one of them, and when a few of the gentlemen looked him in the eye – for by now he had realised he had played cards with a couple of them – he did not know what that meant, and thought he would die with the agony of waiting. When the foreman said the words 'not guilty', he watched Alice drop like a stone a few yards away.

'And then what happened? Tell me again.'

'A great gasp went up from the crowd. I thanked the jury, and then I fainted.'

I laughed and clapped my hands together. I was sitting up in bed, in a clean white nightgown, beneath fresh bedding – the previous had to be burnt, along with yet another mattress. Little Richard was in my arms, and although he was small, he was perfect in my eyes. He had threads of black hair, fine as silk, and rosebud lips, and cheeks round as apples. The first time I fed him, when I had time enough to look over every lovely bit of him at length, I noticed something on his arm, and was about to call the nursemaid when I realised what it was.

In the crook of his tiny elbow was a brown birthmark, no bigger than his little fingernail, in the shape of a crescent moon. It matched the scar I had in the same place, where Alice had drawn blood from me. I checked the next morning to see if it was there, and it was, as much a part of him as his fingers and toes, and I folded his neat little sleeve down again and smiled to myself.

'And then?'

I sipped my warm milk, spicy with healing herbs.

'Well, then we had to wait for the rest of the verdicts,' Richard said.

Half-heartedly, he jangled the rattle he had bought all those months ago. It was not all happy news.

Richard had been unable to read John Foulds' final sentence, scrawled in a drunk's shaky hand in that pitiful candlelight, absolving Katherine Hewitt of any blame. The poor woman, a friend to Alice and her mother, had been found guilty, and hanged. Richard told me how after he had spoken for Alice, Katherine's arraignment came next, and Roger had become hell-bent on seeing his own agenda served. He bullied the jury, he shook his fists, and spittle fell from his lips as he drove the point home again, again, again how that woman, alias Mould-heels, who had delivered so many babies and made so many women mothers, killed a child for no reason other than the Devil told her to.

It was too much for Alice, and Richard said she cried out with more anguish than if the verdict was her own. After her chains were removed, she left the castle without looking back, weeping all the way to Gawthorpe, clinging to Richard so tightly she ripped his jacket. She was free, but her freedom had come at a terrible price.

The Pendle witches who were hanged that day included

Elizabeth Device, her daughter Alizon and her son James, leaving Jennet alone in this life. Seven more went with them. All were present at Malkin Tower. Alice was the only one of the group to be set free. One woman was found guilty and given four days in the stocks and a year in gaol as punishment. Her name was Margaret Pearson, whose servant had seen a toad climb out of the fire. She was not present at Malkin Tower, so Roger was only half-interested in her fate, and was not prepared to go to great efforts to see her swing.

Richard told me that in Bromley's parting words to Alice, he urged her to forsake the Devil. That would have been easy, because as soon as she left the room, she was free of him.

'Someone is here to see you,' Richard said to me a few days later. 'Shall I send them up?'

'Who is it?' Hope bloomed in my chest.

Richard smiled. 'You shall have to wait and see.'

Fatherhood suited him; he was besotted with his son. Somewhere he might have another one, or a daughter, but I pushed the thought from my mind.

'I will come down,' I said. 'I haven't been downstairs yet and am forgetting what it looks like. Richard?' I said before I lost my nerve. He paused in the doorway, one hand resting on the handle. 'I'm sorry, but I shall have to buy you a new gun.' He looked puzzled. 'I took yours the night I . . . The night I came back here. I lost it in the forest.'

'You took my musket?'

He seemed more astonished than annoyed.

'Yes. I didn't intend on using it – I didn't know how. It doesn't matter. It got soaked, besides, so I ruined it anyway.'

He smiled. 'You surprise me every day, Mistress Shuttleworth.'

'Richard . . . One more thing. There is something I want to ask you.'

I handed the sleeping baby to his father and climbed carefully out of bed, going to my cupboard in the corner of the room.

I pulled out the doctor's letter, which was torn and flimsy as an old rag by now. I held it in my fist and looked out of the window at Pendle Hill. Then I handed it to Richard.

'Why did you not tell me about this?'

He frowned and took it with the hand not holding the baby. I watched his eyes move over it, then understanding cleared his face, and he frowned.

'Where did you get this?'

'James gave it to me months ago.'

'You were not meant to see this.'

'Did you not think I would wish to know that my own life—'

'You were not meant to see this because it is not about you.'

I fell silent. 'What do you mean?'

Richard sighed. 'This letter is about Judith.'

'*Judith?*'

He patted the bed next to him and I went to sit. Months of turmoil were ringing in my head, and it took all my effort to listen.

'You were not visited by this doctor; he is from Preston. I had him visit Judith at Barton when she lost . . . She lost the first child. I tried to stay away after that, but . . . I went to her one more time, and she was pregnant again.'

I closed my eyes to let his words sink in.

'But it says your wife.'

Richard bent his head, and said very quietly, 'I had to tell him she was.'

Black ink from the ledger swam to the front of my mind: *Mr William Anderton to bring marriage licence from York.*

'Why did you have a marriage licence brought?'

Richard frowned. 'That was for James' niece. She married last month. There is nothing now you do not know, I promise you.'

I sat quietly, letting his words sink in.

'Why do you go to her?' I whispered.

He seemed to consider his answer for some time, and covered my hand with his. His rings glittered, and his voice was almost a whisper.

'I saw how you were when the babies died. I saw how ill it made you. I was afraid of hurting you again.'

Even then, after all I had been through, I could not hate him.

'And now I could not be happier that we have a son.'

Holding the baby in one arm, he took up the rattle again, and smiled down at him. I watched them sadly, and happily, and wretchedly. It was too much to take in.

'Remember your guest downstairs. I will leave you to dress.'

He planted a kiss on the baby's head and left soundlessly.

I stood and twisted my hair into a cap. It had stopped falling out, and was now strong and thick as a rope. I put a sleeveless gown over the top of my smock, and picked the baby up again to show him the rest of his house. I paused briefly on the stairs beneath my portrait and remembered how Alice had said I reminded her of someone. I realised she must have meant Ann. My son might never know the woman who saved our lives, but perhaps it was better that way, because while she stayed disappeared, she was safe.

Alice had left when I was asleep, and the blood washed away and the baby wrapped, slipping out of my chamber without anyone noticing. Richard said it was a full day and night after our son was born, and the house was so busy with people coming up and down the stairs, bringing bowls of hot water and fresh linen, nobody noticed. She was there, and then she was gone. She had not said goodbye, though she had kissed me with a mother's tenderness I'd never known.

Though I knew it was nigh on impossible, a tiny, glinting part of me hoped it would be her sitting in the parlour now. As though to put off being disappointed, I made my way very slowly down the stairs, rocking and murmuring to the baby. The servants were enamoured with the new addition to the household, and could not stop beaming at me. They assembled in a little group in the entrance hall to smile and watch me carry him down the last of the stairs, and I smiled back.

The parlour was empty.

'Mistress?' one of the kitchen girls said at my back. 'She is in the dining chamber; she is hungry from her journey so asked for food.'

My mother rose from her seat the moment I entered, with her face serene and arms outstretched.

'My grandson,' she cooed, and came to take him.

I hesitated, then passed him over. My mother's eyes raked over my skin, my hair, my body.

'You look well, Fleetwood. Your pregnancy was not a kind one.'

'No.'

'You are recovered?'

'I think so. I lost a lot of blood, so cook has me eating meat almost every hour. This is my first time downstairs.'

She smiled and put her face to little Richard's. He

blinked slowly and flailed his tiny fists, and she placed her finger inside his palm.

'A little boy,' she said happily.

But there was something she was hiding; I knew it in her voice.

'What is it?' I asked, and she turned to me, and smiled bravely.

'Richard is a father twice over.'

'Why are you telling me this?'

The feather in her hat trembled.

'Because I wanted you to hear it from me, and not some newsmonger in the village, or in someone else's dining chamber.' She sighed. 'I know you might never forgive me for keeping what I did a secret, but I thought it was the right thing to do, and knowing would only bring you unhappiness. Who would want that for their child, if they could help it?'

She looked down at the baby, and I noticed the lines around her eyes and mouth as she spoke.

'When your father died, I was . . . adrift. I was alone with an infant daughter, and . . .'

'You could not wait to be rid of me,' I said dully. 'You married me off straight away.'

She shook her head. 'That was a decision your father and I made together. Your father was ill and we needed a man to take responsibility for us. What would have happened to us? When Mr Molyneux came to your father with an offer, he had little choice but to take it.'

'I did not know Father arranged it.'

We sat in silence for a minute or two, looking at the fine black hair on Richard's head, and his pink ears like little seashells. Already I missed his weight in my arms, which hung uselessly in my lap.

'I was so unhappy in that house,' I said. 'I spent every day of my childhood worrying that the next day you would send me to him.'

'I would not have done that.'

'You threatened it when I misbehaved.'

'For that I am sorry. I would never have done it. It's difficult, raising a child without a father. You will say anything for a moment's peace.'

'You know he . . . When he came for the first time, he . . .' My voice shook. 'You left the room.'

My mother looked away. Her eyes grew darker than ever, and her mouth turned down at the corners, though her hand went on automatically patting the baby, who she was rocking very gently. I had never seen her with an infant before, and he seemed to slot into some ancient maternal part of her that I had never known.

'That is why I had the marriage annulled.'

I stared at her. 'You knew?'

'When I came back, I could tell what had happened. He looked guilty as sin, and your little face . . .' For the first time in my life, I watched my mother's eyes fill with tears. 'It was all my fault,' she said, her voice thick with emotion. 'I didn't know what to do, how to get out of it without your father there to tell me. I knew, though, I could never, ever hand you over to that man.'

'I thought it was annulled because Richard was a better match.'

My mother composed herself, and smiled weakly.

'And wasn't he?'

Slowly, I sat back in the chair. Sunlight streamed in through the windows – it was a beautiful late summer day.

'I am glad Richard put his woman in there because now I never have to go back.'

'I hated it too,' said my mother, surprising me. 'I never settled there. I hoped that when you married you would put me somewhere else, and you did.'

Richard did. I had nothing to do with it, had no interest in my mother's desires then.

'Well, now it has a new mistress. Judith Thorpe of Barton. She is welcome to it.'

My mother leant in.

'I took all the best silver before I left.'

We smiled at one another. I was about to ask if Judith had had a son, or a daughter, then decided I did not want to know. The servants began bringing in dinner, and Richard joined us, and we sat down to a joint of roast beef and a huge wood pigeon dripping in sauce. My appetite was unrecognisable from five months ago – I could have eaten the whole pigeon myself.

'I saw on my way through Padiham a woman in the stocks with a bag over her head that had "witch" on it,' my mother said as we ate.

'Margaret Pearson,' said Richard.

Since attending the trials he'd taken a keen interest in the events of that summer. He even had a theory about our old friend Thomas Lister: that Jennet Preston was his father's mistress, and with his mother still living and frail, he wanted her out of sight and out of mind. Either that, or she knew something about him, and he would rather have her dead than have it known. As for Roger, our paths would certainly cross again, but the magistrate had disgraced himself slightly on his voyage for power. He had shown himself as a man who traded lives for a comfortable retirement: souls for new furnishings afforded by the king, all for the sake of adding a final few glory days to a golden career in justice. Among the gentry of the north, such ruthless ambition was considered rather desperate, and many dining chambers had closed to him.

'She will do four market days in the stocks and then go to gaol, where she will probably die, because she will not be able to pay her bail once her sentence ends,' Richard was saying.

'Why was she not hanged?' my mother asked.

Richard shrugged.

'A shred of sense prevailed? I know not.'

My mother shuddered.

'I heard there were thousands in Lancaster on hanging day.'

'Nothing excites the living more than death,' I said.

'What happened to that girl Jill? Or was it Alice? Was she not arrested?'

Richard and I shared a glance.

'She was found not guilty.'

'Well, that's remarkable, is it not? I certainly thought they'd find them all guilty if they found one. Weren't they conspiring to kill Thomas Lister?'

'Who knows?' I said. 'There were no witnesses, apart from a child. Besides, Alice was innocent.'

'How do you know?'

My hand went to the scar at my elbow and traced it over my sleeve.

'All she wanted to do was help people,' I said.

'Where is she now?'

'I wish I knew.'

'She didn't tell you?'

I shook my head.

'Has she family?'

I thought of Joseph Gray, drinking himself to death in his house made from mud.

'No.'

At that moment the baby began crying from his bed in front of the fireplace. The nursemaid was eating with the servants, and my breasts were full and threatening to spill, so I got up and went to lift him from the oak cradle my mother had given me all those years ago. I stood up slowly and came face to face with the set of engraved panels on the mantelpiece.

I blinked, and looked all along them, then stared again. I could not believe what I was seeing. Next to Richard's initials, in the space that had been left blank since the house was built, was the letter *A*.

I would recognise it anywhere, had seen it scrawled dozens of times in the shaky hand of someone learning to write. But there it was, whole and clear. I stood frozen in astonishment, and then I began to laugh.

'Fleetwood? Whatever is the matter?'

I spun around, lifting Richard up above my head and dancing with happiness as my husband and mother looked at one another in baffled amusement.

'She is well!' I cried. 'She is well.'

Alice Gray was the only friend I ever had. I saved her life. And she saved mine.

CHAPTER 26

Five years later

Richard was dressed to hunt. He put his head into the great hall, where I was sitting mending Nicholas' silk stocking. With two sons, I had grown much better at embroidery because of the rate at which they poked holes in things, or skidded on the floor and tore their cloaks, or ripped their collars climbing through branches. At one elbow was the mending, and at the other was an ever-growing list of things I wanted James to fetch from London. Whenever something came to me I would take up the quill and scribble it down. I had just remembered I needed ambergris for my perfumes when the boys, who were clashing wooden swords together in an attempt at a duel, dropped them to the floor with a clatter.

'Father, will you duel with me? Nicholas fights like a baby,' said Richard, thrusting his brother's toy at his father. He took after me, with coal-black hair and serious dark eyes.

'He *is* a baby,' I said, smiling at Nicholas, who was as different from his older brother as I was from Richard. He had his father's warm gold hair and grey eyes.

'I will when I'm back, so don't splinter them before then.'

Richard pressed a sword into each of his sons' arms and wandered over to me. He looked distracted.

'What's the matter?' I said, briefly looking up from my sewing.

'The king is touring the north.'

I stared at him. 'When?'

'Next month.'

'And does he plan to stay here? He is not welcome.'

'Thankfully not, although to refuse him would be treason. I'm glad the tour is not next year when I am sheriff, because he almost certainly would. But he does plan to lodge at Barton.'

'At *Barton*? Why?'

'Your guess is as good as mine. He is staying at Hoghton Tower before that, and Barton is halfway between there and Lancaster.'

'But it's empty.'

'The king does not concern himself with inconveniences.'

I put down Nicholas' stocking.

'We would have to furnish it, and hire servants . . . It will bankrupt us. The king travels with a party of a hundred or more.'

'It's the king,' Richard said simply. 'I am no more happy about it than you.'

'That house,' I muttered. 'It's like a curse.'

Richard ignored my remark. I knew he kept Judith and their bastard somewhere in Yorkshire now, but I had no interest in where. As long as she was out of sight, and I had my boys and my home, I could quite easily ignore the whole thing. Richard nodded at my list on the table.

'You know what ambergris is, don't you? Whale vomit.'

'Richard!'

I batted him away and he darted out of my reach, straight into the sticky grasp of his sons, who pawed at his legs and again begged him to play.

'Enough! I am going hunting and if you do not let go of me this instant I am using both of you as bait.'

He picked Nicholas up by the ankles and tipped him upside down. He shrieked and squealed, helpless with laughter, as his brother pretended to jab him with the sword, crying, 'Die! Die!'

Puck, who was used to their noise but declined to

participate in his old age, watched lazily from the carpet. Sometimes they forced him to take part in their japes, but today he was spared.

'Why are boys so loud and badly behaved?' I asked. 'Why could I not have had two lovely daughters to sit and sew with me?'

Nicholas collapsed to the floor, breathless and giggling.

'Father, take me hunting with you!' Richard demanded, pulling at his father's cloak.

'Not until you are older.'

'What do we say to Father when he goes on a hunt?'

'Don't kill the foxes!' they both cried, each trying to be the louder.

I smiled, and Richard sighed in a playful way.

'Even though they kill the hares and rabbits, and make it much harder work for my birds, I think your mother would turn the musket to *me* if I came home with a fox pelt.'

I nodded sternly and smiled, but I was troubled by the news he brought.

I woke before dawn, leaving Richard snoring gently. The bag I'd packed the night before I'd hidden under the bed, and I swept it up silently and went to dress, arriving at the stables at first light. The morning was clear and fine, with a bright sun and a slight chill. One of the apprentices appeared in a doorway at the sound of hooves in the stable yard, and was startled to see me.

'I am going to spend the day with Mistress Towneley,' I told him as he blinked sleepily, reminding me of my own boys. 'Please tell the master to expect me back by nightfall.'

The road was deserted, and I made a good start. By the time I arrived a few hours later, my thighs were aching, my corse was digging into my stomach, and I was drenched with sweat. I hadn't ridden this far in years, and felt it in every muscle. When I got down, I leant against the horse for a moment, its coat hot and gleaming under the midday sun. I tied it to a tree out of sight, and trudged the last few hundred yards with the string of the bag digging into my wet palm.

I fumbled inside it for the key, and unlocked the door. The last time I was here it had been night-time, with shadows dancing everywhere, but now its mystery was gone. It was just an old, dusty, empty house. The final few pieces of furniture stood listless, and I went to the old cabinet in the hall that had been my father's, running my hands over its grooves and edges. But I could not take it, or anything else, so I patted it as though it was a pet, and moved on.

I looked in every room and opened every cupboard. No doubt the servants would have been through them after Judith left, taking candle stubs and needles and broken vases, as well as every scrap of food. I wanted to avoid the parlour, where I'd been taken away from my dolls to meet my first husband, but I went in and appraised it swiftly. There was the fireplace in front of which Mr Molyneux had sat, but with no furniture it was merely an empty room. I saved my chamber for last. There was just one bed frame in there – mine. My mother's had been moved to a different room. I thought of her sleeping near me every night; I had thought it torture, but now knew it to be something quite different.

I went to the window and looked out at the waving trees, and the farmland stretching flat behind them. It was a beautiful summer's day, with barely any wind. I made sure all the doors were open before I went back downstairs to the great hall, where I had met Judith five years before. It was as though the ghost of her was here, watching me as I went to the large windows overlooking the front of the grounds. The curtains were still there, thick with dust, no doubt too high and heavy for whoever had cleared the house to get down. There was no chair to rest on, no table to set down my things. I knelt on the cold stone floor beneath the window, and the sunlight streamed in and bathed my face. I lifted it up to feel the warmth, closing my eyes.

Then I set to work. I took the little silver tinderbox from my velvet bag and opened it, and bunched the charred cloth in the bottom to air it. I was pleased to see my hands were steady. I took out the flint and the steel and began striking them together. In the empty room, the clinks rang as loudly as they did in a blacksmith's workshop. After half a minute of effort, a spark caught the scraps in the tinderbox, and I leant in to blow it gently into a flame. Fearful of it going out, I held a splinter to it, and when it had caught, put it to the bottom of the curtain. Flames bloomed immediately on the dry, dusty fabric, and I cheered silently as fire licked the bottom of the scarlet threads, rising like damp. There were no mattresses, no firewood in the house – I had counted on this working, and it was. I sat and watched it for a minute, and by the time I stood up the curtain was half-covered in flames. I thought of the time my skirts had caught in Joseph Gray's house, and I stepped backwards and gathered up my things, shutting the front door behind me and locking it.

The king could not stay in a house that had burnt to the ground.

I stood on the front lawn for a long time, watching the front room swell with flickering light that was hard to see in sunlight, but would be magnificent at night. The wainscoted walls caught easily, and when the windows were black with smoke and I felt sure the fire was powerful and furious enough to attack the rest of Barton, I turned to go home.

Someone had been watching me. I jumped, startled, as a movement caught my eye at the edge of the trees. A stunning red fox fixed me with its wide amber eyes and placed a hesitant paw on the grass. We stared at one another, and time stood still. The fire raged on behind me, and my breath caught in my throat. Then I blinked, and it was gone.

ACKNOWLEDGEMENTS

If it takes a village to raise a child, it certainly takes a hamlet to raise a book. To start with, thank you Juliet – friend first, agent second – for making my dream come true and holding my hand through all of it. In no particular order, the following people deserve my utmost gratitude: Katie Brown, Francesca Russell, Felicity Jethwa, Becky Short, Felicity White, Kate Hilsen, Claire Frost, Catriona Innes, Cyan Turan, Ed Wood, Lauren Hadden, Beth Underdown, Rosie Short and John Short. Thank you for your sharp eyes, bright ideas and enthusiasm. There aren't the words to tell my editor Sophie Orme and all at Bonnier Zaffre how thrilled I am that *The Familiars* found its home with you. I knew you were The One as soon as I met you, and you've made the whole process a joy. I am grateful to Rachel Pollitt at Gawthorpe Hall for answering my questions and Robert Poole for modernising Thomas Potts' account of the trials. Last but not least, thank you to my parents Eileen and Stuart and brother Sam for your endless support and love, and Andy for being my No.1 cheerleader in life. You're always there when I need you, and I always will.

A LETTER FROM THE AUTHOR

Dear Reader,

The inspiration for *The Familiars* came when I visited Gawthorpe Hall in Padiham, Lancashire, and noticed Pendle Hill out of one of the bedroom windows. I grew up in the area and the hill is synonymous with the folklore of the Pendle witches. That's when the idea came to me of writing a novel about the events of 1612, told from the point of view of a young gentry woman living at Gawthorpe. I began to research the history of the house and the Shuttleworth family, and found out that the mistress at that time was a 17-year-old woman named Fleetwood, and my story sprang to life.

The more I found out about the Pendle witches the

more intrigued I was. Lots of them were neighbours. All of them were said to have familiar spirits – some of them shape-shifting. One claimed to have met the devil. Many of them admitted to witchcraft. They knew the penalty was execution, so why would they admit their guilt?

The Familiars is an attempt to answer my own questions, and while it's a work of fiction, most of the characters were real people and the book is based on the historical timeline. I hope it's made you want to know more about the Pendle witches as well as Alice and Fleetwood.

If you'd like to receive more information about *The Familiars*, you might be interested in joining my Readers' Club. Don't worry – it doesn't commit you to anything, there's no catch, and I won't pass your details on to any third parties. You'll receive updates from me about my books, including offers, publication news and even the occasional treat! You can unsubscribe at any time. To register, all you have to do is visit www.thefamiliarsbook. com.

Another way of reaching out to me is via Twitter @Stacey_Halls. I hope to hear from you soon, and that you continue to read and enjoy my books.

Thank you for your support,

Stacey

HISTORICAL NOTE

Fleetwood and Richard Shuttleworth, Alice Gray, Roger Nowell, the Device family and many other characters in the novel were real people, but *The Familiars* is a work of fiction. Fleetwood Shuttleworth (born 1595) was mistress at Gawthorpe during the witch trials, and had her first child in 1612, but there is nothing in history to connect her with Alice. However, her husband Richard was present at the assizes – at which Alice Gray and the other ten Pendle witches stood trial in August 1612 – possibly because it generated so much interest at the time. Very little is known about Alice Gray other than from Thomas Potts' account of the trial, *The Wonderfull Discoverie of Witches in the Countie of Lancaster*. For some unknown reason, Alice's transcript is not recorded in Potts' book. Why she was the only one of the Pendle witches to be acquitted remains a mystery.

READING GROUP
QUESTIONS

1. Women were disproportionately targeted as part of the witch hunts of the period. Why do you think this was?
2. Alice and Fleetwood are from very different backgrounds, but their lives have many similarities. Discuss what they have in common – is one 'better off' than the other?
3. The familiar spirits in the book are ambiguous. Do you believe they played a real part in the story or were the imaginings of suspicion? And why is Puck never considered to be one, when he shows supposed signs of being a familiar, such as sucking his mistress' blood and attacking on demand?
4. Fleetwood did not tell anybody about the abuse she suffered as a child because she feared nobody would

believe her, yet she is mistrustful of Jennet Device, who is a child herself. Do you think she should have had more sympathy with Jennet?

5. Roger's pursuit of the Pendle witches evolves from a display of authority to a sinister obsession, like 'collecting cards at a table'. Do you think he truly thought them to be witches or something else was at play?

6. Fleetwood's relationship with Mary is complicated, but typical of a teenager and her mother. Was Mary justified in keeping her silence, and might Fleetwood have been a little hard on her?

7. Richard is not an archetypal romantic hero, nor is he a villain. But is he more of one than the other?

8. Do you think Alice was a witch?

Please turn over for an exclusive extract of

Foundling

by Stacey Halls

Coming February 2020

CHAPTER 1

Bess

Late November, 1747

All the babies were wrapped like presents ready to be given. Some of them were dressed finely, though their mothers were not, in tiny embroidered sleeves and thick shawls, for winter had arrived, and the night was biting. I'd bound Clara in an old blanket that had waited years to be darned, and now never would be. We stood clustered around the pillared entrance, thirty or so of us, like moths beneath the torches burning in their brackets, our hearts beating like papery wings. I hadn't known it would be like a palace, with a hundred glowing windows and a turning place for carriages. Two long and splendid buildings were pinned either side of a courtyard that was connected in the middle by a chapel, as though it was wearing sleeves. At the north end of the west wing the door stood open, throwing light on to the stone. The gate was a long way behind; we had come this far and would go further still. Some of us would leave with our arms empty; some would carry our children out into the cold again. For this reason we could not look at one another, and kept our eyes on the ground.

Clara was clutching my finger, which neatly slotted into her tiny palm as a lock does a key. I imagined her reaching for it later, her hand closing around thin air. I held her tighter. My father, who Ned and I called Abe because mother did, stood to the right and slightly behind me, his face in shadow. He had not held the baby. Earlier, the midwife – a wide woman from a neighbouring court, who was as cheap as she was discreet – had offered her to him as I lay beached on the bed, shimmering in pain, and he shook his head, as though she was a hawker proffering a peach.

We were shown inside by a slim, bewigged man with reedy legs, and through an entrance hall unlike anywhere I'd been. Everywhere surfaces gleamed, from the walnut banister to the polished grandfather clock. The only sound was our skirts rustling, and our shoes on the stone – a little herd of women swollen with milk, bearing their calves. It was a place for hushed, gentle voices, not hawkers' ones like mine. I wondered if I'd grown up here whether or not I would be quiet, too. Our little procession made its way with silent boots up the claret carpet of the stairs, and into a high-ceilinged room. Only one skirt and bundled infant could pass through the doorframe at a time, so we lined up outside, like ladies at a ball. The woman in front of me had brown skin, and her black hair curled beneath her cap. Her baby was unsettled, making more noise than the others, and she shook him with the unpractised air we all had. I wondered how many had mothers to show them how to swaddle, how to feed. I had thought about my mother fifty times that day, more than in a year. I used to feel her in the creak of the floorboards and the warmth of the bed, but not anymore.

The room we had entered was papered green, with elegant white plaster piped below the ceiling. There were no flames in the fireplace, but it was warm and brightly lit with glowing lamps and pictures on the walls, framed in gold. A chandelier shivered at the centre. It was the finest room I had ever stood in, and it was crowded with people. I had thought we might be alone, perhaps with a fleet of nursemaids who carried off the babies that would stay, but a score of faces lined the walls – mostly women, who were certainly not nursemaids, fanning themselves and smiling curiously. They were very well-dressed and interesting to look at, and they were very interested in us. They might have climbed out of the paintings on the walls; their necks flashed with jewels, and their hooped skirts were bright as tulips, moving in some private breeze. Their hair was high and cloudy with powder. There were half a dozen men scattered about, silver-buckled and pot-bellied, not like Abe, with his drab coat like a horse's feed bag. The men appeared more stern, and many of them were eyeing the Blackamoor girl, as though she were for sale. They held little glasses in their gloved hands, and I realised for them this was a party.

I was still bleeding. Clara had been born before daylight that morning, and every part of me felt torn. I had not been her mother a day, yet I knew her as well as myself: the smell of her, the little patter of her heart that had beat inside me. Even before she was pulled from me, red and squealing, I'd known what she'd feel like and how heavy she would be in my arms before she was pulled from me. I hoped they would take her, and I hoped they wouldn't. I thought of Abe's lined face, his eyes on the floor, his calloused hands holding the door for me. He was the only father in the room. Most of the others were alone, but some had their mothers, who looked sadder than the girls themselves. Abe would not meet my eye, and had not spoken much on our slow, sad walk from Black and White Court in the city, but his being there was as good as a hand on my shoulder.

A hush fell over the room as a man standing before a huge fireplace began to speak. His voice was as rich and thick as the carpets, I stared at the chandelier as he told us how they drew the lottery: that a white ball admitted a child, a black one did not, and a red one meant we had to wait for an admitted child to fail the medical examination. It took all my energy to listen.

'There are twenty white balls,' the man was saying, 'five red, and ten black.'

I shifted Clara at my breast. The ladies at the edges of

the room were looking on us more boldly now, wondering which of us would be lucky, which of us might leave our babies on the street to die. Who among us was unmarried. Who was a whore. I thought of their sons and daughters in their grand houses in Belgravia and Fitzrovia and Mayfair, lying beneath warm blankets, brushed and washed and full of milk. Perhaps they would visit the nursery before going to bed tonight, grown sentimental at our plight, dropping a kiss on sleeping cheeks. Who were they?

A nurse began moving about the room with a cloth bag for us to reach inside. By the time she arrived at me, my heart was stomping around my chest in boots, and I held her indifferent gaze as I shifted Clara to one arm and put the other in the bag. The balls were smooth and cool as eggs, and I held one in my fist, trying to feel its colour. The nurse shook the bag impatiently and something told me to let the ball drop and take another, so I did.

'Who are the people watching?' I asked her, pushing them around.

'They were invited,' was her bored reply. I clutched another ball and let it go, and she shook the bag impatiently.

'What for?' I asked in a low voice, aware of the many pairs of eyes on me. One woman was staring hard at me, as though willing me a particular colour. She was large and wide, and held a fan in one hand, a little glass in the other. She wore a blue feather in her hair.

'They're benny factors,' was all the nurse said, and feeling as though I couldn't ask another question, and knowing I needed to choose a ball, I settled on another, weighing it in my palm. I drew it out, and the room was silent.

The ball was red. I would have to wait.

The nurse moved to the next woman, while the rest watched her procession around the room, their jaws set in tight, anxious lines as they tried to work out what had been drawn, and what was left. We had been told at the gate that our babies must be two months old at most, and in good health. Many of them were sickly, starving things that their mothers had tried to nurse. Some were six months at least, swaddled so tightly to look smaller they cried out in discomfort. Clara was the smallest of them all, and the newest. Her eyes had been closed since we arrived. If these were her last moments with me, she would not know. All I wanted was to curl around her in bed like a cat, and go to sleep, and come back the next month. I thought of Abe's silent shame, how our rooms at Black and White Court were thick with it, how it stained like coal smoke. I thought of taking her to Billingsgate, sitting her on my father's stall like a miniature figurehead on the bow of a ship. A mermaid, found at sea and put on display for all to see at Abraham Bright's shrimp stall. Briefly I fancied taking her hawking with me, bundling her to my chest so my hands were free to scoop shrimp and cockles from my hat. I'd seen some hawkers with their babes strapped to their fronts, but what happened when they were no longer the size of a loaf? When they were fat little things with fists and feet and hungry, empty mouths?

A woman began wailing, a black ball clenched in her fist. Her face and her child's were the same unhappy masks of despair, and the child began crying. 'I cannot keep him,' she cried. 'You must take him, please.' While the attendants calmed her and the rest of us looked away for her dignity, I yawned so widely I thought my face would crack. I'd not slept for more than an hour since two nights ago, when Clara began to come. This morning Ned sat with the baby before the fire so I could shut my eyes, but I was in so much pain I could not sleep. Now, every part of me ached still, and in the morning I had to work. I could not walk home tonight with Clara in my arms. It was not possible. But neither could I leave her on a dung heap or a doorstep where the rats might get her. As a girl I'd seen a dead baby on the roadside, and had dreamt about it for months.

The room was very bright, and I was very tired, and suddenly I was aware of being led to a little room off the side, and told to sit and wait. Abe followed and closed the door behind him, shutting out the sobs and the tinkle of sherry glasses. I wished they would give me a glass of warm milk or some beer; I did not know how I could stay awake.

A nursemaid appeared from nowhere and removed Clara from my arms, but I had not been ready, and it was too soon, too sudden. I was vaguely aware of her telling me there was a space for her, because a lady had brought an infant of at least six months, which was far too old, and did she not think they could not tell the difference between a babe of two months and one of six? I thought of the woman and her child, and wondered idly what would happen to them, and pushed away the thought. The nursemaid's frill cap disappeared through the door, and I felt delirious, too light without her in my arms, as though a feather could knock me over.

'She is not yet a day,' I called after the nurse, but she had gone. I heard Abe shift behind me, and the floor creaked. When he reached for his coat at home and said it was time for us to leave, I had almost cried with relief; I had not thought he would come with me.

A man was now sitting before me, writing on a ticket with a fat feather, and I forced my eyes open, and my ears too, because he was speaking. 'The doctor is inspecting her for signs of ailment . . .'

I unstuck my mouth. 'She was born at quarter past four this morning.'

'. . . If she shows signs of ill health she will be refused admission. She will be examined for venereal disease, scrofula, leprosy and infection.'

I sat in dumb silence.

'Do you wish to leave a token with the memorandum?' The clerk finally looked at me, and his eyes were dark and solemn, at odds with his eyebrows, which sprouted from his head in a rather comic way.

A token: yes. This I had prepared for, had heard how the babies were recorded with an identifier, left by the mother. I fished in my pocket and brought out mine, placing it on the polished desk between us. My brother Ned had told me of the Foundling – a home for babies, on the edge of the city. He knew a girl who'd left her child there, and cut a square from her dress to leave with it. 'And if you leave nothing and go back?' I asked him. 'You might be given the wrong one?' He'd smiled and said perhaps, but the idea had chilled me. I imagined a room piled high with tokens, and mine being thrown on a heap of them. The man took it between his finger and thumb, and examined it with a frown.

'It's a heart, made from whalebone. Well, half a heart. Her father had the other.' I flushed furiously, my ears scarlet, aware of Abe standing silently behind me. There was a chair next to mine but he had not taken it. Until now he'd known nothing of it. The size of a farthing, I had the right hand side, smooth at one edge and jagged at the other. A B had been scored into it, and below it, more roughly, a C, for Bess and Clara.

'What will you use it for?' I asked.

'A record will be made should you wish to reclaim her. Her number will go in the ledger as 627, with the date, and a description of the token.' He dipped the feather in ink and began to write.

'You will put that it's half a heart, won't you?' I said, watching the words spill from his quill, but not under-standing them. 'In case there's a whole one, and they get mixed up.'

'I will put that it's half a heart,' he said, not unkindly.

I still did not know where my baby was, or if I would see her again, and I was afraid to ask.

'I will reclaim her, when she's older,' I announced, because saying it aloud made it true. The floorboard creaked behind me. We had not yet spoken about this, but I was certain. I straightened my skirt. Streaked with mud and rain, on washing day it was the milky pewter of an oyster's shell, and for the rest of the month the dirty grey of a London paving slab. The nursemaid came to the doorway and nodded. Her arms were empty.

'She's fit for admission.'

'Her name is Clara,' I said, feeling overcome with relief.

A few months before, when my belly was small, on one of the more genteel streets around St Paul's where the townhouses stretched up to the sky and jostled for space with the printers and the booksellers, I'd seen an elegant woman dressed in a deep blue gown, glowing like a jewel. Her hair was golden and shiny, and at the end of one plump, pink arm was a little hand attached, belonging to a little girl with the same yellow curls. I watched as she tugged at her mother, and the woman stopped and bent down, not caring that her skirts were brushing the ground, and put her ear to the little girl's lips. A smile broke out across her face. 'Clara, you are funny,' she had said, and took up her daughter's hand again. They moved past me, and I rubbed my growing stomach, and decided if I had a girl I would name her Clara, because then, in a very small way, I would be like that woman.

The man was unmoved. 'She will be christened and renamed in due course.'

So she would be Clara to me and no one else. Not even herself. I sat stiff-backed, clenching and unclenching my fists. A clock somewhere in the room ticked patiently.

'And how will you know who she is, if her name changes, when I come back?'

'A leaden tag is attached to each child on arrival, bearing a number that refers to their identifying records.'

'627. I'll remember it.'

He regarded me, and his eyebrows fell into stern furrows. 'If your circumstances change and you do wish to claim your child, the fee for her care will be payable.'

I swallowed. 'What does that mean?'

'The expenses the Hospital incurred caring for her.'

I nodded. I had no idea what sort of cost that might be, but did not feel as though I could ask. I waited. The nib scratched, and the clock ticked. The ink was the same colour as the night sky in the window behind him; the curtains had not been drawn. The quill danced like some strange exotic creature. I remembered the large woman outside with the blue feather in her hair, and how she had stared.

'The people in the room,' I said. 'Who are they?'

Without looking up he replied: 'The governors' wives and acquaintances. Lottery night raises funds for the Hospital.'

'But do they need to watch the babies be given over?'

I asked. I knew my voice did not sound right here; it made him sigh.

'The women are very moved by it. The more moved they are, the more donations are made.' I watched him come to the end of the paper and sign it with a flourish, and he sat back to let it dry.

'What will happen to her, when I go?'

'All new admissions are taken to live in the countryside, where they will be cared for by a wet nurse. They return to the city at around five years old, and live at the Foundling until they are ready to work.'

I swallowed. 'What do they work as?'

'We prepare girls for service, and set them to knitting, spinning, mending – domestic pursuits that will make them attractive to employers. The boys work in the ropeyards making fishing nets and twine to ready them for naval life.'

'Where will Clara be nursed? Which part of the country-side?'

'That depends on where there is a place for her. She could be as near as Stoke Newington or as far as Berkshire. We are not at liberty to reveal where she has been placed.'

'Can I say goodbye?'

The governor folded the paper over the whalebone heart, but did not seal it. 'Sentimentality is best avoided. Good evening to you, Miss, and you, Sir.'

Abe moved towards me and helped me from my chair.

Want to read
NEW BOOKS
before anyone else?

Like getting
FREE BOOKS?

Enjoy sharing your
OPINIONS?

Discover

READERS FIRST

Read. Love. Share.

Get your first free book just by signing up at
readersfirst.co.uk